W9-AWZ-981

Bedford High Media Center
Section 5A

EVA'S COUSIN

Eva's Cousin

SIBYLLE KNAUSS

Translated from the German by
Anthea Bell

BALLANTINE BOOKS
NEW YORK

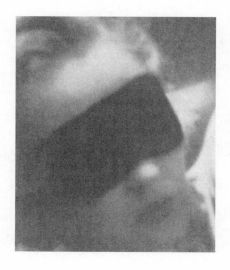

A Ballantine Book
Published by The Ballantine Publishing Group
English language translation copyright © 2002 by Anthea Bell

All rights reserved under International and Pan-American Copyright Conventions.
Published in the United States by The Ballantine Publishing Group, a division of
Random House, Inc., New York, and simultaneously in Canada by Random House
of Canada Limited, Toronto. Originally published in German as *Evas Cousine* by
Claassen Verlag, a division of Econ Ullstein List Verlag GmbH & Co. KG, Munich,
in 2000. Copyright German text © 2000 Econ Ullstein List Verlag GmbH & Co.,
KG, Munich. This English translation is published by arrangement with Doubleday,
an imprint of Transworld Publishers, a division of the Random House Group Ltd.,
which originally published it in Great Britain in 2000.

Ballantine and colophon are registered trademarks of Random House, Inc.

www.ballantinebooks.com

Library of Congress Cataloging-in-Publication Data
Knauss, Sibylle, 1944–
[Evas Cousine. English]
Eva's cousin / Sibylle Knauss.— 1st ed.
p. cm.
ISBN 0-345-44905-3
1. Braun, Eva—Fiction.   2. Germany—History—1933–1945—Fiction.
3. World War, 1939–1945—Germany—Fiction.   I. Title.
PT2671.N327
833'.914—dc21   2002019410

Title page art © Thurston Hopkins/Hulton Archive

Book design by BTDnyc

Manufactured in the United States of America

First American Edition: September 2002

10 9 8 7 6 5 4 3 2 1

For G.W.,
who had the courage to face her past.

With my gratitude to her for trusting me, and for her wise advice
during my work on this book.

This story is as true as the facts on which it is based—and as
fictional as any novel.

For readers who know and respect the mystery of fiction.

PROLOGUE

BEYOND MUNICH YOU SEEM TO PASS THROUGH a gateway into another world. A world of more beauty and greater promise. You feel it at your first sight of the mountains: You look forward to arriving, staying here, waking up the next morning with that view of the snow-covered peaks. Even if you are only passing through you sense something of it.

I take the Bad Reichenhall exit road. Who now remembers the seductive power such place-names once had over us? Bad Reichen-hall . . . Berchtesgaden . . . Our yearning for the extraordinary pleasure to be found only in traveling used to be directed that way. When you are as old as I am, you see that humanity's desire to travel is itself in transit, restlessly wandering from place to place, over the Alps, the Mediterranean, the Atlantic, all over the world, with the crowd following on behind. I am a part of the history of twentieth-century tourism myself, and that history begins in Berchtesgaden.

A very popular destination. Long before the period I am about to describe it was fashionable to go to Berchtesgaden, and if possible to make a home there. Trendsetting city dwellers like Carl Linde the refrigerator manufacturer and Carl Bechstein of the piano-making firm bought holiday houses in the area. So, unwisely, did a manufacturer called Eichengrün. Could he have picked a worse summer holiday resort? He must have been happy here, with exactly the kind of happiness he dreamed of: wooden balconies with geraniums, Alpine sunsets and sunrises in the sky above the house. He wanted his children to breathe plenty of healthy mountain air. People swore by mountain air at the time. It was a remedy against tuberculosis, chlorosis, and other evils of city life. It was no remedy for an evil that forced the Eichengrüns to leave their refuge a couple of decades later, selling their house at far below its market price. Only then did Berchtesgaden enter its prime.

It is a beautiful place. Set among the gentle meadow-clad slopes of the hills rising to the sheer heights beyond them, the bare mountain peaks. A broad valley with the little river Ache running through it. The river name means "water," and is evidence that the place was inhabited in primeval times, that people settled beside the water and for a long while did not even know that there were any other rivers in the world, finding everything they needed to sustain life here: shelter, food, wood, rich meadows. A Garden of Eden. The valley narrows toward the south, where it is closed, sealed off. The steep mountain walls approach each other here, the Watzmann, the Jenner, beyond them the Kahlersberg, and between them the lake, the Königssee— narrow, deep green, surrounded by steep rock walls, as good as inaccessible except at its northern extremity. A place at the end of the world. If you take the boat from Schönau to the southern tip of the lake you find yourself facing it.

This place used to be the ultimate goal of tourist ambition. I still remember seeing framed photographs in people's living rooms showing the church of St. Bartholomä with its onion domes on the solitary promontory jutting from the foot of the Watzmann, which cannot be reached except by boat. Once a legendary spot on the sight-seeing map, on a par with the Blue Grotto of Capri or the Eiffel Tower, it, too, is forgotten now and has been crossed off our private wish lists. The great flood of tourists, although it has swelled to immeasurable proportions, is diverted elsewhere. Not that the place is entirely unvisited today, but only the stragglers come. Pensioners, day-trippers. Me.

I drive over the Ache. To the left of me lies the center of Berchtesgaden. I know I must keep right. The woods come down to the valley here, and I see the signpost directing me to "Obersalzberg," as if it were some kind of village like all the others around it. And so I know it once was. I savor the sound of the old name, its lost innocence, its innocuity. Then the road begins to rise at an inclination of first seven, then eleven, then twenty-one percent. On my left all of a sudden, and sooner than expected, I see the corpse of a hotel, as empty of humanity as the world after a nuclear war, abandoned, emptied, doors locked, shutters closed, with pale plaster the color of bleached animal bones peeling away here and there.

"Guests Only" says a notice beside the entrance. They must mean rats or ghosts.

Ghosts. Balls held night after night at the Hotel Platterhof. Do the lights come on? Do the old bands play? Softly, softly, a sound like the worn grooves of gramophone records, a hiss indistinguishable from the sound of passing time, the inaudible falling of the dust to which all will return in the end. Is that Dr. Morell leading the lovely Frau Bormann out on the dance floor? The lenses of his glasses shine as if to hide the absence of eyes behind them. And Gerda Bormann herself, hair parted in the middle, a gentle figure, is eyeless as well, has only two black sockets with something implanted deep inside staring out of them, something eerie, horrible, indescribable. There goes Albert Speer. He's carrying a roll of architectural drawings under his arm, as if on his way to renovate Hell. Just behind him comes Hermann Göring in his white uniform, red socks, and the order *Pour le mérite* on his breast. He is leading a lioness whom he calls Emmy by her collar. And there's Heinrich Hoffmann. And Eva. And all the others. All of them; they're all there. How they love the fun. Parties all the time. Champagne. Lavish wardrobes. Nights full of music, romantic affairs, passion. A ball at the Hotel Platterhof. Shall I be there, too?

The car park in front of the hotel is empty. It's early in the afternoon. The winter season is over now, the fourteenth of April, and the summer tourists won't begin arriving until the middle of May when the road to the Kehlstein is open again. Dirty remnants of snow are piled around the sides of the car park. Nature is still holding back up here, lingering in a kind of interim season that is neither winter nor spring, for spring will come late and then turn swiftly, headlong, into early summer. A few warm May days and the meadow grass will be tall and full of flowers. April is a gray month in this place, with the snow retreating but spring not yet on its heels. A month full of the past, full of grief and rage. Full of memory.

As I am about to switch off the engine of my car my eye falls on the signpost saying "Hintereck." Suddenly all the weariness of my long drive drops away. I must go on. I haven't arrived yet. The Stone Age art of reading tracks preprogrammed into us is activated. I am wide awake and ready to look for signs in everything around me, secret indications to be interpreted only by the expert, the well-informed.

I follow the signpost left, a little way downhill. The ground is remarkably level below the little road. A sports field? An exercise ground? A barracks square. I go on. There's something close. Very close. Trying to hide. But I am here to track it down in its hiding place. After fifty-four years I am on my way.

The Café Hintereck looks as if it were waiting in vain for customers today. The buses up to the building on the Kehlstein aren't running, but the barrier to the car park is up, and the car park attendant's little hut is empty. Parking is still free at this time of year. Nonetheless, I am not the only person to have parked my car below the concrete wall, once the foundations of the greenhouses where food was grown for Hitler's vegetarian diet. Biologically cultivated vegetables, irrigated with the purest mountain spring water.

Who else is here besides me? I look at the numbers of the cars. A Mercedes from Darmstadt. A VW Passat from Munich. What are they doing here?

It's a strange place for a tourist outing in the year 1999. There is no indication of its nature. No commemorative plaques, nothing to help you get your bearings. No explanation of exactly where you are. A chance-come visitor would assume that people had come for the sake of the Kehlstein itself. A mountain station like so many in the Alps. Unsuitable for winter sports, too perilously sited for that, too much like an eagle's nest perched on the narrow peak. A place for a summer outing, a viewing area to be reached only by the elevator that runs the last 126 meters up through the rock.

From there you can view the world from the Titans' vantage point: the Berchtesgadener Land, with its valleys shrunk to toylike dimensions, the Königssee a puddle, Salzburg a hazy blur barely perceptible to the north. But close to the observer and clear as day is the imperious manner in which its architects imposed their structure on the mountain. Their defiance. The terrifying statement that it was a present for Hitler's fiftieth birthday. A present from whom? From those who fell to their death in the shaft? Who exactly paid the thirty million Reichsmarks said to have been swallowed up by the building costs?

A giant's toy. A thing millions of years old set down in 1939 by visitors from outer space, on a mountain almost two thousand meters high. Perhaps a secret space ship disguised as a mountaintop dwelling, in which the aliens found at the last moment that they could not take off again? A tearoom, a study for Hitler, the octagonal hall for social gatherings, a dining room—surely that can't have been all. The presumptuous violence of the act, building that road up the mountain, overcoming eight hundred meters of gradient, the blasting, the tunnels, the consolidation of the slopes, the building of bridges, all for this?

Come in, come in, enjoy the Nazis' view. You have to admit it is magnificent.

The Kehlstein house is a magnet for tourists. But now, in April, it still lies spectral and abandoned on the mountainside.

I leave the car park, walk a little way farther along the former greenhouse at the foot of the wall, and come up against a barrier beyond which a sloping meadow rises to the top of a gently rounded hill. I wonder why the road should be closed to me just here.

Not that it was really a road up to this point either, more of a beaten track that has come into being because so many people insist on walking this way. In time they tread a path that continues beyond the barrier. Is there anything to be found here?

I realize that this is the way in which modern visitors take possession of Hitler's Berghof.

There's nothing here, claims the absence of plaques, signposts, any other clues.

Oh, but there is something here, say the beaten tracks bearing witness, all too clearly, of the presence of many curious visitors. There must be something here somewhere.

And I know what it is, too. I know what I am looking for as I set off up the hill. They've planted trees where Göring's house once stood; you can make out nothing but its concrete foundations. A little farther downhill you can see the leveled site of the pool, which was not called a pool at the time but a swimming-bath. The Görings had a swimming-bath, and their house stood on easily the most beautiful spot on the Berg.

We just said "the Berg" at the time, in the same way people used to say "Monte" instead of Monte Carlo if they wanted to show they belonged. This is the language of courtiers, of those still almost unable to absorb the fact that they have actually made it to the place they believe to be the center of the inhabited world. Here. The inner clique of the court itself does not need to use it.

When Hermann Göring came he unerringly appropriated the best piece of the Obersalzberg cake for himself, the Eckerbichl, also known as the Göring Hill. He saw it lying there, seized on it, and in no time at all had made it his own, as he did with everything he desired. Never the shadow of a doubt that they were rightfully his. He grabbed them all like a happy baby, convinced that people liked to watch him stuff himself to the point of satiation. A fine example of a greedy baby. A little monster who grew and thrived until it was an enormous monster. The Eckerbichl was only a small appetizer on the menu of his life.

From up here Hitler's Berghof, that bombastic cross between a barracks and an Alpine chalet, looked like a garden summerhouse, and Bormann's villa, situated a little below the boundaries of Göring's property, like its adjunct. The view moves on, like the simulation of a bird's flight, not just down to the valley and over to the walls of the mountain range in the west, but southwards along the valley, too. Smaller hills move into the foreground of the picture, with little groups of trees growing on them. This is where the royal palace of the little kingdom of the Obersalzberg ought to have stood, basking in the morning sunlight, catching the last light in the west, whereas in fact the Berghof was always bathed in evening shadows early.

I suddenly see that I'm not alone up here. A man is standing over there beyond the site of an old ski lift, glancing my way. He may be a hundred meters away from me, yet I feel that he is looking at me.

Now that I have grown old people do not often look at me. There's something to be said for it. After all, it can be a nuisance to be the center of as much attention as younger women are. The target of so many questions: What's she doing here? Who is she expecting? Is she waiting for someone? You have more freedom when you're old. The young probably don't know that.

But this man is looking at me. He does it openly, shielding his eyes with his hand and staring in my direction. He is asking the crucial question: What is she doing here?

I continue on my way as if I hadn't seen him. But in my own turn I have begun asking myself what *he* is doing here. A tourist on the track of memories? A souvenir hunter? A man who will bend down and then straighten up with a surreptitious handful of the soil of the Obersalzberg? A pilgrim, perhaps? Can you trust anyone who travels from Darmstadt or Munich to this of all places?

And what does the man think of me? Has he assessed my age? Has he worked out how old I would have been when the Obersalzberg was in its prime? What does he think may have brought me here?

I realize that something of the spirit of the place arouses this distrust, this latent readiness to feel mutual suspicion. What business do we have here, that young man and I, an old woman? Listen, I feel like calling out to him, it's not what you think!

But is it, after all?

I slowly retrace my steps without looking around. My pace is uncertain. I know that I have fallen out of step with myself. It happens, as I remember, when I know that someone is staring at me.

A little way below my parked car I see the hotel Zum Türken, on the other side of the road leading down the valley. The place looks deserted. Only the faded national flags in front of the main entrance, European flags and the flag of the United States, seem to indicate any readiness to accommodate guests.

But the guestrooms are empty. Obviously not much has changed here since the place was rebuilt after the war. Even the artificial flowers on the tables look as if they date back to that time. Checkered tablecloths and curtains made of some artificial fiber resembling wool have gone slightly grubby, even in the pure mountain air. No, thank you, I don't want to see one of the single rooms with a view down the valley. I try ordering a coffee.

They're not serving coffee at the moment.

But the bunkers are open, the landlady tells me. Would you like to see the bunkers?

I don't know what it is about her that makes me uneasy. She is by no means unfriendly. She tells me to feel free to walk around the building. That's where the entrance to the bunker will be, and sure enough, here it is. Still no information, no plaque, nothing. But then, suddenly, you are where they want you to be. In a kind of museum foyer, with brochures, videos, a grating over the entrance to the bunker. It can be opened with a token for which you pay five marks. This place is a little gold mine to the landlord and landlady of the hotel Zum Türken. They don't need to renovate their premises; this is what people come for. They'll come in any case. And now I know what I didn't like about the woman: She was waiting for me. She'd known I would come some day. Everyone comes some day, says her expression; I've stopped asking why, it says, I just have to wait and take their five marks. They all want to see it.

But I am the only one today. I start on the downward climb. I am still impelled by a curious hunting instinct, as if I had to find and then follow a trail. The whole place is a system of signs and symbols, but no sooner have you spotted them than they seem to blur again. However, it is different underground. Here they address visitors in plain language. The staircases and passages are adequately lit. Notices on the walls tell you where you are.

So now that you're here, the message seems to be, climb down and discover the secret of this place.

Except that there isn't any secret. All you discover is that there's nothing there. Nothing except that the mountain is hollow inside. All that hush-hush mystery up above is to conceal only this: a system of subterranean caverns and galleries. A structure of delusion. A profound, internal void.

Soon I am approaching the first barrier, with peepholes and openings for guns in the wall. No intruder would have survived. They had supplies to last a hundred years: dried milk powder, champagne, medical supplies, oil, cane sugar, wheat flour, nail varnish, liqueur chocolates, Liebig's Meat Extract, washing powder, shampoo, gramophone records, canned foods, rice, noodles, the German classics, and everything else you need for life underground.

They were well-equipped, well-fitted-out, fully prepared. It was pleasant here. Blue-and-white-tiled bathrooms. Wooden paneling on the walls. Oriental rugs. Furnishings like those in the Berghof aboveground. A parallel world, and very comfortable. No sunlight, unfortunately. Hitler wouldn't have minded. He didn't usually get up until around the middle of the day in any case, he tried to avoid the sun as much as possible. A mole of a man. He had strictly forbidden his mistress to sunbathe. He thought he could go on reigning underground if need be. A mole state with mole subjects. In the end, he couldn't see what would be so terrible about that.

I suddenly notice that I have made my way deep into the labyrinth. I have climbed several levels down. Following signposts pointing to the stores and the rooms for the staff personnel. At some point I find myself standing in front of a brick wall. They don't let visitors any farther in. An old trick: They never show you the innermost catacombs, the deepest dungeon, the final burial chamber, for fear of admitting that there's no secret at all. The Nazi hideouts in the Obersalzberg have been cleared and are empty, as everyone knows. Not a water tap, not a light switch, not a nail was left. By the time the Americans came it was all gone. Looting is a job to be carried out fast. It has to be done before you yourself realize what you are doing. Anyone as old as I am remembers that.

I am seized by a fear that the light might go out suddenly and unexpectedly. Suppose the hotel landlady thinks I've left already? I was the only visitor. And how will I find the way back? Luckily I see the arrows on the walls pointing to the exit.

I look at the time. Just five. Closing time in the bunker? I begin hurrying along the passages and up the steep stairs. I hear heavy breathing, my own. Yet I begin to feel that it is separate from me, a noise like the sound track of a horror film. The echo of my footsteps on the stone stairs adds to the effect.

When I reach the entrance at the top, I see the hotel landlady in conversation with the young man from Göring Hill. There's something like mocking recognition in his eyes. As if he knows who I am.

And then I remember. It's a trick my memory plays. The same mocking glance. The malicious amusement of the knowing smile: Well, well, so we meet again. Don't you remember me? I remember you.

I have been afraid of these remarks all my life. I've been in flight from them all my life. They are part of the repertory of my anxiety dreams. Someone pursuing me, catching up with me, someone who can destroy every weapon of self-defense I have with a single sentence: I know who you are.

I dismiss the memory. I control myself. I know it is this place, its curse, that makes me see things that are merely figures from my nightmares. I ought not to have come.

Haven't I carefully learned to forget? Haven't I trained my faculty of forgetfulness, just as other people train their memory? Haven't I practiced silence as if it were an art, an art to be perfected like any other?

Must I learn to talk about it now? Now that the last secret is out, the last veil that lay over the past raised? Now, when news has reached me bringing what happened then in front of my mind's eye again, before that eye closes forever and no one knows any more about it?

You go a little way down the road and then turn left for Hitler's Berghof, says the woman.

Thank you, I say.

I hadn't asked her. I know the way to the Berghof.

NINETEEN FIFTY-TWO WAS A GOOD YEAR FOR ME. The past was long enough ago to be over, and the future began with an engagement to be married, a common phenomenon at the time.

Dark-haired, tall, a motorcyclist, handsome—the man was a prime catch. A medical student. On course for a future career as a specialist. Just imagine how comfortable, successful, replete with prosperity his life would be. I'd been very lucky.

Good-looking young men intact in mind and body were rare commodities at the time. And even all the one-armed men, those who had suffered head injuries, the wheelchair-bound, the blind, and those who had had a piece of their minds shot away, they could all find wives. All of us had to be nurses in our own way at the time, in a world full of women whose task was to soothe, heal, and comfort. The nursing profession was highly regarded, and I had taken it up myself instead of continuing to study physics. I wanted to be like everyone else. I didn't want to be noticed. I didn't want to be special in any way.

And my success showed how right I was. I was getting engaged to a future doctor. What more could anyone ask a few years after the end of the war? It didn't even bother him much that I wasn't a virgin. I told him that my virginity had been a parting gift to a fellow pupil, motivated by a premonition that he wouldn't come back. He was generous enough to understand. I might perhaps tell him the truth much later, once we were married.

I went to Wiesbaden with him, and he introduced me to his parents. They owned a cigar shop near the station and lived above it. Their flat occupied the whole second floor, and the building had suffered almost no damage. That sounds modest enough today, but at the time it was a dream—an almost intact postwar existence. The building where they lived had been spared, and so had their only son. They gave the impression that it had something to do with their own upright character, and the worst threat to their existence seemed to be summed up in the idea of compensation for those who had suffered in the war. They spoke of such compensation with nothing but agitated and quivering indignation.

The second worst threat was probably me. The forthcoming "official" engagement was spoken of as something inevitable, to be accepted whether they liked it or not if there was no alternative. My future mother-in-law, thin-lipped, addressed me by the familiar *du* pronoun. Of course we slept apart in their flat, my future fiancé in the living room, I in the bed where he had spent the nights of his adolescence. We hardly dared look at each other.

Then a significant day came: They asked us out to dinner, to a restaurant with a view of the water-meadows on the banks of the Rhine. It was an evening in July, summery and mild. We sat out on the hotel terrace, and it was so firmly impressed upon me how unusual an occasion this was, and how grateful we should be to my future father-in-law for his generosity, that I knew I mustn't order anything expensive from the menu, and I decided on meat broth with an egg garnish.

And for the main course? asks the waiter.

The waiters even wore white jackets here.

The young lady only wants the soup, didn't you hear? says my fiancé's mother, casting me a glance in which I think I see a trace of approval for the first time.

But all the same I notice that something is not quite right. The waiter is staring at me.

Young man, says my future father-in-law, what's the matter with you? I asked if asparagus was still available.

Well, well, says the waiter. So we meet again.

It's me he means.

Don't you remember? he says. We met at the Hotel Platterhof. The Obersalzberg. A few years ago, right? Don't you remember me?

No, I say, I'm sorry. I can't think that we ever met before.

My apologies, says the waiter. I must have made a mistake.

He bows slightly, smooth as an eel, odious.

Asparagus? he asks. No, sir, no asparagus left in July. But I can recommend some nice tender French beans with the rump steak.

I do remember him, very well. I remember the zeal with which he escorted us to our table. Please sit down, *gnädiges Fräulein*. Of course, *gnädiges Fräulein,* naturally. His obsequious manner. The scorn and contempt he seemed to conceal behind it.

The Obersalzberg? What's all this about? asks the cigar-shop proprietor when the waiter has moved away again. What would you have had to do with Hitler?

Reinhard, says his wife to her son, sternly, Reinhard, have you been keeping something from us?

I feel the inner circle of the family closing again, a circle that had only just hesitantly opened to let me in. Now I'm shut outside.

No, I say. He doesn't know anything about it.

So I explain what I was doing on the Obersalzberg. Why I was there. Who wanted me there. And why I stayed.

I had meant to tell my fiancé at some point or other. Some time when we were entirely on our own and wouldn't be disturbed. He could have asked me more questions about myself earlier, too. Where do you come from? What were you doing while I was in the army? He never did. I didn't know much about him either. I knew nothing about the two years he had spent in an English POW camp. Nothing about the time before that. It was as if there were a general prohibition against turning to look back. The cities burned behind us, the wounded screamed, the damned shouted curses at us, Sodom and Gomorrah, the judgment on the cities of the plain— and we stared fixedly ahead, determined to escape into a future where we would be saved. We didn't want to be turned into pillars of salt.

I never understood the story of Lot's wife. I mean, she was the one who deserved to live. Memory and compassion. Emotion and perception. Do you have to abandon all those if you want to get away? How long is it before you can bear to look back? Someone has to be able to say what happened. Now. Is it long enough ago now for me to turn back slowly, and say what I see? But will anyone still listen to me?

When the waiter returns I rise and go to the ladies' room. I can hear him asking whether he should keep the soup hot for me.

Don't bother, says the cigar-shop owner.

When I return to the table I hope for a moment that my fiancé will get up and come toward me, perhaps even put his arm around me. But he is sitting with his head bent over his plate, just like his parents. So at least I can pronounce sentence on myself: We're not engaged any longer.

Was there something the matter with it? asks the waiter, taking my untouched soup away.

I have remembered his name, Heinz.

(Your favorite table, *gnädiges Fräulein*. And would *gnädiges Fräulein* like the usual to drink?

Yes, the usual. Thank you, Heinz.)

No, it was fine, I say.

A little later I am on my way to the station carrying my suitcase. I have turned down the offer of an escort. No good-byes. No explanation. Nothing.

Now I know that I must never, never talk about it.

ONLY ONCE, a few years later, am I to break that commandment. I shall close my eyes, turn my face away, and speak of it clearly, but almost tonelessly, as if it were a confession forced out of me.

What did you say? he will ask, the man I would like to love me still if possible.

I shall repeat what I said. And he will take my head between his hands, and I shall keep my eyes closed and wait for what comes next.

We'll never mention it again, he will say. Not a word to anyone, ever. Is that clear?

And only then will he kiss me. And I shall think that I've been lucky with him. I shall tell myself I can't expect any more. He has passed the test for which he gets me as his prize. That's more than I could hope for.

And I stick to his one condition, even if I sometimes still dream of being loved unconditionally. But that's an impossible, foolish wish for someone like me. Would he stand up for me? Would he be my knight in shining armor if people knew all about me? At times I feel almost tempted to betray myself, just to put him to the test. That small stipulation in our marriage contributes to its difficulties. We shall never discuss it, even in the silence of the bedroom. He will never ask me what it was like. And if I ever, for instance in front of the children, make the slightest reference to it, in so coded a way that only he and I can know what I mean and the children don't even guess what I am talking about, I shall see his face flush dark red with anger, and know that I could make him hate me.

So only after his death, when my children are long since grown up, shall I tell them about it, and they will tell me that they knew.

But how can you? I shall ask. We never mentioned it.

Exactly, they will say, looking past me as if it didn't matter.

Obviously this is how family secrets get passed on.

And there are the old photographs up in the attic. He even saw Hitler in one of the photos, says my son.

But why did you never ask me about it? I say.

We didn't think it was all that important, says my daughter.

Oh, I say. Have you mentioned it to anyone else?

Why should we? says my son. Everybody's got photographs like that in the attic.

And suddenly I realize how much time has passed. It will be as if I had spent a hundred years inside the Berg, in the deepest dungeons, the lavishly equipped bunkers under the mountain, in that bewitched, accursed, parallel world without daylight, where a single night is like a hundred years, and a hundred years seems like a single night. It will be as if I had only just climbed out to see how the world had changed in the interval. Children grow up; there they stand, looking at you as if you were a ghost from the past.

And I shall not know what to say to them. How am I to explain what it meant when a phone call came for me from Berchtesgaden one day?

CHAPTER *1*

THE TRAINS WERE STILL RUNNING IN THE SUM-
mer of 1944. I even had a reservation, which proved to some degree
superfluous, since the closer the train came to Munich the emptier it
was. Not many people wanted to go into the cities at that time. They
wanted to get out. As far away from the bombs as possible.

But I wanted to go in. I knew very well that I was going to survive; at the age of twenty everyone is sure of surviving. It was a great
promise, a promise made to me, a most-favored-person clause in the
contract of life. Something told me that of any two possibilities, the
better must always be intended for me. Sometimes I was quite surprised to have come into the world a girl, as if in that other world
before birth there had been a version of myself who failed to pay attention just for a moment, and now had to get by as best she could
with being born a woman.

In fact, being born a woman was a considerably healthier prospect
at the time. Of the twenty-two boys in my class who had taken the
school-leaving exam with me a year ago, ten were already dead, and
the litany of their names, a monotonous chant now running in time

to the rhythm of the train passing over the sleepers, came into my mind of its own accord and almost unremittingly: Hans, Waldemar, Wilhelm, Klaus, Otto, Wilhelm the second, Ernst-Günther, Rudolf, Walter, Max . . .

I suppose they, too, had firmly believed themselves fundamentally invulnerable. Or would they have marched when the order came to march, would they have run when they were told to run—into the gunfire, into ambushes, into minefields? Wouldn't they have dug themselves in like foxes, coming out again only when it was all over? Hans, Waldemar, Wilhelm, Klaus, Otto, Wilhelm the second, Ernst-Günther, Rudolf, Walter, Max . . . Not one of them would have known the knack of dying.

When the first bad news began to arrive, pages of death notices in the Jena newspaper inserted by parents describing their pain as "grief and pride," only occasionally revealing the unutterable depths of misery that had afflicted them—"Our dear big boy," they might say, or "Our only child, loved above all else," and then a name that brought back to me all the remembered atmosphere of summer afternoons on the bathing beach or at dancing class—when such news came I had walked aimlessly through the woods for hours on end. The wind ruffled my hair, night came on. I wanted to be close to them, to feel what it's like to be out of doors, without shelter, and with no chance of going home. I began to hear their voices whispering, as if they were in the middle of some old, familiar scouting game to be played only by the dead and those destined to die. I tried to imagine the moment when you assent to your fate. It must come only just before death, I thought. I intended to spend a night in the wood, freezing cold as my friends had been. But then I went home to bed after all.

Hans, Waldemar, Wilhelm, Klaus, Otto, Wilhelm the second, Ernst-Günther, Rudolf, Walter, Max . . . The staccato rattle of the train going over the railway sleepers was a hollow, ominous accompaniment to that chant. A distant, unreal corps of drummers. It seemed to grow louder as the journey went on, as if something unavoidable were approaching. It had accompanied them, too, on their way east.

Ernst-Günther was my boyfriend. When the news that he had fallen came I locked myself in my room to cry. But all I really felt was enormous anger to think that he had died before we ever really did it. I think most of those boys hadn't done it yet. Max might have. Maybe Rudolf. Just possibly Waldemar. Ernst-Günther? If he'd ever done it, it would certainly have been with me. It simply wasn't fair to let them die before they really knew what it was like.

I was sorry now that we hadn't been engaged. If we'd been engaged I might have done it. I probably would have done it. I blamed myself for not being more in love with him. Now that he was dead it wouldn't have matter if I'd pledged mad, undying love for him. We'd known each other so long. Since primary school. Perhaps it was because I'd really always imagined doing it for the first time with another man some day.

Nonetheless, I still wanted to make Ernst-Günther a present of myself somehow or other, so I went to see his parents and told them we'd been secretly engaged, we hadn't told them only because we knew they thought we were too young, but later on we'd certainly have married and set up house together and all that.

That made them both weep dreadfully, and I wept, too, much worse than when I heard the news that he had fallen. They didn't want me to go, and begged me to call them Mother and Father, which was not easy for me. But they had no one left to call them that, and they even wanted me to move in with them, although they realized that was going too far. Instead, I promised to come and have supper with them once a week. And although that wasn't so bad, and in fact it was very generous of them since they had no ration card for me and it meant I could save up my rations at home, my decision to go to Munich was made partly so that I could escape the consequences of my well-meant lie.

I didn't want to be a widow yet. I was full of curiosity about living men. I was twenty years old. Twenty at a time when the men were being sent away to die. If just one of them had been left alive after the war, I'd have wanted him for myself.

It was May 1944 when Ernst-Günther fell. I know that because of the cockchafer incident not long afterward. There were huge swarms of cockchafers that year. There have never been so many since. They've almost died out now anyway, and no one but us elderly folk can remember what it was like when they descended like a plague.

It was during one of my grief-stricken wanderings, those long walks I took in memory of my dead school friends and in their honor. I was walking down an avenue of beech trees when all of a sudden I heard a strange whirring in the air. It was like an aircraft approaching to dive-bomb me. And then they descended on me in their thousands. They fell from the trees like rain. The street was covered with cockchafers. I couldn't put my feet down anywhere without hearing them crunch underfoot. I walked over the corpses of countless cockchafers as their shiny brown chitinous shells cracked open. They bounced off my shoulders, they slipped down inside the neckline of my dress.

But my hair was the worst. It was long, and I wore it pinned up in what we called the Gretchen style, a kind of wreath plaited around the forehead and the back of the neck. That was the fashion at the time. There was a suggestion of solstice bonfires about it, a suggestion of harvest festivals and Hitler Youth girls. It suited me. I never needed a perm. My hair is strong and quite curly to this day, and as resistant as the feet of the cockchafers that got caught in it. It was as if they had grown into my hair with their whirring and rustling and crackling. As if I were wearing an invisible fire on my head, and I could feel it constantly burning.

At home they had to cut my hair off. There was no other way to get them out. Now I really did look like Gretchen, but in the last act of *Faust*, ready for her execution. A hairstyle of shame, my father called it, and I was indeed ashamed. Such a thing as shame existed in those days. Something somber, bad, secret, something that must never come to light. Defilement, racial impurity, and something else, too: One must not acknowledge or guess at its possibility, yet one feared it. This other thing lurked behind everything you saw and heard and knew, a shame so deep that no disgrace, no penance could ever atone for it.

Sometimes we asked each other: What will happen if we lose the war?

What would happen? They would come down on us like avengers; they would torture and kill us. They would enslave our unborn children and make them work in their mines. And God have mercy on you if you were a girl.

So I was thankful to the soldiers for giving their lives for me. What would become of me if they didn't? My life for the lives of Hans, Waldemar, Wilhelm, Klaus, Otto, Wilhelm the second, Ernst-Günther, Rudolf, Walter, Max? Not just my life, my honor. Was I worth it? And what exactly was my honor, also called innocence? What was I innocent of? Apart from the hairstyle I now wore, and there really was nothing I could do about that.

She looks as if she's been branded, said my father.

I myself felt as if I'd been branded. As if I'd had my head shaved and been driven through the town so that everyone could see my shame, the way they did with women who slept with Jews or foreigners imported to do forced labor. Yet I hadn't slept with anyone, even Ernst-Günther. And now that he was dead that seemed remarkably unimportant.

Of course my hair soon grew back. But when I arrived to stay with Eva in July, I still saw something in her eyes like mocking amusement at my inability to be as pretty as she was. I knew that, as she saw it, I'd never learn. She was wrong there, however.

Eva was a good teacher of the art of outshining other women by showing yourself off to fashionable advantage, not so much to impress men—that's not the point, that's more of a desirable side effect—as to make other women wonder what they're doing wrong when they set eyes on you. Oh, my dear, don't you know that headscarves are worn over the forehead now? No one, but no one ties them under the chin anymore! She was always catching you out in ignorance of this kind, as if you belonged to a banned political party and still bore its visible signs and tokens about your person. Such women do exist. All efforts made by others to be fashionable are poor copies. These women sweep their followers along with them this way and that, in a factional struggle that passes entirely unnoticed by men, and my cousin Eva was one of them. She was one of them to the very last hour of her life, for which she made herself beautiful.

Good heavens, child, what do you look like? she said when we saw each other again. Well, there's a good hairdresser here. I think I'd better make you an appointment with him straightaway.

But I am running ahead of myself.

When the train drew into Munich I was almost alone in it.

Two days earlier there had been an air attack on the station and its surroundings. The main building had been partially destroyed. Rough board partitions separated the rubble from those areas where it was safe to walk. Notices were still hanging at an angle. Lighting had been torn out, the roof above the platforms was propped up on makeshift posts. I was probably risking my life when I got off the train, but we did that almost all the time anyway.

Every farewell could be forever. Every arrival could be for the last time. Every departure could be final. The young Wehrmacht soldiers boarding the train on the opposite platform knew that many of them would never come back.

I made my way through embracing couples, swaying as they stood there in sorrow and bewilderment, I passed mothers raising their hands lightly to wave good-bye, just sketching the gesture to spare their sons the sight of the collapse they would suffer as soon as the train began to move, one mother with her hand pressed to her mouth, another with her hand still raised in the air, as if she had spent years taming a hawk and had now let it fly free. And there it went, there it went, and who knew if it would ever be seen again?

I tried to push through the crowds of people taking leave of each other. I sensed the pain and despair around me as you sense the climate on reaching your journey's end, a breath of air in which alien and curiously familiar messages are mingled. I saw the train on the opposite platform begin to move, I saw the platform emptying, I braced myself against the current of people seeing travelers off who were now making for the exit. I stayed until I was the last person left. Only then did I realize that no one had come to meet me.

I still remember my disappointment at Eva's absence. It was partly shame, a hollow, mocking echo of my earlier misplaced delight. How could I have thought that seeing me was important enough to get Eva to the station on time?

So there I stood with my suitcase, and I had overdone it there, too: The case was too big, too heavy, stuffed too full. Unable to make up my mind what to take, I had packed far too much. Now I wished I had an elegant little bag instead of this monster, a suitcase of my mother's. I could already hear Eva's mockery: *Good heavens, little one, that's a wardrobe!*

I didn't yet know that she herself was in the habit of traveling with far too many bags. I think she felt the most important thing in life was always to have the right frock for the right occasion, and even on her last journey she took a wide assortment of clothes and several suitcases.

Since then I have practiced the difficult art of traveling with hand baggage, less and less of it. A single unnecessary item in my case can spoil all my pleasure in a journey. I strive for the ideal of total, minimal, almost mathematically precise perfection in packing. Everything necessary must go in, everything unnecessary be left out. Perhaps this obsession began there in Munich, when I was conscious of both the excessive weight of my suitcase and my shame at not being met. I began to haul the case in the direction of the exit.

Then I heard my name over the loudspeakers.

It's odd the way you react with alarm to the unexpected mention of your own name. You feel suddenly caught in the act of something, but also one of the elect. For a moment anything seems possible. Who's that speaking? The god of railway stations? Who does he mean? Me? How does he know me? How does he know I'm here?

All I could do was follow the instructions and go to the Holzkirchen station exit. Eva would be waiting for me there, I thought. My beautiful cousin. The only member of my family I admire. The only one I want to learn from. The woman whose riddle I would like to solve. Whose mystery interests me, just as love and passion and their forbidden side interest me. The woman who is Adolf Hitler's lover.

She'll hug me. She'll inspect me critically, with mocking amusement. She'll notice that I have grown since we last met. (At least, I hope she'll notice.) Her attention span is always short, so she'll soon turn it to something else, and we'll go back to her house in Wasserburger Strasse, and I shall be at my journey's end.

But she isn't there.

There's an SS man waiting for me at the Holzkirchen station exit instead. He takes my case while another SS man opens the door of a gleaming black Mercedes-Benz. I sink into the leather upholstery of the backseat.

All this happens with the startlingly heavy emphasis of the opening shots of a film, where the first scenes overpower you whether you like it or not, eliminating any other ideas from your mind and leaving nothing but a passionate interest in finding out what comes next. An absolute desire to decode what is going on. All beginnings are emphatic.

We have instructions to take you to the Obersalzberg, says one of the men.

They don't seem to be expecting me to say whether I want to go or not.

MUNICH HAD CHANGED since I was last there. All cities were changing at that time as they fell to dust and ashes before our eyes.

Part of the station area was closed off. Squads of men were at work sorting out the ruins, putting steel with steel, wood with wood, broken glass with broken glass. The rest was still lying around: bits of masonry, splintered fragments, the ragged ends of electrical wiring. Doors boarded up, windowless facades with nothing left behind them. Stairways projecting into this void.

Today, it seems to me incredible that I drove through such devastation and was still full of questions and expectations about the rest of my journey. Shouldn't I have been more shaken? Shouldn't what I saw have upset me enough to make me forget the aim of my journey, my fears, my hopes, my wish to find out what happened next? Shouldn't it have canceled out my own restless ego?

Several times we had to drive around roadblocks with towering mountains of rubble or bomb craters behind them. Several times people barred our way where the pavements were no longer passable: young antiaircraft personnel hurrying to their posts, Red Cross nurses on their way to the hospital, bent old ladies pulling little hand-carts behind them. They were all looking at the ground, as if there were a ban on looking up and seeing the destruction around them. They all seemed to be in a great hurry, as if they had to cross some no-man's-land quickly, without delay. It was only when my driver hooted, as he frequently did, that they suddenly looked up and stared through the car windows at me. Not with hostility but with surprise, as if awakened from a dream. Where are we? their glances seemed to ask. And who are you? Where are they taking you?

I saw in their eyes that I was important. Valuable, irreplaceable. Some kind of precious object. And I liked that, I liked it enormously.

Where's my cousin? I asked.

The men sitting in front of me were just lighting cigarettes.

Want one? the driver's companion asked me.

Yes please, I said.

There was nothing I wanted more just then.

Even today, memory can make a recidivist smoker of me. I remember how I leaned back. How I inhaled deeply, inhaling the poison of that moment.

When did people ever smoke as greedily and fervently as we did then? If you watch old films today you can still feel something of the atmosphere. The fraternal tie between us addicts. The passing of half-smoked cigarettes from hand to hand. The way we carefully took them between thumb and forefinger and raised them to our lips. We smoked like chimneys. It was the fire that lured us, the fire to which we were addicted. Unhealthy? Yes, of course. As unhealthy as life itself; you can burn your fingers on life.

Eva smoked, too, although the man she loved had forbidden her to do so. She smoked with the petty, illicit satisfaction of schoolboys smoking in the lavatory, relishing her forbidden freedom with every inhalation, enjoying the delicious giddiness it induced in her. There's always a certain arrogance about smoking. A defiant attempt to snatch from life what it won't give freely. In essence it is similar to lying: a nothingness that is still harmful.

German women do not smoke, we had been told. German woman do not drink. German women do not wear makeup. What a laugh! If I'd been told I could have three wishes granted: A cigarette, I'd have said. One wish gone. A lipstick, and perhaps a cream cake if possible. Oh yes, I almost forgot: I wish the war would soon be over.

How sad that this test of character was always bound to fail.

Isn't my cousin in Munich? I asked.

Only when the men answered no did I remember that they had said we were going to the Obersalzberg.

Did I know where they were taking me?

Oh yes, I knew. We all knew about the Berghof. It was—how can I put it—a place as familiar as a childhood scene, yet at the same time strange and full of secrets.

That towering flight of steps leading up to the reception terrace: We had seen Göring and Ribbentrop, Bormann, Himmler, Goebbels, and Speer climb it, eyes raised aloft; we'd seen them disappear to the right among the colonnades, where we assumed the entrance to the house must be. We were always left at the foot of the steps along with the common herd, the cameramen, the chauffeurs, the hangers-on. We were the infantry. The newsreel cinema audience. Now and then, from that vantage point, we had seen the master of the house emerge from the colonnades to welcome his guests, going a little way to meet them, a pace or so over the terrace, even down a few of the steps, depending on who they were, never too far, better not to go far enough. Lloyd George, Edward VIII and his lover Wallis Simpson, Mussolini, Chamberlain . . . we leaned back in the cinema seats. We were there. From far below we watched them climb the steps, a steep and sweeping flight that might have led the way to some mighty monument, an Aztec citadel, a place not made for mortal men unless they approached with the intention of offering prayers, bringing gifts, or accepting instructions from on high. And there he stood, the master of the house, watching their faces flush with the strain of the climb, hearing their chests wheezing. They were always out of breath when they reached him, while he was perfectly composed and at his ease.

He went only as far as the top step even to meet Chamberlain. The old gentleman, almost seventy years of age, had traveled by air for the first time in his life in order to comply with Hitler's wishes in every respect, and was still rather bemused by his bold and spirited venture into the modern age when he found himself at the foot of the steps, with Hitler high above him in the unexpected pose of a man waiting impatiently, as if he supposed that a visitor invited to see him might get a move on. And even as the British prime minister struggled to achieve the thin smile he habitually assumed for the photographers on such occasions—they were allowed up to the terrace in front of the house this time—Hitler had already turned his back with an economical gesture, a backward wave of his right hand, which appeared strangely limp and undecided, as his gestures, surprisingly, often were, indicating that if his guest insisted on a discussion he had better follow him. You should never try appeasement with anyone who receives you in a place like that.

Everyone who visited Hitler's Berghof had to face the stairway trick at the start.

I would never have thought I'd climb those steps myself hundreds of times in my life. They were not in fact as steep as I had always imagined them, but something of their inimical nature, the hostility inherent in them, was conveyed to me. If you wanted to run up a flight of steps two at a time, as I usually did in those days, they were recalcitrant. Sometimes the steps seemed too broad, sometimes too high. You couldn't get any rhythm going. There was something malicious in that flight of steps, and it was the same going down. It seemed to have been built on purpose to make you stumble, and none of all the guests who went up and down it can have been spared occasional nightmares of falling farther than they had ever thought to fall, into an abyss of misfortune, a true inferno of defeat, with Hitler laughing scornfully from an unattainable height overhead. When they were descending the steps toward their waiting limousines they all carefully looked down, even Hitler himself kept his eyes on the toes of his shoes, and anyone authorized, as Mussolini was, to close ranks and walk beside him would voluntarily hold back slightly, carefully sounding out the stairway step by step, and shuffling a little.

Even now I sometimes dream I have to climb down the flight of steps outside the Berghof. And there is no handrail, nothing. Only the endless steps going farther and farther down. It is one of those dreams that you can end only by casting yourself into a void. There is no other way of returning to the present and to waking life.

Of course I knew where I was going. I knew about the huge mechanically operated window in the Führer's great hall with its view of the Untersberg, looking toward Berchtesgaden and the Watzmann massif beyond. The window before which even the Führer himself looked forlorn and curiously small. This was his window on the world. The world presented itself to him there, a mighty stage set consisting of the sky and the mountains, high and lonely peaks, remote from mankind, cold, covered with snow most of the time, a wooded zone below, and farther down, very small and very far away, the tiny human world, scattered dwellings, ephemeral, marginal, of little importance in this image of impressive, overpowering force. A flicker of his eyelashes would wipe it out.

The caption in our cigarette card albums read: "The Führer has made great decisions here." I had been a passionate collector of these cigarette cards. I owned the full set. I knew that Hitler's living quarters in the Berghof were of gigantic dimensions, divided into two floors by a flight of dark-veined marble stairs. The lower story looked out on the valley through the great window, so that anyone coming down and into the hall from the upper story caught his breath, understanding how the world must look to a man when he has it at his feet. And I knew about the hearth at the far end of the hall, its surround made of the same marble as the stairs. I knew about the coffered ceiling of heavy, brown wood with elaborately staggered panels and the two gigantic chandeliers hanging from it, one in each part of the hall, encircled densely by tall, candle-shaped electric bulbs on round frames. It was these chandeliers that gave the room a perceptible suggestion of the *Nibelungenlied*, as if knights of the ancient chivalric orders gathered beside the fire by night to swear secret oaths and plan new acts of violence, revenants risen from their tombs of old, tombs that had never been entirely sealed, sworn brothers in

arms like the men in Agnes Miegel's poem, which we had learned by
heart: .

In that hall sat many a lord
While the flames burnt ever higher,
Hagen Tronje with his sword,
The kings assembled by the fire . . .

I loved that poem. It sent shivers down my spine. It was an intoxicating singsong, chanting of strange things. Gold and blood, the
flicker of flames. It contained all the sex appeal of downfall and ruin.

Softly Lady Fiedel sighed, / rapt in thought and dreaming still; /
Sang Volker: In the forests wide / flows a fount, flows a cool rill—I
imagined Eva sitting in the flickering firelight of the hall, like Fair
Kriemhild—Beside the flames Fair Kriemhild stood, / her slender
hands held fast / the quivering light, like gold and blood, / which on
the walls was cast . . .

Oh yes, Eva fit into that picture. She fit into this hall. I knew it
even before I saw her there. Its architect had shown a feeling for
atmospheric detail. The paintings on the walls in their heavy gilt
frames, the Feuerbachs, the Bordone, on the other hand, were like a
concession to a more or less alien civilization. Like items of loot displayed in the conqueror's palace to show everyone that they, too,
were his.

This was Hitler's living room, no more and no less. The place
where he felt at home. It covered 285 square meters and was furnished
with comfortable sofas and armchairs. The domestic arena of his private world.

Later I saw such places portrayed in James Bond films. The villains
lived there, powerful and ruthless characters working on great proj-
ects for ruin. It was remarkable how easily I recognized the aura
again.

Those were remote dwellings: Goldfinger's ranch, idyllic, close to nature, a place where privileged guests were received. Mettlesome cars and horses. All the harmless amusements of the rich and powerful. But the great wood-paneled hall, deceptively welcoming, can suddenly turn into a prison. At the touch of a button walls open and close, windows fold away and disappear, the floor moves. Beneath it lies a world of dangerous passages, unlit cells, subterranean dungeons. Woe to anyone who ventures in. A world of bunkers.

Dr. No's hideout in a nuclear reactor under the sea. The security airlocks that have to be overcome. The thickly armored doors through which you reach the living area, as if entering a huge refrigerator. The well-trained staff welcoming you, making you comfortable. The master of the house is expecting you. All the plush splendor of his private rooms, given the lie by plain granite-colored walls of natural stone. Gold-framed paintings. A touch of the rococo. Lace, tapestries, cut-crystal glasses. Brass candleholders. A whole battery of the choicest alcoholic beverages in the bar. And the view? A window about the same size as the window on Hitler's panoramic mountain view, but with the creatures of the sea swimming beyond it, much magnified. Dr. No's maritime zoo. His aquarium.

Minnows pretending they're whales, just like you and me, says James Bond. One feels safe in here, though.

It depends, Mr. Bond, which side of the glass you're on, replies the master of the house with grim humor.

Back in the sixties, when I saw these films in the cinema, I knew I had once been in such a place myself. But how did Ian Fleming know so much about them? Or is the pattern an old one? As old as the dreams in which we must go down to the deep, dank dungeons of the underworld? Are the architects of evil habitual offenders, carrying out to the letter instructions that are always the same?

I shall know the place again in Hell: seven square kilometers, guarded and enclosed by a double barbed-wire fence. The uniformed men. Their anonymity. Their omnipresence. The checks carried out before anyone was let in, the steep uphill climb, the breathless hesitancy with which you approached, that panic-stricken sense of being an intruder who cannot escape punishment. The friendly welcome from well-trained servants. The guestrooms that could have been in a hotel. The wooden paneling, the fireplaces and tiled stoves, the floral furnishing fabrics, the comfortable club chairs actually inducing a sense of discomfort. The aspirations to art and culture, the Bechstein grand, the brocade tablecloths on all the tables, the hothouse flowers always rising a little too far from narrow-necked curving vases, flowers fanning out in cobweb shapes, red tulips, white lilies, constantly replaced by fresh blooms like a statement that is no more valid for all its repetition. The underworld below, where no daylight could penetrate. The gratings over the shafts, the heavy armored doors, the fear of having to go down there some time or other.

And you always do have to go down. There's nowhere else to go once you arrive in the country house of Evil.

IT WAS A HOT AFTERNOON in the middle of July—the fifteenth, I think. The sun blazed down on the roof of the black Mercedes, and I was sticking to the smooth upholstery. But I still felt that the airflow was uncomfortable, creating violent eddies where I sat in the back and making me shiver. However, I didn't feel brave enough to ask the men to wind up one of their windows. Next day my tonsils would be swollen, and all the time I was on the Obersalzberg I felt I had a lump in my throat alternately swelling and subsiding again. My tonsils were taken out later, but that was years after the war, and even after the operation my throat was still sensitive and vulnerable to chills.

We had left the city behind and were suddenly in the untouched peace of the foothills of the Alps. At first sight of the mountains the laws of the lowlands appear to be suspended, or so I felt then. It seemed unthinkable for the war to reach this place. Somewhere a herd of cows crossed our path, which my driver obviously saw as some kind of act of sabotage, an insult meant for him personally. The radiator grille pushed the mass of bovine flesh ahead of us out of the way with the merciless demeanor of a tank rolling forward. Bellowing cattle. Panic, cries of alarm from the lads herding the cows. Then we accelerated away again, tires squealing.

This was the Führer's domain, a kind of superior private road, although unavoidably available to the other residents of the area, too. Its surface was first class and its condition intact, something by no means to be taken for granted at the time. Our car had absolute right of way here. It was unwise to obstruct us.

I saw the black backs in front of me. Those were not shoulders you could tap, saying: Please turn around. I don't want to go where you're taking me. I was not in a taxi. I was in an official SS car. It was much too late to resist anyway. What would be, would be. There was something curiously pleasant about slipping into the role of a woman abducted; it had a faint touch of the alluringly forbidden about it.

I had felt it ever since I heard what Eva said on the phone when she invited me:

The Führer would like you to come, too.

I wasn't wrong. That's what she had really said. And every time I repeated it to myself it carried more weight, became more irresistible.

He has to go away in the next day or so, she had said. To some ghastly spot in East Prussia where he'll be closer to the war. He's worried about me because I'm left on my own so much. . . .

He was worried. He wanted a playmate for his mistress. Me. This would be my war work. I wasn't fit for Reich Labor Service because of a knee injury. But now the Führer had summoned me.

Father won't let me, I told Eva. You know how he . . .

It'll be all right, she said firmly. I realized that this was the wrong telephone line on which to explain that my father was not a Nazi.

And that was putting it mildly. The fact was that he regarded Hitler as he would go down in history: a monster, a criminal on a gigantic scale. Someone ought to assassinate the man, he used to say.

To which my mother would respond: Oh, hush, you'll get us into terrible trouble.

We're in it already, replied my father, hasn't anyone noticed?

He would be beside himself if he knew where I intended to go. My daughter is not going to enter the house of such a criminal, he'd say.

So we only mentioned Munich.

Do come, Eva had said. Then we can both stir the place up a bit.

As if Munich hadn't been stirred up enough by the war already.

But I knew Father wouldn't agree to that either.

Munich! he cried angrily. There are air raids on Munich night after night!

She has a bunker of her own under her house, I said, a proper air-raid shelter with a gas filter and power generators. The most modern air-raid shelter technology you can get.

I knew the technology argument would carry weight with my father. He worked in the research and development department at Zeiss, and had invented a range-finder that was of great significance for war technology. At the time, however, he was trying to keep his invention secret, so that after the war, as he said, he could make it available for peaceful uses.

Does that fellow think he can salvage his affair from the hostilities?

Father, I said. She *is* my cousin.

Anyway, there's nothing to salvage, he said. Do you honestly think we can lose this war and everything will still go on as before?

Everything always goes on somehow, said my mother, in the pacific tones with which she intervened in Father's and my conversations.

No, snapped Father. No. It will all be over. This time there'll be no going on.

I wish he'd take that back, I thought. I wish he'd take that back.

For his words still had power over me. If he cursed me, then I was accursed. When you're twenty you still need your parents' blessing as you go on your way, you need them to believe in the future ahead of you.

But there's rebellion, too. You need that just as much. You need to march out, spurn prohibitions, set off into the unknown against all reason, making light of the dangers involved.

You can't forbid me to do anything! I said. I don't need your permission!

At heart I knew that I wouldn't be coming back in a hurry. What began as a short family visit seems today to have been my great venture into adult life. My childhood was left behind. On that journey to Berchtesgaden my adult existence began. I am approaching the end of it now, and it started with a mistake. With naive misunderstanding and distorted ideas. But when did such a venture ever begin otherwise?

Don't go, said my father. Don't do it.

And the gentle tone of his voice, the deep sadness in it, really should have made me think again, should have touched me as it touches me today when I remember my father and how he said those words.

I never saw him again.

Later, after the war, when people spoke of guilt, an incomprehensible form of guilt beyond all normal criteria, a burden never to be lifted, I knew what they meant. I recognized my share of it. And I, too, had to learn, very slowly. I had to look back to understand what I had done when I ignored my father's prohibition on a day in July 1944.

I was going to see Eva. Wasn't that what I wanted? Most of all I wanted to know why she hadn't come to the station herself to fetch me, as she'd promised she would. Had she sent these men? She must have. Had she really forgotten that we were to meet in Munich? I mean, she'd invited me to her house in Munich. Perhaps she was waiting for me there now. In which case this was something like an abduction. Did they perhaps keep virgins down in subterranean dungeons in Hitler's Alpine fortress, had I been chosen as an addition to the stocks they were laying in for coming times of shortage when they, the last of the faithful, besieged by the rest of the world, would defend themselves in the Berghof as, in my father's view, they actually intended to do?

The mountains closed in around us beyond Siegsdorf. We drove into their shadow. I was wearing a light summer dress. My jacket was in the trunk of the car, and my fantasies about virgins in freezing cellars were probably no more than symptoms of the chill I felt. I withdrew into myself around a hard, concentrated core, as you do when there is no other weapon against the cold outside. Only Eva's embrace could save me now.

As the car drove through Berchtesgaden I felt for the last time that I could still ask them to stop and let me out. I could have taken a room for the night with the money I had on me, and then gone home the next day. As if saying good-bye, I looked at people sitting on benches outside their houses with children on their laps, I saw young men raking hay, I saw farmers' wives wearing big, shady hats and bending over the beds in their gardens.

But the last houses in the place were behind us now, and our way wound up the mountain, far, far into the shadows of its northeast flank. Soon afterward we stopped at a barrier. We had reached something like a forbidden region. The carefully shielded, closely guarded home of the man my cousin loved.

IT WAS SIX YEARS since I had last seen Eva. I was fourteen then, wearing lace-up shoes and hand-knitted kneesocks, a dark blue skirt with broad braces, and a bodice like a bib over my flat chest. I was to go and visit my aunt Fanny in Munich. Aunt Fanny felt so lonely now that her three daughters had left home.

I must be nice to her, said my mother.

She's got Uncle Fritz, hasn't she? I said.

But I realized that Uncle Fritz was not much of an argument.

So I went to Munich, and was bored. I imagined my absent cousins' lives. I slept in their beds, sometime in Ilse's, sometimes in Eva's, sometimes in Gretl's, and I thought of them as you think of beings inhabiting other worlds, worlds where wonderful, un-dreamed-of things happen. Ilse had just married, which as far as I was concerned raised her to a sphere of everlasting bliss into which, even in my wildest dreams, I could not follow her. But one day, of course, I, too, would infallibly reach that place.

At the time I did not stop to wonder how bliss of such a nature leads at some point or other to life as I saw my mother or even Aunt Fanny leading it. Aunt Fanny who slept alone night after night in her stately double bed, while Uncle Fritz had withdrawn to a narrow, tunnel-shaped guestroom that he left only for meals, and in which he must never be disturbed. No, marriage as I envisaged it for Ilse and me was something quite different: the definitive happy ending. The ultimate freedom. Adulthood. Something surpassed only by Eva.

Nobody had told me about Eva. Nobody discussed it with me. But of course I knew all about it. I knew about it just as I knew all about sex at the time. I knew everything. Heavens, when I think of the sex education of today! Did we get any back then? We didn't even know a word like sex. Luckily my mother had never tried telling me the facts of life. Like any intelligent child, I worked them out from hints here and there, and had long since drawn my own conclusions.

It was something like that with Eva.

One day—I couldn't have been more than eight or nine—I opened a newspaper and saw a photograph of my cousin. "Hitler's current favorite Eva Braun," said the caption under it, "daughter of a

Munich teacher." I was sure at once that this was the main news of
the day.

I went to my mother and asked her what a favorite was. Although
I did not in fact have to guess; I knew perfectly well. I'd like to see
the adult who can tell a child anything she doesn't already know in
answer to such questions.

What do you mean? asked my mother sharply.

I told her the circumstances.

Such nonsense, cried my mother. Where did you get that newspaper? Who gave it to you? It's not the sort of thing you ought to be
reading! Give it to me at once!

I said, guilelessly, that I had found the newspaper by chance and
thrown it straight in a waste bin after reading it. In fact, I had been
reading it in front of my mother's very eyes in our dentist's waiting room.

All lies, she said.

Thanks. I knew all I needed.

Those were the hints I mean. Now I knew all about my cousin,
just as I knew the things men and women keep secret from their children. No one could pretend to me any longer.

Eva. Twelve years my senior. I couldn't imagine anything more
grown-up. Or anyone more beautiful than my beautiful cousin. Or
anything more secret than her secret, which wasn't a secret at all.
Everyone knew it.

One afternoon the bell at the door of the Hohenzollernplatz apartment was rung hard several times, and in burst Eva. Uncle Fritz, who
had just come out of his room for tea, went back into it without a
word and closed the door behind him.

Uncle Fritz wasn't speaking to Eva now that she was Hitler's
favorite.

I couldn't understand. Didn't he think it an honor? Wasn't he
proud of her?

No, said Aunt Fanny. Uncle Fritz would like the girls to come home. Unmarried daughters ought to be with their parents, you know, she added. Don't you understand that?

Where are they, then? I asked.

That was how I found out that Hitler had given my cousin a house.

But then he's sure to marry her soon, I said. I mean, if they already have a house.

I don't know about that, said Aunt Fanny.

And what about Gretl? I asked.

Gretl's gone to stay with her, said Aunt Fanny. So that Eva won't be alone so much.

But she's got Hitler, I said.

Yes, well, said Aunt Fanny.

Oh, I said.

Is it a nice house? I asked, to put Aunt Fanny's mind on a different track. I loved her. Secretly, I wished my mother were like Aunt Fanny.

I don't know, she said. Uncle Fritz has forbidden me to visit them.

I had never seen her so upset before.

Only later, many years later, did I understand the sorrow of Aunt Fanny and Uncle Fritz.

Uncle Fritz shut himself up in his room and wrote letters to the Führer saying nothing about the way he missed his daughters, nothing about the silent meals he shared with his wife at the kitchen table now that the girls weren't there, nothing about the nights he spent in agitated conversation with himself until his indignant murmuring rose to such a volume that Aunt Fanny heard it in her lonely conjugal bedroom next door, where she herself was directing pleas, complaints, and adjurations at her absent husband, she, too, was involved in a hopeless conversation with herself every night.

So Aunt Fanny implored Uncle Fritz, and Uncle Fritz implored Hitler, and no one paid any attention, even though Uncle Fritz did sometimes send off one of the letters he wrote with a trembling hand in the pale light of dawn to the Reich Chancellor and Führer in Berlin. These letters went on at length about masculine honor and civic pride, and the fact that even the great of this world were subject to the moral commandments laid down since time immemorial.

Fritz Braun never received a single answer to these letters, and in the still hours of the night that silence revealed to him all the annihilating scorn and deep contempt felt for senior teacher Fritz Braun, retired, the contempt so present in his mind. He felt dishonored, crushed, exposed. His adversary had triumphed over him. Both of them, Fritz Braun and Adolf Hitler, knew what it was all about. As always when a daughter is seduced, it was about the question of satisfaction, which can be offered only in the form of marriage.

So all the letters Uncle Fritz wrote to Hitler were nothing but an unspoken plea. All his verbose appeals to honor and morality and decency just meant: Marry her! For heaven's sake marry her! And in the silence of the night Uncle Fritz himself knew it. Hitler spoke very clearly to him by preserving his silence. Herr Braun, Hitler was saying, let's put an end to this farce. I know you'd be glad to have the Reich Chancellor of Germany and your doubtlessly beloved Führer as a son-in-law. Well, what senior teacher wouldn't? But you see, I just don't have time to answer your letter about this matter. And what makes you think I'd have the time, or shall we say the inclination, for the matter itself, or come to that even the faintest intention of doing it? Herr Braun, may I please ask you to stop bothering me? My uncle Fritz contemplated shooting himself through the head. But for one thing, he lacked the courage, and for another, who would look after his daughters' lost honor if he was gone?

So he shut himself up in his room. He said very little and he hardly ate. He was dying of shame.

It had not, perhaps, been very wise of my mother to send me to their home, a place incomprehension haunted like a ghost, dividing spouses, destroying sleep, silencing conversations, closing doors, making daughters into remote, fleeting visitors. For the first time I felt that behind everything I saw that something else was hidden, something the grown-ups did not merely seek to hide from me but in fact kept secret from themselves and each other.

And here was Eva. She was wearing a pale blue coat and looked a vision. I have wanted a pale blue coat like hers all my life. I did own such a coat once, but I hardly ever wore it. It got dirty very quickly, and always somehow looked as if I had borrowed it. A handsome article of clothing hanging in my wardrobe, no doubt about that, but not so good on me. It hung there for years, and finally, at some point, I gave it to my husband's secretary. But I don't think she wore it either.

Eva looked breathtaking in her pale blue coat. Like a film star, I thought. A touch of Marika Rökk, a touch of Kristina Söderbaum. Women who come into a room, fling their coats down on the first chair to hand, and turn everything upside down within a few seconds before dashing off again, always at top speed, leaving some indefinable trace of themselves behind, a breath of perfume and perplexity . . .

She called, "Mami!" Mami. Nobody said "Mami" at the time. She could only have got it from a film. I made a note of it at once, but later decided it didn't suit my own mother. Nor Aunt Fanny, to be honest. Eva burst into the kitchen, opened all the cupboards, looked for the "secret hoard," as she called it. Finally she found it: a tin in which Aunt Fanny always kept a supply of peppermint creams obviously intended for Eva. She immediately fell on them greedily.

I realized that she was Aunt Fanny's darling, the daughter for whose visits she was always hoping, and for whom she jealously guarded a little treasure. Her tomboy, her whirlwind girl, her princess. I could tell from the way Aunt Fanny hastily took off her apron and closed the doors of the kitchen cupboards again. I could tell from the frank pleasure with which she watched the peppermint creams disappear.

Would you like one, too? she asked me.

Then it turned out that it was because of me Eva had come.

Let's have a look at you, little one, she said. I still had a bit of puppy fat, too, when I was your age. Well? Aren't you bored? What do you do here with the old folk all day? It must be awful!

And she invited me to come and stay with her for a few days.

In . . . in that house?

Yes, she said, Gretl's there, too. We have no end of fun. There's a gramophone, a wireless, a telephone. You can phone your mother in Jena every day if you like. I phone my own mother almost every day, when Father isn't around . . .

Oh, how I wanted to accept!

We must ask Father, said Aunt Fanny. I don't think he'll let her.

Mother, said Eva, it's nothing to do with Father. She's *your* niece.

At that moment I saw the figure of Uncle Fritz in the doorway. I don't know how long he had been standing there.

Well, I don't care, said Eva, putting a bitten peppermint cream down on the table.

I think . . . , said Aunt Fanny. But she didn't know what she thought.

Oh, do as you all please, said Uncle Fritz, waving us aside and going away again.

I think this was the only kind of contact he still had with Eva; his manner of greeting her when she came home.

She can come back here to sleep, said Eva, loud enough, perhaps, for her father to hear, too.

So we came to a working compromise. I could go to my cousins in Wasserburger Strasse for the day, but I must be back in Hohenzollernplatz in the evening. I would spend the night in one of my cousins' formerly virginal beds. By day, however, I would see the place where Hitler came visiting. At last I would know what a favorite's life was like.

★ ★ ★

I KNEW NOTHING ABOUT MALMAISON, but I had imagined some kind of palace. Mirrored halls. Servants . . .

However, what Hitler had given my cousin was an ordinary family house, the kind with a front garden where crocuses flower in spring, where leisure, freedom from care, and a reasonable amount of prosperity seem to dwell behind the net curtains. At the time such a house was given the grand name of a villa only by those for whom possession of anything like it was an unattainable dream. Wasserburger Strasse was inhabited by people who had done rather better in life than my uncle Fritz. It was an address beyond the reach of senior teachers.

Perhaps that was one reason why he never visited his daughters there. In what character would he mix with the neighbors? As Hitler's father-in-law? He wasn't Hitler's father-in-law. On the other hand, no one could have approached him without the greatest respect, because in a way he *was*, all the same. No one could slight him with impunity. Fritz Braun was deeply sensitive to the scorn that was equally inherent in either respect or disrespect for his person.

He did not know that his daughter Eva felt that scorn just as deeply. If she met her neighbors she greeted them with an almost obsequious friendliness that had in it something like a plea to be forgiven for living here among them—she, a mere office girl, not even a secretary, as she was described in the telephone book entry. Only a former assistant in Heinrich Hoffmann's photographic business, employed sometimes in his studio, sometimes in the office, sometimes in the shop—where one day, when she was sixteen, a dark, gruffspoken man had come in and asked her for something in a low and husky voice. She served him as obligingly as she could. He intimidated her, and the familiar and expected shyness of her manner was irresistible. For the first time she felt her shyness giving her power, and when she fetched a ladder to look for what he wanted on the top shelves she did it in the full awareness that she was obeying an order, and let him get a look at her legs under her skirt.

She knew who Adolf Hitler was. In 1929 he was already the most important customer a man like Heinrich Hoffmann could have— Hoffmann could even sometimes refer to him as a friend. But there was no calculation or ambition to rise in the world involved when she immediately offered herself to him for the first time. It was not that. As some people are brilliant at dissembling, or friendship, or business, others are brilliant in their timidity. They are looking for a master, and once they have found him they can hold him by a degree of self-abnegation that even the most experienced men of power, those most practiced in the subjugation of other human beings, would scarcely think possible. And sometimes a bond develops between the timid and their masters that looks like the bond of love yet is something quite different, such a perfect interplay of command and obedience, subjugation and submission, always and unresistingly in collusion, that the submissive partner acquires as much power as the dominant partner, the timid woman finds herself suddenly facing an intimidated man, the master faces a mistress, and they both recognize themselves in each other, and demand both timidly and imperiously to be loved.

At the time, of course, I knew nothing about any of this. I did not know that tyrants are in fact shy people and like to entrust themselves to the shiest women they can find, in order to be dominated by them. Nor did I know how severely they blame themselves for turning to women of this kind in their timidity, still less how many other people must suffer for the fact that such a woman knows them for what they are.

I thought shyness was my own problem and mine alone. Like all girls of fourteen, I was tormented by the idea that I was the only girl in the world who felt insecure, inhibited, and lacked the self-confidence that everyone else seemed to display, while I dreamed of someday seeing the world at my feet, offering me respect and admiration.

For only the shy entertain a wish to make a big splash at some point. My cousin Eva had done it, or so I thought at the time.

But I was severely disappointed when I first saw her house. A porch, a small entrance hall, a kitchen, a living-dining room with a sliding door separating the two halves, two bedrooms on the first floor and another in the loft. The furniture could have come straight from a furnishing showroom, every room complete in itself like a little in-store display, the dining room furnished in mahogany, the living room in dark oak, the sisters' bedrooms matte-lacquered white with a bed, a chest of drawers, a wardrobe, a dressing table, and flowered bedspreads. This was how young families set up house at the time if they had the money. It was clearly the deceptive realization of Eva's idea of an average, self-contained, manageable lifestyle. This was the setting in which she had dreamed of living. And her friends, Beppo, Kathi, Mitzi, Mandi, and the others all fitted in here.

The idea of Hitler entering this house seemed to me unthinkable even at the time, and to this day I think he didn't often go there. It was very much Eva's house, a present, the only present from the dictator that she made entirely her own, regarding it as a present he had given her of life. A large portrait photograph of Hitler did hang in the hall, and you faced it the moment you came through the front door, but all of Eva's friends thought he looked very strange and ghostly in it, pale and unreal, with a curious gaze that cast its spell on the observer, seeming to come from another world into which he would spirit us some day.

It must have been one of those photographs by Hoffmann that had pleased its subject, or he would probably not have given it to his mistress. To me, however, it seemed then, and still seems in my memory today, like an evil phantom, not a real likeness, a ghostly apparition that would come to life in the middle of the night, step out of its frame, and visit nightmares on the occupants of the house.

I was glad Aunt Fanny had said I couldn't stay overnight with my cousins, and whenever I came back in the evening to the Hohenzollernplatz apartment, where one of the three abandoned beds of the daughters of the house awaited me, I felt a sense of relief and security.

And how are my girls? Aunt Fanny would ask me if Uncle Fritz's door was shut.

Terrific! I replied. It was a favorite word among the young people in my class, so I made it my favorite, too.

I mean are they well? asked Aunt Fanny.

Yes, I told her.

In the afternoon we played the card game Eleven Out. I don't know if they played it when I wasn't there, or just to kill time with me. It's a stupid game, and I hated it. All the same, I got caught up in the tempo that even pointless games can generate, a kind of compulsive repetition, a paroxysm of pedantry in which you submit yourself to a strict system of rules. No sooner was a game over than we reached for the cards again like addicts to reshuffle them.

Eva sometimes went out of the room and came back a little later in another dress. Even then she had a mania for changing her clothes, and did it six or seven times a day, often for no perceptible reason. It was as if she were working on some major and difficult task that called on all her powers and sometimes exceeded them: the necessity of finding more and more ways of dressing, more and more attempts to be herself. If you ever saw her at the time thinking hard about something, you could be sure she was wondering what to wear next, and every impressive entrance always outdid its predecessor.

I was particularly fascinated by her blouses. Silk had a sinful charm at the time. The blouses my mother wore and those she bought for me were made of cotton, and provided evidence of meticulous domesticity. You soaked the collars, then you bleached them and starched them. They rubbed your neck sore. Eva's blouses were soft and shining, a second skin clinging gently and perfectly to her shoulders and breasts. A higher form of nakedness. I wanted nothing more than to touch them.

One day she came back into the room with a blue-gray wool dress over her arm.

Take your clothes off, little one, she said.

When you are fourteen there's nothing worse.

Come on, take your clothes off, little one, don't be shy. It's only us. She wanted me to try the dress on.

Not for the world. I had my reasons. Take my clothes off? Never!

Look, said Gretl, you can't go around in that pleated skirt and those terrible blouses the whole time. It's just not chic.

Gretl herself looked like a rather blurred copy of her sister. She was three years younger than Eva, and neither as beautiful nor as elegant. In fact, she had only one outstanding quality: devotion, and her devotion was exclusively to Eva. She lived with her, wore her cast-off clothes, and was kept out of the allowance that Hitler gave to Eva. She was a professional younger sister, having broken off her training as a photographer—in this again resembling Eva. She seemed happy to share her sister's life and did not, as far as I know, have a lover of her own. She was the woman who comes into the relationship as part of the deal when a man marries her sister.

Men never develop an appetite for such bargains. They have too little appeal to the male as conqueror, since such women will come into his possession anyway. With time, men may perhaps feel at ease with them through the habit of familiarity, and will appreciate their boundless loyalty to themselves so long as they, the husbands, respect the marriage.

For professional sisters keep a fanatically watchful eye on the marriage, like little guard dogs, and the only savagery of which they are capable is aroused if their sisters are betrayed. Then they become avenging goddesses. Their own husbands, if they have them, have nothing to fear. Their husbands are free to do as they like, and if they take advantage of that freedom it is no more than their wives expect, considering themselves not worth the trouble of fidelity.

If Eva had been fated to grow old she would have grown old with her sister. They would have lived in her house on Wasserburger Strasse, and after many years they would have looked like elderly twins holding hands as they went out for a walk, offering hesitant greetings, afraid of not sounding friendly enough, although they know no one except themselves anymore, two old ladies with the same dismal hats on their heads, clinging to each other with the identical movement when a gust of wind blows. . . .

It could just as well have been a salesman, a teacher, or a chimney sweep who came along and wanted one of them for himself. But it was Adolf Hitler.

There I stood, clutching my blouse with both hands, as my cousins had fun trying to undress me. I didn't think it was funny at all. I had something to hide. I defended myself with all my might from letting them reveal my source of deep physical shame. They almost ripped my blouse. Then they let go of me.

Whatever is the matter, little one? said Eva suddenly, in the changed voice I can still sometimes hear today if I try hard. I have only to think of that moment as I stood there facing my cousins, rigid with outrage, tense with resistance—and I hear Eva's voice as it was then, as I can still conjure it up, recorded somewhere on the hidden audio system of my memory.

What's the matter, little one?

And suddenly, at her tone of voice, the ice of my outrage and resistance melted, I surrendered, and I showed my cousins the instrument of torture that I wore. Suddenly I even felt I very much wanted them as my confidantes. I didn't yet know that having confidantes is the first step toward liberty in a woman's life. That evening I would leave Wasserburger Strasse as the woman I was to become, the woman I am now.

Nobody has even heard of a chest brace these days. It was a garment like this that I wore under my blouse, a structure made of stout cotton and whalebone enclosing my torso, and not just compressing everything budding and swelling there when it threatened to show, but hiding it under a perfectly flat front. Not a bra, more of a breastplate such as perhaps only St. Joan of Arc wore before me, and for the same reason that it had been imposed on me: to keep us from leading men into temptation. There was to be nothing swelling and bouncing about when we faced the fray, St. Joan on the battlefield, I in gymnastics lessons as the only girl among the fourth-year boys at the Jena grammar school I attended at the time.

My father wanted me to wear one of these garments, and my mother had taken me to a shop selling sanitary items and bandages to be fitted with this armored carapace when my breasts began to grow. They grew fast, and seemed to do so all the faster in the constraint of their imprisonment. When I undid all the metal hooks and eyes in the evening, they were sore and marked by deep red weals, and they swelled up like balloons that start out crumpled and unattractive and are then pumped full of air. They hurt whenever I moved, and I didn't know what I would do if they didn't stop getting bigger and heavier, if the day came when I couldn't endure them either with or without the breastplate.

I knew there was no help for me, and when my cousins watched, speechless, as I unbuttoned my blouse and then undid hooks and eyes and exposed the sore, tormented flesh underneath, slowly swelling to its full shameful size, when I saw in their faces first horror, then incredulity, and they shook their heads, it confirmed my suspicion that I had some kind of monstrous growth that would slowly kill me, like a cancerous tumor, and for which there was no cure on earth. Then they began to laugh, and suddenly I realized that I was laughing, too, and Eva helped me undo the last hooks and eyes, peeled the thing off me, and tossed it away. Instead, she wrapped me in her arms. I felt her breasts soft against mine, and realized at that moment how things were supposed to be.

What on earth's the idea of that, little one? she said.

I told her about the gymnastics lessons.

Then they gave me my first bra, light and soft as silk. It was one of Eva's. I tried it on, and it fit. It had adjustable straps crossing over the back, and champagne-colored satin cups. I wore it for many years, for the growth of my breasts soon stopped giving me cause for concern.

LATER, WHEN WE HAD NOWHERE TO TURN, when we wandered aimlessly through a country that offered us no home anymore, through devastated cities, ruined stations with trains that had nowhere to go, nowhere to arrive, when we all carried our lives around with us in little cases that we never put down anywhere, always keeping a watchful eye on them, cases full of letters, broken hand mirrors, empty tubes of cosmetics, single stockings whose partners had been lost in another life, I always carried Eva's bra with me—a little soft, silky thing—in my hand baggage, light as a feather. Yet one day, when I remembered whose it had been, it seemed to me a heavy burden. I didn't want it anymore. I wanted to be rid of it, as one would wish to be rid of the corpus delicti, leaving no trace behind. I threw it in a waste bin, and then took it out, because you didn't throw away used articles of clothing in those days, not while there might still be some use for a button, a piece of elastic, a scrap or so of fabric. Finally I threw it on the fire, and tried not to think of the bits that wouldn't burn, the metal clips for adjusting the straps. The Austrian farmer's wife with whom I was living at the time must have found them in the ash box of her kitchen stove.

No one asked questions in those days. Uniform buttons lay beneath all the rubble that was being removed; stinging nettles grew and fed on disintegrating cotton drill trousers and black coats, ferns and coltsfoot spread over weapons thrown away into roadside ditches in haste. The black boots under which the roads once echoed were lost somewhere in a swamp, sinking deeper into it year by year, until nothing was left of them. No archaeological dig would ever bring them to light. Only now and then did a warhead still explode, tearing apart children who had been playing on a bomb site. No one could dig among that detritus with impunity.

I didn't want anyone to ask me where I came from or who I was. You dare not turn around if you are suspect. Everything depends on passing unrecognized. The trains were full of people who wanted to pass unrecognized. Most of them hoped for a future spent incognito, somewhere no one knew about them, a place where the seeds of liking and trust could be sown again, where everything they felt to be good in themselves could be brought to flower. For we all feel that we are good. We feel it too deeply to believe any evidence to the contrary. Some men turned up their coat collars when the train came into their hometown and did not get out, but traveled on somewhere else, anywhere, and their wives went to the social services, registered them as dead and applied for their pensions.

And there were plenty of others who did not go home, and now and then one of these took another man's place. Is that you? a woman would ask, and he said yes, and slept with her, and she told the children, don't run away, this is your father, come along, don't be frightened, and something in the children knew that they would never love him and could not stop waiting for another father to come back; a vague sense of grief lingered on in them, and now and then they would feel a convulsive desire to sob for no apparent reason.

So many of the dead were never buried. People tried desperately to imagine the site of some kind of grave. Crosses set up in nowhere, crosses over which the wind of the steppes blew in its never-ending passage, driving grains of sand and matted tufts of dry grass before it, soon to cover the crosses, until only one last piece of wood stuck up like the hand of a dead man who has failed to rise again. The living need graves in order to believe that the dead are really dead. What else protects us from meeting them once more?

For a long time after the war was over, we lived in a world full of the undead. They came and went. They mingled with us. Somewhere in a busy shopping street, in the gloom of an underpass, outside a railway station, our footsteps would suddenly falter, because we had recognized someone. A passerby had the profile or the shape of someone we had lost. It was his way of walking, his hair . . . it was him. We quickened our pace to tug at his sleeve, and then, no, it wasn't doubt that held us back, something else made us hesitate to address him: Is that you? Oh, what a surprise! What are you doing here? Rather, it was a sense that it was too late to meet again. We had changed so much, all of us. Only the dead still resembled themselves. They were the same as they had always been. They would not recognize us now. That was what made us hesitate until it was too late. The person we had seen turned a corner and was lost in the crowd. Only then did the doubts set in, and they would never entirely let one go again.

Now and then I met Eva.

She stood above me on an escalator, riding up to the clothing department on the top floor of a big store. She wore the New Look these days. Long, swinging skirts and tailored jackets. Her little hat was jauntily perched over one ear. A peroxide blond lock of hair swung free on the other side of her head. She'd grown no older. How could she? She was trying the Marilyn Monroe style these days, although she was a little too athletic and earthy for it. She was playing hide-and-seek with me, luring me down the alleys between racks of clothes, until she turned into one of the shop dummies standing there with their empty, lascivious smiles. Once again, I was too late to recognize the game she was playing.

Then I met her in a hairdressing salon. She was sitting under the dryer, looking odd, disfigured by the rollers. She glanced at me in the mirror with a familiar, knowing smile, considering me in a rather resigned and weary way. Do you think it's any fun for me, haunting your life? she seemed to be saying. Then they washed my hair, put it in rollers, and installed me under the dryer, too. When they let me out again, another customer was sitting in her chair, casually looking through a magazine.

On other occasions she was standing on railway platforms as I sat in a train just coming in, or the other way around: I was on the platform and Eva was just closing the window of her compartment as the train drew out, or she walked down the corridor past my own compartment, and when I looked to see where she was going she disappeared into the lavatory and didn't come out again until I had given up waiting.

I was not the only one to whom she appeared at that time. There were always rumors that she was still alive. Hitler had gone to Argentina with her in a submarine, said these rumors, and they were convalescing in a sanatorium there.

Eva would have liked that. I know for certain she would. That was the picture she had imagined of their survival after the war: a sanatorium where Hitler could recover from all the stress and strain. And she would be with him, a cross between nurse, Wallis Simpson, and dietitian, walking arm in arm with the former dictator along well-tended garden paths, or taking down his memoirs on her shorthand pad. It would have been sheer heaven for her. At heart she saw happiness as a sanatorium, a place set apart where all your decisions and responsibilities could be delegated to people in white coats.

Eva had no grave either. Could it not be true that she had really escaped after all? That her suicide with Hitler had merely been staged, and she had not bitten into the capsule of cyanide found lying on the ground like a lipstick? Could Goebbels, the first to enter the room, not have taken her out immediately and given her the forged passport she would need for a life after Hitler? Couldn't she have escaped from the bunker while they set up the legend of the double suicide, bringing out two corpses wrapped in blankets and burning them in the Chancellery garden? Anyone could be inside a rolled-up blanket with only a pair of ladies' black suede shoes sticking out of it. That legend would have made it possible for her to go on living. Eva Hitler would be dead. That way she could have lived on.

I imagined her disappearing into the underground railway tunnels of Berlin, a fugitive, a nonentity among other fugitives. I imagined her slowly realizing that she was nobody now, no one's daughter, sister, or cousin anymore. Most of all, not a widow. At least, not the widow of the man she had married two days earlier. I imagined her putting on a headscarf, tying it not over the forehead but under the chin like a farmer's wife, so that no one could see her hair, permed and dyed blond, later to grow back straight and light brown. She would have it cut very short, as women do when luck goes against them—I've often observed it. It's like a cry for help. Self-mutilation, forcing others to feel sympathy. But Eva couldn't have counted on sympathy from anyone.

She would surely have tried to go south to Bavaria, where else? They all wanted to go to Bavaria, as if Bavaria, where it had begun, still offered them a refuge, a place where they would be inviolable and safe, something like the sanctuary mark in children's games of catch that bestows immunity if you can only reach and touch it. But there was no such sanctuary now. The Obersalzberg had turned back into the nonplace it had always been. A lunar landscape. A field of rubble. A desert. A place no longer of this world.

Today I meet her only in the past. The longer ago that past is, the more clearly I see her: a very pretty blonde with something not quite right about her eyes. An athletic girl, not as young as she once was, not as invincible as she had been, "smart," as they put it at the time, a term that also suggested the pitiless cheerfulness she would assume, her mischievous merriment, her positively heroic determination to be amusing at any price. The self-discipline with which she forced herself to keep coming up with new ideas, to be active all the time. Her slender and androgynous figure, although that was endangered now. Some of the fatty tissue that would have made her look matronly later had already accumulated on her upper arms and thighs. Everything about her seemed like a false claim that could be upheld for only a limited amount of time. That was how I found Eva when I arrived in Berchtesgaden on the fifteenth of July 1944.

CHAPTER *2*

GREAT TYRANTS HAVE CASTLES IN THE MOUN-
tains from which they come down to strike terror into the world.
And they go back there from time to time to consider their work,
while the smoking ruins on the plains still bear witness to their pitiless acts. Now and then they bring abducted princesses to their castles
and have them guarded by sinister characters released from their duties of killing and looting for this task. All this is yours, they tell the
princesses. Make yourself at home. Taste the delicacies so lavishly
provided for you. If there's anything you want don't hesitate to tell
me. All my ministering spirits are here only to satisfy your discrimi-
nating mind. Look at this—there's no jewel that I would think too
costly for you, dear child. Tell me what flowers delight you, and I'll
order all the vases in the palace to be filled with them even if they
have to be brought from the ends of the earth. You have only to
open your mouth. Speak to me, lovely child. End your silence. I
don't want anything from you. Nothing that you will not grant me
some day of your own accord. For you will, never doubt it. But now
I must leave you for a while. Remember, when I am not here, you

are mistress of this place. Give your orders and they will be obeyed.
It's a pretty game, as you will see. For a time, anyway. Until I come
back. You will be longing for me. No? Oh, but you will. In the end
you will be listening for nothing but the sound of my horse's hooves,
you will have forgotten that only one thing is not permitted to you on
pain of death: to leave my castle. And why would you want to? It
seems to me there is no better place in the world for a beautiful young
princess with no one to protect her. How well your anger suits you! I
would like to stay with you, believe me, but a man like me has little
leisure to do as his heart desires. We have to fight, conquer, destroy all
opposition. There are so many things of which you have no idea,
Princess. But if you're lonely I will happily allow you to choose a girl
for your playmate. Do you have sisters, relations, young friends, even
cousins? Any of them will be welcome as my guests.

Hitler left the Berghof on July 13, 1944. The motor convoy was
ready, the men of his escort stood by the open doors of the cars. He
came down the flight of steps, stopped briefly, and then climbed the
steep stairway to the entrance again. My cousin stood there. She had
already said good-bye. He walked past her, entered the great hall,
crossed it, stopped in front of the huge panoramic window, allowing
one to suppose that he was taking his leave of the Untersberg spread
out before his eyes, the mountain under which, so the story goes, the
Emperor Barbarossa sleeps waiting to be recalled to life—a farewell
between two men who had guided the destiny of the world, a word-
less greeting outside space and time, a farewell made in the void
where it is easy to die, to destroy, to perish. Then Hitler turned, ig-
noring the fact that my cousin had joined him, and went over to
Feuerbach's *Nana*, who looked into the distance above his head, with
a stern and permanently injured expression.

Who knows if one will ever come back, he said.

He liked to use the impersonal pronoun in speaking of himself.
My cousin Eva, half fainting with the hope that he had come back to

take leave of her once more, as he had done already in the usual mer-
cilessly casual manner that always made her determine to take her
own life the moment he had left, so that he would have to come
back, burst into lamentations, take her in his arms even if she was already dead, and once, just once, speak those passionate words of
farewell that she was never destined to hear—my cousin, so close
now to the fulfillment of her dreams, which were not of happiness
but of ecstasy in disaster, renunciation, separation, the long good-
bye, thought he was addressing her, and was about to fling herself
on her lover's breast in tears when Luftwaffe Adjutant von Below
joined them.

Let's go, said Hitler.

Von Below bowed his head slightly, to show that he understood
the Führer's feelings but at the same time dared not take any notice of
them, or not insofar as they might be taken as a sign of weakness.
And when Hitler turned and, bestowing not one more glance on his
mistress, left the room followed by his adjutant, there was much sol-
dierly concurrence between them in that, too. Much of it is the cruelty that separates men from women, not only determining the form
of their farewells but making those leave-takings acts of exquisite
cruelty in themselves. The pain of parting weighs light in the balance
compared with the distress of the woman left behind, recollecting
the indifference of the man as he left, and now she must endure day
after day, month after month, with that memory in mind. The pain
of parting may diminish with time but the distress never will. It will
renew itself whenever it is remembered. It grows with time. Like revenge, it wants satisfaction.

He didn't look back at me again, Eva told me later, adding at
once: We're never alone when we say good-bye.

As if that were a mitigating circumstance. Like any woman whose
feelings are hurt, she sought exoneration for herself by exonerating
the man who had hurt her.

I was too young to understand. The only farewell I could remember was when the young soldiers from my class at school left:

A chilly April morning. We were freezing. We recalled jokes from our schooldays. Do you remember how . . . ? There was a sense of setting off, as if for a class outing. The expectation of something sure to turn out greater than anything we had ever known. An attempt to act as if it meant nothing special to us, as if we'd been through all this a thousand times before.

And in the middle of the crowd Ernst-Günther trying to make his way toward me, the few moments we stand close together, laughing at jokes, not exactly jokes, references that no one but our classmates would understand, silly, scrappy little remarks, all of a sudden unbearably comic, revelations suddenly illuminating our shared experiences in a lightning flash, positive chasms of comedy that now, at the latest, we have fully explored.

We share our knowledge of those comic depths. It links us that morning as only those who have studied in the same class at school can be linked, and I don't need to look at Ernst-Günther to know that he, too, has tears of laughter in his eyes.

And when the train finally comes in, and there is a crush that will carry off Ernst-Günther with the others, it's too late to kiss. I'm suddenly left alone, listening to someone saying, don't cry, don't cry, and I realize that means me and try to put the last of those do-you-remember jokes out of my head, because otherwise I think I'll go crazy.

That was the farewell I remembered. How was I to understand my cousin Eva's distress? The rage of a woman left behind, without comfort, without a glance or a touch, without anything . . .

Her feelings were hurt. She had a great talent for hurt feelings. In every other way she was moderate, reasonable, average. Only when it came to feeling hurt was it granted to her to break the mold. She was extraordinarily good at it. And in Hitler she had met her master, the man who would give her the occasion for hurt feelings on a grand scale.

He was seldom at home, had little time for her, liked and indeed preferred to be seen with other women: Magda Goebbels, Winifred Wagner, Annie Ondra, Leni Riefenstahl . . . women with whom my cousin could not compete in any way at all. He neglected her, although it was not certain that he betrayed her. In fact, I am inclined to think he was faithful. But she had plenty of opportunity for hurt feelings. In Berlin she had to use a back door to the private rooms in the Reich Chancellery. On the Obersalzberg she was expected to make herself scarce when official visitors were announced. She could show herself only in Hitler's most intimate circle. He did not take her traveling with him.

The one time she did accompany him, on his visit to Rome, she had smuggled herself into the retinue of secretaries without his knowledge, and was consequently excluded even from the official program arranged for the ladies until she let the Italian organizers know who she was: Hitler's companion. So she did watch a parade of warships in the Gulf of Naples, an event ladies were not really supposed to attend at all, with the result that she had to be explained away once again as a secretary and had yet another reason for hurt feelings.

As a macho man, in fact, Adolf Hitler was only average. Albert Speer records such comments as: "Highly intelligent men should choose a simple, stupid woman. . . . I want peace and quiet in my leisure time."

Remarks such as this, made in Eva's presence, could nonetheless have been made by any factory owner, any editor of a provincial paper, any university professor.

The unusual aspect of their relationship was entirely Eva's. She was a heroic and accomplished exponent of the art of putting up with things. She toed the line, she stayed in her room when there were married couples present—Goebbels and Magda, the Görings. She very correctly avoided even meeting them on the stairs. The film clips that exist of her show that as soon as Hitler came on the scene she stepped back. She is never seen coming to his side, she is always retreating from the picture, airbrushing herself out.

Wait a moment, she seems to be saying, and then I'll be gone. Don't put yourselves to the trouble of noticing my existence.

But she stepped aside in the hope of being called back. That was what she was waiting for. She was the kind of woman who never puts out a hand to take what she wants, the kind who always waits to have it offered to her, and who is mortally injured if it never is.

Eva was absolutely unbeatable in the art of nursing hurt feelings. All the passion, all the gravity, all the endurance of which she was capable showed in that skill. She swallowed humiliations, compressed them into a small space inside her to make room for more, swallowed those, too, compressed them again, she couldn't get enough of them. Until the pressure inside her rose to such a pitch, became so intolerable, that she was ready for the next suicide attempt. In November 1932 she had shot herself with her father's service revolver, just missing her carotid artery. In May 1935 she took fifteen Vanodorm tablets—too few to kill her. I don't know about the other times, but I suspect they were even more symbolic in nature.

Yet she had experience. She was no amateur suicide. Suicide was the one profession she had really mastered, the only skill she had made her own. Extinction of the self. And I am sure that at the end it was she who taught Hitler the art of suicide, she who, with the solicitude and readiness to oblige peculiar to her, showed him how to set about it.

When I met her again she was a case of hurt feelings at an advanced stage. They're a strain. They take all a person's strength. She needed support at this time. She needed company, and I think now that this was the reason for her invitation. I was to be a diversion. I was her excuse for going out and about, on expeditions to Munich or to bathe in the Königssee.

For, you see, Gretl had married, or rather had been married off. Women like Gretl, born to be the shadows of their sisters, don't marry of their own volition. It takes persuasion, intrigue, not to mention a hint of threat and coercion, to bring them to the point of marriage. They finally agree for fear of harming their sisters if they don't.

So Gretl Braun married a courtier, Hermann Fegelein of the SS, Himmler's liaison officer at the Führer's headquarters. She had lived at court too long to escape the fate of being handed over to a courtier. The function of courtiers is to do their masters bidding, out of the loyalty and assiduity with which they pursue their careers at court. Fegelein was prepared to marry the favorite's sister, a fact that said nothing about any feelings he might entertain for her, but a great deal about the ambition driving him. According to certain rumors it wasn't even clear if he preferred women at all, let alone the pale and rather timid Gretl.

At the time, of course, I knew nothing about any of that. Nor did I know how much Eva feared life without Gretl. She hated Fegelein. She hated him as one hates a victorious rival in love. He had taken away what was dearest to her, the companion of her empty life, her comrade in the isolation of her days and the luxury that was too much for her to bear alone. She wanted a substitute sister, she wanted me, because her friend Hertha Schneider, who normally took that role, had been hurt in a motor accident when she was flung out of her car and had to stay in bed. That was why, on a sudden whim, I had been invited. That was why I was here now.

WHERE THE ROAD TO THE BERGHOF turned off to the left there was a little lodge for the guards. They came out and stopped the car.

My assumption that my two companions were sufficient guarantee of my identity turned out to be wrong. I was asked to get out and go into the guardroom while the two men stayed in the car. Clearly what happened next was none of their business.

It was the first but not the last time in my life that my things were searched. Not that there's anything so bad about that, is there? They unpack your case and pack it up again. There's even something slightly flattering about it. One's indignation is always mingled with a sense of importance. Here's someone who takes me seriously. Who's looking for a secret behind my facade. Who thinks there's something to be found out.

And perhaps it's this terrible confusion that makes the whole business so horrible. You feel like laughing: What on earth do you suspect? Do you think I'm traveling with my luggage full of explosives, weapons, heroin (it would have been morphine in those days)? Do you really think me brazen enough for that? At the same time you have to watch them exposing your most intimate, personal things to the light of day. Between the two sets of feelings, you very soon lose your personal dignity. You let your unsuitability to play your part show. And then, but always too late, you realize: that's what they were after.

The men did their job well—that is, they did it thoroughly. They unrolled my silk stockings, let them drop to the floor like obscene and lascivious snakes, unfolded my knickers and held them up in front of their faces. (These days, although some people condemn the infiltration of the German language by anglicisms, we use the pretty little monosyllable *slip* for that item of underwear, but we didn't have it at the time; we had only the coarser-sounding word *Schlüpfer* for knickers.) They came to my bras, and dropped them, too, on the floor, where they lay like dirty little remnants of snow. Finally they even opened my toilet bag and found some sanitary towels in it. (They were the washable kind we used then. Only a few old women like me still remember them. You took them down to the cellar and hung them up there in the most secret corner to dry. Only sluts dried them out on the balcony.)

You can pack your things again, they said.

Their tone of voice said: We're not used to rubbish like this.

Then they gave me a piece of paper with a signature and a stamp to show that I was a "guest of the Führer," and could pass.

Right, *gnädiges Fräulein,* said the men, holding the door open for me and carrying my case back to the car. The piece of paper seemed to have transformed me. I was now the Führer's guest.

My escorts dropped me off at the foot of the steps up to the Berghof, putting my case down beside me. I carried it up the steps. I was exhausted and breathless when I finally stood at the door to Hitler's house.

I didn't know that once you have got to that point, the doors of a tyrant's castle will open of themselves to let you in. I was looking for something in the nature of a doorbell, some means of drawing attention to myself, but the guards had phoned up long ago to say I was on the way, and now, when the door opened, I felt sure that Eva had been looking out for me, waiting impatiently.

But for the second time I was disappointed to find it wasn't Eva who welcomed me in. It was the housekeeper, wife of the domestic manager of the Berghof. She greeted me with the routine, casual friendliness of a well-trained hotel manageress.

When I asked where Eva was, she told me the *gnädiges Fräulein* had gone for a swim in the Königssee. She sent her love and would be back soon.

A housemaid took my case, and I was led up a broad, carpeted wooden staircase to the second floor.

The guestroom was like something out of a middle-class Alpine hotel. Geraniums at the windows. The famous view of the Watzmann.

I've never reached the end of any journey without feeling disappointment. It's a kind of reflex: I didn't want to come here at all! An elemental homesickness, a black melancholy overcomes me on my

arrival in hotel bedrooms and holiday cottages. The place may be delightful, luxurious, wonderful, the sea may be blue and the beach
white, yet I still feel like going straight home. Very likely the dominant, home-loving part of me is simply rejecting having a change of
scene forced on it. It hates traveling, but as soon as it realizes its
protests are useless it starts making itself at home in this strange place.
Since we've fetched up here, it says, we might as well build ourselves
some huts. Come on, settle in. Put some roots down. Imagine you'll
be staying here forever. This is your table, your bed, your chair. Your
view out of the window forever and ever.

But I hadn't reached that point on this first afternoon, and if I was
ever disappointed by arriving at my journey's end it was then, at the
Berghof. I thought of nothing but whether to leave again at once, or
maybe spend one night in this admittedly hospitable bed, soft as
down, fragrant, made up with white sheets. Just a single night.

I wasn't as familiar as I am now with my impulse to take flight
when I reach the end of a journey. When you're young you take
your own moods at face value. Tomorrow morning, I thought. I'll
get those men to drive me back to Munich tomorrow. Or I'll take a
train. Or I'll walk. I must be able to get away from here again somehow. I was already practicing the anecdotal version of my experiences that I would give when I was home.

Guess where I slept the night!

But then Eva arrived.

Oh, you're crying, she said. Why are you crying?

I'm so glad to see you, I said.

She was even more beautiful than ever. Even blonder, livelier, more
high-spirited than I remembered her. She was bronzed by the sun.

The fashion for a suntan was just coming in at the time. When our
mothers were young they still valued a delicate, white skin. But we
felt ourselves the daughters of a new age, daughters of the light and
the earth, breaking out of the constraints of city life, capable, strong,
close to nature. Turning to the sun. Eva was a trendsetter of this new

image. Trends are always thought up by people with the time for them. The image of the strong, healthy woman, efficient at work and a good mother, is best embodied by women with no children and no job. By women like Eva. She had all the time in the world for sun-bathing and sport.

You're so pale, little one, she said. You need fresh air! Sunlight! You look like such a little stay-at-home! Is it really true you're study-ing physics? Oh, you clever girl! You must tell me all about yourself.

She kept saying that: Tell me about yourself! I want to know every single little thing about you! But whenever I started talking, some-thing would distract her. There was a will-o'-the-wisp restlessness about her. Her mind was always in flight, looking for something new, something different. As if it were deadly dangerous to linger more than a few seconds on any one subject. I never knew any-one with such a craving for novelty. And never again did I know anyone with such restless eyes.

She had something of the look of a bullfighter, seeming to test the wind all the time, as if to counter the danger that something might escape her. When something did claim her attention for a second or so, her glance went straight to it. She opened her eyes wide, stared as if she intended to penetrate the object with her piercing gaze. It was meant to be comical, but wasn't. I didn't remember her being like that before, and all of a sudden I felt afraid she might have gone mad. I dismissed the idea, but it kept coming back to me over the next few months. It kept coming back until at last it stayed for good.

Good heavens! she cried, that piercing gaze on my feet. For a mo-ment she really did look like a bullfighter raising both spears to the level of his head and taking aim before attacking. Good heavens, what on earth are you wearing? Platform soles! Take those shoes off this minute, little one! Nobody, but nobody wears platform soles anymore! What's more, they make you almost as tall as me, and that will never do!

I was very proud of my shoes, which my father had brought back for me from Budapest. They really did make me taller, and at the time I still hated being short. At the age of twenty, I still hoped I might grow a little more. I liked those shoes, and up to that moment I'd thought them acceptably elegant, too. But how could I contradict Eva in matters of fashion?

She pressed a bell beside my bed, and gave orders to the maid who soon appeared. The girl came back with a laundry basket full of shoes and put it down in front of me—it held boots, sandals, pumps, oxfords, ankle boots, all very smart but much too small for me.

Oh, don't worry, said Eva, you'll walk them in. Now then, which do you like?

Perhaps I ought to say how valuable shoes were to us at that time, in the sixth year of the war. It was ages since shoes had been available at all. Not to us women, anyway, unimportant to the war effort as we were. We went on wearing our prewar shoes, and as my feet had grown a size larger since the beginning of the war that meant I usually wore a pair of my mother's old flatties. I'd been saving my platform-soled sandals specially for this visit.

Here, have these, said Eva, handing me a pair of low-heeled white pumps. At least I could just about squeeze into them.

And I was far too exhausted that first evening to contradict. We went for a walk to the Tea House on the projecting crag of the Mooslahner Kopf, a few hundred meters from the Berghof. I didn't yet know that we would be taking this walk every evening, and every evening Eva would announce it with the same brisk enthusiasm:

I tell you what, little one! Let's go to the Mooslahner Kopf! There's a simply wonderful view from there, especially in weather like this (sunset, rain, snow, the alpenglow, or whatever . . .). You've never seen anything like it!

And every evening she would change her clothes first. Always a new outfit for a familiar old habit. Beautiful coats and skirts with just a touch of traditional Bavarian costume about them. Braid, staghorn buttons, collars lined with flowered fabric. And dirndls, full, drawn in at the waist, the bodice with a deep décolleté. Or smart plain gray suits cleverly set off by pastel-colored blouses. She ordered them from the most expensive tailors in Berlin. Imagine what a Jena country bumpkin I looked beside my cousin!

That first evening I walked my feet sore in her shoes, which were much too small. I had raw blisters on my heels and bleeding toes.

Next morning I leave my room in my mother's oxfords, themselves slightly too large for me. The house seems deserted, quiet. I don't know where I'm supposed to go. My footsteps, which I can't muffle because my heels hurt so bad, echo like an intruder's as I go downstairs.

On the second floor I suddenly find myself outside a room with double doors standing wide open. I go in, with a sense that this is forbidden territory. A massive desk dominates the room, the walls are paneled in wood, with bookshelves built into them. Gilt-framed paintings hang between the windows. I don't know who the painters are, but I suspect these are artistic treasures. There's a corner seat with red-and-green-flowered upholstery. A round faience stove on the inside wall. Hitler has a very comfortable place here. This must be his study. The books piled on the edges of the desk, presumably reference works, suggest that a scholar who usually works here has gone away but will soon be back. There are vases of carnations. The whole Berghof is in suspended animation, ready to welcome back its owner. Soon this will seem as natural to me as it does to everyone else. It's as if he might suddenly spring out of the ground.

All at once the telephone on Hitler's desk rings.

Should I pick up the phone? Is it for me?

There's something urgent, something imperious about the sound.

Suppose it's Stalin? Or Churchill? Or Roosevelt. Shouldn't someone tell them Hitler isn't at home?

As I move toward it, I hear the footsteps of someone entering the room behind me, making haste to the telephone.

Yes, says the man, yes, all right.

It's the domestic manager, to whom Eva fleetingly introduced me the previous day.

You're to come and have breakfast, he says.

I don't know if this was the message he was given over the telephone, or whether it's his way of throwing me out of Hitler's study.

In the dining room, he says. Downstairs.

I've no idea where the dining room is. Does he mean the great hall? It is dark and deserted. The huge curtains over the panoramic window are closed. Light comes in only through a narrow gap at the center like a spotlight, giving a dark red-velour glow to the whole gloomy place. I feel as if I have entered some forbidden temple where strange and mysterious rites are celebrated by night, rituals in which those who intrude unauthorized are sacrificed without mercy to a cruel deity.

I step back, almost colliding with a housemaid carrying a breakfast tray.

Where's the dining room? I ask.

Am I mistaken in thinking she gives a scornful sniff? Doesn't she realize I'm new to Hitler's Berghof?

I follow her, and see the huge table in Hitler's dining room, covered with a white cloth, and with a little bunch of pinks in the middle, looking lost and much too small. Is this where we have breakfast?

The breakfast table is in the rounded bay looking out over the valley. The Watzmann massif lies bathed in morning light, with the sky above it the translucent pale blue of an Alpine summer's day. I try opening one of the bay windows. I want to feel the fresh air outside.

Let me do that, says the maid.

She opens the window herself. Then she lays the table. I rehearse the role of pampered guest. It's new to me. I'm still not sure: Is there anything I can do for myself, or isn't that allowed? I still feel like someone looking around a museum or a castle, aware that visitors mustn't touch. Am I permitted to sit on one of the chairs at the breakfast table? Or will that set off an alarm immediately? Will the security men arrive, unmasking me as a dangerous intruder?

Only after a few days shall I discover what I did wrong that first morning. I was up too early. I was a guest in the house of a man who was a late riser. Breakfast was never served at the Berghof before ten. Later I became accustomed to this, made use of the early morning hours to go for short, solitary walks, filling the time until Eva, who observed Hitler's daily rhythm even when he was away, put in an appearance between ten and eleven, perfectly groomed, well-rested, vibrating with activity as she is on the morning of that first day.

Goodness, you're up already, she says.

I don't like to say I've been sitting at the breakfast table for two hours, with the maid constantly asking what else I would like, gradually registering the shift of emphasis in her tone to the word *else*, until I realize what a nuisance I am to her. I never thought of just saying: Thank you, I don't need you anymore. Those are the magic words she was waiting for to release her from attendance on me.

One of the things I shall learn on the Obersalzberg will be the magic words for dealing with the domestic staff who minister to us: The words to summon them up and dismiss them again. I shall learn this lesson from Eva, along with a great many other useless skills: the art of plucking your eyebrows until there isn't much left of them at all; the art of not crossing your legs but keeping them perfectly parallel when you sit in an armchair. I shall have little need for these skills in the life that lies ahead of me. But uncertainty of the kind that overcame me on my first morning at Hitler's Berghof encourages the learning of such lessons.

I admire the way Eva gives orders as a matter of course, asks for a soft-boiled egg, wants stronger coffee. I admire the way she ignores the open reluctance with which those orders are carried out. The slight lack of assiduity, the tiny touch of condescension with which the maid says, "Yes, *gnädiges Fräulein*." I think this is inevitable.

Fascinated, I observe Eva granting the housekeeper an audience when she comes in with suggestions for our lunch menu.

What would we like to eat? A half-chicken each, maybe? Or French beans with bacon? Perhaps some soup to start with?

What would you like? Eva inquires.

She's asking too much of me. I find it absolutely impossible to entertain any wishes in this place, let alone express them.

I don't know, I say.

At home in Jena my parents have an extra ration card now, and one less mouth to feed.

Chicken? I say, more astonished that such a thing can exist than assuming we can really have it.

You heard, Eva says to the housekeeper.

The woman turns back in the doorway. But do please be punctual this time! she says sternly.

I look at Eva. She doesn't appear annoyed.

I tell you what! she says. Let's go swimming.

She speaks in a conspiratorial tone. As if swimming were a forbidden frivolity. As if we were a couple of children planning to play truant from school on a fine summer's day.

Soon afterward we meet outside the door with our bathing things. There is a black limousine at the foot of the flight of steps, with two security men leaning on the doors. They drop their cigarettes on the ground when they see us.

Our taxi, says Eva. Now, listen: We're going to shake them off! See that mail van? That's our bus! You just do as I say. Come on!

We go back into the house and through a door on the left of the entrance hall that leads to some steps going down to the basement. We walk along a passage, come to the end of it and so to a narrow path that leads down to the road—this is a tradesman's entrance to

the north wing of the Berghof—and we come out exactly where the
mail van is parked. I catch a glimpse of the two SS men, one at the
foot of the stairway, the other a few steps up, both of them looking
for us, wondering where we can be. But by now we're in the back of
the mail van.

When the postman who delivers mail to the Berghof five times a
day comes back, Eva taps the pane dividing the driver's cab from the
back of the van, and the postman's grinning face briefly appears.
Then we're on our way. Eva is using the belt of her beach robe,
passed through one of the door handles, to keep the back of the van
shut; the doors can be closed securely only from outside. Through
the crack between them we see the SS men still staring up at the
main entrance to the Berghof.

It's the only way to shake them off, says Eva.

I have become part of a plot. It is a childish, ridiculous plot. Eva
has entered into a petty conspiracy with a postman against the power
to which she is delivered up. She is not defying that power, just
thumbing her nose at it. She expects me to enjoy this small victory
along with her. And I do. I tell her what a good time we're having. I
don't know why this makes me feel sad. Something about Eva
touches me. Something seems to be wrong. We are pretending to be
keener on this bathing trip than we really are.

But then, when we get out of the van on the banks of the lake,
when we untie the rowboat lying ready for us at one of the landing
stages in the Malerwinkel, when we take off our shoes and feel the
planks of the boat under our feet, the wood warmed by the sun,
when we dip the oars into the deep, cool, dark green water, when we
hear the faint splashing that mingles with the creaking of the planks,
the sound of the oars against the side of the boat, wood on wood, all
of it combines into a symphony of pleasure, and I, too, am convinced that this is the most beautiful place in the entire universe.

Eva knows a spot on the eastern bank where the precipitous rocks do not come all the way down to the water, but leave a narrow, stony strip of beach in front of it, and that is where we are making for.

They'll never find us there, she says. We'll be invisible there.

We can go skinny-dipping here, she suggests, taking off her clothes. Come on, haven't you ever bathed with nothing on? she asks. It's lovely.

I have not, indeed, ever bathed naked before. It seems to me an outrageous idea—outrageously exciting, new, bold. I watch Eva from the bank as she goes into the water. I've never seen another woman naked. I hardly expect to be as beautiful as Eva.

My nakedness seems somehow pitiful to me. I plunge right into the lake, seeking cover for my nudity there, while the water climbs very, very slowly up around Eva's thighs and hips, a tender touch to which she surrenders herself calmly, securely.

We swim far out into the lake to where the water is cold with the chill rising from the depths. I think of the profound abyss opening below me, going far down to the bed of the lake. It's a kind of vertigo that comes over me when I'm swimming, a fear of the depths and something trying to pull me down there. I hate swimming in deep water.

Eva! I call.

I can't see her anymore. I turn around. As I am about to get out by the bank, I see the two men sitting just above the place where we have left our clothes. They're smoking and looking out over the lake with bored expressions. Our guards have found us.

I support myself with my hands on a rock in the shallow water and keep still, as still as a crocodile. I wait. I'm waiting for Eva to come back and find some way out of our situation.

The men take no notice of me, although I am sure they've seen me. Would they have jumped in to save me if I'd been drowning out there in the lake? Is that what they're here for? Who gives them their orders? And just what are those orders? Are we prisoners, or are they only meant to make sure we're safe? Is this a privilege for them or an irksome duty? What do they say about it when they're in their barracks? Do we feature in their jokes? Isn't that just what I am, a joke personified for masculine amusement, naked, with my clothes out of reach?

If they do think it's funny, at least you can't tell from their faces. Their expressions show nothing but the gravity of two men doing their job, however uninteresting it is. Then I suddenly see them stand up and go down to the bank, turning their backs to me and moving a little way farther off. At the same time I hear Eva coming back. She emerges from the water beside me, shakes herself, wrings out her hair.

Those men! I say.

Oh, there they are, says Eva. They always find me. Well, after all, we have to get back to the Berghof somehow or other.

We go over to our clothes, and while I get dressed faster than ever before in my life, I see the two men down beside the water, playing the old game of ducks and drakes with flat pebbles. They still have their backs turned to us.

In the car, Eva begs cigarettes from them for both of us. I feel embarrassed.

But why? asks Eva later. Isn't that what they're there for?

I don't know what they're there for, I say.

Oh, little one, you worry too much, she says. One gets used to them.

I noticed that she doesn't even know their rank from their stripes. They have to set her right; they insist on it. Rank is no laughing matter. Their rank expresses the core of their being. I can sense that.

I also sense, in Eva's ignorance, something of her unsuitability to be a wife. Wouldn't a wife have known how to interpret the men's stripes and give them their proper titles, even if the indications were subtle, hidden, revealed only to the eye of an initiate?

Wives become expert at this sort of thing. It's their job. Eva, on the other hand, was innocent of the art of interpreting any signs of rank whatsoever. She paid no attention to them, favoring VIPs and the unimportant with the same kindness, the same charming smile, labor squad foreman, storm trooper captain, and squadron leader alike. Did she think that would bind them to her? It was a mistake appreciated as little by the underdog as by the military commanders. She had no instinct for such things. And yet she had not chosen the most powerful man in her world with her eyes shut. That was part of the puzzle she still represents to me today. She was avid for the power that a man can wield, and had not the faintest idea what to do with it.

By the time we get back to the Berghof it is early afternoon. We're as hungry as children after a day on the beach when they've stayed in the water too long. I am thinking about the chicken we were promised.

Tell you what! says Eva. Let's take a look in the kitchen.

There's no one around in the Berghof kitchen. It looks as if it had never been used at all. White as newly fallen snow. Uncompromisingly clean and tidy. Odorless as a laboratory. There's nothing to suggest that someone was roasting me a chicken a little while ago.

We look in the pantry, which contains a walk-in fridge. I've never seen such a thing before. Surely the chicken must be somewhere around the place. I'm perfectly ready to eat it cold if necessary. I'm crazy to get at that chicken.

What are you looking for? a voice suddenly asks, from the kitchen. It's the housekeeper.

We were so hungry, says Eva.

Then you ought to have been back in time for lunch, says the woman sternly. Or if you'd told me you were going for a swim I'd have had a picnic basket packed for you. But this really won't do. I can make you a ham sandwich if you like. The staff are having their afternoon break now.

Oh, yes, please, says Eva. How kind of you.

I'm surprised that Eva will put up with this. Isn't she the mistress of the house? Aren't they all here to do her bidding? Doesn't Hitler's lover have an army of devoted servants at her command?

Later, I understand what at this point I only guessed, for there was something in the air. A breath of insolence, a small, lurking, barely perceptible resentment that could turn back into a show of respect at any time.

They were still all feeling the relief of Hitler's absence with his whole retinue—all of them, the domestic manager and the house-keeper, the servants, the chauffeurs, the guards were alive with a dreadful exuberance, with pitiless, insatiable high spirits. They would have liked to hold a wild celebration, throwing furniture out the windows, slitting mattresses, lighting a great bonfire, and they would have enjoyed tormenting someone a little, just for fun. When the cat's away the mice will play.

The pressure of authority exerted by Hitler's presence must have been enormous. Nothing mattered but the readiness to be of service. There was no other idea in the minds of the people around him. Every emotion, every passion, every dream led only to the dread of censure from him. His displeasure was feared more than any misfortune in this world. Even a casual expression of disapproval uttered in passing was shattering. And as for his anger—his boundless anger—they would do anything, anything at all, to avoid it.

Then there was a wonderful sense of relief when he wasn't around. The little postmidnight feasts described by Speer. Champagne corks popping, muscles relaxing once Hitler had gone to bed, shortly after sending Eva up first. Someone would go to the piano, pick out a soft tune, and here and there small, trivial remarks would drop into people's glasses like pearls of sudden wit, warmth, and quick repartee.

I was not to know at the time that I had fallen into one of these power vacuums when I arrived at the Berghof. With a few interruptions, Hitler had been based here since February. Everyone had been terrified for months of making a mistake. They had been punctual, assiduous, blameless in their conduct. They hadn't laid themselves open to the slightest charge of negligence. They had been on the alert day and night. They had excused any betrayal on the grounds that they were on duty, and they had hated themselves for it.

Now they wanted to be themselves again for a while. And a little rude and unpleasant to someone else, anyone.

There could have been no better target for this playfully bad conduct than Hitler's mistress. They were using her to see how far they could go. They had been commanded to address her as *gnädiges Fräulein*, but while Hitler was away they could venture to lay a little more stress on the *Fräulein*, pointing up her single state, than on the respectful *gnädiges*. For wasn't she really more like one of them? Even below them, in fact, considering she wasn't married?

Did they have to hurry to fulfill her wishes? Did what she thought was right matter so much? Couldn't they just say, now and then, Look, *Fräulein* Braun, can't you see I'm busy?

All they had to do was ensure that she had no actual ground for complaint. They were, so to speak, working to rule in serving her. Eva always felt that more keenly in the first days of Hitler's absence than at any other time.

A mistress cannot take advantage of the privileges conferred by her lover's status except when he is around. Only marriage will transfer such marks of status to the woman herself. Only marriage can keep them in force during the man's absence, even after his death. No such prospects had been held out to my cousin Eva.

("I could never marry, said Hitler . . . it's the same with a film star: If he marries, he loses a certain attraction for the women who worship him, he's not so much of an idol anymore.")

She hated her status as mistress, the defenselessness to which it condemned her. But that defenselessness in itself was a part of her attraction for Hitler. He loved defenselessness. Like all tyrants, he couldn't get enough of it. So my cousin Eva endured what she hated. She did so with a charm peculiar to the defenseless, and with the acumen of the experienced mistress who knows that this is exactly what she is loved for.

She was the woman of Hitler's dreams. Pretty, young, vain, and completely ignorant of power politics. She learned nothing at all from mixing with the Bormanns, the Himmlers, the Speers around her. Nothing rubbed off on her even from the lower-ranking courtiers, the compliant Schaubs and von Belows. She always retained the sulky little air of willfulness with which she would inspect Hitler, her head on one side, and say:

You look like a chauffeur in that cap.

Everyone would hear her and suddenly realize how intimate she was with him. And every time they became aware of that they would feel afraid again, just as I still feel afraid today.

All the lies, the dirty little keyhole views: suppositions founded on too little rather than too much imagination, not enough imagination for anyone to suppose it possible that a monster of a man can also be average, the lover of a girl whose own average mind but above-average beauty appeal to him. Not enough imagination for anyone to see that her awkwardness, devotion, dependency can set off in him something that persuades him, erroneously, that he is a human being capable of feelings and emotion, resulting in a kind of susceptibility and consideration that always needs the woman's extreme inferiority to kindle it and make it perceptible.

There was a lot of his love for his dog in it. Sentimentality. A touch of self-pity. An admission that he was lost from the first, and could not even imagine real happiness.

Speer, he said, the day will come when I have only two friends, Fräulein Braun and my dog.

Are those the words of a man confident of victory who will subjugate the rest of the world?

The doglike pet name he gave her. Embarrassing. Revealing. Just as the pet names a couple give each other are always revealing, the ordinary kind just as much as those with some claim to be unique. A word like a wet, slobbery dog's tongue suddenly licking your face. I am glad I was never present to hear it spoken. Let's forget the word. Extinguish it. Let it never have been heard from the first.

WE HAVE OUR EVENING MEAL SERVED on the great terrace. There can be no lovelier setting. The pink mountain range. The birds of prey circling high above the valley of the Ache, the vague awareness of human settlements down below us, somewhere to the southwest where Berchtesgaden lies. It's all so far away. The inhabited and uninhabitable world, the war. We know it can never, ever reach us. Not here, not where we are. Not up here on the Berghof, where Eva and I sit under the slowly darkening sky in which the stars of summer are beginning to show. We get them to bring us out a lantern. Soon we can see only our faces in its light.

Now, tell me about yourself, little one, says Eva.

I know she's thinking of something else. I feel very clearly that something else is taking hold of her with ever-increasing power. Something removing her from me. Putting her out of my reach. I understand that the questions she asks me are nothing but a defensive wall behind which she is disappearing. An attempt at concealment, obscuring the path along which she is moving away from me.

Tell me all about yourself.

All the same, I try to interest her. The farther away she moves, the harder I try. I tell her about my parents. About my engagement that was not really an engagement. About Ernst-Günther's death, and my wanderings in the Thuringian Forest, mourning for the boys I knew.

And what else? says Eva from far away. Your studies? What are you studying?

I know she is only trying to keep me talking so she can devote herself, undisturbed, to the other subject that entirely occupies her mind. I trip over my own words. I tell her things she can't understand. I talk about optical polarization, about the nature of all electromagnetic radiation resulting from the transversal character of electromagnetic waves. I know perfectly well how useless this is, but I fear the silence that will fall between us otherwise. I tell her, with increasing enthusiasm, that the polarization in long waves, medium waves, and short waves is vertical, but in the ultra-short waves of radio communication it is horizontal. I draw diagrams on the tablecloth with my thumbnail. I begin explaining how a radio works.

Suddenly a change comes over Eva. She leaps to her feet.

Quiet! she shouts at me.

A telephone is ringing inside the house.

Put it through to my room, calls Eva as she disappears through the door to the little living room.

A few minutes later she is back, relaxed, relieved, as if she had just finished taking an exam. I can tell at once that she has attention to spare for me again. She's been speaking to Hitler on the telephone.

Hitler sends his regards, she tells me.

Thank you, I say.

I am ashamed to have told her so much about myself and my own interests just now. I decide to be more understanding in future. I have yet to find out what conduct is appropriate for me.

As time passes by, I get used to the evenings when she's waiting for that phone call. It doesn't come every day, but with every evening when there is no phone call Eva's uneasiness grows. I know now that I am there to help her bear it. At the same time I sense that I myself am more than she can bear on such evenings. I talk so we won't hear the silence of the telephone. I talk too fast, too loud. Everything I say drops into that silence.

Can't you keep your voice down a little? asks Eva. I'm not deaf, you know.

The transformation comes at the moment when she is summoned: Telephone, *gnädiges Fräulein*. It's the Führer for you.

Oh, my God, cries Eva, leaping up. Oh, I don't know what to say to him! Tell me what to say to him!

Love over the telephone. The fact that he calls is what matters. They get through the conversation itself as best they can.

(So what are you doing?

Getting people killed. How about you?)

Once, when the door to Eva's room is left open, I overhear a couple of sentences. They are about her dogs Stasi and Negus, two black miniature schnauzers given to her by Hitler, who are scuffling around her while she talks, trying to climb up on her lap.

Down, Stasi. Down Negus. Don't do that!

A happy yapping and squealing. I close the door quickly. I don't want to hear any more.

I am sure she has never asked him what he was really doing. Not on the telephone, not when he was with her.

I mean, what do you really do?

The most obvious question to ask. And at the same time the form of words that would have released her. Afterward, she would have been free. Free to leave him and get on with her own life. She went to join him and died with him instead.

Tell me who you are. Not: Do what you like with me.

It would have been so easy. When I realized that, later, I tried to tell her who he was. I heard what our enemies were saying on the radio. I told her about it. I spoke of the dead we saw in the Böhmerwaldplatz. I offered to take her into the mountains, to the place where the deep tunnels had been dug. I wanted her to see this shadow world and understand who had made shadows of us, so that we no longer recognized ourselves, and could not ask the simplest questions: Tell me what you are really doing!

But I couldn't save her. She didn't even say good-bye to me when she went to him to die. Not a word from her, not a greeting. To hell with her!

And that was where she went.

MEMORY IS A WHORE. It is solicitous, obliging. It's ready to do everything that has been agreed, but no more. You want it to look real? That's a little more expensive. You want it to *be* real? The truth? Which truth, pray?

Once, a few years ago, I gave an interview. Some radio station or other called me. I've no idea how they found my name. They had probably discovered that I was Eva's last surviving relation.

You're Eva Braun's cousin, said the voice on the telephone, and as I had not expected to hear those words until the Day of Judgment I admitted to everything.

We'd very much like to talk to you, said the voice, and since that sounded as if a commission of investigators had tracked me down it didn't even occur to me that I could just say no. This was what I had always feared, and now I would simply have to face up to it.

Petra, in her early thirties, arrived a few days later. I liked her. We were on friendly terms at once, calling each other *du*, and we drank cup after cup of coffee. I didn't even notice her putting her microphone on my living room table. I showed her my only memento of Eva, the little china rouge pot Hitler had brought back from Paris for her. Then came the questions, and all the time I was answering them I was aware that I wasn't telling the truth.

Not that I was lying, but there's a world of misleading answers in between the truth and an outright lie.

We ordered a pizza when we had finished. Petra didn't like the cake I had baked specially for her. Finally I took two quarter-bottles of sparkling wine out of the fridge. We told each other how well we had got on. After she had left I began to suspect that they always act like that to get to where they want, extract from you what they want to hear. I was left with a curious sense of depression, like a hangover. I never listened to the broadcast. I shall never give another interview.

Memory is a whore. She's ready for everything. And if she ever really tells the truth, who would notice? In the last resort, truthfulness is only another pose. It shows up incidentally. By chance. Unnoticed.

What do I really remember?

I remember the even tenor of our days on the Berghof.

Is that all?

I remember the boredom I felt.

Is that all?

I remember the sense that time was standing still. As if every new day was just a repetition of the day before. A kind of curse, a magic spell from which it was impossible to escape in any way.

And what else?

Our flights when we escaped to Munich.

We'll be coming to that later. What else?

There wasn't anything else. There really wasn't.

Oh yes, there was.

Well, yes. There was. But I can't explain it.

You don't have to explain it. Just remember. What do you see?

I see a girl. I can't believe it's me. She looks so young.

Never mind about that. Just say what you see.

She's lying in a deck chair on the great terrace. The sun is blazing down on her skin, and if she opens her eyes a little way she sees a world of glittering white with deep, black shadows at the edges. She'll have a sunburn that evening.

Something else will happen that evening. Remember.

We went down to the lake.

That's right.

We rowed out from the Malerwinkel to the place where we usually bathed. There was a waterfall nearby. We climbed a little way up the rocks to the top of the three basins that had formed there. We plunged down with the water from one basin to the next until we reached the lake. I was scared when I first did that, but Eva laughed at me. It was just the kind of thing she liked. In fact, now that I come to think of it today, she was too old for it at thirty-two. Not too old to do it, just too old to get so much fun from it as she was showing me she did, with her shrieks of delight and screams and her announcement of her firm intention to do it again at once. How could she insist so obstinately on enjoying life?

Stick to the point. What happened that day?

Something spoiled it.

What?

News. Someone or other came along and spoiled the summer's day for us.

News?

Alarming news. We were suddenly ashamed of having had such fun. We snatched up our things, the picnic basket, our beach robes, and ran barefoot to the place where the boat was tied up. We called to the men to row faster.

What was that news?

I don't remember.

Don't try to remember the news, remember yourself. Was it a secret pleasure you felt? A kind of relish of all the excitement? A readiness to meet what was coming, whatever it might be, head on? Wasn't there something of all that in it?

Maybe. Possibly. But I was afraid, too. Afraid for myself, afraid for Eva.

If you remember how you felt, then you can remember the news, too, what it meant, all the rest of it. Stop airbrushing yourself out of the picture! Now, close your eyes and remember!

I remember. It was the twentieth of July. I can still feel my bathing suit clinging wetly to my skin, the puddles that formed under me in our guards' official car. We'd had no time to change. And the thought suddenly occurred to me that this might be the last time we ever sat here, the last time we had a chauffeur, the last time we'd be asked: Anything you'd like, *gnädiges Fräulein*?

If Hitler was no longer alive then we would be totally superfluous, two young women who would have to disappear as quickly as possible. The whores of dead rulers are always the first to be thrown out of the house. I see myself running barefoot up the great flight of steps after Eva, racing through the door, which as usual has opened as if of its own accord. I hear the housekeeper's whispered words, yet I can't make out what she means. The lines are all busy at the moment. What does that signify? The two dogs are barking somewhere in the house. I want to stand by Eva. That's how I see my part in this drama, however it turns out. I determine not to move from her side.

Leave me alone, she says, when I have followed her into her room. Please go away!

My feelings are hurt. She kneels in front of the telephone on her bedside table. She keeps on and on dialing the operator and hanging up again.

When I close the door behind me I don't know where to go. If I stay in my room I'll miss finding out what happens next. I'm still wearing my wet bathing suit under my dress. The lump in my throat is my swelling tonsils. I keep swallowing to find out how the pain is developing.

Was that the week I spent in bed with a temperature, when the doctor had to be called? Did he come the next day? I think that was it.

I am so absorbed by my role as comforter, by my duty to be there for Eva, that I still don't venture to change my clothes. I go down to the great hall. Hitler is receiving Mussolini, listening to his expressions of sympathy and his congratulations on such a piece of luck; he has already given orders for the merciless settlement of accounts with the conspirators, and a nightmare begins in Berlin in which the protagonists of the Resistance recognize one another in growing horror as they watch themselves moving incredibly slowly, dreamers who simply cannot move from the spot in an attempt to save themselves. All this time I am standing by the gigantic window, a very small figure looking out at Hitler's panorama, the jagged mountain crests like military defenses behind which the sun has disappeared. My skin is glowing, but beneath it I'm trembling with cold. I hope Hitler is dead. I passionately hope so. Not for my father's reasons, but because I hope that then, at last, Eva will realize that she needs me.

Let's go, I shall say when she comes down. Let's get away from here as fast as we can.

I am not prepared for what she will tell me soon afterward. Now that she knows what has happened she wants to go to Rastenburg to join Hitler. Tomorrow. She is like a madwoman in her determination. I realize that I can't stop her.

You must stay here, she tells me, imperiously.

The experience of finding that her lover is actually vulnerable has made her strong. She has become another woman in the last few hours. I don't recognize her.

Misfortune is Eva's own domain. It gives her radiance, strength, personality. She is made for misfortune. On its arrival she straightens her back, acquires a firmer outline, shows style and self-assertion, not to avert it but to welcome it. There is no saving her, but I don't know that yet. She is mistress of the art of self-destruction.

Eva is an oracle. It will be obvious on the day when she appears in the bunker of the Chancellery, calm, relaxed, beautiful, totally self-confident. There will be nothing left to remind anyone of the shop-girl she once was. Everything nervous, rapid, blurred about her will have given way to supreme clarity. She will step on stage with the utmost assurance, as if she had been rehearsing all her life for this one entrance. And this time she will not remove herself from the scene by withdrawing to the prescribed distance from Hitler; she will place herself beside him, to the fore of the picture, and all present will see and understand with horror. As the survivors will say later: When Eva Braun arrived we knew it was all over.

But we haven't reached that point yet. When she is still there on the Berghof the next day I actually believe she has stayed for my sake. I feel as if I were still wearing my wet bathing suit. I have shivering fits. I can't get warm even under the two eiderdowns Eva has them fetch for me. The housekeeper makes me compresses as if I were a child.

But I am wrong: Hitler has forbidden her to do anything so stupid as to come to East Prussia. If there is one person he doesn't need there it is Eva. Now he has the proof of his own invulnerability. He feels fortified. Confirmed. Authorized to proceed with the work of destruction upon which he has embarked. She will have to wait a little longer before she can join him in his downfall.

To cheer her up, he sends her his ruined, bloodstained uniform. Kind of him. Here, you can enjoy a little of the feel of the disaster that just missed me. Well? How do you like it?

Did he know her, then? Did he know what she needed?

But then shouldn't I remember this unappetizing item of clothing, said to have been among Eva's possessions at the time of her death?

I don't.

Shouldn't I remember how disgusted I felt?

I don't.

Disgusted by the smell of it? The smell of Hitler? Of the sweat he shed in fear? Of his blood?

If I remembered any of that, I would go into a nunnery and spend the rest of my days inhaling the scent of incense. Or perhaps I would have killed myself long ago. But I don't remember it.

I do remember something else, though.

I remember what Eva was like. She hated dirty clothes. Stains. Grime. The smell of sweat. She never wore anything of her own more than once before having it laundered or dry-cleaned.

She could be utterly nauseated. She was not the nurse type who will mop up other people's body fluids. She was fastidious.

If there had been such a . . . such a thing, if Hitler had really thought it a good idea to send it to her, whether to create a holy relic of himself or wanting to be close to her in that way—no, my cousin Eva would have wrinkled her nose, held it away from her at arm's length between the tips of two pointed fingers, her head turned aside, and would have burned it in the hearth. Anyone who ever looked into her wardrobes and saw the meticulous order in which she kept her outer garments and underclothes, from which the delicate, slightly dry scent of lavender rose with uncompromising cleanliness, knows that she would never have kept a . . . a thing like that.

CHAPTER 3

AS LONG AS THE UNIVERSE GOES ON EXPANDING nothing is irretrievably lost. What was once so always will be. The past hurtles through space at the speed of light. Fifty-five light-years away is the point where, seen from that viewpoint, I am twenty years old, a pale young woman wrapped in rugs, lying on a mountainside terrace in a deck chair, convalescing from a nasty attack of tonsillitis. Fifty-five years away, Hitler's Berghof still stands, the chimneys of the concentration camp incinerators are still smoking, the tanks are rolling on, the sky is still fiery red with the light of burning cities, the echo of death-dealing commands still lingers in the air.

The young woman gets up from her deck chair now and turns to the rather older woman who has joined her.

I don't want to go in the least, Eva, she says. I'd rather stay here with you.

But you must, says the older woman. The chauffeur's waiting. Your suitcase is in the car. You'll be back in a few days' time.

Goodness, do you want to get rid of me? asks the young woman. I wonder why?

She means to sound lighthearted, but it's easy to see that she is un-sure of herself.

Don't make jokes, says Eva. Give Gretl my love, and mind you be-have! Listen, it's all men there, they'll try to turn your head. I don't want any complaints—don't forget you're upholding the honor of our family, so watch your step, understand?

When she's in the car, turning back once more to look at her cousin, she sees her racing up the great flight of steps at top speed, as if expecting something that she absolutely must not miss.

She really did want to get rid of me, thinks the young woman.

It's a longer drive than she had expected, and when they reach Zell am See her chauffeur has to ask the way to Schloss Fischhorn, which comes into sight only a little farther on, at the southern end of the lake and to the left of the road to Bruck.

She had imagined something Austrian and Baroque in nature, something lighthearted in the Habsburg style. A little lakeside castle, Eva had said, which suggested pastel colors, Mozartian merriment.

But what she actually sees is a darkly forbidding citadel of gray stone rising above the valley. It could have been formed out of the dreams of men who regard themselves as invincible. That's how they want the world. They want it the way you see it from the castle tower: land tilled and cultivated for them, land governed by them, land over which they hold sway from such citadels as this—stern, fortified, pitiless. These are men born a few hundred years too late, soon to be swept away, but over the distance of the light-years they look as if they had settled within these walls forever. As if they were masters not only of the Salzach valley, of the Pinzgau, but lords of the whole world, that's what it looks like.

The guards at the lower gatehouse wave the car through, and the young woman is let out at the bottom of the stone steps up to the main castle gateway. There she stands, slightly dazed from the drive over winding roads, which made her feel sick several times. Low clouds hang over the valley. A fine drizzle is falling.

She fills her lungs with a deep breath, trying to stabilize her circulation. She looks up at the walls and the tall lead-glazed windows, wondering what awaits her behind them. She would give a good deal to be able to get back into the car and return to where she came from. This is the way a new pupil stands outside an old and venerable boarding school, hesitating to go in. The well-tended turf, the landscaped park extending over gently hilly terrain, with old trees and carefully clipped brushes, it all fits this interpretation of her situation, and so does the riding school exercise ground that can be made out from here, the silhouettes of riders trotting in harmony, the stable buildings stretching out along the hillside.

Come along, says the chauffeur.

At least he carries her suitcase for her. Two uniformed men emerge from the castle gateway to meet them. Her chauffeur, who wears the same uniform, comes to some understanding with them. She can't follow exactly what they are saying. He hands over her suitcase, and if she is not much mistaken he is handing her over, too. He goes back to the car without any good-bye.

This way, please, say the two men, indicating that she is to go first.

When she steps inside the tall entrance hall, paneled in dark, almost black wood, the only familiar feature greeting her is the big black swastika on its red and white banner on the wall. Of the various doors standing open, from which a babble of male voices reaches her, she chooses the largest, a double door. She looks around before going through the doorway, but cannot see the two men with her suitcase. Young men in uniform pass her now and then, carrying trays with bottles and glasses and ashtrays, although she cannot see where they are coming from and where they are going.

The room into which she hesitantly ventures, almost expecting someone to turn her back, suggests a hall in a hunting lodge, its walls densely covered with trophies and pictures of the chase, crossed spears over the fireplace framing the head of a wild boar with huge, straight tusks as if they were rammed into its invisible flanks. The benches running down the longer walls of the room, as if in a chapterhouse, are unoccupied. The men are standing around the room in groups, smoking cigarettes, brandy glasses in their hands, deep in conversations of muted agitation. The scene is more like a kind of interlude than anything else, the sort you might see during a break in a political congress, where the participants debate with each other in galleries and corridors, in anterooms, forming groups as if by chance to negotiate the real subject of the conference. Their eyes pass over the young woman and look away from her again, as if they had noticed her only inadvertently.

She goes through a door that would usually be concealed but is standing ajar, and enters a kind of game room. A billiard table stands in the middle of it, surrounded by several men, once again smoking and commenting on the frame being played by two older men. One of them has a limp. Nonetheless, he moves around the table with remarkable agility, his stiff leg tapping out a syncopated rhythm on the wooden floor. He is the player dictating the course of the game, holding the spectators spellbound. There's no doubt that he is in charge at this table.

She need not fear being noticed here, and makes her way across the room like a dreamer looking for the way out of this false reality. She stops by one of the poker tables and lightheartedly picks up the cards. She can already feel the satisfaction of invisible spirits roaming reality, giving off just a few sparks to show they're really there. When she puts the stack of cards down again they change position. Something shifts, the pack fans out, the top card presents itself to her line of vision.

As if this were the signal recalling her abruptly to reality, she suddenly hears the footsteps of the man with the limp behind her.

So what are we doing here, young lady?

All at once there she is in person, highly visible, the card still in her hand. As she quickly puts it back, the man with the limp can see for himself what she, too, has seen. The image is burned into her memory for all time. It is the Hanged Man; she knows about the tarot pack, and that this is one of the twenty-two great arcana. Except that he is hung up not by his feet but by his neck, from a piece of wire that has dug deep into the flesh. The hook from which he is hanging, an abattoir hook, a butcher's hook, rises above his head like a question mark, replacing the aureole around the Hanged Man in the tarot pack. She wonders, but only briefly, why they are playing with photographs instead of ordinary cards here.

Times of trial, she thinks automatically. Caution. Danger somewhere close. She knows the meanings of the cards. A neighbor in Jena once dealt out the tarot pack for her. It's a game, she thought, only a game, that's all. It doesn't mean anything. But she knows that here and now she cannot rely on the borders of reality.

You're expected, as far as I know, says the man with the limp. Not here, though. The ladies are up on the second floor. Didn't anyone tell you?

No, she says. I don't know my way around here at all.

Well, you'll soon learn, says the man with the limp, and it suddenly sounds like a threat. Now she sees that she is in the center of a circle, surrounded by men. Their faces express an interest in her, although she does not really understand why, and it seems a moment too long before they step aside to let her through. When she leaves the room she has a feeling that they are sitting in judgment on her. She hasn't the faintest idea what the verdict may be.

Going upstairs to the second floor, she reaches a broad corridor full of chests and heavy Renaissance cupboards. She can't imagine what is kept here. Why in the world would anyone need so many cupboards? The doors along the corridor on both sides are closed. Should she knock? Or should she open them and walk in? Neither idea seems right. The loud creak of the floorboards under her feet makes her feel awkward. It also prevents her from making full use of the only one of her senses which is helpful at the moment. She tries finding her way by sound. She thinks she can hear voices behind the doors.

All the same, she decides to turn around, and reaches a wing of the building with an open door at the end, leading into a room. After the gloom that has surrounded her since her arrival, this room seems flooded with light and air. For that reason alone it attracts her. And now she can hear the laughter coming out of it. Women's laughter.

The two women are sitting on a tall four-poster bed covered with rugs, a four-poster with a wine-red canopy, and one of them is her cousin Gretl.

There you are at last! cries Gretl. We were waiting for you.

She pats the bed beside her as if the new arrival were a dog she is inviting to jump up and join her.

Make yourself at home, she says. This is Frau Höss.

The name means nothing to the new arrival. She doesn't know it. She won't even remember it. Only a kind of faint echo of the name will stick in her memory, clinging there with little barbed hooks, and she will suddenly feel them years later at a chance touch, when she is unable to remove them. Where did I hear that name before? she will think at that later time, seeing a black-haired woman under a wine-red canopy, looking at her with an expression that seems to say: You see, you'll be one of us, too!

She remains standing.

Sit down, do, says Gretl.

She rests her buttocks on the edge of the bed, but is still really on her feet, since it is so high and she is so short that if she sat down she would lose contact with the ground, which she is reluctant to do. During the days she is to spend at Schloss Fischhorn, she will not succeed in relaxing even for a few moments. There will always be something about the place to make her feel she should be on her guard, and never again will she leave any place as happily as she left that castle.

How's Eva? Gretl asks her. Is she feeling calmer now?

Yet she knows perfectly well that the two sisters telephone each other daily. Each of them always knows how the other is. Among other things, the new arrival has to discover that when questions are asked the answers do not matter. Not in this place. It is one of the lessons she is taught promptly in swift succession.

Vinegar? says Frau Höss

She appears to be picking up the thread of a conversation interrupted by the young woman's arrival.

Cider vinegar, says Gretl, a glass a day.

You drink it? asks Frau Höss.

What else? says Gretl.

I was only thinking, says Frau Höss.

One's not meant to think, says Gretl. Thinking makes you ugly. Cider vinegar makes you beautiful.

The new arrival's sense of not knowing the rules here grows stronger. Except for her, they all seem to know what is going on and what regulations you have to observe so as not to make yourself conspicuous.

I don't know where my suitcase is, she interjects.

Oh, don't worry, says Gretl, nothing goes missing here.

Thereupon she turns back to the black-haired woman. The young woman thinks the two of them look like bosom friends from whose pact of intimacy she is excluded. Later she will learn from Gretl that they met only at lunch that day, and have no idea what to make of each other.

Oh, I'm so glad you're here, Gretl will assure her.

But without Eva she is curiously distant to her cousin. After copious assurances that it's just so wonderful for them to have each other, nothing more will come of it.

Nonetheless, Gretl helps her to find her way around the labyrinth of suites of rooms and corridors and locate her room on the top floor, where her suitcase is on the bed. She wonders who occupies the other bedrooms. Except for the chambermaid, she will never see anyone in the corridor, and she isn't sure which would be worse: to be all on her own up here, or to have complete strangers just the other side of both her bedroom walls.

In the night, she will hear voices. The sound of booted footsteps. The creaking of a door. If this castle were inhabited by ghosts, that is just what it would sound like.

That afternoon they have arranged for her to go for a walk with Gretl. She waits for her in the entrance hall. She has had nothing to eat since breakfast on the Obersalzberg, but she doesn't dare ask for one of the pieces of cake she sees carried past her now and then. Once again, she gets the feeling that she is invisible, and if she isn't invisible then she ought to be, as if the director of this drama had not foreseen her presence here.

Undecided, she looks at the suits of armor standing around the walls while Gretl keeps her waiting. Gretl is one of those women who are never punctual.

She suddenly thinks she sees the living eyes of alert and suspicious warriors looking at her from behind the closed visors. Going up to them, she tries to see behind the iron masks, looking far in, into the very depths of the souls once enclosed there, souls that had to escape through the slits and hinges of the helmets, or perhaps were obliged to stay inside them and watch what went on around them, unredeemed, full of a mad blood lust, full of a desire to avenge their own death agonies, full of an uncontrollable craving to be part of life and present in it still.

Just as, having lost her timidity now, she is putting a hand out to one of the visors and trying to raise it, the eyes of the knight in armor suddenly flash. She flinches back, and a reproachful, indignant, metallic sound comes from him. He sways on his plinth, and for a moment she fears he is about to fall on her. She knows at once that she has gone too far, and already she can hear footsteps hurrying up, and a woman's cross, angry voice:

Whatever are you doing? Don't you know not to touch things here?

I'm sorry, she says.

She can't explain to this woman why she was so startled. Only later will she be able to account for it by thinking that just as she was raising the visor the clouds outside parted, and a ray of afternoon sun shone through and glanced off the helmet as it moved.

I do apologize, she says.

The woman, approaching her with a click-clack of high heels, is no taller than she is, and has the plump, coffeepot shape of many women over fifty. She wears her iron-gray hair pinned up in a wreath on top of her head. Everything about her is rounded, apple-shaped, including her face, everything is full and firm, her tubby figure squeezed into a tight-fitting, almost ankle-length black dress that reveals all the outlines of her body. The feet under its hem are surprisingly small, and her small shoes so delicate that you wonder how they can carry the weight of that body so nimbly.

At the moment when she reaches the young woman Gretl finally arrives.

Mama, she says, emphasizing the second syllable, this is Marlene. You remember.

She speaks in a tone of voice indicative of earlier discussions. Well, she's here now, Gretl's tone of voice indicates, and you can't do anything about it.

She ought not to be touching things, says Mama. Have you met my son yet? she asks by way of a greeting.

No, says the young woman.

Find your husband, Mama orders, and as Gretl immediately sets off she adds: And don't forget he doesn't hear well!

I know, Mama, says Gretl.

Poor boy, says Mama Fegelein, turning to the young woman. Did you know he sacrificed his eardrum to the Führer? He was standing right beside him when the bomb went off. It's always the best who bear the brunt of it. That's life. And as for the Führer—no, unthinkable. It injured his eardrum. In my view those criminals ought to be wiped off the face of the earth. What do you say? Men who think so little of human life! If you ask me the death penalty's too good for such scum. Ah, here comes my boy! The Führer's sent him home for a few days to recuperate from his terrible experience. I can tell you, the Führer's like a father to him. Well, he has no children himself. I always knew something great would come of my boy. A mother senses these things, believe you me.

As the young woman watches him approach, followed by Gretl a few steps behind, she looks for some mark, some distinguishing feature to allow her to recognize Hermann Fegelein again among all the other SS officers.

He looks remarkably handsome. As do they all.

He is so tall that in other company he would tower above most of the men, but not here.

He has a bored, haughty expression on his face. Just like the rest of them.

So she will know him again only from the fact that Gretl keeps her conjugal gaze bent on him, a gaze in which anxious skepticism mingles with a frenetic willingness to agree to anything at all. Among all the men here, he is the magnet attracting Gretl's eyes.

And his mother's eyes, which are without any skepticism whatsoever.

This is Gretl's cousin, she shouts in his ear.

He looks at her with complete indifference.

Take care of her, he tells his mother sternly. It sounds like an order of some magnitude, curiously enough intended not for Gretl but for his mother. The task is apparently of such import that her husband thinks it will be beyond Gretl's capacities and sense of responsibility. As a result, Mama Fegelein attaches herself to the two cousins on their walk in the park and does not move from their side all evening, or over the next few days.

Do you ride? she asks at supper, which the ladies take separately from the gentlemen in what is called the breakfast salon. Besides Mama Fegelein, Gretl, and Frau Höss there is a girl of twelve present; the young woman cannot work out whose daughter she is. She has been trying for some time to understand who they are talking about around the table: Paladin. October. Semiramis. These persons are discussed with great warmth and intimate knowledge. Then she realizes that they are horses.

No, I don't ride, she replies.

What? says the child, rolling her eyes scornfully.

Oh, my dear, then it's high time you learned, says Mama Fegelein.

She demurs, but soon realizes that she has come up against a blank lack of comprehension.

Even Gretl, says Mama Fegelein, even Gretl has made some progress.

She speaks of Gretl in the unmistakable tones of a mother-in-law, not concealing the fact that Gretl fails to come up to her expectations in more than one respect. Just imagine: She can't even ride, and she invites cousins who can't ride either!

The next morning the visitor is taken for a riding lesson after one of the chambermaids has brought her a pair of jodhpurs, a pair of boots, and a red jacket. The boots are tight, but she finds the jodhpurs and jacket an exciting costume, allowing her to resemble the uniformed men around her, and she suddenly thinks that it can't be impossible to talk to one of them. And as she walks down the path through the park to the riding ground a few hundred meters away, with the man who has been detailed to accompany her, she suddenly feels that she wants to stop and look at his face.

It is a blue morning of the kind found only up in the mountains in August. On one side of her and down below, the southern end of the lake shines brightly; the meadows are deep green; and here and there you see the scythes of the mowing farmers flash in the sunlight. The whole scene suddenly strikes her as a kind of Garden of Eden, a new morning, a new world in which the old precepts, the old constraints, the old setbacks no longer apply.

She looks sideways at her companion, and sees how young he is. He can't be more than two years older than she is herself. And as she notices this she no longer finds him strange and intimidating. Behind the masculinity on display she sees his still childish face. His shyness. His homesickness. His awkwardness because there is a girl walking beside him. We could have been at school together, she thinks suddenly, and wonders why the idea is so surprising, why it has never occurred to her in connection with any of the other men she has met recently.

And she cannot resist the temptation. It is like the desire to do something forbidden, kick over the traces. For a moment she feels it is possible to say: Come on, let's just leave all this behind us. Let's go.

Instead she asks: Do you like it here?

That in itself is a bold remark. As far as she can possibly go, even in view of their closeness in age.

(Fifty-five light-years away, on a planet called Earth, the two would now take hands, shouting in high spirits, and run down into the valley, where they would stand by the roadside and wait for a car to stop, a car in which they disappear from our view. The screenplay of life changes at the speed of light, too.)

What do you mean? asks the young man.

I mean, she says, emboldened by the morning, the blue air, the scent of hay, I mean it's a bit like being on holiday. You feel like going for a swim. A pity one can't just do what one likes here. Have you ever been up there? she asks, pointing to somewhere up in the mountain peaks, which appear to her suddenly close, as if you could walk on them.

Up there? says the young man. Well . . .

Do you know anything about the history of the castle? she asks, trying again.

History? says the young man. No, no idea.

All the same, he, too, suddenly seems to want to talk. But in everything he now tells her about himself she hears nothing but a litany of military ranks, promotions, and decorations for courage that he was nearly awarded, or nearly was not awarded. His Austrian accent makes it even harder for her to understand what he is talking about. It is as if he were talking not about life but about some kind of sport with which she is unfamiliar, so that she cannot appreciate his triumphs in it either.

Where do you come from? she says, trying to change the subject.

The East, he says proudly. Kiev. Vilna. Minsk. Anywhere we were needed.

She had meant his home.

And don't you ever get frightened? she says.

Frightened? he asks. Frightened, well, yes. When they scream so loud. Especially the women. The women scream so hard when they have to hand over the children. Enough to frighten anyone. But we in the Black Corps have to be particularly brave. Anyone can shoot a man dead. It's different with the women. . . .

They have come to the big dairy farm located above the valley, with the men's barracks and the stud farm. It is a proud and ancient building, displaying the centuries-old wealth of the lords of Fischhorn. A little lower down lies the riding ground, from which the sound of hooves and the wonderful warm snorting of the horses are heard. There is a smell of hay and manure and equine sweat in the air. Men's voices rise, good-humored laughter, commands, scraps of remarks full of pride and appreciation. Agreement. Jokes. A whole symphony of lively activity, healthy and in harmony with itself and everything else, with nature, with animals, with their attitude to one another.

To her surprise, the young woman meets the limping man from the billiard table here, and she realizes that this is Fegelein senior, Gretl's father-in-law, head of the SS cavalry school that is conducted here. Yet again she marvels at the agility with which he moves.

He lets his glance wander over her from head to toe and back again. He is assessing her, but as a riding master, not as a man. He sums her up and matches her in his mind with one of the horses.

Snow Queen, he says.

This is an order to her young companion. Soon afterward he emerges from the stables leading a horse by its bridle. The young woman cannot imagine getting up on the creature's back. It is far too high. Anyway, she has not missed seeing the hostile look in the mare's eye. She knows the two of them are not going to get on. She knows it, and so does the mare. Involuntarily she retreats as the horse approaches her.

Up you get, says the limping man.

He believes in the bareback method of learning to ride. It is his view that a novice must feel the horse under her, feel its warmth, the play of its muscles, its flesh. She must feel it between her thighs. He swears by this method.

She is rigid with fear and distaste. She does not want the insides of her thighs in contact with the animal. She doesn't even want to go close enough to touch its twitching flank, that convulsively moving mass of muscular flesh from which the acrid smell of horse rises, one of the typical aromas of life here, immediate and powerful, both familiar and strange.

Her companion puts the reins into her hand and holds out his own linked hands to help her mount the horse. There is no way she can get out of it now, so she steps into this living stirrup. Her desperation and fear have turned to anger instead, although she does not know what she is angry about. But something has given her a reason to feel anger and contempt. Something monstrous that shapes the monstrosity of her fury.

She senses the hands raising her with extraordinary ease. For a short moment she really does feel like a horsewoman about to gallop away on the back of her mount, leaving everything behind her, free and wild. Very briefly, she is at one with the impulse of the movement raising her to the horse's back, experiences the intoxicating novelty and startling intimacy of the situation. Then, with the same willfulness that inspired her to feel like a horsewoman, she lets herself slip off the other side of the horse again.

You have to be patient with the ladies, she hears Fegelein senior saying, everyone knows that.

It's always different with women, that's what, says the young man.

She gets up and simply walks away. Only much later does she notice the pain in her knee. No one is going to persuade her to mount a horse ever again in her life.

At dinner she feels what a burden she is to her cousin. Her failure makes Gretl's position, weak enough anyway at this court, no easier. After all, who is Gretl Braun? Is she Hitler's sister-in-law? Obviously not. Still, one can't behave as if she were not, to some slight extent, his sister-in-law. She fulfills that role just enough to have made it impossible for Hermann Fegelein to refuse when she was suggested to him as a wife, although in herself and without Eva she appears even more pallid. And she does not improve matters by her efforts to please everyone and be constantly obliging. Even Hermann Fegelein sometimes simply fails to notice when she speaks to him, and only when something is repeated does he pull himself together and say:

I'm sorry, darling. You know I've not heard well since then.

"Since then" is a phrase they frequently use, and they all know what they are talking about.

You know he hasn't heard well since then, repeats Mama Fegelein, as if it were Gretl who was hard of hearing.

The young couple are seldom to be seen together here at Schloss Fischhorn. Life in the castle, on the riding ground at the dairy farm, at the stud farm, on the bridleways and paths through the park is a man's life. Women are merely peripheral to it, marginalia scribbled in at the edges, pale, barely perceptible. Imagine them absent, which is easily enough done, and there wouldn't be much difference here. Cooks, chambermaids, a few wives. The most noticeable female presence is that of Mama Fegelein. She has what it takes to be a chatelaine, the lady of the castle, except there is no such position here. She herself doesn't seem to know what is really going on, what exactly is the focal point and meaning of all the activities pursued around her.

Cars drive up and drive away again, new arrivals stride with lithe footsteps through the hall, carrying under their arms slim briefcases the contents of which appear to be of incalculable importance, shrill telephones ring, boots creak on the wooden floor, double doors swing open and shut, briefly revealing groups of men in black uniforms bending over tables behind clouds of cigarette smoke, letting out the regular buzz of a constant exchange of views, which immediately seems to be muted when the doors are closed again, a roar rising and then receding again, like the sound of a swarm of insects going about its business somewhere in the building, moving from place to place, settling somewhere or other and rising in the air, without sense, without meaning, without purpose.

Gentlemen, is the word repeated over and over again, the leitmotif. If I may say so, gentlemen. Thank you, gentlemen. Gentlemen?!

It is a world in which the gentlemen mix only with themselves. A world in which they relate, in a curious manner, to one another and nothing else at all.

Young Fegelein moves in this world like a fish in water, smooth,

quick, and agile. He is in his element. Only late at night is he to be
seen climbing the stairs and approaching the bedroom into which
Gretl disappeared hours before. He does not seem to be in any hurry.
Not until the last game of billiards or poker is over does he join
her. He lights a cigarette as he goes up, putting it out again, half
smoked, in a vase of flowers in the corridor. He is straight and
smooth in every way, seen like this. His dark hair, combed back, is
straight and smooth, not a strand ever out of place except when he is
riding. The skin of his face is taut, gleaming, and very pale, so that
the idea of touching it produces a chilly sensation. His uniform tunic
fits smoothly and faultlessly, molded to his body.

Now, at night, he has unbuttoned its collar, just the top button,
which gives his appearance that certain something, that touch of the
casual, which is essential to true elegance. There's the inimitable cut
of the riding breeches he wears under it, emphasizing his thighs and
buttocks. The promise of power and intransigence expressed in his
appearance. All the sex appeal of martial virility. And oh, those
boots. They, too, are black and shiny. See how he walks in them.
Long, sure, firm footsteps. Even the mighty oak staircase of Schloss
Fischhorn groans beneath that tread.

Only Gretl knows who he is when he gets undressed, or perhaps
not even Gretl. Perhaps the light is always out when he approaches
her. Darkness is appropriate to the lovemaking of two people who
know each other so little. They married in Salzburg two months ago.
Hitler was there. Bormann and Himmler were witnesses. Such were
the men who stood sponsor to their married bliss. A dream wedding for Gretl Braun, thereby socially elevated above her sister. An
SS-Gruppenführer to whom one is married trumps a Reich Chancellor and supreme warlord to whom one is not, anyone can see that.

Gretl did not want this triumph for herself, but what Gretl wants
is not the point. Not even with respect to what happens after the
wedding. The dark nights when she lies alone in the double bed until

the boots come creaking upstairs, and shortly afterward, somewhere near her, a belt buckle is undone, while a cloud of horsiness wafts her way, mingled with the odor of leather, cold cigarette ash, and the exhalations of a man who has drunk too much cognac. Signals from a world in which she has no part, a world that alarms her, in which she senses something like contempt, even hostility toward herself.

At the time of their marriage she had only one night with him, the wedding night. Then he left. This is a time of separations, brief moments of happiness, and moments of unhappiness, too. The rest of your life for a single night. Or two. Or three. And the opposite may be true: another three nights. Another two. Another one night. And then it's over—perhaps forever, but for the time being anyway.

Let it never end!

Or, make it end!

This is the time in which the silent prayers of women are heard. Men come and go, and women pray for both their coming and their going.

In this world of superfluous females the young visitor is even more superfluous than anyone. Nonetheless, people occupy themselves with her, although she cannot see why. Why can't she simply go for a walk? There's no need for them to go to a great effort to fill her time.

The fact that they do makes her suspect that she is the one intended to be driven away. Driven away? From where? Driven away from the scene of the crime. What crime? She doesn't know.

Take care of her, Fegelein junior told his mother, and his mother is taking care of her now.

What about going for a climb in the mountains tomorrow?

The young woman doesn't want to go for a climb in the mountains. Her knee hurts, and she is afraid of climbs in the manner of a Luis Trenker film, with women falling down crevasses in glaciers to be rescued, half dead, by intrepid mountaineers, children of nature to whom they are then delivered up for better or worse. She likes mountain movies, but only while she is sitting comfortably in the cinema.

Anyway, her shoes would be a problem again. She has only her oxfords from Jena with her, and they are not at all suitable for climbing.

Unfortunately, it turns out that Gretl wears the same size shoe as the young woman, and can lend her a pair of climbing boots.

Doesn't Gretl want to come climbing in the mountains herself?

No, Gretl has been there before. But Mama Fegelein will go, and nothing will induce her to abandon this plan, as if it were the performance of a patriotic duty. The young woman realizes that she must go along with it.

NONETHELESS, HER INTERNAL RESISTANCE is still strong as they set out early in the morning, the two women and their inevitable male companion, wearing climbing boots with his uniform trousers, a combination the young woman thinks looks rather silly, somehow out of place. Without their riding boots these men forfeit much, indeed almost all, of the elegance of which they are so confident; much, indeed almost all, of the intimidating influence they exert and which they themselves feel as a kind of aura surrounding them, keeping their bearing erect, every muscle taut, endowing their bodies with a dimension not their own, but lent to them as members of a collective identity. Like this, the man looks rather overdressed for a climb.

The reluctance dominating the young woman saps her strength, imparts itself to her muscles. She feels none of that inspiring lift of the spirits required for walking and climbing mountains, when you are in pursuit of yourself, part of you always running slightly ahead, making haste to the summit. Instead, she is lagging behind herself, rebellious and unenthusiastic as a naughty child dragged off somewhere against its will.

The Hundstein, says Mama Fegelein, who is walking ahead with remarkable agility, not what one would expect of her sofa-cushion figure, the Hundstein has the best view for miles around. On a clear day you can even see as far as the foothills of the Alps.

The young woman feels no desire to see the foothills of the Alps. She fancies dawdling and being tiresome, an obstacle in the way of Mama Fegelein, who is now privately rehearsing her enthusiastic account of the beauties of nature she has seen, to be delivered on their return.

All the same, the climb brings the release of high spirits even to the young woman, that sense of lightness, that feeling of freedom and intoxication induced by any expedition into the mountains. Her own spirit spreads its wings when she sees Schloss Fischhorn, the lake and the villages in the valley, Bruck and Taxenbach and Maria Alm, lying at her feet, the lake like a puddle glittering in the sunlight, the castle like a toy, soon to be entirely lost from view. But her exuberance, her sense of a greater liberty than is permitted down in the valley, is expressed in an urge to behave badly.

I can't go any farther, she says, and since she says it, it is true.

To her surprise the man accompanying them turns out to be chivalry itself. He takes her rucksack and insists on a rest so that she can recover. Mama Fegelein, on the other hand, agrees to rest only reluctantly. Her bosom is heaving, her face is flushed an alarming shade of red, but her small person will allow no sign of weariness to show. She is possessed by the energy of the uncompromisingly domineering who are used to getting their own way, even in competition with themselves. Only much later will the young woman realize what strength of will animates Mama Fegelein, and what plan she is pursuing at present with such effort that it is driving her to the limits of her strength.

Early in the afternoon they reach a mountain hut, and the young woman says she doesn't want to go any farther. There is something about her two companions she doesn't like. It's the way they are both doing her bidding, serving her, anxious always to give her the best place, to make sure the old herdsman who brings them milk and cheese is aware what glorious radiance she has shed on his poor hut. What is it that unites them? They know something about her that she doesn't know herself.

At any rate, they know where they are going, and they assure her that it isn't much farther now.

So she sets off on the last stage with them. The path now leads almost smoothly over a narrow ridge from which steep scree slopes drop almost vertically on both sides.

This is really beautiful, says Mama Fegelein, this wonderful view of the Hohen Tauern with the Dachstein range in the distance. Striding out with a firm step, she looks all around them, pointing out the rugged beauty of the Leoganger and Loferer Steinberge.

There, look! she cries. Just look at that! Isn't it grand?

Fantastic, murmurs the young woman, wonderful, as she keeps her gaze fixed, with superhuman watchfulness, on the path in front of her. She is concentrating entirely on staying alive, while Mama Fegelein is obviously one of those people who never suffer from vertigo at all. She dwells securely in the middle of her rounded corporeality, steering it skillfully and purposefully through life, her lack of imagination never allowing her to think how far you could fall.

Careful, their companion sometimes says as he goes ahead of them.

Then there will be a few loose stones on the path, or with increasing frequency it shows little fissures, cracks reaching into the middle of it, small ravines over which they must step and which go all the way down to the infernal chasms below.

All her life she will dream of this climb, will walk that path above the abyss, ahead of her the back of a man she does not know but who nonetheless provides her with protection and support, the only protection and support she has. And behind her someone else will be walking, someone pushing her and urging her on, preventing her from turning back. In these dreams she will suffer a terrible sense of vertigo, a perception of a danger that is also a temptation, and while she follows the dark back the word *Obersturmbannführer* will take shape in her dreams, a monstrous word, a word full of dark violence, full of lurking danger. The name for a mysterious, disguised, faceless masculinity, which she is following.

In the mountains, evening, although predictable, always comes as an unpleasant surprise. It falls quickly. A shadow races up the mountain slopes from valley to summit, and like the finger of God it changes what it finds, as if someone had said: Let there be darkness.

Like all lowlanders, she has always thought the climb down from an ascent must be child's play, something that would come of itself, you would simply have to let yourself go downhill along the path without making any effort. Like all lowlanders, she is obliged to discover that this is not the case. All the same, she thinks someone might have warned her in advance.

Oh, my dear, says Mama Fegelein, surely you don't seriously want to go back today? We're nearly at the hut. We'll stay the night there.

This is not the back of a horse off which you can slip and land on the other side, this is the top of the Hundstein, and the young woman realizes that she is going to spend the night in a mountain hut with these two strangers.

They are the only climbers out today. They find the key to the hut, and their companion lights a fire on the hearth. Until now she has avoided addressing him by his rank, as is usual down in the valley. Now, to her surprise, she discovers that Mama Fegelein calls him Hans. A relation, perhaps? Only now does the familiarity of the two with each other strike her, a familiarity in which she feels she would like to be included. She is too tired to be as watchful as she was in the morning. Up here, after all, they are a kind of mountaineering team, relying on one another, alone beneath the stars like the remnants of a tribe that has fled from war in the valleys to safety among the mountain peaks.

And enthusiasm takes hold of the young woman, too, an ecstatic sense of being so close to the sky. The deceptive purity in which you feel removed from everything that would soil you and drag you down. Now, sitting outside the hut, eating their provisions and watching the night as it falls fast, she cannot maintain her sulkiness and reserve.

Mama Fegelein finds some gentian spirit in the hut. They all drink from the same bottle, an act that brings them closer to one another. The Obersturmbannführer talks about his childhood on the banks of a river. Stories of wild duck, beaver lodges, and perch-fishing. Not a word about Vilna, Kiev, and Minsk. You travel light in the mountains. And anyway, the war doesn't reach up here.

Isn't it beautiful, children? says Mama Fegelein. She has the world below her at her disposal, as if it were her front garden. She has the night at her disposal, too, and the stars and the firmament.

It is early August, a night of shooting stars. The little miracle of light comes with increasing frequency. Far out in space worlds are in movement, opportunities are open.

Are you making a wish? asks Mama Fegelein.

Yes, says the young woman.

What are you wishing for? asks the Obersturmbannführer.

A husband, says Mama Fegelein.

She says it in a voice that suggests she is the authorized recipient of wishes made when you see a shooting star. As if it depended on her alone whether they were granted.

A lovely girl like you must take good care of herself, she says. It must be the right man. Watch out for yourself! Don't throw yourself away, my child! As a German woman your responsibility is not just to yourself but to our country, you see.

Then she withdraws for the night, irrevocably, as firmly as she has spoken.

Good-night, children.

Rather bemused, the young woman is left with the Obersturm-bannführer under the starry night sky. Then she, too, rises to her feet.

There is one room containing four beds in the hut, and one single bedroom. The single bedroom is for the older lady, as befits her status. The young woman lies down on the bed next to the wall, in silence. She keeps on everything she is wearing except her boots, and pulls the dark woolen blanket up to her chin. A faint red light comes from the hearth in the main room, where the fire is still burning.

Would you leave the door open, please, she says to the man who follows her into the room. It's so cold in here.

She shuts her eyes, with her eyes closed she hears the click of his belt buckle, a sound so familiar to many women of her time, but this is the first time she has heard it, soon after that comes the noise as it falls to the floor, the hollow thud of the boots, the sound of fabric against fabric, the rustling of a straw mattress as a male body lies down on it. She smells the strange odor of a strange man near her, an odor that also rises from the straw and the blanket of the bed on which she herself is lying. She holds her breath, hears him breathing all the louder beside her. She tries to form a shelter around her out of her held breath, her stillness, her closed eyes, she tries to simulate absence.

But she can do nothing about the presence of the man near her.

A kind of breathing duel develops. The quieter and more shallow her own breath, the more audible and deeper is his. And there is the whispering and rustling of the straw in the mattress on which he is lying. She knows that a single long-drawn breath, the faintest movement from her could decide the duel in his favor. Any rustling of the straw beneath her would deliver her up to him.

It is a long struggle. Her muscles are cramped, the blood pulses in her with muffled beats echoing so noisily between her temples that she cannot believe they are not audible outside her body as well. Sometimes she thinks she hears him hold his breath and listen quietly to see if she will give herself away. Then his breath, the movement beside her that she dreads, start again.

She tries all night not to go to sleep, but her wakefulness keeps slipping into a dream, a dream the subject of which is that she mustn't go to sleep, a curious, light hovering above herself as she lies on her bed, sleeping deeply, exhausted after the unaccustomed climb.

When she wakes up she is startled by the beauty of the world outside. Mountain peaks tinged with rosy pink in the morning sun, the sky changing from the blue of night to the blue of day, one last star fading as it stands above the mountains. The bed beside hers is empty, the blanket neatly folded, as if no one had spent the night there.

She goes out, washes her face in a channel of water that now, in high summer, contains only a trickle running into a hollow beside the hut.

No one around.

Soon afterward, Mama Fegelein comes out of the hut.

Oh, you young people, she says. Up already?

The young woman walks around behind the hut and goes a little way along a path through the scree and mountain thistles. With amazement, she drinks in the overwhelming purity of the world up here, the magic of a perfectly white light that seems to emerge from the rock itself. Nothing is dirty when you have made your way so far up. Around a bend, a black figure appears in the white light, the man beside whom she spent the night. She cannot avoid him, and does not want to go back. So she goes toward him, just as she would rather go toward a danger than turn her back to it.

Good morning, says the Obersturmbannführer.

Good morning, she says.

I've been over to the lake, he says. Did you know there's a little lake in the cirque up here?

No, she says.

Would you like to see it? It's not far from here.

Is there anything but water to see? she asks.

Take a look for yourself, he says.

Around the next bend she sees the lake a little way below the path. It is deep black in color, a black slowly tending toward green as she looks down on it, an ever-open eye gazing straight at the sky above.

Then she sees that she is alone. Her companion is climbing a scree slope to the left of the path. She goes down to the bank of the lake. She wants just to dip her hand in the water and look into its black and green depths. It is icy cold, much too cold for bathing. As usual, she immediately loses interest in any stretch of water once it turns out unsuitable for bathing.

As she goes back to the path she realizes, with surprise, that the Obersturmbannführer has begun climbing the rock wall rising above the scree.

She wonders: Does he have a rope?

This is the one thing that, as a lowlander, she knows about mountaineering: You need a rope to climb a vertical rock wall.

Then she takes no more notice of him and goes back to the hut, where Mama Fegelein is already having breakfast.

Do you know where Hans is? she asks her.

See that? says the young woman. That black dot up on the rock face? I think that's him.

For heaven's sake! cries Mama Fegelein. Is he out of his mind?

She jumps up and runs along the path.

The young woman sits down calmly and eats her breakfast. Bread. Milk. Cheese. A hard-boiled egg from her rucksack. She keeps her eye on the rock wall as if watching some kind of sport that does not interest her, with rules she doesn't want to understand. She has no idea how she got into this Luis Trenker movie, but at least she is now playing the right part, the part of an observer, and she is relying on the story line that keeps characters alive if they are still needed for the plot, just as she relies on it at the cinema.

Slowly, the black dot moves onward and upward, finally disappearing from her sight, and Mama Fegelein reappears, bosom heaving, struggling for composure.

I can't understand it, she says. I just can't understand what's come over Hans.

When he comes back he places an edelweiss in front of the young woman without a word.

The Führer's favorite flower! cries Mama Fegelein, quite transported. My dear child, it looks to me as if you've made a conquest!

Oh, but how could you run such a risk, how could you be so careless? she adds, turning to him with pretended indignation.

She is captivated, delighted, girlishly flattered, as if it were for her that he had ventured up the rock wall.

Are you cross with me? he asks the young woman.

Let's go now, she says.

On the way down she is silent, refuses the helping hand reached out to her now and then, and she leaves Schloss Fischhorn that same evening.

She has mislaid the edelweiss on the way down. On purpose? By accident? She is not sure herself. Most things just happen.

LATER, BACK AT THE BERGHOF, I understood what had happened to me. Or rather, I never entirely understood it. It remained mere supposition, and the longer I thought the less sense there seemed to be in it.

Why had Eva sent me away at all?

What was I supposed to be doing at Schloss Fischhorn?

Why was Mama Fegelein so extraordinarily concerned about me as to subject herself to the strain of a climb in the mountains?

When I came back, dropped off by the drivers from the motor pool at the front door of the Berghof, which was opened to me in a moment by one of the housemaids, I was told that my cousin was in her room waiting for me. She had been anxious, and was just telephoning Schloss Fischhorn to find out when I had left.

I could hear her talking through the closed door, and quickly entered the room without knocking, sure she would be relieved at the sight of me.

I heard her saying, in agitation: And suppose she's pregnant?

Then, suddenly lowering her voice: Well, I must ring off now.

Our conversation on meeting again was dull and meaningless. I told her I was tired after my mountain climb.

Only later in my room did a suspicion occur to me, one that haunted me for the next few days. I tried to suppress it whenever it came into my mind, but suddenly, while reading one of the novellas by Storm I was enjoying at the time, or swimming in the lake, or in the middle of watching one of the films they screened for us in the great hall, I would think of something, something that would not leave me in peace, like a dog pushing its muzzle against you now and then to make sure it is not forgotten. There was something else. And I knew what it was. Eva had been trying to marry me off.

I turned the hypothesis this way and that, tested it against all my experiences, and saw that it made sense. I had been on offer to one of the courtiers.

Poor Eva. She could think of nothing but to weave a little web of relationships and spin herself into it. Since she couldn't have the big wedding she had longed for herself, was she trying to make up for it with a couple of lesser weddings? Did she perhaps hope Hitler, too, would be caught in her web? Or did she want to consolidate her own position at court independently of him?

It was the only intrigue upon which she ever ventured, her single and fundamentally misconceived attempt to meddle in domestic power politics, marriage being the only means to the end she had in mind. Just as she could think of no other aim for herself but to marry

Hitler. No other dream. No other plans. Only this one fixed idea: to be Hitler's wife.

And she was not even concerned for her position, or the power it would give her, or the wealth she would acquire by the marriage. She wasn't thinking of any of that. Except perhaps sometimes in weak moments, after suffering a snub, when she was told to use one of the side entrances to the Reich Chancellery while Frau Goebbels swept in at the front in a grand dress, or when she was sent to her room at the Berghof, and looking through the curtains she could see Emmy Göring standing at the top of the steps beside Hitler to receive distinguished guests. At such moments she may perhaps have dreamed of saying to those ladies some day, with a little smile: Oh, my dear, that hat, don't you think it's just a bit out of date? We're wearing those little hats that perch on the side of the head now, don't you know?

But her imagination would reach no farther when it came to avenging herself for injustices suffered. Her ardent wish to marry Hitler was only loosely connected with a desire for social rehabilitation, it was more of a pipe dream of the definitive, unreserved, great affirmative! Her ardent wish to marry the worst man in the world was romantic through and through.

It was a wish straight out of the movies. It fed on the films we watched. Films by Veit Harlan, Carl Froelich, and the other directors of our collective lifestyle fantasies. They were the masters who taught us the art of love. They had dreamed our dreams before us. We dreamed them again in the directors' versions every evening at the Berghof.

We were given the list of rolls of film in the Berghof archives at breakfast in the morning. We knew it all by heart. Still, we went through it solemnly, often agreeing on the film we would watch that evening only after long discussions.

There were about two hundred films for us to choose from, but we watched only a handful. We always plumped for the same favorite movies, spelling out the same enchanting dreams, when the projectionist arrived in the evening—the only man in civilian clothes I remember seeing there—to roll up the large tapestry in the hall and reveal the screen of Hitler's private cinema behind it, whereupon he disappeared into the cabin behind the opposite wall, and a bright light would soon shine from its projection window.

I remember the flickering white light, the soft hum of the projector, the first notes of the choruses we heard when the opening credits rolled. I close my eyes. I still remember those films. I remember them frame by frame, take by take, line of dialogue by line of dialogue. I have a small movie house inside me with a Nazi repertory, a cinema that will show me films of love and death night after night if I want.

And yet again I am Kristina Söderbaum. I am a wild creature. Untameable. A child-woman. My voice is shrill, high, piercing. I get everything I want, and what isn't freely given I simply take. Men like me. My childish innocence arouses their protective instincts. I can flirt, but I am not a femme fatale, never that. In the end I make myself rather than them unhappy.

I'm greedy for life. I want all of it. I want it without making compromises, an impossible dream. The child in me can be incredibly happy. I am direct, wildly enthusiastic, vulnerable. I can be radiant with happiness like a match flaring up.

I must hold my heart in place or it will jump out! I cry at the sight of the Hradschin, the river Vltava, the whole city of Prague.

After this scene, obviously, my director will fling his arms around me and praise me for my intensity of expression. In real life he is my husband. He doesn't ask me to be more withdrawn, more reserved, he encourages me to come out of my shell.

I am not beautiful. It's just that I'm so intense. There is something strongly muscular, powerful, earthy about me. But you see that only when, at the same time, you realize that I carry the germ of a tragic illness deep inside me, a mortal illness that will afflict me in almost all my films and make me prone to feel a great, all-consuming love.

That is what I offer the public, a chance to see this spectacle and the way in which, despite my blue eyes and robust appearance, the sickness mows me down. Every attempt to save me is bound to come too late.

Have I disappointed you all? Didn't anyone see how much I needed help? Didn't you realize that the liveliness you liked so much in me, my strength, my wildness were only the reverse of the extraordinary tenderness animating me, were its cover, its disguise?

I am the woman for whom men go to war, not Zarah Leander, still less Lida Baarová and Marika Rökk. They are the kind of woman to whom men hope to return some day. Alluring. Ever-changing. But I am the kind who deludes them into thinking it is worth dying.

I am on familiar terms with death. The stronger the temptations with which life approaches me, the closer death comes, too. I suffer a terrible vengeance for my actions and innocent wishes. A short trip to Prague comes to a fatal end.

All I want is to see my mother's native city, where she was so happy before she went into the marshes.

That golden city! That captivating film in Agfa-Color into which I have found my way! The sinful red of the cheap dress I wear there instead of my demure traditional blue costume!

There is a powerful struggle going on in me between my mother's blood, which makes me susceptible to urban temptations, and the blood of my father, calling me home to the soil.

The opposition of town and country. Their irreconcilability. The definitive border, the border one may not cross with impunity. It will be the death of me.

My end is tedious, accompanied by choirs of angels and screen monologues of a kind the public has not had to suffer since then.

Mother dear, I say, you are calling me. I'm coming to you. I must go the same way as you went.

My mother, to the sound of angels singing, tells me I am doing the right thing.

May God forgive you, I say, meaning my seducer, for I have forgiven you.

My countenance is already hovering over the marshes in a dissolving shot. I am as good as dead. So I can now be more generous than is really right in view of what my seducer has done to me: He has taken my honor, made me pregnant, and left me. Shame on him! I ought to be saying. Let him be accursed! But that doesn't suit the character of the angel I am about to become.

Forgive me, Father, says the angel, for not loving my homeland as much as you do. Forgive me for giving you such pain.

And I see the light coming over the marshes. The rescuers are close! But the screenplay, supported by the heavenly choir, insists that I assume that light to be a kind of heavenly radiance.

Finally I am lying on my bier, pale with the pallor of death and my regained innocence. And now my father understands the message of his loss, the message of the entire film.

Drain these foul marshes, he says. And then, hand outstretched like a prophet:

Let the rye grow here!

And so it does. Cut. The grain is seen waving in the wind around my grave to the sound of Smetana's music. Where there was once marshland, rye grows all the way to the horizon. The true gold of the ears of corn against the false gold of the city!

I need no projectionist now, no projector, no screen to see that film. It is inside me. I am forever in the cinema where it was shown.

I'm sitting there with my cousin Eva. It is Hitler's living room. The projectionist switches the ceiling light on again in his cabin. For a while we still hear the hum of the machinery rolling back the film.

We hardly dare look at each other. We've been crying. Crying our eyes out.

The few members of the domestic staff who sometimes join our film shows, which is permitted even when the master of the house is at home, have already stolen out of the room. They've been crying, too.

We feel ashamed, but we know crying is permissible. It is desirable. It is the right reaction. We are meant to be shattered. Spellbound. Harrowed. We are meant to see that there's something worth giving your life for.

Oh yes, we see that. We understand that a country girl can't visit the big city with impunity. We know that vice dwells there. We guess at the presence of dives where people dance hip to hip, to the music of saxophones. Alcohol. Bad smells. Sex in unmade beds. Dirt.

What is good, genuine, and true, on the other hand, has its natural home in the country. The dirt of cowsheds and farmyard dunghills is clean dirt. Something ancient, reliable. Something we want to preserve for the future. Something familiar, redolent of home. Even those of us who are not from the country—and Eva and I are not country girls ourselves—believe that all this is a part of our souls, the true, the better part. The farmhouse is our spiritual home.

We are young people born for the land. Our cities, the cities we shall build after the war and live in forever, will be clean. We see broad avenues. Buildings like manor houses made of great stone blocks. We will suffer no one but ourselves there. A healthy race, strong, hardworking, reliable, and honest to the point of idiocy. Only Germans can be like that. Only their roots go deep enough.

That's what counts: knowing your roots and defending them once you know them. We want to call out and tell this to Kristina when we see her falling for the seducer. We involve ourselves in the ensuing tragedy. We experience it as if it were our own tragic story, and she is suffering it in our place, so that we are spared.

We understand that it is dangerous for blood to mingle, for the blood of those who come of the soil to mix with the blood of those who don't know their roots. We know the seducer has no conscience. We wax indignant on seeing him make a beeline for the pure country girl. We curse him. We curse the city that produces such monsters. We go back to the country and call it our home. We would rather be dead than anywhere else. We vow to die for our land. Our eyes are wet, we have a lump in the throat. We join the singing of the choir of angels that Kristina hears from heaven as she dies.

The feeling that inspires us, our deep sensitivity, is honestly felt. Nothing is further from our minds than hypocrisy. We are genuinely moved. We long for something similar to this Veit Harlan movie for ourselves. Fate, I come!

Homeland, The Call of the Mountains, Sacrifice, Romance in a Minor Key are titles we would like to give to the operatic libretti of our lives. We consider the metaphysics of kissing a universal truth, like the magic of the announcement, "I love you." Both come with inevitable finality, authenticated by the tragic or happy ending to which they lead.

It is something very much more elevated than kitsch, since it is the true substance of our dreams. If anyone had told us that three decades later love would be less revered, would no longer appear as the force of destiny but simply as what it is, we would have thought that person was speaking of some other planet.

We Nazis were a generation of a thoroughly melodramatic cast of mind, and only when the choir of angels failed to strike up in the last act did we realize what kind of film we were in, and realize that what we saw was not some bad tragedy but hell itself. Nor was it a film at all. It was the play in which we had acted the part of ourselves. Suddenly we found ourselves personally involved in the showdown, saw that it all boiled down to saving our bare lives, which we did, and when it was finally over we crept offstage very quietly.

We remember everything. The great crimes committed in our

names. The small acts of treachery and cowardice that were our own part in it. We remember the lies we heard, the stern order instructing us to spread them, and we remember that we carried out that order. We remember gray-faced people whom we saw passing by, and we remember that we saw them in the knowledge that they were lost. We remember.

But there is something that is too shameful to be remembered, even after all the years that have now gone by. No one can expect that of us! It is easier to admit to guilt than embarrassment. The memory of a spurious emotion is horrible, shameful, humiliating. And hidden deep down, disguised and camouflaged out of all recognition, the evil of which we were capable lies in the same memory. That is where it hides.

CHAPTER 4

WHEN I CAME BACK FROM SCHLOSS FISCHHORN we resumed our old habits. Our outings to the Königssee, our evening walks to the house on the Mooslahner Kopf. And it was here that I made a curious discovery one evening.

Eva had a key to the Tea House. She kept a little hoard of cigarettes there, and used to go and inspect it like a squirrel checking on its winter provisions. It was in a cupboard in the anteroom of the circular tea salon, which you reached by going up a few steps. Sometimes we sat there smoking while our guards stood outside the building and smoked, too.

The Tea House lay hidden in a part of the woods a little way down from the Berghof. There was a spurlike area in front of it looking out over the valley, with the rocks falling precipitously away below. The view from here had none of the Alpine grandeur that Hitler and his visitors admired so much. It was an idyllic view, hemmed in by the tall trees to left and right, a friendly picture of a friendly world, a river valley with lush meadows where grazing cows were dotted about, and bordered by the forest that began here at the foot of the Untersberg, whose massive heights cut off the horizon. Now and then, as if dabbed on the canvas by an amateur painter, you saw the rooftops of barns. This was the place where Hitler liked to take his guests, rather than the Kehlstein house. He seldom went there; he came here daily.

He was never as private anywhere else. It was here that he sometimes nodded off in an armchair with a flowered linen cover, while the conversation died down around him until all present were preserving an awkward silence as they listened to his breathing, trying not to notice when his facial expression slipped and his chin sagged.

A tyrant's nap, even if it lasts only a few minutes, can be endless for his companions, and it was Eva who at some point would gently touch his lower arm and get him through the dangerous moment when even he was a child, helpless and vulnerable, the moment everyone must survive when waking up in company. To bridge that moment he would put his hand to his forehead and smooth his hair. He did not put it back from his brow as a man whose hair had fallen into his eyes while he was asleep would have done, but used the palm of his hand to plaster it where it would always belong, at a slant over his forehead. A hairstyle sui generis, marking the physical appearance of evil in the world for all time. A masterpiece of the spirit of the age acting as barber.

It was a gesture that, although intended to be energetically disciplined, looked curiously awkward and affected. For an unplanned, unguarded moment his lack of grace and elegance was visible, and with it all the arrogance of the lordly bearing he assumed. He was neither a bear nor a god. His paw was white, fleshy, weak. People would have laughed if it had been allowed. But laughter was not allowed even in the Tea House.

A part of Hitler's power lay in his peculiarly distinctive appearance, which was an extraordinary phenomenon.

No picture of him comes as a surprise. No picture suggests that

there is anything else there, a face behind the mask, a character looking over his own shoulder. He is always the same. No smile, no gesture, no item of clothing, no state of mind or body can add anything
to his appearance. Nor can age or the signs of failing health—he does
not change. Not since then has anyone of such a dominant physical
appearance been seen. An appearance in which every single feature
was ordinary and bore witness to the ordinary. An appearance that
has outlasted its time. His physical death could not affect it. It stares at
us down the decades. Hitler, always the same. A face as phenotype. If
we forget everything else, even if death extinguishes all our memories and we take none of them into the underworld with us, we
shall recognize him in Hell. There is no draft of oblivion for that
memory. And although I never actually set eyes on him, he was
as present to me then on the Obersalzberg as is the master of a
household who has just gone out for a walk and is expected back
for dinner.

That day we found that the cigarettes from Eva's hoard were missing. The cupboard in the anteroom was open. Someone must have
been there.

First, Eva got our guards to give her a cigarette. Then she fell into
a kind of detective frenzy.

She told our guards to search the surrounding area while we ourselves set out to look for clues in the building.

In the kitchen I found the door of the fridge left ajar. I quickly
closed it before Eva noticed. There was nothing in it but a few cans
of milk anyway, as I knew, and I didn't want to give Eva new grounds
for her childish suspicion that someone had broken in here. None of
the windows were damaged, nor was the door leading to the cellar
below the house on the valley side. The cellar windows were barred
anyway. I knew how happily Eva would have worked this up into a
little anecdote. I knew she was already polishing up the text for
Hitler's benefit.

A break-in on the Mooslahner Kopf! Just what she needed to spice up her evening phone conversation with him. As if strange things were part of our experience. As if we, too, were a little head-quarters for issuing orders and making decisions.

Perhaps there's still someone in the house, she said.

At that moment we both heard the voice in the next room.

It was a quiet, regular voice, male and monotonous. After a short pause it began again, still speaking in the same monotone. At first it sounded as if it were saying a prayer. Then we realized that it came from a radio.

Eva recovered first and opened the door. In a room furnished as a single bedroom a radio stood on the small table by the bed-head. It was playing as if some invisible hand had switched it on, and the voice speaking to us from the radio was our enemy's voice. The man was speaking German, but very obviously in the way educated British people speak German, almost without an accent, but their vowels are just a little too long, and the *a* and *e* sound slightly nasal.

Our enemy was saying that we were going to lose the war.

Who switched that radio on? cried Eva, and I saw the bullfighter look in her eyes again, lids wide to dart glances that this time con-veyed not an assumed but a genuine wish to attack. I explained that it must already have been switched on when we entered the house, be-cause the BBC was broadcasting its German-language program at intervals.

There was one of the breaks between transmissions until just now, I told her. That's why we didn't hear it sooner.

How do you know? Eva asked sternly, as if she were a teacher who had caught me out trying to cheat.

My father, I said. My father listens to the BBC.

I knew she wouldn't give him away.

But somebody must have switched it on some time or other, she said.

That's right, I said, somebody switched it on.

When had it struck me that there was no radio in Hitler's Berghof? Or not for us, at least. Not while I'd been there.

Not a single People's Wireless Set in Hitler's own home. In every other living room in Germany, but not his. Radio silence reigned there.

I have never been anywhere so quiet since then. There was nothing but the wind blowing around the houses that stood in isolation on the mountain heights, a whistling wind, rising and falling, always in the same key, and although it is always there, always audible, it is the song of nothing, it speaks of nothing but the vacuum surrounding every building set high above a valley floor, where your neighbors are the abyss below and the air above it, nothing but air as far as the eagles fly. You get used to it. You call it silence, yet sometimes you hear that piping sound as if it were a confusion of airwaves gone into overdrive, shrill, sending messages into the ether that are never received.

But there was something else. A recurrent rumbling from the depths. Sometimes the ground under our feet seemed to quiver as if an earth tremor were announcing itself. The mountain appeared to be laboring.

What is it? I asked Eva.

No idea, she said. Just take no notice.

There was no point at all in asking Eva questions.

(Do you love him?

Of course.

Does he love you?

Yes, I think so.

Would you like to be married to him?

Why not?

Aren't you afraid, then?

Afraid? What of?

Afraid we'll lose the war. And afraid of what happens after that. Let's talk about something else, little one. You're so serious.)

Sometimes the rumbling seemed to come from the depths right below us. It was as if the mountain itself were telling me something I ought to know.

Why weren't we given a radio?

We got everything else we asked for: smoked goose breast; banned Duke Ellington records (because we did have a gramophone); Tyrolean hats, one for Eva and one for me; lily-of-the-valley perfume, it made no difference to us where it came from; Merano figs; as many of the Salzburg sweetmeats called Mozart balls as we wanted. But no radio.

The truth is that we didn't ask for one.

Didn't we want to know what was going on?

Well, we did know. We were on the spot. We were the news ourselves. Its center, the whole secret point of it. Could anyone be closer than we were? Wasn't it here, where we were, that all the strands of world events came together, wasn't this place their end and their beginning? Any theater of war, whether in the East or the West, was only a sideshow of a battlefield. Every command post could be regarded as expendable in an emergency except for the place where we now were.

It was the innermost citadel, the real fortress for which the Second World War was fought, the "Alpine Fortress," the most profound and precious heart of Hitler's Reich, and at the same time the safest place in it. Anyone waging a war of conquest starts out from somewhere, and intends to return there either victorious, with the world in his baggage, or beaten. This was that place.

It was the object of every military engagement, every exchange of firing in this war, every attack and every defense. All the men's courage was mustered for its sake, all the blind will to achieve with which our soldiers set off for foreign lands—Africa, the Balkans,

Russia, Finland, and Norway, all those places where their whole business was to kill and to die. Places where they were ordered to run uphill while marksmen posted above them had them in their sights, finger on the trigger. All that remained of life was crammed into that moment. It was not for that hill they were fighting, however, it was for the mountain from which their commander had set out to conquer the world and to which he meant to return in the end. That was what they were dying for. This place was the center, the place where I was now, and everything else was peripheral. Outworks in front of it, worth defending because this place was being defended.

It was the last home of the Nazis, their inner refuge, their own place. It was here that they all intended to survive. They wanted to be here if the end should ever come for them. They could not imagine that retribution would ever track them down here. Whenever discussions of the situation and new reports from the front made them a little uneasy they would think of the Berghof and how close they were to it, of its full cellars, its flower-bedecked balconies, the stocks of wood behind the building. Nothing could happen to them. Not really, not while they knew of a place of total security for themselves. After all, what did the reports from the front have to do with them?

No, we didn't need a radio. We were the message ourselves. If there was anything we thought of in connection with the vision of victory, which we called not just victory but "the final victory"— why "final"? Doesn't that suggest the end of victory, the diabolical converse of everything conveyed by "victory" itself?—if there was anything we thought of then it was a whole series of Berghofs scattered over the wide expanses of the East, their dark battlements lit by torches held in iron shafts, with the shafts fitted to tall walls built of mighty blocks of stone. The next fort would always be visible on the horizon, set on rising ground, a day's journey away by horseback, while the outworks around these forts spread over the plains, blameless areas of the agrarian economy where a servile people would do the work for which it was fit: tilling the soil, hard physical labor carried out under the stern direction of their natural masters. They, too, would be content, oh yes, they would be grateful.

Ah, the life on those Berghofs! One imagined it well-disciplined, severe, ornamented by gentle women in dirndls with their hair wreathing around their heads: harvest festivals, midsummer bonfires, winter evenings by the blazing hearth, to the accompaniment of melancholy songs for which Slavonic throats and German feeling would be cultivated. A soldier needs something to fight for, something worth giving his life for. It was the Berghof idea for which they died. It stalked ghostlike through the speeches of Joseph Goebbels, it had echoes in the modest, rhetorically simple addresses made to the troops by their officers before battle.

Something hallowed by time, cozy as a tiled stove, solid, reliable, fortified by shutters over the windows, something Alpine, Sunday-smart, summer-flowered, something built in natural stone, crafted of straw and wood carving, with old folk costumes and the lusty singing of brand-new tunes—the Berghof ideal was their defense against the affronts of modernity.

They discovered that the word *Gemütlichkeit*, a term for that very German sense of being snug and comfortable, existed only in their own language. They shivered at the thought of a world pressing closer, rootless, homeless, brand new—a world of the future. They had been so far from home for so long that their homesickness weighed more heavily on them than their fear of dying. All the *Ungemütlichkeit*, the lack of home comforts to which they were exposed, that life in dirt and danger and humiliation was tolerable only while they had a purpose in the war such as the defense of the Berghof before their eyes. Something warm and comfortable, something snug.

We were there. We lived at the one place in the universe for which they all longed, a fortified refuge and the aim of the war combined. The still center. We didn't need a radio.

From now on our walks to the Mooslahner Kopf were made in the cause of our inquiries. I loved them. I loved this leak in the hermetically sealed world surrounding us. It was surprising to discover that the self-contained system within which we lived could be infiltrated. Was that what attracted me to the Tea House? Was that the reason why I began to imagine myself living there in my fantasies?

It was a pretty place, small, as if made specially for me. There was a room for the guards, as there was everywhere—a room the tyrant himself used to frequent—a small bedroom, the kitchen, an anteroom leading to the round structure beyond, built as a massive tower and containing the tea salon itself, with its tall, narrow, panoramic windows. It was the ideal of a small private house, and that part of me which likes the idea of a hermitage, a house on a mountain slope built with its back to the forest and its front high above the valley, with the human world lying at my feet like a toy, a little house where I can be just myself and I am entirely alone at home, that part of me had its beginning here, and even today I sometimes find myself settling into Hitler's Tea House in my mind. One of the secret rooms of my heart is built in its image. I go in. I am not afraid. I feel safe there. I am alone, although I know there is someone else in the place with me. I am not alarmed when I find myself facing him. My secret and I live in the house together.

The dwellings of our life are built in the image of the dwellings in our minds, and whenever we suddenly feel at home in a strange place, in tents, in inns, beside a lake by night, we have entered one of our inner rooms, and sometimes we see a house at the far end of the street in a strange town and know we still carry the key to it, we could go in and find everything just as if we had never left.

Hitler's Tea House is more than a memory to me. I can go into it. I still have the key. I unlock the door and go through it. I open a window. Like all houses not constantly inhabited, it smells of itself. I have access to this house at any time. One of my unlived lives was played out in it. And sometimes I am alarmed by the clarity with which something reminds me of it: a slab of snow slides off the roof, a linen curtain with flowers on a pale background moves in the wind. I hear someone breathing but there's no one there . . .

The detective game soon seemed to lose its charm for Eva, like everything else on which she embarked, particularly as we found nothing else suspicious on our visits to the Mooslahner Kopf. Or at least, so Eva thought, since for some reason or other I did not tell her that the next time we went there I found a towel lying on the bathroom floor. I retrieved it and hung it up again. It felt damp. Someone had used it. Perhaps the cleaning women had simply forgotten it.

On another occasion Eva was looking for the chocolates that, she assured me, were always here. Mountains of chocolates. Hitler loved to present lady visitors with gifts of sweets. It suited his notion of gallantry, his idea that women lived in a café society world of the mind. But there were no stocks of chocolates left, only a box that had been opened.

But we always throw chocolates away once the box is opened, she said, as if stating a basic principle of Hitlerian policy.

I'd like one all the same, I said.

She watched me eat it with an expression of distaste on her face.

August was over, and the days were getting perceptibly shorter. Summer in Berchtesgaden comes to an early end. The sun now reached us only in the afternoon, and soon the Berghof would be sunless throughout the day. Hitler was a creature of the night. He went to bed in the small hours of the morning, when day was approaching. Autumn was his season, and the Berghof, built on a slope facing northwest, was his house. While Göring's and Bormann's houses basked in the midday sun on the west-facing side of the mountain, the Berghof lay entirely in the shadow of winter. It didn't trouble

Hitler. He did not realize what was missing, and when autumn began to approach he couldn't understand Eva, a natural sun-worshiper who suffered severely from melancholia at that time of year.

Let's go to Munich, she said, more heroically determined than ever to have fun.

Can we?

You silly little thing, she said, we can do anything we like.

I clearly still hadn't understood the rules of the game governing our life here.

Tomorrow? I said.

Tomorrow . . . she said. Well, that depends.

What do you mean? I asked.

Wait and see, said Eva.

Hitler phoned that evening.

We're off tomorrow, Eva said later. I've ordered us a car.

I thought she had asked Hitler's permission. Only later did I realize what it was all about. If he rang one evening, then his next call could be expected two evenings later at the earliest, so that until then we were more or less at liberty. After that, however, Eva must be back at her post. It was simply unthinkable that she wouldn't be, and I believe it never once happened.

She was as much afraid of him as everyone else was. Like all true despots, he had the ability to spread fear that ultimately was not the fear of any threatened punishment, not fear *of* him but fear *for* him, fear for his injured feelings. It was so terrible to disappoint him, to fail to come up to his expectations. He could be so inordinately, uncomprehendingly disappointed in someone that his uncontrolled anger, the quivering indignation that filled him, seemed justified, and by comparison with the suffering caused in Hitler himself by inadequacy and disobedience, the suffering of the person punished, however pitilessly inflicted, seemed hardly worth mentioning. Nothing takes more courage than to disappoint a despot. Nothing inflicts

more cruel pain on him. Should he ever discover that free human beings with free will exist, it would surely be the death of him.

And he would certainly not discover it through his mistress. So we
improvised.

Next morning there was a car ready for us. They actually did
take us where we wanted to go, on our own orders. So we were not
prisoners.

Suppose we wanted to go to Paris? I said.

I realized that this was a stupid remark in the September of 1944.
Or Berlin?

When I go to Berlin it will be without you, said Eva.

Munich, she told the chauffeur, and we set off as if for a nice drive
into town, a little escapade of the kind Eva liked so much. We were
just two young women who, after a stay of some length in the country, wanted to breathe a little of the big-city air.

SEPTEMBER 1944: the air of Munich smells of the aftermath of fire.
It smells of wet lime, of smoldering beams, of the odors rising from
cellars that have filled up with groundwater. It smells of death.

The way to Wasserburger Strasse is like an obstacle course. Whole
streets are blocked, impassable, clogged with mountains of rubble,
metal, glass, broken tiles, bent metal girders. The buildings still standing look uninhabited, most of their windows boarded up, including
the shop display windows. There are no shops left. Only the old
names from another time: Ladies' Outerwear, Delicatessen, Oriental
Rugs. They stand there like the inscriptions in a desecrated grave-
yard. The city is gray. The end product of every act of destruction is
the dust that settles on everything.

The people are gray, too. They appear singly, separately, moving as
if in flight. A race of beings coming up from the cellars, venturing
briefly into the light to perform rapid tasks, eyes lowered to the

ground, making haste about it, disappearing down into the cellars again. They snatch up something to take with them, some pathetic possession that they intend to hide away. Something retrieved from the rubble, something acquired for an incalculable price. This is how thieves move. But they are not thieves. They have stopped appearing to be what they are. They are indifferent to it now.

The only way you push a pram is at a run. The wheels of the prams wobble. The little bodies inside them are shaken all over the place. But not every pram contains a baby. It could hold cabbages, old clothes, cooking utensils. You're lucky if you can wheel a cabbage home. The ruined city of Munich is a city full of prams. They are the prime method of transport. They are low-built white wicker baby carriages, with massive wheels and hard rubber tires. When they have been wheeled to the point of disintegration you snatch up their contents, whether a baby or some other item, and just abandon them. Someone or other will chuck it on top of the rubble pile along with broken grandfather clocks, shattered lavatory pans, and bathroom fittings.

The fate of the trees: Here and there a tree stands defoliated, shattered, violated, dead. They share in our experiences. I am instantly aware of the monstrosity of it. The one thing I take in on our drive through Munich is the monstrosity inherent in the death of the trees along with us. Birds sit in their scorched branches like messengers from another world. It is an image from the mind's picture book of horror, clear and grisly, although these are not ravens but the migratory birds that visit Munich every year at this season.

The triumphal gate is barred by the fallen masonry lying around. One of the bronze lions is lying on its back. Our pity could not be greater if it were an animal of flesh and blood.

We still wax indignant over the suffering of animals and trees. When the elephant Wastl died buried under the ruins of the Berlin Zoo after an air raid in November 1943, the whole country grieved.

The picture of the dying colossus, lying helpless on his side crushed under several steel girders, once again embodying in death all the awkward, beguiling charm of a baby mammal, was printed in all the papers, and if the people were ever united by a single emotion it was by their indignation at the death of Wastl as a result of the Allied air raids on Berlin. None of the fallen soldiers was mourned so much. None of the suffering of those buried in the ruins touched us so closely. Would we let war be waged on animals in the zoo? Bombs on Hellabrunn? Never! We suddenly understand the meaning of human suffering through the suffering of our fellow creatures.

Eva's house is intact. Everything in Wasserburger Strasse is still just as it was. The fridge is full. The SS provide for us here, too. No sooner are we through the door than the protective cocoon closes around us again. We are invulnerable. In the gray world of death surrounding us we are the colorful exception, enclosed in a shimmering little soap bubble floating merrily along. Nothing can happen to us. We're having fun.

We exercise with the gyro-wheel in the garden. Eva is proficient with the gyro-wheel. She goes the whole way around the circular lawn with the cherry tree in the middle of it, whereas I am happy if I can perform a single revolution on the device. Our cheerful squeals echo through the neighborhood.

The Führer's lady-love is back.

We invite Eva's friends around. Mitzi comes, Mandi, Kathi, and Schorsch. They come at midday and stay well into the evening. Their conversation is all about clothes, people, fashion magazines. There are chocolates in the afternoon, and for supper we have the dry-cured beef we found in the fridge. We drink champagne with it. There's always chilled champagne ready when Eva comes here.

Got anything? they asked as soon as they were through the door.

Of course, said Eva, I always have something nice for you.

Mitzi bites the chocolates, tries them, and if they have centers she doesn't like she deposits them in the ashtrays with the cigarette ends.

I spend some time struggling with myself, wondering whether to speak up.

Finally I say: There's butter in those, you know.

Yes, I know, says Mitzi. Fact is, I don't like butter.

In 1944 that sounds like blasphemy.

The air-raid warning sounds in the afternoon. It's the second that day.

We must go down to the shelter, I say.

You go, says Mitzi, you're just a scaredy-cat, nothing's going to happen.

I don't see why we can't stay up here, says Schorsch, it's cozy up here, he says. Cozy and cheerful, that's the ticket.

They sing. It's a drinking song claiming that the cozy cheerfulness of Munich will never die, not as long as Old Peter, the name of the bell tower of the church of St. Peter's, still stands . . .

But as far as I am aware it isn't standing now.

I try to cast Eva meaningful glances, but she doesn't respond. I get the feeling that when she's with her friends she shuts me out. I feel excluded. I don't know what they're laughing at. They laugh almost all the time. I feel my face contorting into a grimace, as if I were laughing, too. The women's laughter, as I sense without being precisely able to account for it to myself, is a sign of their sexual readiness. It is unbridled, shrill coloratura laughter, giving evidence at its height of their own ability to climax in orgasm. I have heard it since then in many other women, particularly in middle age. It stops after sixty at the latest. Even today hearing it still makes me angry. It makes me angry because I feel that it exposes me.

At the time I watch, with the inward wrath of the excluded, to see if I can catch Eva joining in this laughter. The expression on my face is intended to stifle it in her throat.

But I don't catch her at it. Nonetheless, my fear of air raids takes the form of a sense of deep injury, of exclusion.

I'm going down now, I say.

My sense of injury is so strong that it almost paralyzes me, and I make for the cellar entrance with stiff, unsteady steps.

Off you go, then, says Eva. Come back when the all-clear sounds.

The hell with her.

While I sit in Eva's bunker, that expensive luxurious air-raid shelter fitted out especially for her, I think of Hitler. If he only knew, I think. She's insulting us both, Hitler and me alike. Neither Hitler nor I feel happy with the company she keeps in Munich. But I realize that Hitler has other things on his mind just now. I have to endure this on my own.

And as if mocking me, the all-clear comes quite soon.

Hey, look, says Schorsch. Here's our little chickabiddy again.

Out of every thirty or forty air-raid warnings and alerts, only one portends a real raid. I'm a little chickabiddy because I didn't know that. I'm a provincial, with my correct High German accent contrasting with the Berlin dialect. I'm a Prussian. I'm just a nuisance and a hanger-on.

Cheers, says Schorsch to me. Have a drink, love.

All I know about Schorsch is that his work is important to the war effort, so he is exempt from service in the national army or even the territorial army. Later I learn that he is in the wines and spirits trade. It's a job that suits his natural inclinations. I wonder whether it's my patriotic duty to inform Hitler.

I cast Eva a warning glance, which she fails to notice, and go to bed.

Before we drive back to the Berghof the next morning we go to see Eva's parents. I am surprised by the warmth of Uncle Fritz's welcome. No dour silence now, no reproachful withdrawal, as I have feared.

In fact, he long ago forgave Hitler for loving his daughter. And Aunt Fanny even seems to have blossomed a little herself in the sun of power and its warming rays. She looks distinctly younger than six years ago. There's something flirtatious, roguish about her. A kind of determination to be happy at any price, which stands up to the air raids now coming at shorter and shorter intervals.

Now and then it does happen that the success of their daughters in love reflects so much on mothers that they become reconciled to their own modest lot and raise themselves, unasked, to their daughters' social eminence. Aunt Fanny would not have been Aunt Fanny if she hadn't eventually succeeded in persuading Uncle Fritz that there was no point in resisting good fortune, particularly when it is pursuing you so tenaciously. Any daughter can bring home a husband. But a Hitler is something else. Once, when Uncle Fritz finally showed himself ready to be a guest on the Obersalzberg from time to time, Aunt Fanny had rewarded him with herself, with an Aunt Fanny enjoying a second springtime, clearly rejuvenated and slimmed down in the air of her social and geographical high altitude.

It was an act of seduction she performed on her husband, who no doubt would have tired of his celibacy in the guest bedroom at some point, and no longer felt like resisting the siren song of all the female voices in his family. He half sank, Aunt Fanny half dragged him back into the marriage bed, and there he was sleeping with her again. He joined the Party, a step that was rewarded with the honor of a membership number containing only a few digits, putting him on a par with the early members, the Party veterans. And if Fritz Braun did make a great effort to remember the past, he sometimes actually did believe he had always been a member, and after suffering a slight injury on the occasion of Georg Elser's attempted assassination of Hitler in the Bürgerbraukeller in November 1939 he considered himself one of the martyrs of the movement. In other words, he gave up. He aged. No one took him very seriously.

Not so Aunt Fanny. In the autumn of 1944 she still was in excellent form. The ship of her life had a favoring wind in its sails. She was long past dreaming of a wedding between her daughter Eva and the dictator. She liked the status quo. Indeed, she rather relished the risqué nature of the situation. It rubbed off on her, too. She flirted. She would talk to any men present in front of her daughters, and her comments were cogent and sometimes daringly irreverent. None of her daughters had inherited her native wit. Ilse, the cleverest of the three, came closest, but her cleverness had told her to leave the nest early, and she still kept well away. And Fanny Braun need not expect competition from her younger daughters, nor indeed did she expect much of anything else from them. She laughed a little too loud.

The greatest day of her life was the wedding day of her youngest daughter and Fegelein. At heart, she herself was the bride. It was she who, with an air of inimitable confidence, received the congratulations of the powerful, which were as good as a promise of happiness, a kind of policy to be paid out when it matured.

But it was not really material advantage that my aunt Fanny Braun expected to reap from her daughters' connections; what she really liked was the fact that at last, if rather late in the day, she had a chance to show her talent for making a big entrance. Did she not feel the ground beginning to get hot beneath her feet?

Eva urged her parents to join us on the Obersalzberg, where they would be safe from the bombs, and they arrived a few days later.

My word, said Aunt Fanny, you girls are very comfortable up here.

But I soon realized that we bored her. She lamented the days when Hitler held court here. State visits. Receptions. The whole circus, she said dreamily. Yet I felt fairly sure that Eva had seldom invited her when Hitler was at the Berghof. Women like Eva are considerate in love, considerate to an extent verging on self-denial. She would not have done anything to upset her lover in the least, anything that would have seemed like an imposition. If necessary, she was even ready to spare him the imposition she herself embodied.

Her parents didn't stay long this time either. After a few days, they decided to go on to Schloss Fischhorn and their younger daughter. I imagined Aunt Fanny taking riding lessons and flirting with the young SS officers. I could well believe it of her. The Fegeleins would have to revise their opinion of the women of the Braun family.

In time Eva's parents took to shuttling between Schloss Fischhorn and the Obersalzberg. When they returned to the Berghof, Aunt Fanny would indulge in peculiar references to me. I had made quite an impression, she said. I wasn't forgotten at Fischhorn.

I didn't ask for details.

I still loved her. I still wished my mother were like Aunt Fanny. But I was disappointed in her. Her inflexible determination to amuse herself, her alert cheerfulness, both fascinated and repelled me. I was surprised to recognize in them her similarity to her daughter Eva. The same determination to counter misfortune by claiming that one had never been happier. The same strength expended on proving that claim. I have seen it since in many other women.

Yet at the time a day's excursion to Munich should surely have been enough to mute the cheerfulness in which I myself shared. Didn't we see the extent of the destruction? Weren't we afraid? Had we no sympathy for the disabled, the injured, the victims buried under the rubble? Didn't we feel for the starving? That meant almost everyone but us. For deportees bound for the camps? For the suffering of those who, to us, were nameless? And surely to be "nameless" is the worst anyone can suffer. We guessed it was so. Even my cousin Eva and my aunt Fanny guessed it was so.

None of this, however, could rein in my aunt's and my cousin's desire to be out and about. Or put a damper on their pleasure in a boating expedition, a snowball fight, a day spent climbing. Or the childish enthusiasm with which they devoted themselves to a game of nine-men's morris or pinned up the hem of a skirt Eva wanted to alter. Aunt Fanny could work magic with needle and thread. She was an expert dressmaker.

All their passion, all the potential creativity in them, went into these trivial activities. All the serious thought of which they were capable was devoted to having fun. There was nothing left over for anything else. They made sure of that. And there was even a grain of heroism in their superficiality, their inexcusable lack of integrity and responsibility. Can I call it courage? The courage that keeps a child from bursting into tears although it has reason enough to weep?

There's nothing good in falsity, so no, not courage. Except, perhaps, with respect to the strength it cost them to be always good-humored, amusing, cheerful. Full of merriment and initiative. We laughed all day long. It was dreadful.

THE HOUSE WHERE EVIL THINGS HAPPEN has the forest at its back. It is not isolated, yet it is some distance from other dwellings. You can see it is empty. The summer visitors it once sheltered left long ago. There is a feeling of neglect about it. The terrace and the steps leading up to it are covered with autumn leaves. The house is cold. Of its nature it cannot be warmed. Darkness lives within it, even by day. Sometimes the stairs creak softly. Horror lies in wait behind curtains, doors left ajar; it lurks in the corners between cupboard and wall. The house has a cellar that is better not thought about. All the same, it's there. Perhaps it hides no secret. But you would have to go down there if you wanted to make sure of that.

Sometimes, in the smiling south, close to a village full of grapevines, barking dogs, pots of geraniums, and laughter you see such a house. It is hired out to tourists as a holiday villa. I recognize it at once. I know what it is like inside. Why am I so afraid of it? Why can I imagine nothing worse than to be on my own in it? It's as if someone had a rendezvous with me there, someone I can't remember, don't want to remember, but that person remembers me and has known, all this time, that I shall come sooner or later. He is waiting for me there. He has time. He is patient. Evil always has time.

This is the other, the menacing side of the house on the Mooslahner Kopf. Like every house, it has a daytime and a nighttime aspect, it harbors its ghosts, its own darkness. It is a place of death.

Wouldn't you be scared to sleep there all on your own? Eva asks me.

As soon as we got back from Munich I told her about my decision to go and stay in the Tea House.

Scared? No. What of?

Could any seven square kilometers in the world be better guarded than this place? (And yes, of course I'm scared.)

Scared that someone will notice what broadcasting station you're secretly listening to, says Eva, laughing.

Of course she knows I want to listen to enemy broadcasts. I want to know what's going on. Since we went to Munich it seems to me as if I had merely been dreaming in all the weeks I've been here on the Berg. How could I survive so long without news? To be honest, I must admit to myself that I've never read the newspapers or listened to the radio much. While I was living in Jena all my political information was derived from my father. It was through him that I learned what was going on. It was through him that I knew what to think about it. So I'm not weaned yet, I'm still unable to look after myself in such matters. Well, I have to learn, and now is the time for it. My decision to stay in the Tea House is a first step in that direction. I take it, as one takes any first step, with a certain overconfidence in my abilities. But I want to know what's going on.

I want to find out what our enemies are planning. I want to face the enemy. It's better than having him behind you. I sense that instinctively rather than thinking it out. At heart I know that Eva is on my side. I'm her little scout, her spy. She can't do it herself.

What interests her, I realize later, is to find out not how to save herself but how to be there when the end comes. She doesn't want to be deceived now, any more than I do. Through me, she wants to discover how far gone we are, how far advanced in the process of dying, annihilation, extinction. From now on she will be setting the clock of her life by the news I bring her over the next few weeks:

Romania, formerly our ally, has declared war on Germany and agreed to an armistice with the Allies in Moscow.

Bulgaria is changing sides.

There's a revolt against the German troops in Slovakia.

A retreat from Greece.

From Albania, Macedonia, Serbia. The Red Army takes Belgrade.

Finland agrees to an armistice with the Russians and Great Britain.

The Eastern Front is coming closer.

The last German battleship, the *Tirpitz*, is sunk in Tromsö Fjord.

And my cousin Eva is on her way to her marriage bed. As long as the war pursued a victorious course it was none of her business, just one of those wild, mysterious games that keep men away somewhere far from home. But now she must be vigilant. Now she must arm herself to be ready at the right moment. My cousin Eva is in her own state of mobilization now that she realizes Germany is losing the war. And I am her scout.

So I know she will have no objection to my moving into the Tea House. She may even think I'm doing it for her sake. I have nothing to fear from her if I tune in to the BBC. Quite the contrary. When we meet she questions me. She wants to know all about everything.

Be careful of the guards, she says. They patrol the woods around the house even at night.

Of course I'll be careful, I say.

I put a blanket over myself and the radio. It's like being in a tent, just the radio and me. We whisper. We conspire. The tuning button calls for great delicacy of touch as I move it. Our enemies' voices can be heard only if you're very careful. Move the tuner only a little farther, and all I get is a slight crackling. It's not so easy to receive them up here in the mountains anyway. They are also disturbed, distorted, interfered with by our own transmitters. Often I can hear nothing but the rushing sound that contains all the frequencies audible to the human ear. The news I want to hear is hidden in there. I know it is. I listen for it. I feel that I can hear the music of time in the rushing sound. That white noise is the present. The present is entirely contained in it. Explosions, screams, orders, volleys of firing, sirens, the whistling sound just before a bomb drops, curses, groans, the roaring engines of the Lancaster bombers, psalms, prayers, lies both merciful and unmerciful, whispered words of farewell, marching songs, the cry of *Sieg heil! Sieg heil!* toward which they flow, the voice of a senior judge, high-pitched and furious, sweeping through the People's Court like a whiplash: "Aren't you ashamed of yourself?"

All this is hidden in the persistent rushing that I hear most of the time. But now and then, and always suddenly, I succeed in picking out individual voices:

The curtain has risen on the last act of the German tragedy, says Hugh Carleton Greene, head of the German-language service of the BBC.

He is talking about the territorials, the Volkssturm, our last reserve of men.

The boys and old men of Germany, he continues, are being asked to face armies equipped with the keenest and most modern of weapons. The fact that everyone between sixteen and sixty is to be called up and sent into battle, he says, proves that Hitler and Himmler intend to drag the whole German nation down with them in a disastrous act of suicide.

But thereby, says Hugh Carleton Greene in his correctly accented British German, thereby Hitler and Himmler have given the Germans a way out: Anyone who carries a gun, he says, is no longer defenseless, has no excuse left. Anyone who carries a gun can turn it against his real enemies, the enemies at home.

The real enemies at home—he means me. In my mind I see an

army of children and old men storming the Obersalzberg. A disorderly mob of madmen who have heard too many BBC broadcasts. They don't even reach the lowest guard post. They fall to the machine-gun fire of our guards. They fall the way I've seen men fall in films of the First World War, jerkily, twitching, literally mown down. I hope, for their sakes, they resist the blandishments of Hugh Carleton Greene. They know, or so I hope, how well our position here "at home" is guarded and fortified.

I think of Hugh Carleton Greene in his London studio. He'd better watch out for himself. We have been attacking London since September 8 with V2 rockets against which there is no defense. I am afraid for Hugh Carleton Greene, Lindley Fraser, and the others at the BBC, because I need them. I wish I could talk to them. I'd have so many questions to ask. I feel so lonely in Hitler's Tea House. What will happen to me if we lose the war? Who will I be then? I wouldn't mind being a domestic servant to Hugh Carleton Greene. That would be all right. But it could be worse, much worse. I simply cannot imagine what will happen when we lose the war. I hear my father saying: This time there'll be no going on.

But that's not possible. I don't believe Hugh Carleton Green wants me to be shot. I just don't believe it. His voice sounds pleasant. I'm sure I'd get on well with him.

Dear Mr. Greene, please may I ask you a question . . . ?

I imagine him as a man of around fifty, old enough to be my father although a little younger than my real father. He might be stern with me.

Do you have a gun? he would ask immediately.

No, of course not.

You should do something, all the same.

But what, Mr. Greene? What can I do?

Keep your eyes open.

I'm trying to.

Suppose he knew I'm here with Eva?

What did you say? asks Hugh Carleton Greene. With Eva Braun? Hitler's mistress? The woman he phones in the evening? And you ask me what you can do?

I am afraid Hugh Carleton Greene takes too simple a view if he thinks Eva would resist the disastrous act of suicide of which he spoke. Eva will fling herself right into it, that's what she'll do.

I ask her at supper: What will you do if the Allies come here?

Here? she says. You mean here to the Berg?

Yes.

That amuses her.

They won't come here.

But suppose they do?

What will I do? Nothing. But do be careful no one hears you talking in that defeatist way.

Eva laughs, and looks at the open door of the dining room.

But seriously, I say. Don't you think we're losing the war?

Yes, says Eva. I do.

So what about you? I ask. Where will you go then?

I'll go to him, says Eva. Whatever happens.

She follows this remark with a little laugh, the kind that says: I meant it seriously, but you can take it as a joke if you like.

I tell her that Aachen has fallen. The Americans are outside Düren. Eva sighs.

Do you know what Hugh Carleton Greene said? The city of Aachen no longer exists. And other German cities will go the same way. He says we ought to have surrendered them at once rather than risk such losses in what is a hopeless struggle anyway. An order leading to the destruction of our German homeland, said Hugh Carleton Greene, is a treasonable order.

That's enough, little one, says Eva. I think you've forgotten where you are.

But she says it in the tone of cheerful banter that is usual between us.

Now! says Mr. Greene. Now, he says. Do something!

Do you think the Führer knows about all this, I ask Eva innocently.

He knows everything, says Eva. You'd be surprised how much he knows.

Because otherwise you'd tell him, wouldn't you? I say to Eva, nodding as if there can be no doubt about that.

For a moment I believe I have succeeded in setting up a link between Hugh Carleton Greene and Adolf Hitler, a kind of conference circuit through which they can talk to each other, so that Mr. Greene gets a chance to convince Herr Hitler.

You're out of your mind, says Eva, suddenly serious. You don't think I talk politics to him, do you? How naive can you get!

(Suppose I had a woman meddling with my work, Herr Speer! I need peace and quiet in my leisure hours. . . .)

Well, there you are then, Mr. Greene.

AT THIS SEASON THE MOUNTAIN was surrounded by thick autumnal mists. It was the time of year that makes you think of staying where you are for the winter. Autumn tempts you to linger, at least until the coming of spring.

The winter semester had begun in Jena. I was still determined to go back soon. But whenever I mentioned it to Eva, she begged me to stay, as if she felt God knows what depended on it. Her fear of being alone, without the excuse I offered her for little diversions, must have been boundless. And some of it had rubbed off on me, too. The life we lived here, like two princesses, its curious mixture of tedium and amusement, the luxury surrounding us, there was something seductive about all that, something that sapped my will and drew me along with it, repeating daily what was always the same, like those afternoons playing cards in Eva's house in Munich years ago. Once you begin you can't stop.

Sometimes I phoned my mother. My father always puts the receiver down without a word, and I could talk to my mother only when he was not at home. If he was she confined herself to short answers.

We're all right.

Well, there's a war on.

She dared not ask how I was when my father was around. But when she was alone she urged me to come home.

And bring Eva with you, she said. You girls can't stay where you are when the war ends!

I asked her to send me some warm winter clothes. She promised, but I waited for the parcel in vain. My father must have forbidden it, and she was no heroine who could hide things from him.

I could just hear him saying, if she's feeling cold she'd better come home. I knew it broke his heart to know where I was.

In the end Eva lent me all I needed from her own wardrobe. She had plenty of clothes, and I was never in my life as elegantly dressed as in that last winter of the war.

Now that I had moved into the house on the Mooslahner Kopf I spent the morning studying the physics textbooks I had brought with me. The bathing season was over. Eva respected my going back to the Tea House after breakfast. She never asked what I was doing there, but she let me off the task of keeping her company. I didn't know what she herself did during these hours. We met again at the Berghof for lunch and spent the rest of the day together.

I used the round tower with the view of the valley as my study, and I have never again had such a beautiful study. Mist dripped from the larches outside my windows. The yellow of their needles shone through the grayness, and just before the mist rose and dispersed entirely the Watzmann came into view behind its veils, while the solution to one of the exercises in my textbook revealed itself with majestic clarity, and I was rewarded with a correct answer that could be verified.

I loved these hours that I had all to myself. I loved the indestructible happiness they brought me, a happiness raised above all suspicions, uncertainties, and doubts. I was sure I would go far in my scientific career. I saw a future as a researcher before me. Experiments, laboratories, scientific conferences at which I would be much admired for the delivery of my findings . . . I had no idea that these proud hours alone in Hitler's tea salon were my last excursions into the pure, clear world of the natural sciences, my last experience of a happiness bought at the cost of nothing but enjoyable intellectual effort.

I was sorry for Eva, who was unable to experience such happiness. I tried again and again to share it with her, at the same time training my ability as a teacher by guiding her interest to the miracle of the polarization of light, or explaining the way in which electrophoresis functions—only metaphorically and as a general principle, of course.

She reminded me slightly of my mother in her reaction to my attempts to lead her, with missionary zeal, to the marvels of the world and of life, hoping at least to elicit from her something like amazement at the scientific approach to these subjects.

I'm really pleased it gives you so much fun, dear, my mother used to say.

It was hopeless.

Eva reacted similarly, if not in such a calm maternal way, at least with just the same friendly indifference. She thought it "very sensible" of me to be studying, because getting hold of a husband could be very difficult, look at her, the living proof of it. But she didn't understand that the field I had chosen genuinely interested me, and once, when I talked about the pleasure of my mornings, when I tried explaining what I felt—pride, independence, a certain sense of invulnerability, as if I were made immune to all humiliations, as if my study of physics was a kind of dragon's blood in which I could bathe as often as I liked—when I tried explaining this Eva looked at me as if I were out of my mind. She did not understand the slightest part of what I was trying to tell her.

The only person who did understand me was Albert Speer.

He turned up one day, walked into the hall of the Berghof, where I was sitting with Eva by the Nibelungen-like hearth—it was a rainy autumn afternoon, and we had got them to light a fire—he kissed Eva's hand, paid her compliments, asked if he could be of service to her, she knew, he said, that if there was anything he could do for her she only had to say so, and then he came over to me and kissed my hand, too. I think he was the first man who ever did.

What's that you're reading? he asked, and I saw that he was asking only out of politeness. He obviously thought nothing of the intellectual activities of women. Then his eye fell on the book's author and title: Werner Heisenberg, *The Physical Principles of Quantum Theory*. He looked at me in surprise, and decided, I suppose out of a kind of embarrassment, to address himself to Eva, saying something like: Well, imagine your cousin reading that! Only then did he turn to me, asked me what course of studies I was taking, whose lectures I had attended in Jena.

Could I perhaps talk to him about Hugh Carleton Greene? I felt sure he knew about him. I felt sure he would know more about the war than Greene did. He was the cleverest man I'd met for a long time. Self-confident. Superior. A little restless, in too much of a hurry, too *distrait*, as if someone had just summoned him and he was already on his way. Did Hugh Carleton Greene know that Hitler had men like Speer around him?

I hoped suddenly that he had news of some kind for us. A message, just for us, secret news of an imminent change for the better. Something along the lines of: Ladies, not a word to anyone else, but the war will soon be over. I'd have believed him. I'd have believed him more readily than anyone else. His praise, his lively interest in my work had led me to overestimate myself. His interest was always lively, and always moved on quickly to something else, but I wasn't to know that.

Herr Speer, I said, Eva and I would very much like to see the new bunkers.

Your cousin, he said, rising, knows where to go for that kind of thing.

He suddenly seemed irritated.

I'm afraid I'm too short of time to put myself at your disposal any further.

Are you crazy? Eva snapped at me when he had left. Acting the blue-stocking! Speer hates it. All men hate it. *Physical Principles,* she said in an affected tone of voice, and that quantum thingummy. Didn't you see him roll his eyes? Now he'll think that kind of thing runs in the family. And what did you mean by saying: Herr Speer, we'd like to see the new bunkers? I suppose you thought that would make him regard you as an expert on air-raid shelters!

Did Eva herself actually know what was going on underground? Like me, she had heard the rumbling inside the mountain, felt the ground tremble under our feet. Did she really not want to know what it meant? Didn't she, like me, see the trucks driving along the access road to the Obersalzberg day and night? Did she really not know who lived in the huts on the Antenberg, five hundred meters away from us as the crow flies? Didn't she sometimes see the lines of gray-clad men from a distance, marching in step as they were taken out to work and then back to the huts?

From a distance. We saw them from a distance. From where we were—at the very center of events—we saw everything that happened only from a great distance.

If you really want to know, said Eva, I've seen the plans and that's enough for me. Schenk came here and asked how I wanted the bath-rooms tiled, and if the wooden paneling in my bedroom should be natural or white. I told him I didn't mind. I shall never go down there anyway, I told him.

Schenk?

Bormann's head administrator. If you ask me, the whole idea of the bunkers is a whim of his. You don't know Bormann. He's a real slave-driver. He likes to have other people working themselves to death for him. When those catacombs he's having driven into the mountain are finally ready he'll think of something new to plague his workmen with, something that'll let him tyrannize over the engi-neers and craftsmen. Did you know that almost the whole mountain belongs to him personally? Not to the Führer. To Bormann.

Once, she said thoughtfully, before the war, when everything was still different, the Freidinglehen stood down there on the way to the valley—an old farmhouse, but it was empty.

Who used to live there? I interrupted. Where had they gone?

No idea, she said. There wasn't anyone living up here anymore when we arrived. That's to say, well, there was, but they . . . sort of moved out. The Freidinglehen people were the last of them. And the house got in the way of our view. It was annoying, you see. The windows were all broken. They'd been broken at some point when the house was being cleared—I mean when the people who lived there moved out. Well, you see, they weren't moving out of their own accord, not really. Many of the families had lived up here for several hundred years. Anyway, the house was in the way. So the Führer asks Bormann how long he would need to demolish it. Three days, Führer, says Bormann, or more precisely three days and three nights. Good, says the Führer. The Aga Khan is coming in three days' time. And when the Aga Khan arrived there was nothing but green turf where the house had stood. That's Bormann for you. There's nothing he can't do. He could have the whole mountain removed in a day and built again next day if he wanted. I don't like Bormann. Have you ever seen Gerda?

Who?

Gerda Bormann. She lives here on the Berg, too. Her garden goes almost all the way down to the Tea House.

I've sometimes heard children's voices, I said.

She has ten of them, said Eva. I feel sorry for her. Imagine being married to a man like that. It must be terrible.

And is she unhappy? I asked.

Children's voices. Suddenly I remember hearing shouting one day at the end of summer. It wasn't children shouting. I had heard the voice of an adolescent boy—it had either broken or was just breaking—and a woman shouting "Martin! Martin!" I went out of the Tea House. I heard something like the sounds of the hunt, the noise of something crashing through branches, the branches breaking, the running and hard breathing of a hunted animal trying to escape through the undergrowth. Then the hunter caught up. I heard the whistling sound of a whip cutting through the air, the precise noise of the whip hitting a body, the scream that followed every lash. And I saw them. It was all going on not far away. I saw the boy clutching a tree trunk, his arms around it, I saw the man, no taller than he was, chastising him. I saw that the boy could have defended himself, that he was quite strong enough to wrench the whip from his father's hands. I saw that he didn't know that, hadn't realized yet, was letting himself be beaten the way he had always been. I heard his screams of "Stop it! Stop it!" And I saw the woman who came running down the hill calling out "Martin! Martin!" For a moment she saw me, too. She stopped and we stared at each other before I turned and went back into the house.

She's the saddest woman I've ever seen, said Eva. And the most beautiful.

I wanted to say, You're the saddest woman I've ever seen. But instead I said, Well, what about it? Shall we go and look at the bunkers?

If Bormann is building them, she said, I'm not setting foot inside.

Yet there was everything there she needed. She'd have had a big wardrobe. A wardrobe with mirrors inside the doors and indirect lighting. She could have changed her clothes seven times a day in Hell. But there is no day in Hell. It's always night. I should know. I've been there.

IN THE EVENING, after the showing of a film, I set off on my way to the Mooslahner Kopf. I heard the voices of my companions somewhere behind me. They were always there. I saw their cigarettes glow in the dark. Nothing could happen to me. When I closed the door behind me I heard their footsteps as they patrolled around the house.

I knew they had a key to the Tea House. I was the best-guarded virgin in the whole German Reich. Early in the morning, when I was still half asleep, I heard them again.

So I was not greatly alarmed when, one morning, I suddenly heard someone enter the house. I thought of Eva—perhaps she had sent me a message. But I had never before seen the woman standing just inside the door.

How did you get in? I asked.

The first thing I felt was her furious dislike of me.

The same way as you, she said. I still have a key.

Who are you? I asked.

The woman had been walking through the rain. Her small hat was dripping. Her coat, slightly too short, was clinging to her. She was shivering. She wore very high heeled shoes that were much too thin. I wondered how she had ever made her way to the Tea House in those shoes in such weather. She was no longer in her first youth, it struck me at the time, perhaps twice my own age.

Instead of answering she just stared at me.

What do you want? I asked.

Nothing, she said. I just wanted to see who it is now.

Her voice dropped to an indistinct murmur. Was she ill-wishing me? Was she telling me a secret I couldn't understand?

Then she turned and hurried away. I heard the click of her heels on the wooden flooring and the catch of the front door as it closed. I followed her.

What did you say? I called after her.

But she had already disappeared around a curve in the path.

It was freezing cold. By now the rain was pouring down. It would turn to large snowflakes as the day went on. The woman was much too lightly dressed. Her silk stockings. Her shoes. Everything about her was chosen for the wrong occasion. And I was the wrong person to be the object of her anger and disappointment. Her . . . her jealousy, was it? But why be jealous of me? And why had she come to the Tea House? Where did she get the key?

Was I really as safe here as I had thought? Or were there loopholes for the unexpected after all in the faultlessly guarded, hierarchically ordered world of the Obersalzberg? Was there a parallel world of uncontrollable passions whose existence I had not previously suspected? The scene between the Bormann family. The sly recalcitrance of the staff. A strange woman in the Tea House. I decided not to tell Eva about the incident, but to be more watchful.

The first snow fell that day. It was around this time that the German troops stationed in Albania surrendered Tirana. American units took Metz and Strasbourg. Hitler issued a special order stating that if the commanders of sections of troops that had been cut off wanted to stop fighting, they must hand over command to any subordinate determined to hold out. I could imagine what Hugh Carleton Greene would make of that: Hitler was now staking everything on the last madmen in his army. He had given the command to them. To those like himself, the deranged and merciless.

When I was a child I saw the first snow with a child's eyes. The world was putting on fancy dress for my delectation. I was enchanted. But since the war, and to this day, when the first snow falls I see a shroud. The endless snowy steppes out in the East. The weary men for whom there is no shelter, no safety. Their slow steps. Their isolation. The white storm against which they will defend themselves a little longer, and which will finally bring them to their knees. No rescue. Nothing.

Since the war, and to this day, I have known nothing sadder than the first snow. The wet, black, treacherous tracks in it. Hungry, wandering animals, some hunted, others hunting. Black patterns in the snow, the traces suddenly made visible of an otherwise hidden world bent on getting a little food, on domination, on warmth. The world of stray cats, foxes, pine martens, and homeless human beings.

I wake up from terrible dreams in the night. I have been dreaming that I was in Hitler's Tea House.

I *am* in Hitler's Tea House. If this isn't a dream, how will I escape the terrors of my nightmare? In that dream there was someone else in the Tea House with me. Someone watching me like a secret camera. A strange consciousness observing me. It was there.

It *is* there. I can hear its footsteps. It is moving along the passage outside my bedroom door. It is not wearing shoes, and is trying to keep as quiet as possible. All the same, I can hear it stealing into the kitchen. The door creaks softly.

I want to wake up, but how can I when I know I'm already awake? In my dream, I cautiously get out of bed, taking care not to make any noise either. Then I hear a clatter as something drops to the kitchen floor. Suddenly I am wide awake. At the same time I think of the woman that morning. The woman who hates me. She's come back, I think. She wants to kill me. I have no idea why. But I dredge up from my dream the assumption that she must want to kill me.

I have nothing to use as a weapon. I must get to the tea salon somehow before she finds me. I am planning to defend myself with the fire poker that's in there. I am still acting on the logic of my dream. But what is going on outside me follows the same logic, too. I make my way along the wall to the tea salon. Only when I have the poker in my hand do I realize it is a murder weapon. I stand there in the dark, listening. All is quiet in the kitchen, but then I clearly hear a chair being moved. If she wants to kill me, what is she doing in the kitchen?

I can see in the dark now. My fear ensures that my pupils are wide open. From the passage I see that the kitchen door is open. And I see the figure sitting at the table.

What are you doing here? I ask.

No answer.

What do you want? I say.

For a while nothing happens. It is as if neither of us knows what to do next. Then I hear a sound, and can make nothing of it at first. Heavy breathing, in and out, with a kind of trembling in it, a suppressed sobbing, and I realize that someone is weeping. I put the light on, and then I see him.

It's a boy. He can't be more than fourteen years old. His head is bent, and he is half turned away from me. He is trying to cover his face with one arm, like a prisoner in the dock ashamed of his crime. His head is shaven, and he is indescribably dirty. You can hardly make out the badge sewn to his jacket through the dirt, but I see what it is. The oval sunflower garland, the badge of workers from the East.

I know that badge, everyone knows it, and I also know at once what its position on the breast of his jacket means: It tells me he is a bad slave. If he were a good slave he would wear the badge sewn to the top of his left sleeve.

At the time a single glance was enough to tell you who a person was: a member of the master race or a slave, a Party member or a foreigner. Or a Jew. When I see a badge on a breast pocket today, for instance the badges worn by the Eismann or McDonalds employees, I still feel an instant reaction of alarm. I still think: What plans do they have for these people? Then I remember that there are no slaves in the country now. It makes no difference whether the badge is on the breast or a sleeve, I tell myself. It means nothing. At the time, however, it showed whether someone was human or nonhuman. Only nonhumans wore their identity badges on the breast. Everyone else wore them on the sleeve.

We Nazis were world champions at the invention of signs of rank and recognition. If we had not been halted in our tracks, no one would now step out of doors without an identity badge on his clothing. The Star of David was only a beginning, and an inspiration, too. We ourselves saw the Star of David disappear from our streets, but it had given us ideas. Shouldn't one be able to tell at a glance how many children a woman has borne? Perhaps a badge consisting of the appropriate number of stripes on the upper sleeve, aping the signs of military rank? A childless woman's badge, in contrast, to be sewn to the breast, denoting her shame. A small mortarboard sewn to a university graduate's sleeve? An *M* for a millionaire? An *S* for a recipient of social security? And of course an *A* for *Ausländer*, foreigner, to be worn on the breast in the national colors of the foreigner's land of origin?

We were working on it. If we'd lasted a little longer, perhaps I'd have worn the stylized outline of the Kehlstein house on my jackets and coats as an emblem, as the badge of the Führer's guests. On my upper arm, of course, where else?

At that time, in Hitler's Tea House, I look at the boy and I know where he belongs. He belongs in the hut encampment on the Antenberg. And I know what will happen to him if they find him. It is knowledge that I carry in my mind and accept as the most natural thing in the world: They shoot workers who try to escape. I have never been troubled by knowing that before. It is part of the system of rules in force. That's how we live.

But I had not known before that there were children among the slaves working for us. Later it turned out that he was in fact sixteen. But a sixteen-year-old who never gets enough to eat and has done forced labor for two years looks more like twelve than the fourteen I had taken him for.

What are you doing here? I ask, in as friendly a tone as possible.

My fear is slow to die away. I am still in a state of alarm. I take a couple of steps toward the boy. He suddenly lowers his arm and looks up at me. His face is distorted with terror, smeared with dirt, snot, and tears. He stares at me as no one has ever stared at me before. The sight of me has never struck mortal fear into anyone, and I realize that I am still holding the poker. I drop it. The noise with which it hits the tiles alarms us more than either of us can bear at this point. The boy jumps up. He is like an animal in a trap. I bar his way to the kitchen door. I see him taking stock. I see his glance move back and forth between the window and the door. He is looking for a way of escape. I sense that he is ready to rush me.

I won't hurt you, I say.

I raise my hands and show him their upturned palms. I do it without even realizing that I am making this ancient gesture whereby strangers assure one another of their peaceful intentions.

Sit down, I say. They'll catch you outside there straightaway.

I have no idea if he understands me. Perhaps he grasps the essentials, if only from the conclusions he draws. I see him beginning to weep again.

Don't cry, I say. Do you want something to eat?

I have bread, a little butter, and milk in the fridge. Everything I need for breakfast. Only now do I see that a chair has fallen over. That must have been the noise I heard.

We do not take our eyes off each other as I open the bread bin and put a plate of sliced bread on the table in front of him. He snatches it the way a hungry cat snaps at something you hold out to it, greedily, uncontrollably, used to the constant presence of others who will snatch it from him. He digs his teeth into it immediately, swallowing as much as he can.

I pick the fallen chair up again and put the butter in front of him. He looks at me incredulously, as if he had seen me work a miracle. But before he can gulp the butter down, too, I draw it toward me again, take a knife, and butter a slice of bread. I hold it out to him. I feel that his suspicion and caution cannot hold out; I see his ferocity capitulate. What I am offering him is too miraculous. Slowly, in a manner now far removed from feline greed, he takes it, amazed, overwhelmed. He takes a bite, looks at me, takes another bite. Then he abandons himself entirely, without further reservations, to enjoyment of the bread and butter, while I butter another slice for him.

What's your name? I ask.

He does not answer.

I repeat the question. I hold a slice of bread and butter out to him and withdraw it when he is about to take it. Now I know how to make him do as I want.

Mikhail, he says.

I reward him.

I'm Marlene, I say.

Lene, he repeats.

Mikhail, I ask, how did you get in here?

He doesn't seem to understand me, but perhaps he is only pretending not to understand. I take the bread and butter away again.

How did you get in here? I repeat.

Now he puts his hand in his pocket and puts a key on the table.

I pick it up at once. I reach for it the way Mikhail reached for the bread, hastily, like an item of loot. This is the second time today

someone with no right to it has proved to be in possession of a key to
the Tea House.

Where did you get this key? I say.

But I see that he is no longer hungry enough for me to continue
my interrogation. And I realize that he is my prisoner. I can question
him as often as I want. He will belong to me. To me or the SS, who
will kill him.

That night I hid him in the cellar. He followed me without any
will of his own, and I realized how exhausted he was. I gave him a
mattress and all the blankets I could spare. I showed him a drain out-
let in the floor for the call of nature. I told him he must keep very
quiet, not put the light on, and come up only when I tell him it is all
right. I hoped he had understood all this. Then I closed the cellar
door, took the key with me, and went back to bed.

By morning I had thought it all out in detail. I would hide him in
the cellar and keep the cellar key on me at all times. There was no
reason for the cleaning women to go down there. Toward morning,
when the guards had made their first round, I would let him come
up to use the bathroom. I would feed him on leftovers from the
Berghof kitchens, if I could manage to get hold of them in secret.
And I could ask the domestic staff for special rations, on the pretext
that I sometimes felt hungry at night in the Tea House.

If he were sensible, and understood the danger he was in, it would
work. For how long? Until Hitler came back? Or until we had lost
the war? Until the end of the world?

I would have to stay here until then. I realized that as well by
morning. And stay I did. I stayed there until the end of the world of
the Obersalzberg.

HE WAS LIKE A WOLF who has fallen into a trap, a pit from which it
can't escape. He was apathetic, sullen, sly, dangerous, and sometimes

as trustful and ingratiating as a child. He was all those things. He remained unpredictable to me. I never knew exactly what mood he would be in when I opened the door down to the cellar and called him up. And I succeeded in taming him only very slowly. A remnant of suspicion always remained in him, however, and a remnant of caution remained in me. And when I met him again at the end, a changed man, no longer the hunted but the hunter, I was not surprised.

That first morning I tried to get him to take a bath. He stank to high heaven.

There was a central hearth in Hitler's Tea House with a fire that heated all the rooms through hot-air shafts. Once the whole house was warm it held the heat a long time. The fuel used was wood and briquettes, which I added when necessary. The stock of fuel was constantly replenished, and the ashes removed. I never had to bother about that, it was done by the two cleaning women who came in every afternoon, whether there was anything to clean or not. But if I wanted hot water for a bath I had to light a little stove in the bathroom itself. There was always wood ready in a basket.

When the boy saw what I was doing, he approached and took the piece of wood I was going to put in the stove out of my hand.

I gave him the matches. When I saw him crouching in front of the stove, blowing on the flame, he looked to me like a child from the early days of human history, a cave dweller who had strayed into the present, a paleoanthropological find. And for a moment it did cross my mind that I had only to tell the morning patrol, and I would be rid of him again.

Here's soap, I said. Do you know what to do with it?

I still wasn't sure how much he understood.

We must wash your clothes, too, I said.

He shook his head frantically.

Later he came out of the bathroom with his dripping wet clothes on. I think he had got into the tub fully dressed in his filthy garments, and there was still more mud than water trickling out of them. Still, it was a start. By now I had put a few logs on the fire. It was hot as a sauna in Hitler's tea salon. I gave him a blanket and said, Take those wet things off.

Suddenly I heard the guards' footsteps outside the house, and next moment there was a knock at the door.

They never came in. They merely patrolled around the house. They respected the presence of a woman alone here. And indeed, they retreated politely when I opened the door.

Everything all right? they asked.

Of course, I said.

We saw footsteps in the snow leading here, they said. Just wanted to ask if you had any reason to feel uneasy last night?

No, I said. No, they must be my own footprints.

Only now did I realize what I must look like: I was wearing a dirty dressing gown, my hair was uncombed, and I can hardly have given the impression of a woman who has just finished putting on her makeup.

They looked at my feet and saw that I was barefoot.

They looked at my face and saw the marks of a night that I had obviously not spent asleep.

What they were thinking couldn't have been clearer to read in their eyes.

Sorry, they said. No offense meant. If you need us you know we're here.

From now on everything they said to me would have a double meaning. From now until the end. I was never to shake their assumptions off. I had aroused something sleeping in them, as if a piece of sweat-soaked clothing had been shown to the pack. The hounds were off the leash. They were on the wrong track, true, but they had picked up my scent. It was going to be dangerous for me, too, I realized at that moment.

Next day I asked one of the maids at the Berghof to get me some louse insecticide.

What? she said.

I repeated my request, and gave her ten Reichsmarks.

Good heavens, she said, and came a little closer to me, but not too close. You're right. I can see them.

And then I, too, suddenly felt my scalp itching.

I gave her another ten Reichsmarks to keep her mouth shut.

I remembered how ashamed my mother had been when I came home from school with lice. I was a disgrace. I had fouled the parental nest. It was the danger of infection with poverty and uncleanliness that she feared. The worst of the little insects was not the way they made you itch but their failure to observe the rules of the social game when they jumped from the heads of poor people's children to the heads of the better-off. Fear of lice expressed a horrified distaste for the mingling of social classes, middle-class reservations about state schooling. I had sensed, without actually being able to explain it to myself, why my mother waged war with such fanatical zeal against the parasites on my head, why she showed no sympathy when she washed my hair with the stinging stuff and it got into my eyes, when she tortured me with a louse comb, its teeth sharp and jagged, which caught in my coarse curly hair and pulled it out in tufts until tears came into my eyes. She was merciless in her hunt for the last nits, their white eggs, the breeding-ground of everything you could catch if you played with the wrong sort of children.

Perhaps I ought to have given the girl even more money. My standing at the Berghof was not high anyway. I couldn't allow myself to risk representing the danger of catching something, who knew what.

Above all, Eva mustn't know about either the guest at the Tea House or the guests on my head. An escaped slave laborer might just possibly have appealed to her liking for the subversive, but she

would never have tolerated nits. She would have sent her special pest
controller to deal with my head lice.

SOMETIMES, ALTHOUGH NOT OFTEN THESE DAYS, I take the book
out. I know just where it stands on my bookshelves. It is different
from all the other books because it is covered in wrapping paper.

That was what you did when I was a child; schoolbooks and textbooks were covered in wrapping paper to protect them. On the first
day back at school after the holidays mothers stood at their kitchen
tables in the afternoon, covering the new textbooks in wrapping paper with practiced movements and inimitable accuracy. Nothing
must be left sticking out. All the edges must be absolutely straight.
Perfect symmetry was the first commandment. Later, as a student, I
must have done the same thing myself. We still assumed that the
books from which we drew our knowledge would accompany us
through the rest of our lives. We could not imagine that the knowledge stored within them would have its own sell-by date. We believed in its durability, its reliable validity. We were convinced that it
was right to preserve the books themselves, the material of which
they were made, from deterioration.

The bourgeois zeal with which I put a wrapping-paper cover on
that book at the time touches me now. I feel as if some other woman
did it. I am as strange to myself as if I were a Turkish woman in a
headscarf.

The wrapping paper has changed color several times over the
years, from its original pale, almost white gray to a greasy darker gray
hue, shiny and black where it was frequently touched. Under the influence of several decades of sunlight it then bleached out again, so
that it now looks like greaseproof paper used and reused for wrapping sandwiches, marked with fat. Does such a thing still exist, I
wonder: greaseproof paper that has absorbed so much fat that it is

practically transparent? Where the paper was folded it is now velvety soft and roughened. It has torn several times at the folds, and indeed tears again every time I pick it up. One day it will disintegrate and reveal the cover of the book itself: Werner Heisenberg, *The Physical Principles of Quantum Theory*.

I never parted with it. It is the one thing I retrieved from that other life. I carried it with me wherever I went, wandering or in flight. My war diary. My piece of evidence. My secret report from the front.

"Experiments in physics and their results can be described in the same way as anything else in daily life: in the terms of the space-time world that surrounds us, and in the ordinary language appropriate to that space-time world."

If Heisenberg was right, then couldn't daily life, conversely, be described in terms of experiments in physics and their results? It was his opening sentence that gave me the idea.

I wrote brief notes in the margins of the book, notes that were in fact diary entries. I recorded the date by underlining numbers in the equations on the page I was using, and wrote with a sharp pencil in tiny handwriting. Today I need a magnifying glass if I am to decipher my notes. I interspersed them with mathematical signs that had distinct meanings in my cipher. The pronoun *I*, for instance, was the infinity sign. I used *xx* for all forms of the verb *to be*, and *yy* for all forms of the verb *to have*. In my system, Eva was the root sign. The Berghof was "greater than." Anyone opening the book would think at first sight that I had been making my own notes on Heisenberg's *Principles*, and I relied on the fact that quantum physics would discourage rather than encourage further reading.

Today I often can't find my way around my own notes, fitted in as they are between equations and functions that I can no longer follow, in the margins of a text that once stood the world on its head and then put it back on its feet again:

"It has been shown that one and the same mathematical array can be

interpreted sometimes as a quantum theory of particle formation, sometimes as a quantum theory of wave formation." And then:

"Our enemies," I wrote in cipher in the margin, barely legible like the rest of my notes, "our enemies must be our rescuers."

Sometimes, when I decipher this comment with difficulty today, it strikes me that the two were synonymous: something both hard to understand and clear enough when you think of it.

11.5

He still isn't talking to me, but seems to understand everything I say. If I only knew where he got that key. If it's the one the woman had when she came that morning—what has he done with her?

11.9

He's coughing. I'm afraid it will give him away when the cleaning women are in the house or the guards are patrolling. I need cough mixture, so I pretended to have a cold myself, not easy. My tonsils let me down when I really needed their help. But Eva has called the pharmacist. He'll send something up tomorrow. I hope he's not going to be seriously ill. I can't get a doctor to him. It's too damp for him in the cellar. Perhaps I'll let him come upstairs at night.

11.10

He spent the night with his back to the hearth. That's how Russian peasants sleep. I wonder if he's a Russian? I did ask him, but he seemed indignant. He understands more than he lets on. Most of the workers from the East are Poles. He's probably Polish, too.

11.14

They're beginning to think it odd in the Berghof kitchen that I'm always so hungry. I can't feed him on nothing but biscuits. He needs meat and vegetables. I wrap as much of what's on my plate as I can in napkins when Eva isn't looking. It's not very appetizing, but that doesn't bother him. What am I going to do with him in the long run?

11.15

He has a temperature. I'm trying to simulate his symptoms to get the right medicine. But my throat feels easier and healthier than it's been for ages. I walked through the snow barefoot, but that only chilled my bladder, which is no use to him.

11.17

I'm giving him the bromide tablets the doctor prescribed for me, and aspirin stolen from Eva. She's suggested a trip to Munich tomorrow. But I can't leave. How can I get her to drop the idea?

11.22

Two days in Munich. I left him provisions and gave him the key to the cellar door so that he could use the bathroom. He seems better. No temperature now. Snow in Munich. Like white ashes left by the fires. No people. Partying as usual in Wasserburger Strasse. We rolled up the carpet and danced. Glowing embers under the ashes. Well, we're only young once. But why now? When I came back he was sitting on my bed and listening to the radio. I punished him with two days on bread and water.

11.23

This morning Eva came here, which was a surprise. She's never been before, not since I took to sleeping here. She says she thinks she ought to take better care of me. I don't know what she means by that. People say that sort of thing without meaning anything much. Most of what Eva says doesn't really mean anything.

11.25

I borrowed a German-Polish dictionary from Hitler's library at the Berghof. Eva didn't notice. Perhaps he'd be prepared to talk to me in his own language. It's worth a try.

11.26

He spoke to me for the first time today. I tried some Polish from my dictionary on him. For the first time I saw him smile. My Polish pronunciation was obviously a joke. He began correcting me, and suddenly we were in the middle of a conversation. He knows German much better than I expected, and when he was lost for a word we looked it up in the dictionary. He's Ukrainian, but his mother is Polish, so we were able to communicate with the help of the dictionary. Now that I know who he is and where he comes from I'm even more frightened for him. And for myself.

CHAPTER 5

I COULD NEVER HAVE WRITTEN DOWN THE whole confused story he told me in the margins of my book. I learned it only in fragments, and some of it I guessed at rather than learned. I had to fill in a good many gaps, and only over the course of time did the connections really come clear to me. Even today, however, much of his story is as real to me as if I myself had visited the village on the Ukrainian-Polish border that was his home. A village at the foot of the Carpathians, surrounded by woods and cornfields. A little village on a little river, where you can spear fish with sticks while you stand up to your hips in the running water. A village of wooden houses, with snow coming up to the eaves in winter; the only stone building is the castle standing behind tall copper beeches and rhododendrons. The castle offers you the only opportunity to dream of another world, where you might be another person. It's a village where your father is a carter, with two horses, and has a few acres for growing barley and potatoes. A village from which you are driven out one day, when your childhood ends forever, and to which you will never return in your life.

★ ★ ★

THE EVENING HE WAS TAKEN AWAY, in October 1942, he had just
been going to feed the dog. It was a young dog, and it was his. Or
not really his. No one had given it to him, and no one even knew he
had a dog. It wouldn't have been allowed; in fact, it would have been
impossible. But a dog decides where it belongs for itself. And once it
has decided, it belongs to you forever and ever and ever, whether you
want it or not.

The dog decides who it belongs to, but not of its own free will. It
is more as if it had to make up its mind against its will. It whimpers,
it whines, it howls. It crawls on its belly and wriggles under the hand
of whoever is now its new owner, whether he wants it or not. Take
me, I've chosen you. There's nothing you can do but be chosen by
me. And while you are still trying to be noncommittal—wait a moment, let's think about this, I'm not at all sure I wanted a dog—you
can't tell for sure whether you didn't, after all, give it the command
to submit to you. You try to get things clear once and for all. You
pick up a stick and threaten the dog with it. That's enough, now, I
don't want you. But as soon as you've turned away it is placing the
stick at your feet, showing you that you have no choice. You, too,
obey the law of man and dog. You are surprised, but you resign
yourself. In the end you accept the fact that you have a dog.

This one was a young hunting dog, a setter with a russet coat that
was soft and smooth and wonderfully shiny despite the hunger he
had endured. He was a gentleman's dog. None of the peasants of
Korcziw had a dog like that. A foreign dog. And there was only one
answer to the question of where he came from: The huntsmen must
have left him behind. They had arrived by car. German huntsmen in
German cars who stayed at the castle for a few days and hunted stags
and wild boar in the surrounding forests. When they drove off again
they took a whole truck full of game with them. God knew where

they were taking it. How can three or four men eat so much meat? Perhaps they were going to send it to the German soldiers to give them strength. They must be getting the strength to fight the war from somewhere or other. Strength to fight and win victories and be pitiless.

His father had died in the winter. He had had a cough. And although Mikhail's mother put compresses made of hot potato on his chest day and night, and the priest came and sprinkled all four corners of the bedroom with holy water, it was God's will to take him from them, and they had to bury the coffin in the snow; they wouldn't be able to dig down any farther into the ground until spring. That was what happened when someone died in Korcziw in January. And in April they had to till the fields. By then death had taken one of the two horses as well, so there were only his brother Jossip and himself and the last horse, an emaciated mare, to do the work, Jossip being almost seventeen and Mikhail fourteen years old. His brother Andrzei was only eight and could scarcely even feed the chickens.

They put as much under the plow that year as they could, the mare, Jossip, and Mikhail. And it would have been enough for the family, too, but for the barley dues to be paid, which were calculated by the size of the fields in cultivation and not the number of workers available. Barley for the breweries that the Germans were planning to run in Ukraine after their victory, to brew enough beer for their soldiers. German soldiers like beer better than potato schnapps. They are always very thirsty from all that marching, and after all, they couldn't bring their own beer from Germany. They had heavy marching packs to carry already.

That was why the German huntsmen had come in September. They were the new brewery managers. While they were out hunting, their men went to every farm and fixed the barley dues. Thirty hundredweight of barley for German beer, and his mother was so angry that she tore the scarf from her head and threw it at the feet of the men who came about the barley dues. It was a gesture of defiance, the utmost she could do as a woman and a mother. If she had ever allowed herself to do such a thing in front of his father, she would certainly have got a beating. For a moment he was terrified for her when he saw it. But the Germans didn't seem to understand what his mother was saying. There! she said. See that? I have uncovered my head, for how can anything worse happen to me than what you are doing now?

May Our Lady help us, said his grandmother, who was equally horrified.

But Mikhail already knew Our Lady would not help with the barley.

Blessed Virgin Mary, intercede for us. And on top of it all there's a German dog, thin as a rake, always ravenously hungry for food and for something else, too, hungry for a response to his devotion.

He must have got lost during the hunt. It was probably the first time he had been out. Mikhail even thought he might have been frightened by the shooting and run away. Such things happen. Dogs like that are no use for hunting, and the hunters usually shoot them when they come back whimpering, beside themselves with delight and joy at being reunited with their masters.

At first he tied the dog up in a wooden shed a little way from the farm. Then, when he was sure the German huntsmen had gone away again, he let him off the leash and gave a short whistle when he visited the shed in the morning and evening. The dog barked as soon as he approached. Finally he left the door of the shed open at night, and the dog would run to meet him when he came early in the morning, very early so that no one would see. Anyone would know at once where the dog came from, and nobody would believe it was his dog now. He knew some people who would probably have shot the dog.

It had not been easy for him to feed the dog. He never had enough to eat himself, and no doubt to the sorrow of Our Lady had to steal from his mother and lie to her more than once. But one morning he found a dead rabbit in the woodshed. He praised the dog and shared the rabbit fairly with him.

He sometimes went to the wooden shed in the evening, laid his head on the dog like a cushion, breathed in his smell, listened to the faint rumbling in his belly, and felt the wet, warm tongue licking his cheeks and nose now and then, while a very quiet growl, a deep, sonorous sound rose from wherever the soul lives in a dog's body. He had called him Fritz because it was the only German name he knew.

Then, one day around the middle of October, when it was already cold and the mist lay over the river meadows all day, but Jossip and he had cut enough wood for the winter—one day around the middle of October the village elder's carter came to the door just as they were sitting down to supper. The village elder was his father's cousin, and the carter said Jossip must clear out at once, he must go away and hide. The Germans, he said, had been asking around in the village about young men who were healthy and fit to work, and were to be employed in their factories in Germany. The village elder had given Jossip's name, and they would soon be here to take him away, but only if Jossip was at home, understand? So he had sent the carter, because Jossip mustn't be at home, or they would be yet another man short on the farm, if Jossip could be called a man yet.

But his mother had already got him into his winter jacket, and put some bread and sausage in his pockets. Jossip would know where to go, and soon they heard the stable door blowing in the wind. As usual, Jossip had failed to shut it properly. Mikhail went to close it, and when he got back to the kitchen they could already hear the Germans coming down the road. There were three men in SS uniforms. They came in through the doorway, ducking their heads. For the first time, Mikhail saw that his childhood home was a hovel. Low-ceilinged and poverty-stricken. It offered no protection.

Jossip Nowak?

Jossip's not here.

When will he be back?

Who? Jossip. Oh, him. He won't be back, he's gone to town.

To town?

To Belz.

And what's he doing there?

If only his mother knew. Probably looking for work. Who knows? Young folk today. They none of them ask their mother's opinion anymore. They do as they like.

So who's this, then? said one of the Germans.

Mikhail was still standing in the kitchen doorway, on the threshold, which may have made him look a little taller than he was. He wore the boots that had been his father's. They were rather big for him, but he liked putting them on, because he felt that when he wore them he walked with a firm and heavy tread, like a man with something important to do.

At that moment his mother's eyes turned to him, and he saw fear flare up in them, fear that made him walk into the kitchen and stand beside her. For it seemed to him that she needed his support, and after all, he was the only man in the house now.

Him? said his mother. He's only a child!

But he could already look down on her if he stood beside her wearing boots. His mother was a very small woman.

How old are you? asked the German.

Nearly fifteen, he said.

He's only fourteen! cried his mother. He was ill in the summer, too! He had typhoid fever! See how thin he is!

And she rolled his sleeve a little way up, took his slender wrist and held it out to show the German.

Don't, Mother, said Mikhail, pulling his hand away. He was ashamed to have his mother making a spectacle of him like this.

Pack your things, said the German.

He's not well, cried his mother. Please! And Mikhail saw her throwing herself on her knees, trying to kiss the hands of one of the Germans. He kept the boots on and went upstairs, followed by one of the Germans, who never took his eyes off him. The other two stayed downstairs with his mother. It was his grandmother who helped him to pack a few things: underpants, a shirt, a pair of woolen socks, what you need when you're leaving home forever. She did not say a word to him, but she kept talking to God and the Virgin Mary, praying softly to herself. He heard her holding the pair of them responsible for everything that happened to him and would happen in the future. If they'd only admit it, they knew perfectly well it was their business to guarantee the boy's safety. Well, who else would do it? His grandmother hoped God and the Virgin Mary were fully aware of that. They'd have their work cut out for them! Fancy letting a boy this age leave home, only thirteen years old!

Fourteen, said Mikhail, interrupting his grandmother's prayers.

He heard his mother down in the kitchen, still pleading with the Germans and making out that he was a little boy, she, too, calling on the Lord God and all the saints to bear witness. It was very embarrassing for him.

Let's go, said one of the Germans when he came down again. He was carrying his things on his back. His grandmother had stuffed them into a pillowcase.

Only now did he notice that the men were holding his mother down on a chair between them. When they saw that he was ready they let go of her, and suddenly she seemed entirely transformed.

Mikhail, she said, as she said in the dream he had dreamt over and over again since then. It was a dream in which he came into the kitchen in Korcziw early in the morning to fetch his breakfast before he went to school. His mother gave him a slice of bread and dripping wrapped in paper. He put it in his school bag and went to the door. But whenever he was about to walk out his mother called him back.

Mikhail, you've forgotten something, she said.

And he knew he had forgotten something, but he didn't know what it was. He undid his bag and took out his slate, and saw that everything he had written on it was wiped away. All the homework he had done the day before. Whatever it was he couldn't remember had been on the slate, but it was no longer legible, nothing could bring it back. What followed next was an agonizing search, an agonizing struggle to win time, to retrieve the irretrievable, which ended with his getting to school much too late, once again with the writing on his slate wiped clean and illegible.

Mikhail, you've forgotten something.

She went to the kitchen cupboard as if she were only going to spread him a piece of bread and dripping for school. She seemed to have calmed down and was now filled only by a great, growing urge to be active. She packed up some bread and sausage for him.

Mikhail, don't forget your cap.

Mikhail, do you have a handkerchief?

Come along, said the German. The other two were already out in the yard.

Mikhail, wait, the socks I was knitting you. They aren't finished. Oh dear. It won't take long, she said, turning to the Germans. Half an hour, maybe only a quarter of an hour. Come back then. Yes, why don't you come back in a quarter of an hour?

Mikhail was already in the doorway.

It really won't take long, she said, as if she were talking to herself.

It was only when the German took his arm and drew him through the farm gate that he suddenly remembered the dog, who had not been fed.

Mikhail, his mother called from the doorway of the house, you've forgotten something!

But they were already hauling him up into the open truck where a couple of other boys from his village were already sitting.

The dog! he called.

And his mother called back: What?

Someone must feed the dog! he called.

But the truck was already on its way, and the sound of the engine swallowed up his words. Although he did not turn back, he knew all his life that his mother had run behind the truck until it disappeared from view. He was never to see her again.

In the evening they were taken to a parish hall, about twenty youths, all older than he was, and they slept on the floor with their baggage as a pillow. All night he kept thinking that it must be possible to make a break for it and at least reach the dog just once, before they picked him up again. He had his mother's bread and sausage, he could feed the dog with that. He strained his ears, listening, but all he could hear was the breathing of the other boys around him. Then he imagined the dog turning up in the morning and going with him. This was late in the night, when waking dreams begin to resemble the dreams of slumber, even when you have your eyes open and bitter grief will not let you sleep. The dog would go with him wherever he, Mikhail, was taken. He would work for them both. They would be inseparable. The dog would go wherever he went, and would never allow anything bad to happen to him, just as he, Mikhail, would protect the dog. He would always share his rations with him, and now and then the dog would bring a rabbit for them both, and they would eat it together by a small fire. He wouldn't need a bed at night if he had the dog. They would keep each other warm and never be alone.

Toward morning he must have slept after all.

Later, he reproached himself bitterly for not using his last night in Korcziw, where he had a dog, to run away, for they were herded back into the truck before it was light. This was because of the mothers, who had waited outside the parish hall all night after word went around the village that they were still there, and who all wanted to give their sons something they had forgotten, caps, prayer books, a cake baked in a hurry. . . . They had not let the Germans send them home until long after midnight, and they were coming back at daybreak. They had been assured that daybreak would be early enough, and only when they got that assurance were they prepared to leave.

Consequently they were now setting off just before daybreak, under cover of darkness. All the boys had spent the night making plans to get away, and had finally slept briefly on those plans, not noticing until they were in the truck again that it was too late now.

I've got a dog, said Mikhail, when the truck was out of the village. It was a confession of the secret he had kept to himself for weeks. He had reached the point of telling his secret.

Shut your trap, said the boy sitting opposite him.

I really wanted to bring him with me, said Mikhail.

Didn't you hear him tell you to shut your trap, said another of the boys, the oldest of them.

Shut up, all of you, said one of the Germans, who spoke a little Polish.

Mikhail wondered how he could jump off the truck as it went along. All the boys were wondering how they could jump off the truck as it went along.

They were taken to Belz, where two doctors examined them.

Take a look at this lad, said one of the doctors to the other when it was Mikhail's turn.

Good Lord, said the other doctor.

Mikhail stood in front of him, naked. Without his father's boots and the padded jacket he had worn on the journey he was a wretched sight.

Any illnesses? asked the first doctor.

Mikhail said he had had typhoid fever in the late summer.

Might just as well send this one home again, said the other doctor. Look at him. He can't work.

And he took Mikhail's wrist, as his mother had done yesterday. Then he pulled down Mikhail's lower eyelid and examined his eyes through a glass.

If you ask me . . . , he said, shaking his head.

This time Mikhail knew what was going on.

I sometimes come over all dizzy, he said.

I bet you do, said the first doctor. You'll be properly fed with us, and then you can work.

They don't get anything to eat, you see, he told the other doctor. This lad's fourteen. He's got some growing to do yet.

Just a moment, said the other doctor. Joseph? Is that right? You're supposed to be seventeen years old?

That's my brother, said Mikhail. There's been a mix-up. I'm here by mistake.

Suddenly he saw everything turning out all right. He could go back on foot. He wouldn't mind that. He'd be home in two days' time. A dog doesn't starve to death in three days.

Don't you lie to us, Joseph, said the first doctor. Good God, they all lie like the blazes. Listen to me, Joseph, he said, you've been ill, and you're not the strongest lad in the world, but a bit of work will do you good. It'll make you big and strong. It'll make a man of you, Joseph.

He punched Mikhail in the ribs. His examination was over.

And Joseph, one more thing, he said, as Mikhail bent to pick up his clothes and took in what had happened. Give up lying. Lies won't get you anywhere.

Mikhail only wished they would, because then he would have told some. Why had he been taken instead of Jossip? He must have done something wrong, and he couldn't work out what it was. If only he had at least told Jossip that the dog would need feeding.

They were taken to the barracks in Hrubieszów, where they slept on straw, and his only comfort was the smell that rose from it. But at this point he was already so dreadfully homesick, thirty miles from Korcziw, that any kind of comfort only made matters worse. He lay on the straw, buried his face in it, breathed in the smell and traced all the odors of Korcziw in it. He picked them out one by one, the smell of ripe wheat still in the ear, the smell of potatoes slowly beginning to rot, the smell of a damp pinewood fence, perhaps showing that a few splinters of pine had found their way into the straw, the ammoniac smell of urine, which overpowers every other smell in a cowshed or stable, the smell of slightly rotting cabbage leaves, God knew where that came from, the smell of sweat from an unhappy animal robbed of its freedom, which he recognized as his own, and finally, stronger every day he slept there, the aroma of the tears he wept into the straw.

They stayed in Hrubieszów for a week, and every day more boys were brought in from somewhere or other, boys who fantasized day and night about escaping and soaked the straw with their tears. They did not talk much, and if one of them wailed out loud he was immediately told to shut his trap. He was in a world where there was no pity now.

On the sixth day he saw Stepan, a boy from Korcziw, not much older than himself. They had been at school together.

He asked him about the dog.

Stepan hadn't seen any dog, but he said that was all right, he was going to escape anyway. He had no intention of going to Germany, and once he was back in Korcziw he promised to look after the dog. Suddenly Mikhail felt he was an old hand at captivity. He had at least got beyond such notions. All the same, he told Stepan how to find the wooden shed, and felt a certain comfort in knowing that someone else knew.

Next day the train left, and he and Stepan tried to get into the same goods truck and actually succeeded, although not side by side. But when his eyes were used to the darkness—only a little daylight filtered through the barred hatches in the sliding doors—he could see Stepan, and Stepan sometimes looked his way. That comforted Mikhail slightly and made up for the loss of the straw bed on the barracks floor. They tried to get a little closer to each other, but changing places was not allowed.

They were on their way all day and all night, a goods truck full of boys between fourteen and twenty. None of them had ever traveled before, they had never been farther from home than the town that held the nearest administrative district center. Most of them had never even been in a train before. They listened to the rattle of the wheels and were bewildered. They had traveled in carts drawn by horses or teams of oxen, and this was their introduction to the machine age, which was inexorably carrying them away from everything they knew. Farther and farther and farther away every moment. They did not feel their hunger or thirst or full bladders, or anything else from which they were yet to suffer, they felt only that they were nothing. Only a few days ago they had still been sons, grandsons, brothers, future smallholders; now they were ground to nothing in this crushing of iron on iron. Foreigners as they would be from now on, foreign workers, they felt increasingly foreign to themselves, anonymous figures taking with them far too heavy a burden of what they remembered and loved, what was familiar to them. They felt it all concentrating into a small, hard kernel that they would now carry within them, with nothing but their weak and freezing bodies to protect it. The hidden, aching core of their desolation.

Once, toward evening, they stopped at a railway station where they were given soup and cold, weak tea. They were told to get out and use the latrine buckets. Every single one of them intended to make a break for it and go home on foot. This was the opportunity they had all been waiting for.

But it wasn't even the guards posted on both sides of the platform with the safety catches off their guns that stopped them. Something

else prevented them from simply running away. If they had all tried, a
few might perhaps have made it. The fact was that they had already
changed. They were no longer the boys who had been willing to face
any danger, any challenge. They were prisoners now, a wretched procession of the dispossessed, and not a spoonful of soup would be
wasted on them over and beyond what was necessary to keep them
fit to work. Ashamed, bellies half filled, they got into the trucks
again. Mikhail and Stepan did not look at each other anymore. They
tried to sleep.

For it was suddenly important to keep their strength up. A little
extra food, warmth, or sleep could be crucial. The boys pressed close
together. Any attempt to claim privacy for yourself was impossible in any case, in such cramped conditions, and was expressed only
occasionally in an unfriendly growl, in an intentional rigidity of the
limbs, the poking and pushing of anyone who got too close to his
neighbor, perhaps let his head drop on his neighbor's shoulder as he
fell asleep, but all such attempts were now useless, indeed counter-
productive. They almost crawled under each others' padded jackets,
breathing on the necks and armpits of the boys next to them. Give
me some of your warmth and I'll give you some of mine. This is the
behavior of slaves. They know they have nothing except their mere
selves. Everything that had previously made up the basis of their
social standing, the victories and defeats associated with them, the
property owned by their fathers, the intimidatory potential of elder
brothers, the beauty of the girls they desired or who had been their
sisters and fiancées, all those imponderables whereby a person's worth
is assessed and which are carried around like an aura, an invisible
halo, counted for nothing here. The first commandment of a slave
runs: Thou shalt not be proud. Or you won't live long.

Mikhail soon learned it, too. When the train next stopped and
they were herded out he was already looking down at the ground, as
slaves do, knowing it is none of their business where they are. No
more rapid glancing back and forth, no spying out the terrain for

possible escape routes. And he would never know the name of the first German town to which they came. He could of course read the Roman alphabet, since they had learned Polish at school. He just didn't look at the signboard.

Here they were deloused, had their heads shaved, and were sorted out according to their usefulness. The strong, well-grown boys for building work and industry, the others for agricultural labor.

Finally there was only Mikhail left, naked, bald, freezing, shrinking into himself with despondency and cold, shrinking into himself like his penis, which was almost out of sight, a pale boy, too weak, too small, and too useless to be fit for either industry or agriculture.

Neither the man in the white coat nor the uniformed man seemed to know what to do with Mikhail. The other youths were already getting dressed again. Their clothes, like their naked bodies, had been sprayed with pesticide, and before they put them on they had to shake them vigorously to make the fleas that had been living in them fall out.

Then Mikhail suddenly saw one of the boys picking up his own jacket. It was the most precious thing he owned. It wasn't just because it had belonged to his father and still smelled of him, it was thick and soft, and on him it was almost as long as an overcoat. It was also his only home, his winter quarters.

Naked as he was, he ran over to the group of boys—they were the strong ones, including the building workers—and snatched back his jacket. Thief, he said in Ukrainian. The other boy bent and picked up another jacket. He, too, was already a slave, indifferent, without any pride left.

When Mikhail was going back to the two men he saw them closing their book, standing up and going out of the door, and he realized that so far as they were concerned the matter was settled. He had made his own choice. The small problem he represented was solved. As easy as that.

Now he was with the young men who had been picked to do the

hardest work. Most of them had even come to Germany of their own free will. All they wanted was to work for a fair wage, the prospect that had been held out to them, and they had promised to send a good part of it home to their families. They believed they had a right to go home on leave once a year, and they had signed contracts assuring them of both these things. What they didn't know was that the provisions of these contracts did not apply to the nationals of an enemy power. No one had told them that.

Mikhail was with the wrong set, as he well knew. But as things stood there was no one around to hear any protests. So he shook the dead fleas out of his clothes as best he could, and put them back on. At least he had his jacket. He resolved never to let it out of his sight again.

The train to which he was assigned was going to southern Germany. It was all one to Mikhail. What mattered was not where he was but his distance from Korcziw. And every time the wheels of the train went round that distance increased.

He tried not to think of the dog. But the dog was thinking of him, Mikhail knew that, and from now on it would be the one thing that distinguished him. It was his secret mark of rank. His pride, hidden deep within him, in knowing that the dog was his. The dog would stray and kill game, grow bad-natured and suspicious, just as Mikhail must be suspicious and bad-natured from now on, relying on no one but himself. That way they would not cease to be master and dog, and in all their misery a tiny kernel of hope would still exist inside a hard shell. He, Mikhail, and the dog had every reason to stay alive.

Even years later, Mikhail would sometimes work out how old the dog would be now, and whether he might still be alive. Seventeen, eighteen years? How long does a dog live? And how long does his memory live, and his desolation and grief, how long do they live on?

He saw Stepan for the last time on the loading platform of a truck.

He seemed to be waving, and Mikhail waved back to him. Then the truck started to move, and Mikhail stood there, arm raised in the air, palm of his hand outstretched, as long as he could still see the vehicle. A motionless wave, a frozen greeting sent the way that Stepan was going, away from him. Then he felt someone shove him in the ribs. Nazi swine, someone hissed in his ear, in Polish, and he, too, was pushed into a truck.

They drove into the mountains. It was October and already cool, with a little snow on the peaks, when Mikhail arrived in Hitler's private domain.

HE NEVER TOLD ME exactly what had happened before he took refuge with me in the Tea House. He didn't like talking about it. But in time, as we came to know each other better—although his distrust always remained near the surface, always ready to hand—I could sometimes get him to talk. And from what he told me about it, just disconnected fragments, observations imperfectly understood, anecdotes that broke off before you could see what the point of them was, delivered in the pidgin language with which he tried to protect himself even from me, the short sentences using only verbal infinitives that he used to conceal his advanced knowledge of German—I be hungry. I not understand—from all this I have told myself his story as if it were my own.

And in a way it was my own story, too. It sent me on a journey of exploration around the place where we were. Through Mikhail I came to see the other, invisible side of the Obersalzberg. Through him I saw that the world is full of loopholes through which you can slip into other worlds, other realities, and that from those other viewpoints things appear in their full terrible light. If Mikhail had not existed, I would have had to invent him in order to get a view of the place where I was.

But he did exist: dirty, greedy for anything edible, cautious, wily as a fox, silent as a cat, desperate as a wild animal in a trap, timid and distrustful.

He had no word for the sickness from which he suffered. No German word, and no Ukrainian or Polish word either. He had no term for the disorder that afflicts the soul and makes it sick. From all I gathered from him over the course of time, I spelled out the word for myself: homesickness. He was deranged, ill with it. He would die of it. He knew that, but first he wanted to be home just once more. To see if the dog was still there. Smell the potato fires of Korcziw in autumn. To tell his mother that you had to obey the Germans, always and unconditionally. Teach her to understand that they had no pity. They were the stronger. They always would be.

He had no doubt that they would pick him up and either shoot him or bring him back. He had no idea that in his native country the Germans had already lost the war and were in retreat. The SS men, the brewery managers, the endless columns of Wehrmacht trucks, all gone like ghosts. He didn't know that they had been superseded by Red Army soldiers, and it was these soldiers whom the people of Korcziw now feared. He didn't know that they would kill him if he came back because they would regard him as a collaborator, and wouldn't ask whether he had gone with the Germans voluntarily. He had no idea that his mother was praying fervently that he would stay where he was. He couldn't know how far, how irretrievably far he had fallen into one of the black holes of the history of the twentieth century.

There was nowhere for him to go, no refuge, no homeland, not even a country of which he was a citizen. His old village on the border, first Polish, then Ukrainian, then part of the Union of Soviet Socialist Republics, was ultimately only as he saw it in his dreams. A stable door. A stairway. A headless chicken fluttering around the yard until it stopped in midcourse, twitching, and fell to the ground.

Sometimes, in the huts, he tried to find the smell of the old wooden house in Korcziw that had been his home. Stones smell of nothing, but wooden houses retain something of the breath of the trees of which they are made. Something of the aroma of their autumns and their springs. It is strongest in sunlight, when the wood expands with a slight creak. In Korcziw it had spoken with a voice as familiar to him as the rustle of his grandmother's skirts. In winter the fire on the hearth made the wood speak. Overnight, as the fire died down, the wood fell silent. You heard nothing but the wind rattling the shingles on the roof. But in the morning, when the fire was lit again, the wooden house moved and expanded.

Mikhail sought the smell of Korcziw in the darkness of the hut in the Antenberg camp, and responded to the familiar voice of wooden beams expanding. He deceived himself as best he could, and lay with closed eyes conjuring up a sense of being in Korcziw. At least he wasn't in a stone building. The snorting and shifting of the other men—they slept eighteen to a room—could in certain circumstances be Jossip and Andrzei. He enlisted the aid of his homesickness and shut out all perceptions that would disturb the illusion. With a bold and supreme effort of the mind he filtered them out, forcing his senses to inexactitude, and there it was, the smell of wood, the creaking of the beams, the sound of his brothers breathing beside him, the grating noise as a slab of snow slid off the roof. And he wept.

He wept almost all the time. He smelled of tears like a damp, musty gallery in a salt mine. The others despised him for it. The odor of tears is repulsive among men. Not much better than the smell of urine, something wet, a bodily secretion, something clinging to his clothes, his breath, from which they flinched away, revolted, as from something disgusting. They were used to a good deal, the men in those huts. They stank of sweat and urine and all other physical emanations. But they hated the smell of tears that clung to him.

Don't whimper, they told him. Be a man.

He wanted to be a man. He knew it was about time for him to become a man. He was growing. He could tell from the clothes he wore, his trousers and his jacket. They were getting too short for him. He noticed his sexual organ changing, too, and saw it grow of its own accord. But the comfort that gave him never lasted long.

There were no limits to his homesickness. It devoured every other feeling in him. Homesickness is an emotion that makes you soft and weak, not hard and strong. It was as if a spider were sitting in his heart, its venomous saliva slowly dissolving him from within, to absorb him into itself by sucking, sucking, sucking. There was nothing he could do about it. Be a man, the men said.

Why don't you go home, then, if you're men, he thought. If I were a man I'd go home.

And so, in countless nights of weeping, his hand on the large penis he had grown, he came to the reverse conclusion: He must go home because he was a man now.

As soon as he had come to this decision his tears dried up. He saw it as confirmation that he was doing the right thing.

He didn't know where he was. He saw the same uniforms that he had seen in Korcziw. He heard the language that he knew was the language of the masters spoken around him, the language of orders that you had to obey, or threats in case you didn't. The language in which the days someone spent in the arrest cell were counted. The language in which rations of food were handed out.

Five o'clock in the morning: coffee, a piece of dry bread; ten o'clock: a piece of bread and jam; midday: soup, twenty to thirty grams of meat with potatoes; supper: warmed-up leftovers from the midday meal, if there were any.

He understood everything. Like all the rest, he knew German much better than anyone suspected. They dissimulated. It is always better not to understand your masters' language too well. Why make things too easy for them? But it wasn't even mere deliberate dissimulation that prompted them not to say a word and look baffled when one of the Germans asked a question. It was also the genuine timidity that affects slaves before their masters. How could they use the language of the Germans? It wasn't right and proper. They themselves felt it presumptuous to do so. And so they stuck to reacting idiotically with brief sentences such as "You the boss," while the gulf between their spoken German and their knowledge of the language gaped wider and wider, and even years after the end of the war Mikhail would still speak his slave's pidgin German, although by then he had long been able to read German newspapers and knew what kind of a country he was in.

At the time, however, in the autumn of 1942, he thought he could be anywhere at all in Germany. The guardhouses along the roads, the high wire fences, the dense presence of SS men, the barracks, the shooting ranges where, he knew, they practiced for shooting people like him, the well-tended properties of the powerful, their wonderful houses somewhere in the neighborhood, at which he guessed rather than actually seeing them, the escorted limousines in which the masters of life and death arrived on the mountain—Mikhail had expected all this when he came to Germany. It did not occur to him that this was a special place. He had imagined Germany as a single Obersalzberg, a kind of guarded open-air Nazi preserve.

The snow-covered mountains surrounding the place, as he saw it, were all part and parcel of the same thing. Their precipitous slopes, their great distance, their inaccessibility. People used to avoid the peaks in the Carpathians. To the Germans, no mountain was too high, no rock too steep for you to build a house there. He looked up with horror at the Kehlstein house. So that's how they live, he thought.

Initially they were put to work moving earth and doing construction work on a housing estate. There were a few of his own countrymen in his troop, and they made sure that he was given the lighter tasks, digging trenches, clearing rubble, mixing mortar. Hey, little fellow, they said to him in Ukrainian, I'll do that for you if you fancy a bit of a rest. And they showed him how you could disappear into a trench for a brief period, until the German overseers had finished their cigarettes and began to make their rounds checking up on the workers again. Then a swift kick from one of them woke him from the sleep into which he could always fall anywhere, he was so exhausted.

When winter came they had to go on working in hard frost. They were given gloves, but the gloves disintegrated with the work they did, and when one of the older workers, hands in his pockets, came over, saying, Hey, little one, lend me your gloves a moment, will you? he knew he had no choice, handed them over and never got them back. So he kept trying to put his own hands in his pockets. This was not easy, for a slave with his hands in his pockets is living dangerously, and knows it. Even his protectors sometimes snapped at him, Don't just stand around. If you don't work you don't get fed, right?

And that was another request with which he was familiar, Hey, little one, lend me your bit of bread, will you?

The same men helped him and despised him, depending on how they felt. That is the law of the stronger.

Yes, right, he would say, handing it over.

The most he would sometimes allow himself was to bite off a large chunk before he gave them his bread. Then they laughed.

That's okay, little one, they said. You need to get something inside you if you're going to grow big and strong.

Although winter in the German mountains was as hard as in his own country, you didn't feel the peace here that winter had always brought to Korcziw. There could be no thought of knocking off work. The Germans were quick. They were restless. Whatever they wanted, they wanted it at once. No sooner had a beginning been made than they wanted the work to be done. It was as if they knew they wouldn't have much more time to finish what they had begun. Mikhail could not understand their restlessness. If the world belonged to him, as it belonged to them, the first thing he would do would be to give himself time. But the more powerful the Germans he saw, the overseers of overseers and their own overseers, the more restlessly they went ahead with the work others were doing for them.

So they erected huge tents over the building sites and put stoves under them. When it grew even colder, so that it was impossible to mix concrete, they kept the supplies of gravel and sand warm by inserting heating coils into them. They heated the water for mixing concrete in huge boilers, and erected large radiant heaters on the boarding. The heating had to be on day and night, to avoid damaging the fresh concrete, and the men in the huts suddenly began to regard work on the building sites as very desirable. They had feared winter more than anything else, and when the next autumn came they thought, with a sense of reassurance, of the radiant heaters for the concrete.

But around this time they were suddenly called elsewhere. The Germans had begun hollowing out their mountain from the inside. It was as if they now wanted buildings to grow into the earth rather than on top of it. Mikhail could not understand what their idea was, which made it even stranger to him. They were setting up their empire even underground.

They were in the air, too. He had ducked under the thunder of their aircraft often enough back in Korcziw.

They were in the water. He had seen pictures of the U-boats with which they shot any ships that still dared put to sea out of the depths of the oceans.

They were in the air, on water, on land, and now underground as well. They were everywhere.

He saw the vast halls they had built below the mountain. Throne rooms of the underworld, linked by a labyrinth of underground passages. He realized that they were working to provide themselves with everything you would need to live deep below the surface of the earth: fresh air, electricity, telephone lines, water, central heating. . . . Now he knew that nothing at all was impossible to them.

He had always been afraid of suffocating. It was a completely uncontrollable fear. To him, the worst part of death was the idea of going down into the grave, and when they buried his father Mikhail felt sure that he was struggling to be free there in his hole in the ground, in the narrow coffin where they had nailed him up, he felt that his father was hoping to the end that he, Mikhail, would come to his aid. And when they handed him the spade and he did what was expected of him, it suddenly seemed as if all the people who had gathered for his father's funeral were really there to prevent him from coming back to life, a sworn conspiracy of the unmerciful that, for some incomprehensible reason, included his mother, his brother, his father's best friends . . . and Mikhail himself. He was one of them, too. They were all standing there cutting off the dead man's way back to life.

Mikhail's fear of suffocating was the fear of being let down, betrayed, exposed, alone in the dark. Everything underground made him anxious. In Korcziw there were only graves underground. The wooden farmhouses had no cellars under them, and there were no underground structures in the country around except for foxes' earths and badgers' setts. Now, however, Mikhail had to work below the surface.

Since he was the smallest of any of them, they made him crawl along the smaller service tunnels running parallel to the main galleries when there was rubble to be cleared away, or if someone had to find where a passage was blocked. It was often so narrow that he could not even support himself on his knees, but had to wriggle forward like a snake, lying flat on his stomach, arms stretched out ahead of him, face on the ground, his mouth full of dust and coughing breathlessly. There was a rope fastened to his ankle. Often he couldn't feel it anymore and didn't know if it was still there. From far away he heard them calling to him.

Little fellow? Got it? Hurry up!

Hey, little fellow! You still alive there?

And he tried to move his foot to tug at the rope, his only link with the world of the living. But then they immediately paid out more. They wanted him to crawl on. The jaws of the mountain had closed around him.

When they finally let him out, he begged them to send someone else next time.

What's the matter, little fellow? they asked. You can trust us. We'll look after you. You're in luck there. You can lie flat on your belly. A cushy job, we wouldn't mind having it. Or would you rather work on the stone-milling machine?

Yes! he said, and they laughed at him.

It was worst after blasting, when the air was full of stone dust and the mountain was still trying to close its wounds. Here and there some scree would fall. Slabs of rock shifted their center of gravity and moved. Everyone knew that the chance of a man's being buried by a rockfall was a calculated risk.

Maybe little Mikhail had better go down and see how deep this crevice goes. Don't worry, little fellow, we'll strap you into a harness and pull you out again.

He knew there was no chance of refusing. Slaves have no right to refuse. They couldn't, anyway. There was always one of the armed German overseers quite close. So he let them tie a rope around him, or a harness when the descent was vertical, and went down into the maw of the mountain.

Once he fainted, head downward. When he woke up a German first-aid man was kneeling beside him. The people who saved your life and the people who derided you were the same. There was no one to help.

Perhaps you got used to such terrors. But he became as little used to them as a torture victim gets used to the torture. Far from it. Like a victim of torture, he wanted to die, but not this way, and that is the dilemma of the tortured. He went on suffering, until one day in the autumn of 1944 the solution lay clear before him.

He had crawled so far into the mountainside that he could no longer hear the voices. Then, suddenly, he saw a faint shimmer of light ahead. It was a white light, not the yellow light of a miner's lamp such as the one, like the others, he wore on his helmet. The light came from another way out of this world, and he could see it.

He crawled toward it until he felt that they had stopped paying out the rope around his ankle. He moved back and tried to pull his knee up under his body enough to allow his hands to reach the rope.

Suddenly he felt that he had experienced this already, this very same thing, and on that first occasion everything had turned out all right. That encouraged him, although he was in the tightest place imaginable, and he made progress only by millimeters until he had finally freed himself from the rope.

At the same moment he instantly regretted it. How was he to find his way back to the entrance of the tunnel without the help of the others, without the rope? All his panic and horror and his fear of death returned. He tried to crawl a little way back to retrieve his rope. But it was gone. They had pulled it in without him. Now they knew what he was doing. They knew he was trying to find the way out. They knew he had set off for Korcziw. And he once again made haste to move forward. He crawled toward the light, which was still very far ahead of him. No one would come crawling after him, he knew that. No one else was as small and thin as he was. And as he moved slowly forward, hands first, pulling his body after them, as he felt his clothes and skin gashed on sharp ledges, he felt the light growing brighter around him. He heard rain pouring down outside, raised his eyes, and then he saw that the opening ahead was much too narrow for him. It was a trap, and he had crawled into it.

He was far too exhausted to try going back. Not now. With the clarity of hopelessness he suddenly knew that his workmates would not give him away. At roll call after the early shift they would show the guards the rope. They would invent a death for him, he knew they would. One of the many deaths he had feared daily. Buried under the rubble. Crushed. Suffocated. One of the many deaths intended for him. But they wouldn't report an attempted escape. They would have been punished in his place. They weren't going to risk it.

And wasn't he as good as dead? Were they necessarily lying if they said he was? Mikhail suddenly realized that he no longer existed. Even if he were to survive, if he found a way out, or back to the main tunnel, he no longer existed. Curiously, this realization filled him with a kind of peace he had not known for a long time.

He felt like a fox that, after a long pursuit in the hunt, suddenly finds a safe hiding place where it takes shelter, while the pack races over it and on. It was impossible for anyone to find him. That was all he asked. Since that day two years ago his misfortunes had all begun with the fact that, unlike his brother Jossip, he was not impossible to find.

He laid his head on a rock and fell asleep.

He dreamt of his dog. The fields of Korcziw. They walked through them together. Together they chased the deer that fled before them. They were as fast themselves, as wild, as bent on blood and prey.

When he woke up the rain had briefly stopped. He knew at once what would kill him: the cold and his cramped position. The two were in league against him. They overwhelmed him. He could not distinguish between pain and numbness. There was no end to either. He would have had to move to feel them. To know where one left off and the other began.

Then he could hear the dog again. He was quite close. He was panting. Mikhail heard him whining as dogs do during the hunt when they have found the prey. The supreme expression of triumph, good fortune in the hunt, bloodlust.

The dog was here. He really could hear him. He thought it possible that he had already lost his mind with cold, pain, and the fear of death. Then he heard voices that did not come out of his dream, voices calling to a dog, sternly, imperiously. Mikhail heard the dog move a little way off. He could sense the effort, the strength of will it cost the animal to obey that human command. He felt the dog's own disappointment and humiliation. The whole extent of the misunderstanding was clear to him. And although in this case he, Mikhail, was the prey, the game to be run down in its hiding place, the fox in its earth, it was with the dog's defeat that he felt sympathy.

He's started poaching, said a voice. If he doesn't stop it I shall have him shot.

What a shame, said another voice. I like that dog.

Two uniformed men came into Mikhail's field of vision where he could see only their heads. He had a view of their faces in profile. He saw a cigarette lighter flare up between them, saw the two faces bend over it in turn, saw two cigarettes begin to glow, smelled the cigarette smoke. Mikhail realized that there was a footpath running along the mountainside below him. He had arrived just where the guards patrolled on their daily rounds. They were here. They were everywhere. They would track him down to the very end of the world. He felt like a man who, having followed an escape route for a long time, suddenly sees his tormentors in front of him again.

Did you really think there was any way of escape? they said. Do you think there is anywhere where we will not be found? Don't you know that our Reich is everywhere you go?

It is the quintessence of every nightmare, the most feared scene in every film, the most terrifying experience one can have. It is shock pure and simple.

Suddenly, seeing the two SS men, Mikhail was wide awake again.

His presence of mind, his concentrated strength, his will to survive all suddenly returned, and as soon as they had gone on he began to move slowly back into the mountain. This was no place to stay, not even in order to die.

And as he made his laborious way back, centimeter by centimeter, forcing his sore body through rock and rubble, lying on his back, dust and debris came falling into his eyes from above, where his fingers had been searching for a handhold. He felt around to find where it came from, discovered a crack widening inward, but had to keep his eyes closed and go on groping blindly as he moved slowly back. He was sure that he could not be seen from outside, which for the moment gave him enough courage to continue, although there was no real hope to justify it. The crack grew broader. Now he could put his arm out through it, and after a few minutes he felt that he could sit upright.

He rubbed his eyes, narrowed them again at once, and remembering his mother's advice never to rub them except from the outside in, he suddenly realized that there was bright if brownish light around him, and with streaming eyes he realized that there was a way out of the upper branch of the passage into which he had moved, a way out overgrown with creepers and ferns, and he could get through it. He hauled himself up on the rocky platform, and saw that it was of the same size and gently rounded shape as the benches around the stoves in Korcziw.

HE SLEPT ALMOST ALL THE TIME. He had come with the winter, and he stayed the winter through. He hibernated in the cellar of Hitler's Tea House, wrapped in the blankets I had provided, hidden under the eiderdown I had borrowed from the Berghof on the pretext that the temperature in the Tea House dropped sharply at night. It was two years since he had had enough sleep. The inmates of the huts would have sold their souls just to stay lying where they were when they were woken at four in the morning, particularly in winter. Now he could do just that, with his heartbeat, circulation, and heat regulation lowered to hibernation levels. He slept and slept. He woke only in order to eat, and then soon fell asleep again.

And something happened to him. When I met him one last time over six months later, with a pistol in his hand and a GI's cap on his head, I saw that he had grown. Suddenly he looked like a man. All the strength of his hibernation was there in him.

In time I stopped locking him in. I gave him the key to the cellar door, and when darkness had fallen he could move about the house. He knew himself that he must never put a light on, and he learned to find his way in the dark with the skill of a nocturnal animal.

On his first explorations of Hitler's Tea House he discovered the radio. He turned the knobs. He was alarmed to hear a human voice speaking so close to him, but with time it became his only toy. His passion. When I came back from the Berghof late in the evening I knew where I would find him: on his knees by the little table in my bedroom where the radio stood, his ear pressed to the fabric covering the loudspeaker. He learned to turn the sound right down.

At first he didn't really understand that the radio was talking about the world in which he, too, lived. Then he heard names. Warsaw. Belgrade. He tried to find out what he was being told about these cities. And Lvov? And Belz? And Hrubieszów? From the fact that no one said anything about those places he concluded that everything was still the same at home.

He could hear the Germans' music. It was wonderful. It was terrible. It brought tears to his eyes to hear their music. There was a stormy wind in it, laughter, a festival, victory. It broke through dams, including the dams of his mind, like a great tidal wave. When he heard the music of the Germans, their victory signal, he knew he was subjected to them forever.

One evening he heard the voice that spoke to him personally. He was greatly alarmed, but there was no doubt about it. It was meant for him, Mikhail, even if his name was not spoken.

And now, just for you, said the voice, alone and far from home as you are, here is your song. Your song, my song, our song. Next comes . . . "Lili Marleen."

Underneath the lantern, by the barrack gate
Darling, I remember the way you used to wait . . .

Mikhail knew the song. Everyone knew it. The men in the huts had sometimes hummed it to themselves. But he had not known until now that it was his song, a song that had been dormant in his soul until this moment. Now it awoke in him, and he realized, happily, that he knew it word for word and note for note, and could join in singing it in his mind with the woman's voice on the radio.

This was the first time such a thing had happened to him. He was sixteen. He had never heard a woman sing except for the women of Korcziw, who sometimes struck up a kind of chant as they did their washing by the river, a chant cursing unfaithful husbands. Mikhail had never before heard anything as beautiful as the song Lale Andersen was singing for him and him alone:

Resting in our billets, just behind the lines
Even though we're parted your lips are close to mine.
When the night mists swirl and churn,
To that lantern I'll return,
My Lili of the lamplight, my own Lili Marleen.

And he saw it: the mists rising from the ground, the rain slowly turning to thick snowflakes like cotton wool. He saw the woman as he had seen her on the morning when he escaped and found a way to climb out of the mountain. He had seen her as he hid behind tendrils and ferns. Her short gray coat, flapping wet and heavy around her thighs, impeding her as she walked, her little high-heeled shoes, the small hat she was clutching to her head with one hand to keep the wind from blowing it away. And then he saw her face, the face of an angel as she raised it to him. He saw the pain in it as mingled rain, snow, and tears ran down it. And he saw her swiftly give him her present. She threw it down among the gorse beside the path, as if to say: There, did you see that? Pick it up for yourself! He noted the place where it fell.

He knew she had been sent to him. He put it down to the prayers they were saying for him at home in Korcziw. Suddenly everything was in league to save him: the earthly part he had performed himself by escaping through the mountain, and now came the part played by heaven, which was necessary for success. And when the next minute she disappeared, in those shoes that didn't allow her heels to touch the ground—he had never seen anything like them before—when she disappeared, floating rather than walking, he immediately climbed down to the path and found what she had brought for him. It was a key. The key to his salvation. He had no doubt of it.

But he was not insane. He knew he must be cautious, and he hid until darkness fell. He had seen the SS guards. He knew that their route passed his hiding place. He knew that if an angel comes to your aid you must still be clever. He knew he must do the rest for himself, with the greatest caution and if necessary the cunning of a thief.

He went back to his hiding place. He made himself a bed of autumn leaves, soil, and flakes of stone as best he could. For the moment he was very pleased with the way things were turning out, and he fell asleep at once.

When he woke it was dark. He did not know how long he had been asleep. It seemed to him that everything was all right, everything already achieved. He felt he had been saved, miraculously brought to the place where he was supposed to be. Then, suddenly, as his mind made an effort, apparently operating on its own and separately from him, he took stock of his position in a crack in the rock, a kind of cave, and realized that he was in the process of freezing. Exerting great strength of will, he opened his eyes and saw that it was still snowing. By now, he could see, the snow was settling, and it occurred to him that he still had some way to go.

He reached the way out of his cave several times, to find that he was really still lying where he had been, and only his dream self had set out. At some point, with another huge effort, he managed to get his body moving as well. Letting himself down to the ground, he saw with all the horror of which his mind was capable that he would be leaving visible tracks in the newly fallen snow.

He set off in the direction from which his angel had come. He avoided walking along the path, but knew it was impossible to leave no tracks behind him, and when he saw the house he realized that he would have to take his last few steps to the door along the path itself. He hoped his footprints would soon be snowed over.

The house was dark. It seemed empty. It must be empty, or would an angel have brought him the key? He put it in the lock and was not surprised when the door opened. Groping his way along a wall in the dark, he reached a narrow passage through a door that had been left ajar, came to another door at the end of the passage, and at once he could smell that there was bread nearby. He was frantic with hunger. His hand passed over a tabletop. He turned to the wall, where he thought there was a cupboard, and a chair fell over. Suddenly pausing, he heard the sound of bare feet in the passage. They moved away, and then came closer again. He had not been wrong. There was someone else here.

He knew he would be too weak to defend himself. The fear that came over him made him even weaker. He felt the back of a chair and sat down. He was finished. He wept. The light came on.

★   ★   ★

WHERE DID YOU GET THE KEY? Tell me where you got the key.

I put it on the kitchen table between us. At night, when I came back from the Berghof, he fell on the food I had brought him. The kitchen was on the valley side of the Tea House, above the steep slope, so that its window was invisible. We could put the light on there.

K-key? he repeated.

His boyish face twisted into the mendacious grimace I was getting used to. Something between weeping and grinning, between slyness and pitiful vulnerability. Boys reaching puberty tell lies all day long. They can't help it. They are practicing how to hide what matters. It is the pact they make with their future, which depends on keeping what matters a secret. They seal the pact with the lies they tell.

I find, he said.

This was the stupidest and most common of all stupid explanations. It annoyed me that he thought he could try that one on with me.

Mikhail, I said, if you go on lying to me I won't bring you any more to eat.

But he stuck to his story.

Where did you find it?

By path, he said.

It made me really furious. Here I was risking everything for him, and he wasn't even prepared to tell me the truth.

So I suppose the key fell from heaven, I said. I would have shouted at him if silence had not been of prime importance here.

Yes, he said.

An angel gave it to you, no doubt, I said. I meant it to sound ridiculous.

Yes! he said. Yes!

Oh, really? I said. What did the angel look like? It had wings, did it?

Then, hesitantly, ashamed, he described it to me. The mist. The rain. The most beautiful woman he had ever seen. Her tears. The shoes in which she didn't walk but instead hovered in the air.

I JUST WANTED TO SEE who it is now, she had said to me. And then I understood. The traces of someone else in the Tea House that Eva and I had noticed before I moved in here—one of the SS men had been using it as a love-nest after Hitler left. He had given the woman he was meeting there a key so that she could wait for him. That might also, perhaps, explain the presence of a radio in the Tea House. Perhaps it belonged to this couple and they liked making love to soft music. For hadn't we found it in the bedroom? And could it not be that they had also, very secretly indeed, tuned in to enemy stations now and then?

Then I had come, and the woman probably thought that I was the reason for the end of her affair. That her lover was now entertaining another woman in the Tea House. And she had let herself be driven to intrude on me. She had been beside herself. Beside herself with hatred and jealousy. I'd seen that she was.

I saw her walk out in the snowy rain, saw her put her hand in her coat pocket halfway down to the path, and fling the key into the bushes beside the path in a passion of fury. I saw her stop, raise her face to the rain for a moment, and try to face the pain of knowing it was all over. I saw the boy watching her from his hiding place. Saw him looking for something a little later among the bushes beside the path, finding it, quickly picking it up, and returning to his hiding place with it.

All at once I myself felt I was serving some kind of higher plan, a plan that had been made long ago and without my personal involvement. There was nothing more to be decided. I was involved in it now.

If the worst comes to the worst, I thought, Eva will help me.

She wouldn't have.

Today, so many years later, I know that she was helping me in her own way, the only way in which she could face the horrors going on around her: She didn't look. She looked in the other direction. I think Mikhail could have walked past her and she wouldn't even have asked who he was.

That is the way in which people like Eva Braun help you. And they help to make evil possible.

I had nothing to fear from her. At heart, I knew that. But when someone who could be dangerous to me did come on the scene soon afterward, I also knew at heart that I could not hope for anything from her.

CHAPTER 6

ON NOVEMBER 20, HITLER HAD LEFT HIS HEAD-quarters at the Wolf's Lair in East Prussia and continued to wage his war from Berlin.

It did not seem to trouble Eva that this meant a retreat from the approaching Eastern front. Soviet troops had already marched into East Prussian territory in October. I knew that from what Hugh Carleton Greene said. But suddenly Eva seemed full of optimism again.

I'm just so glad he's back, she said.

She sounded as if she were speaking of someone who has come home after a long absence. And gradually I came to understand her purpose. She could not have reached him in Rastenburg, where he was in the field. But she could follow him to Berlin; she had access to him there. He couldn't turn her away from the Reich Chancellery. I sensed her restlessness, her readiness to set out.

I could imagine the difficulty Hitler had in persuading her over the telephone not to pack her bags at once and set out to join him. Perhaps he even talked to her, just that once, about the military situation, for she was full of hints to me about an expected turn of the tide in the West.

Christmas, said Eva, eyes shining like the eyes of a child who can't wait. You wait and see—at Christmas . . .

But I could get nothing more precise out of her, while Hugh Carleton Greene was holding out to me and all the people of Germany the prospect of the saddest Christmas we had ever known.

And it would be Hugh Carleton Greene who was right.

When the Ardennes offensive began on December 16 there was no holding Eva. She began preparing for Christmas celebrations with the victorious commander in Berlin, and to this end we were all to go to Munich where she employed—she actually still employed—a dressmaker.

Can one believe it? Were frocks still being made among the ruins? Was someone designing a new pattern? Were people curling their hair? Practicing the cello? Making Christmas decorations? Teaching dance steps? Crocheting borders for handkerchiefs? Embroidering cushions? Writing poems? Building dollhouses? Were they still affectionate? Vain? Scheming? Feeling hurt by a thoughtless remark? Were they still mad with love, ambition, jealousy? Could you still fear making a fool of yourself? Could you be looking forward to a special occasion? Did gossip still flourish, and resentment, and lust?

Yes, they did. Jealousy, ambition, fearfulness. Great longings and small anxieties. Parties. Walks. Fretting over whether your skirt was too short or your hair too long. The whole A to Z of small needs that spell out great events.

The simplest lesson is the most difficult. I didn't realize that until later, when I read the diaries of Goebbels. How injured he felt. How enamored, how enthusiastic. How proud when he scored a particularly great success with one of his acts of arson, one of his lies. How deeply stirred his feelings were! Oh, the pain of love! Heartache. Paternal pride.

Didn't he know that he had no right to such great feelings?

Who says so?

History.

Didn't he notice the Muse of History looking over his shoulder when he wrote of his affair with Lida Baarová, "My heart is sick unto death," didn't he see History falling about with mocking laughter?

No, he didn't notice. Not even he, who dictated to History the lies she needed as a pretext to make herself come about. If we were ever aware that history is on the point of coming about we would try to prevent it. We would try to stop it with all the force at our command. Not just this particular bit of history, but History in general. It's so tactless. It makes us look like fools. It lays all our great passions and small needs open to ridicule. It makes little of them, destroys them, leaving nothing but mockery behind. The insipid flavor of a faux pas that has been committed and, seen in the light of day, suddenly appears a crime.

Looking back, I find it incredible to think of myself walking through Munich with Eva in the pale midday December sun, past mounds of rubble, facades scorched black, former display windows boarded up, notices adjuring people: "Knock to give a signal! How to act in the event of being buried under the rubble." Then walking past the church of Our Lady, which has a hole blown in the vault above the choir, while its entire roof is more or less open to the elements. "Danger of Falling Masonry!" says the notice on the temporary hoarding past which we hurry, soon afterward reaching the food market in a basement entrance, where there are a couple of steps down to the fashion showroom. Here Eva tries on a close-fitting pale mauve suit with a mink-trimmed collar, and expresses her annoyance at finding that the skirt is too short.

Not again! she says, crossly. Not again! Don't you see? I can't afford to show so much leg, not in my position. Don't you understand that?

To which the dressmaker, on her knees, replies: Oh, yes, of course, *gnädige Frau*. We only tacked the hem up. It's easily let down if madam prefers.

Her mouth is full of pins. I admire the way she can talk through those pins.

Madam knows that we always go to a lot of trouble to get everything just as madam likes it. If there's no air raid tonight we can bring it around tomorrow morning. Of course. Heil Hitler, madam!

When the first air-raid warning goes off at around nine-thirty we've already polished off a couple of bottles of Sekt with Eva's friends, who as usual turned up as soon as we arrived in Wasserburger Strasse. The ground-floor windows are blacked out with the thick roller blinds specially made for the purpose. We are sitting by candlelight. Well, it will soon be Christmas.

What a shame, says Mitzi. This always happens just as we're feeling nice and comfortable.

Take no notice, says Schorsch. It's only a nuisance raid. They'll move away soon. And if they're making for Perlach and Harlaching again we won't get hit anyway.

Eva fetches another bottle from the kitchen. The first explosion comes at the same time as the pop of the champagne cork.

No need to go so pale, little one, says Eva. That was miles away.

Mitzi says: I'd really love a good night's sleep for once. Those Yankee bastards are just trying to soften us up. Sleep deprivation, that's their game. But they won't do it, not with us. It's a notorious method of torture, did you know? Cheers! That's what I say. Cheers, you Yankee bastards up there! I hope you die horribly!

As she lifts her glass to the ceiling the whole house suddenly shakes. The china in the cupboards clinks, and Hitler's *Little Church in Asam* falls off the wall. It's a sketch he gave Eva, and is of mainly financial value to her. Art by the Führer, she has told me more than once, will be worth a fortune in twenty years' time. "My old-age pension," she calls the little picture.

I hear something whistling.

That's very loud, I say.

If you can hear them whistling they'll come down somewhere else, says Schorsch.

Suddenly there is a mighty, penetrating howl from somewhere very close, a terrible crashing sound—I don't know how we get down to the cellar. We have to unlock the door to the air-raid shelter first, but luckily the key is hanging from a hook right beside it.

When it closes behind us, Schorsch says: Damn it, I left the bottle upstairs. Do you have anything to drink down here?

Oh, do be quiet just for once, says Kathi, his wife.

The little air-raid shelter is meant to take four people. There are six of us. There are two folding seats against each wall, and we sit crammed together on them.

They just won't give up! They keep on coming and coming, trying to kill us again and again! The loud crescendo of the engines dropping from the sky toward us. The whistling, howling, crashing all around. Our little ark, with us inside it, is drifting in the middle of all this racket.

I look at the faces of Mandi and Schorsch, of Mitzi, Kathi, and Eva, oblivious of themselves, carried away, concentrating entirely on the precious, irreplaceable life within them. Danger places us all on the same level. Whether we like each other or not makes no difference now. As if in a vision, I see us with the eyes through which the gods may view us, examples of a species sharing the common fate of mortality, wanderers between worlds here in this room, a waiting room of death, like every room in which we ever find ourselves. I see it now with eyes unsealed by fear. There is no arrogance in such a gaze, rather the opposite. No one can be humbler than people in a bunker during an air raid. I read in the wide eyes of the others that they know it, too. If eternity is just beginning, then it is beginning now. We don't know for certain whether we are still on this side of the grave. We have lost our sense of time. Have we been down here several hours or only a few minutes? There are no intervals, no measurements of time amid the roar of destruction. It is total.

When the all-clear sounds at about twenty to eleven, we sit there motionless for a moment, like passengers in an aircraft that has just landed. Then we slip back into our old roles as if into a familiar garment.

From the terrace we see fires burning all around. They are brightest on the other side of the Isar, over near the railway station. Next day we shall discover that the worst of the raid was around the food market, and Eva will never get her pale mauve suit now. But flames are flickering up very close to us, too, and smoke rises to the night sky. We can hear the noise of the fire engines now, of rushing water, calling, shouting. Of the men in our party, Mandi has gone off to help with extinguishing the fires at the first note of the all-clear. Schorsch goes on drinking where he left off before the raid.

Come on, says Kathi, come on, Schorschi, let's go to bed.

Oh Lord, says Schorsch. If our bed's still standing.

You can leave out the jokes, says Kathi.

It was a nice evening, she tells Eva, honestly, darling. But tell your Führer we've had enough now. Right, Schorsch? You tell him that.

I will, says Eva.

But don't say anything about us, says Schorsch. I'm not a defeatist.

Of course not, says Eva wearily. I won't say anything about you.

Honestly, says Kathi, when I tell Schorsch we've had enough, then we've had enough. Right, Schorschi?

Right, or I'll catch it, won't I? says Schorsch. I'm not saying just what I'll catch, though.

Bastard, says Kathi.

She puts her arm around his waist, and he leans heavily on her shoulders.

Let's go, says Schorsch.

They move away and out into the night, swaying slightly, making straight for the smoke and the flickering firelight in which the outlines of people running can be seen at the end of the street, and fire engines at the road junction, a platform truck, ladders. A young woman in an unbuttoned coat with nothing underneath but a petticoat is running toward them, both hands pressed to her temples. She stops, turns around again, runs in the other direction, a prey to distraction.

In the morning we can still see the pillars of smoke, rising black into the gray December sky.

Beppo was going to come yesterday evening.

Beppo, she tells me, lost an arm at El-Alamein in 1942. But even with only one arm Beppo's an amusing sort. He used to be a good dancer; there was no one to equal him. He was Ilse's favorite partner in dancing class, and Eva herself knows no one can dance like Beppo. He doesn't want to dance anymore these days. He says your body feels quite different when you have only one arm instead of two. But it's only his left arm missing, says Eva. It makes no difference to her. The only thing is that she has to lead him with her right arm when they dance. Beppo says he feels as if he were holding a dancing partner made of air in his missing left arm. He can't describe it, he says. And you feel pretty silly buttering bread with only one hand, not to mention doing various other things. The right hand knows what the left hand does, and if the left hand isn't there anymore then the right hand doesn't know what to do. Since he lost his arm Beppo has been living with his mother in Böhmerwaldplatz. But Beppo never misses seeing Eva when she comes to Munich.

After breakfast we walk to Böhmerwaldplatz. It is in the direction of the pillars of smoke. The smell of burning intensifies as we come closer. From a distance, it is reminiscent of smoldering autumn bonfires. But we soon plunge deeper into yellowish-gray fumes, which envelop us like fog, lying heavy on our lungs. We try not to cough. We hold handkerchiefs to our mouths. When we turn in to

Böhmerwaldplatz the sky above us grows darker. People are moving through a shadowy underworld. We can't see if any buildings are still standing behind the facades. This is no longer a habitable world, and never will be again.

A man wearing the NSV armband of the Volkswohlfahrt, the public welfare organization, runs toward us waving his arms about. Get back! he shouts. The next moment a facade collapses in a cloud of rubble and dust. We stand there looking at it. As the dust slowly settles the ruin is revealed, dramatic, solemn, emerging from the haze: a doorframe, a section of wall with a hole where the window used to be, and a scrap of torn curtain blowing behind it.

A woman shouts: Roswithaaa . . . A couple of NSV men run toward the fallen wall and start digging in the rubble. Then they carry something to the ambulance standing on the other side of the square. Roswithaaa! cries the woman.

Other women are carrying buckets up in pairs. In their flowered dresses, checkered aprons, bright headscarves they still seem to belong to the world that ended last night. The water they are carrying is like a single drop on a hot stone. Still, a man keeps tirelessly tipping it through a window; flames flare up behind the window, and smoke rises now and then.

You can't go any farther, says one of the NSV men, this place is in danger of collapsing! Spreading out his arms, he forces us back.

We're only going there, says Eva, pointing to the middle of the square, where various items are lying. I assume they are mattresses and parts of beds saved from the burning buildings.

Are you family of anyone here? asks the man from the National Socialist welfare organization.

Friends, says Eva.

All right, says the man. But keep well away from those buildings.

As we make our way through the ruins lying all around, a strange smell that I cannot identify grows stronger. An entirely impossible thought shoots through my head: How, I wonder, can anyone be roasting meat here and now? But there is nothing I wouldn't be prepared to consider possible at this moment. I am new to Hell. Everyone except me knows what's going on. They move through the inferno as surefooted as ghosts. I follow Eva, who is making purposefully for the middle of the square, where an empty truck has just arrived.

I look at the dead. They have been laid side by side on the paving stones, like the kill after a hunt, thirty or forty of them. They are the first corpses I have ever seen in my life. They are disfigured. Many were burning when they died. Others died with their heads, their torsos, a leg torn away. A woman is clutching her baby. They died together. The fire has made a Madonna and Child of them, a statue with a surface resembling dark-stained wood. The woman looks like a death's head; the flesh has shriveled back from her teeth in the fire.

Looking for anyone? asks a man from the truck.

A man who's lost an arm, says Eva.

Oh, plenty of people have lost bits of themselves, says the man. That's why we put them here. When we find something we look around to see whose it is. You'll have to hurry. I'm about to load up the complete ones.

Beppo, says Eva, stopping in front of one of the corpses.

He is one of those who have not burned and whose heads are still in their proper places. Beppo is not disfigured, he even looks happy, as if he had been dancing with an airy partner to the very last.

Well, if you say he only had one arm already, I can take him with the others, says the truck driver, and when he loads up the dead of Böhmerwaldplatz he starts with Beppo.

Let's go home, says Eva on the way back.

Home?

To the Berg.

Where else was I still at home now?

★　★　★

FESTIVE TABLES ARE LAID in the dining hall of the Hotel Platterhof for the big SS Christmas party. The Christmas tree reaches to the ceiling. It is decorated with tinsel and silver balls like German Christmas trees everywhere.

At this time there are no fashions in Christmas trees yet, no special designs and themes for them. They won't be introduced until the fifties, when I shall surprise my family with a new creation every year. I shall begin with a tree of gold tinsel. It will be followed by a tree decorated with wooden figures, a tree decorated with straw stars, then my red-apple tree, until at some point I get to the all-violet tree—violet candles, violet glass balls tied on with violet taffeta bows. The blue spruce that supersedes the Norway spruce will itself go out of fashion, pines and Douglas firs will come in.

One day I shall wonder where this search of mine for new ideas is leading, and I shall remember a poorly lit street, or rather a street that wasn't lit at all: I was standing in the dark in front of a shop window, with nothing on display but a few bottles of eau de cologne, and decorated with some silver tinsel on a fir branch. I read the words *Johann Maria Farina, Glockengasse* . . . Glockengasse, Bell Street. The words themselves have a silvery, Christmasy sound, extraordinarily musical and magical. Something touched me and cast a spell over me once and for all, and it was to fill me with sufficient Christmas spirit for the rest of my life. I would only have to conjure up that picture: the dark street, the little shop window lit faintly from within, the turquoise packaging, the branch of fir, the ornate characters of the script. I can tell, from the surrounding darkness, that it must have been in wartime, and suddenly I know how intense, how irresistible, how once-and-for-all Christmas was at the time. The memory of it has something of the same heartrending enchantment as the memory of an early love.

And perhaps that was because love did come into it. Although it was a love that had nothing really to do with love itself but with fear, with confusion, with inner conflict, with a sense that I was ruined forever, not morally, but ruined for the life I would otherwise have lived.

It began with the big Christmas party at the Platterhof. Oh, the terrible charm of a Nazi Christmas! Outside, the dark world bristling with weapons and our enemies, and here inside, in our world of tinsel-decked fir trees, we are crowding close, warmed, enveloped by all the scents of Christmas. It was beautiful. At the back of the hall, on a large, dark, handwoven tapestry, a picture of Adolf Hitler was flanked to right and left by two swastikas, the great Christmas tree stood a little way in front of it, and the piano to accompany the singing was at one side of the room.

Each of the men got a special Christmas platter: fancy biscuits, cinnamon stars, and a packet of cigarettes set out on white paper napkins decorated with sprigs of evergreen, so that gradually cigarette smoke was superimposed on the Christmas scents, mingling with them and with the smell of leather and masculine sweat to create something that brought tears to their eyes when the first chord was struck:

Germany, sacred name, they sang, ours for eternity, down through the ages the same, dearest land, blessings on thee . . .

And they sang: I had a friend, a comrade true . . .

And when the commander had finished his speech, which dwelt on the darkness that would bring forth light, and the winter solstice that was like a turn in the fortunes of the international struggle facing us—Germany is going through its winter night, he said, to emerge all the more glorious in the end—and when the men felt they were sitting within the heart of that night, as close and warm and as terribly at ease as only a company of men sitting together can be, as close as only such a company can be, then in the exuberance of their unbounded high spirits, their Christmas mood of camaraderie, the sense of well-being warming them to the bone, the defiance filling them as they thought of their enemies and the course of the war, one of them struck up the beautiful old carol "O du fröhliche," and immediately they all joined in, while the man at the piano spread his hands on the keyboard.

O thou happy day, they sang at the tops of their voices, O thou blessed day of grace and mercy at Christmastide . . .

So far, so good. But then they heard themselves suddenly singing the rest of it.

The world was lost, forlorn, they sang out loud. O be glad, good Christian folk, whate'er betide.

A carol of thoroughly defeatist sentiments, in fact. But as no one shouted, Stop! they went on singing, and even the commissioned officers joined in. The carol was more than they could resist. And when it was over the man at the piano, one of themselves, began the prelude to the next carol. For a few bars he played the tune of "Silent Night, Holy Night," and they all felt that they would be incapable of not singing along. But then he changed the key from C sharp major to D major. Something had fleetingly touched them, a memory, a temptation, an emotion, something of all those, and now, glad that it had passed them by and was gone, they joined in their own familiar, politically unobjectionable, ideologically neutral Christmas carol:

O Christmas tree, they sang . . .

Eva and I were sitting in the hotel lounge that afternoon having tea and stollen. There was deep snow outside. Now that winter had come to the mountains, and we could walk only on the roads that had been cleared, we went to the Platterhof almost every day for afternoon tea. They kept a table reserved for us in the lounge.

(Your usual table, *gnädiges Fräulein*?

Yes, the usual table. Thank you, Heinz.)

Sometimes we were accompanied by Eva's friend Hertha, who

came with her two little girls several times to spend a few days at the Berghof, or by Aunt Fanny and Uncle Fritz, unless they preferred to stay at Schloss Fischhorn. There was more laughter at our table than at any other in the Hotel Platterhof. We were never as merry, as determined to have fun as here. To keep it up, we needed a little cognac and the sense that others were watching us. Aunt Fanny in particular was mistress of the art of walking the tightrope that allowed her both to figure as Hitler's mother-in-law and to enjoy the freedom of behavior deriving from the fact that she wasn't. She joked with the waiters, but ordered them around a little more than was necessary.

That afternoon before Christmas, however, Eva and I were alone. We could see the Christmas party in the dining hall through an open double door. We hummed along with the carols, exchanging ironic glances. It's always easy to avoid being carried away if you are not one of the party.

I think we'll leave before they all make for the bar, said Eva. That's when the Christmas celebrations will really begin.

The Platterhof still had stocks of everything that was unobtainable elsewhere: Italian wines, French champagne, Alsatian fruit spirits, sherry from Portugal, Russian vodka, Romanian slivovitz, Bavarian herb-flavored liqueurs, and beer flowing like water . . .

Eva signaled to Heinz to let him know we were ready to leave.

It was always the same:

The bill, please, she would say.

The bill? said Heinz. Very good, *gnädiges Fräulein*. We'll put it on the account.

I don't know exactly whose guest I was. Hitler's? The Nazi Party's? I never went to the trouble of finding out. Everything went so smoothly, was taken so much for granted. I am sure that Eva herself couldn't have said for certain if I had asked her, but in any case she would have regarded such a question as a faux pas. It was one of the questions, one of the countless questions, that were never asked. Eva was very good at not asking questions. It was part of her talent for elegance. She never asked unsuitable questions, just as she never wore unsuitable hats. It was perhaps the greatest talent she possessed, apart from dying. Tact is the virtue of those who leave it to others to decide on the rules of the game.

As we were being helped into our coats, one of the men suddenly came out of the dining hall and approached us, and I recognized the Obersturmbannführer from Schloss Fischhorn. First he greeted Eva, then he took my coat from Heinz and, without shaking hands, helped me into it himself. I felt his hands on my shoulders and his breath on the back of my neck.

We meet again, he said.

I saw the look of amusement in Eva's eyes, and I knew I had blushed.

Well, well, said her eyes.

And my nervous system had gone crazy, some kind of uncontrollable signal set my reactions going, my blood pressure shot up, the sensitive vessels just under the skin of my face expanded, filling with the blood that rose inside me in a huge wave and carrying me away with it, washing me up far, far from myself on shores where I was safe and could not be found, while my other self, delivered up, exposed to view, stayed where it was.

I ought to have told Eva: That's not it at all. You're wrong.

But appearances are always working against those of us who blush easily. It gives us away. And where something appears to be given away, it means that there is something to hide. That's the dilemma of blushing, and at the same time it's what sets the blushing signal off.

May I escort you back to the Berghof? asked the Obersturmbannführer.

By all means, said Eva, while I returned from the momentary fit of distraction induced by my blushing.

So the three of us walked out into the starry winter night. Above us rose the vault of the same clear sky that would decide the outcome of Hitler's Western offensive in the Ardennes: Once the cloud cover that initially favored Operation Autumn Mist had given way to an area of high pressure, the enemy fighter-bombers were able to attack the Panzer divisions moving westward. Eva's dream of a reunion with Hitler in Berlin in the near future was being crushed at this very moment by Allied bomber formations attacking von Manteuffel's Fifth Panzer Army at Bastogne.

I don't remember what we talked about as we walked to the Hintereck above the barracks, the place where all the roads of the Obersalzberg met and radiated out in a star shape, the road to the Kehlstein house, the roads to the residential estates of Klaushöhe and Buchenhöhe, the roads to the private houses of the Göring and Bormann families. We turned left into the road toward the valley, passed the Obersalzberg administrative offices, the building known as the Kindergartenhaus, the former Zum Türken inn, which now accommodated the SS Reich Security Service, and soon afterward we reached the access road to the Berghof. No one had followed us. Our usual companions had obviously been sent off by this higher-ranking officer, countermanding the law that said we must not be left unguarded. I did not yet know exactly what the consequences of this incident would be, and for the time being I registered what was going on with a certain uneasiness. Even unpleasantness begins to become acceptable when you know what it's about.

I could have murdered Eva when she asked me, as we came to the flight of steps:

Well, little one (little one, indeed!), are you coming in?

Which obliged me to say that I was staying not at the Berghof but in the Tea House on the Mooslahner Kopf.

Hadn't I ever spent the evening in the Berghof, then?

Yes, of course, I said.

And suddenly I knew what was making me uneasy.

What? said our escort. All alone in the Tea House on the Moo-slahner Kopf? By Jove! he said, an expression that, like many others, has since gone out of fashion. Like "a good sport." Like "a dashing blade." Like "amazing." Like addressing girls as *Fräulein*. Like speaking of a man as a real pal—all of them terms once loaded with more or less emotional weight, all of them once components of the mental luggage with which we traveled through the Nazi period, a period that is not just part of our political history but also of our minds, a part of our consciousness.

By Jove, says Obersturmbannführer Hans. Aren't you afraid of anything at all?

Now I sense the danger. Someone is on my scent. Someone wants to get on the track of me and my secret.

But why? he asks. Doesn't your cousin have enough room for you at the Berghof?

Here we go.

Yes, I say. But she doesn't want me there.

That's not true! cries Eva. Her eyes dart fire at me. Don't you believe her! She's lying! Ooh, she's dangerous! You just watch out for her.

We have reached the steps up to Hitler's house. The December stars sparkle in the sky above us. Snow crunches underfoot.

I explain that I spend the mornings studying physics. I like the quiet there, I say. The peace. The lovely view. The whole atmosphere, I say.

I can sense how unsatisfactory my remarks sound.

The Obersturmbannführer wants to know more. What exactly am I studying?

Heisenberg, I say. The physical principles of the quantum theory.

I say it not without some vanity. Not without a wish to impress him. I want him to respect me. I would like to build a wall around myself too high for him to climb.

But at the same time I am aware that I've already given myself away. It happened so quickly. My most sacred secret, coded in my amateurish way, is already told. I go quite hot with alarm.

Would you like to come in with us for a moment? I ask.

I say it to lull any suspicion that I'm hiding anything. Please, it means, take a look around, but take it here. And I say it because I expect that otherwise Eva will say the same thing in the next minute. It's meant to show that I am just as adult as she is.

No, thanks very much, he says. Oh no (with a little smile), certainly not.

I can tell from his tone of voice that I have made a mistake. We quickly say good-bye. This time he salutes me in as military a manner as he does taking his leave of Eva.

At the top of the steps, still breathless, she snaps at me:

Are you out of your mind? Did you have to throw yourself at the man's head like that? He saw us home. That was all. Don't you know one says good-bye to men *outside* the front door?

I know I have committed a faux pas. It's a recurrent experience of mine. As a woman, I have gone too far and I regret it. My regret makes itself felt as shame, remorse, a sense of humiliation. I am surrounded by invisible walls against which I bump, injuring myself, until I have understood that on principle you behave coolly toward men. You are standoffish on principle, you take offense on principle. The rules of courtesy, indeed of common humanity, do not apply to men unless your relationship with them is that of a working assistant. You may also be ministering angels as nurses, and again you have a dispensation from the duty of being standoffish. The way lies open to you there. In hospitals you bend over the feverish, stroke the damp hair back from the brows of groaning men, hear their stammering, their murmured confessions, understand what they are begging for, and say nothing but a soothing "There, there," or "No, it's all right"—a world of physical affection surprisingly opening up, a world where the conventions are no longer in force, a subliminal sphere of desperate passions, extravagant dreams, final obsessions, all coming up against only one obstacle, death, in the vicinity of which, like every true passion, they thrive. This was the dark, concealed origin of many postwar liaisons.

But for me on the Obersalzberg, where my presence was tolerated as the guest of Hitler's mistress, and she herself was not much more than a tolerated guest, for me there were no dispensations from the convention requiring me to be standoffish. The undefined nature of our position as women in the male-dominated world of the Obersalzberg allowed no deviation, however slight, from the rules of the game. Our proximity to the SS, which saw itself as a kind of male order vowed to the ideal of uncompromising masculinity, made that position precarious. Eva knew it, and relied on my understanding it, too. Her reprimand was well deserved, or anyway so I felt. Among women, it is other women who check that the rules of the game are being kept, and they do not mince their words.

If you don't know how to behave here, she said, as the door of the Berghof opened for us, you'd better leave.

That struck home. I got the message.

I knew it anyway. Like all young women, I knew it in all its ambiguity. I knew I was attractive. I knew I only had to be around to be sure of the attention of men. Part of them was always intent on me when I entered a room. When I left it. When I was silent. When I laughed. As soon as I opened my eyes I saw theirs turning away in pretended indifference, or not, as the case might be. I knew that, as every young woman knows it. The knowledge of it was expressed not in my consciousness but in the movement with which I put the hair back from my brow, or crossed my legs. It relaxed my hips, spread my fingers, lent my carriage a certain victorious suppleness.

Much of it was imitation, both conscious and unconscious. I had begun imitating Eva at the age of fourteen, and I was still doing it.

Eva herself got it from the films we watched. With every step we took we were Greta Garbo or Lida Baarová, about whose scandalous affair with Goebbels we knew. We were simultaneously lascivious and innocent, a perfect mixture that we Nazi women embodied better than any generation before or after us.

Eva dreamed of a postwar career as a film actress. What part did she want to play?

She wanted to be Hitler's lover in a big Hollywood movie. That was her dream, the utmost to which the former shop-girl aspired in her fantasies. The life of Hitler's mistress as a screen melodrama. She made no secret of it. She came back to the subject again and again.

I just hope it doesn't take us too long to beat the Americans. Don't you see? she said. Then we won't just have the Ufa film studios. Hollywood will belong to us. All those studios! Warner Bros., Otto Selznik. Oh, you know what I mean! she said. It was clear to her that these places were the Mount Olympus of the movie world. It was clear to all of us. She just hoped that when the time came she wouldn't be too old to play herself.

She had grasped the principle of the reality show at an early date. You play the part of yourself. The idea was that life and movies come to the same thing. The great soap opera of Adolf Hitler and Eva Braun. She knew it would run and run. She was planning the grand finale, already working on it. It would be a mixture of melodrama and Wagnerian opera.

When it really happened, she must have been aware that no cameras were running. And yet, and yet . . . I know what she was like. She knew she was being filmed live as she died. She was wearing the long, dark blue taffeta dress she had worn for her wedding shortly before. The setting was right, so was her partner. Filmed live in death. History on the air. She knew it.

At the very end, then, she got the leading role she had dreamed of in the movie of her life after all. Only it was not the society comedy with just a touch of pathos that she considered her genre. As it happened, she was acting in the drama of the century. A Grand Guignol piece.

Young as I was, I had chosen her as my instructor, but a dangerous instructor, from whom I learned how to perform effectively while observing the rules of the game.

Oh yes, we Nazi women knew we were sexy. But we also knew that it was imperative not to know what sex meant. We consistently behaved as if there were no such thing as sex. We never talked about it. Not among women, and certainly not to men. When it happened we abandoned ourselves to it as if to a force of nature at whose existence we had not previously guessed. We acted as if surprised by the desire that came over us, carrying us away, leaving us defenseless. As you may imagine, this was not without its appeal. Not without a certain degree of theatricality that did wonders for our sexual performance.

We hardly talked at all during sex. It wouldn't have suited the style of performance that said we were overwhelmed. We closed our eyes. We arched backward. We sighed. We let ourselves slip into a state of reverie that could rise to ecstasy at will. We had to be out of our right minds, because if we had been in them how could we have answered for the fact that we were having sex? This way, however, we knew nothing of what we were doing. To a certain degree we weren't there at all when we made love.

I suspect we were delightful lovers. Well, of course, all women are. But when I think of our consistent pretense of innocence, the inner urge to experience ecstasy which was all that helped us to do something so strictly forbidden, without exception, I know we deserved applause.

Oh, it was a great time for love when love was still forbidden. When it was still something of a dirty secret. That made it all the more compelling. What actually happened was the same as it is today.

But what *had* happened was indescribable. Indescribably filthy. Indescribably wonderful. We lowered our eyes when we met the man with whom we shared such a secret. We blushed to think that he had the same memory of it. We felt bound to him by it, as only an indescribably shameful secret can bind people together. And so dependency, anxiety, susceptibility to blackmail throve along with love. Insincerity was triumphant. Among us women, too.

With mendacity bordering on self-denial, we maintained our claim to know nothing about it in front of each other. Even Eva, whose bedroom at the Berghof was next to a bathroom that also had a door to Hitler's bedroom on the other side, a more or less concealed but unambiguous zone of intimacy, would never have mentioned her intimate relationship with the Führer to me. It was not just that it would have been unthinkable for her to hold forth about the details; she did all she could to give the impression that there were none.

Only once did she ever hint at something, in an entirely incidental manner, which cast a revealing light on her sexual relationship with him and showed it as what it probably was: a perfectly normal if intermittent love affair, presumably monogamous (on Eva's side anyway). A love affair centering on bed, both frustrated and given new impetus by frequent separations. Nothing else.

You know, Eva said to me one day when I had severe period pain—menstruation, although an intimate subject, was one that we women did discuss openly at the time—you know, she said, I always feel worse when I've put it off.

Put it off? I said.

Yes, said Eva. When I'm going to have the curse and the Führer's coming, I ask the doctor for something to put it off.

Can you do that? I asked.

Yes, certainly, said Eva. I can't recommend it, it's worse afterward. Still, what wouldn't one do!

This was the only risqué remark I ever heard Eva make: Still, what wouldn't one do! I feel as if it summed up her entire love for Hitler in a nutshell: What wouldn't one do!

Otherwise she said nothing on the subject.

(As for love, Hitler is supposed to have said, I keep a girl in Munich for that kind of thing.)

It was as simple as that.

We never discussed love, never. Yet love had us in a stranglehold. And I would never have confided in my cousin, older and more experienced in matters of the heart as she was, when I myself came to feel the power of that stranglehold soon afterward. It's the way we were.

WHEN I WENT MY USUAL WAY to the Mooslahner Kopf late that evening, the bag over my shoulder full of bread and cold roast meat, I saw them with a certain sense of relief: my escorts, who emerged out of nowhere as usual and followed me.

The path to the Tea House had to be shoveled clear of snow every day now. Two men from the work squads were made available for the job, guarded by two more men from the security service.

We never felt bothered about giving other people extra work. At the time it seemed to me hardly worth a thought. Now, however, I find it incredible that at a time when all hands were allegedly needed, when scarcely anyone who could still move at all was not obliged to do war work, when an exhausted, starving population was being required to make a mighty collective effort, four men were occupied every day in keeping a path at least five hundred meters long free of snow so that a young student could read her textbooks in her favorite place. No one saw anything odd about it.

Winter is a good time for the hunted, for people who have gone underground. Provided they are in the warm. Winter holds them fast, protects them against their own carelessness, and stops pursuers in their tracks. Once the snow was thick enough, the guards no longer patrolled around the Tea House but only approached along the path, often turning back once they were within sight of it.

We ourselves were careless, Mikhail and I. He spent more and more time in the rooms above the cellar now. The greatest danger was still the cleaning women. It was because of them that he had to spend the afternoons in the cellar. I had told them the cellar door was always locked, and only the security men had the key. I indicated that there was something secret there, and even I was not allowed to go down.

The cleaning women understood this kind of language very well. There were secrets everywhere on the Obersalzberg. Locked doors. Inaccessible rooms that were presumed to contain important files, valuable treasures, loot taken in war. The whole mountain was a secret. I was a part of it myself. Incomprehensible, mysterious, and inscrutable, at least so far as the reasons for my presence affected the cleaning women.

Later, when the fortress was laid open, the locked doors blown up, the walls reduced to rubble, all those women from Berchtesgaden and its surroundings were the first to come and gape at what had been concealed from them. It was curiosity rather than greed that drove them here. But when they saw what lay behind the doors, and realized it was not so much mysterious as tempting and valuable, all those stocks so industriously hoarded, the silver, the pictures, the linen, the appurtenances of the powerful, they were quick to seize upon it.

At the time, however, in that last Nazi winter, they still firmly believed that not every door could be opened. When I think back to it now, it was extraordinarily easy to hide a human being in Hitler's Tea House, here at the very center of his power, his favorite place; perhaps easier here than anywhere else. It was like wearing the beast of prey's own skin to prevent it from finding you.

We were living in a state of temporary security that had a certain sense of comfort about it. When I sat over my books in the morning, with the winter outside and Mikhail inside with me, leaning back against the hearth, squatting on the floor and carving a piece of the wood that I brought him now and then at his request, I sometimes thought this would go on forever.

He was like a domestic pet, and indeed he crawled around the house on all fours like an animal so as not to be seen from outside. He did not sit on a chair, but crouched on the floor close to the walls. It seemed second nature to him, and when I saw him later at his full height, after everything was over, I was suddenly afraid of him, as if he were someone else. And so he was.

At the time, however, he still had a wood-carver's knife in his hand instead of a gun. He was carving animals for me. A cat. A squirrel such as he saw outside our windows. A dog, a hunting dog. He kept the dog himself. I gave Eva the squirrel for Christmas. How sweet, she said, and never asked where I got it. The cat sat on the mantel-piece. She was asleep, waiting. She had curled up, aware that nothing in life is better than having a warm place. That was the cat's message. I knew what it meant.

ON CHRISTMAS EVE, Eva gave me a dressing table set of hairbrush, comb, and mirror with silver handles. It could have come from a Hollywood diva's dressing room. All I needed was a lady's maid to brush my hair for me.

Oh, we can fix that, said Eva, brushing my hair until it was crack-ling with electricity and stood out from my head like a wreath. As she brushed I felt her increasingly nervous state, about to veer into aggression. I knew what the matter was. She was waiting for a phone call.

She had given the staff the evening off, including the film projec-tionist. Only the two security men were sitting in the room next to the kitchen, playing dice. The cook had left a cold meal for us before she left: Norwegian smoked salmon, chicken salad with mayonnaise, and toast. The greatest independence we were allowed was to make the toast ourselves and carry the trays into the great hall.

As we ate we listened to a record of the Vienna Boys' Choir. After that the insistent silence of the telephone surrounded us, interrupted now and then only by the click of the dice shaken in a leather container and falling on an uncovered wooden table, and the suppressed cry of triumph of one or other of the men when he had won a game from the other.

I could feel the thin ice of Eva's composure. I guessed at the dark torrent of despair beneath it. I felt the burden of the task of diverting her, noticed from her reaction that she was letting a kind of somnambulistic automatism guide her actions. I was sitting at the same table as a suicide. Far, far away from me she was moving toward the darkness, the all-consuming emptiness that had power over her. It was there. It was always there. Eva's love for Hitler had been conceived and had grown under the spell of that power. It was founded on it.

It had been in her from the very first, a fearful void, a vacuum sucking her in, allowing no resistance, no attempt to oppose it. She was that void. She could not remember ever having been anything else.

Oh, she struggled. She erected bastions against the void within her. She tricked it by playing little pranks, even when she was a schoolgirl. She always went about with a group who liked to have fun. She didn't need good marks, she needed fun, small triumphs of insubordination. At the Tengstrasse high school she relished the reports of her schoolmistresses, who considered her a "wild, unruly, lazy child."

She loved sport, or rather the idea of herself as a sportswoman. Her body would do everything she demanded of it. She did gymnastics. She swam. She went skiing. She had mastered the basic figures of ice skating. She liked to show off in these sports. She was proud of her body, and lived in it as you might live in a magnificent and imposing house, but a house that nonetheless is haunted after dark. The void in her felt at ease there.

She also had a talent for dressing well. She was amazed by women who were perfectly happy to be badly dressed yet were obviously attractive. The nothingness in her insisted on an elegant wardrobe, and she obeyed it.

She cultivated appearances. It satisfied her to make photographic copies of appearances and keep them. She was an enthusiastic photographer and cinematographer. She took photographs as mothers do. Everyone in her pictures seemed to have been snapped for a family album, and even when she happened to have history in front of her camera, as she did in the days before the outbreak of the Second World War, she carefully stuck the pictures in her albums and wrote little captions under them, such as:

". . . and then Ribbentrop went to Moscow"

(Hitler, Bormann, Julius Schaub, and Luftwaffe General Bodenschatz talking in front of the hearth in the hall of the Berghof)

Or:

". . . but Poland still refuses to negotiate"

(Goebbels, with Hitler apparently lunging at him in a blurred movement as if to press him to his heart, and in the background the entire entourage in front of the drawn curtain of the great window of the Berghof.)

In Eva's photo albums all this looks like a child's birthday party.

Sport. Photographs. Clothes. She did not give up without a struggle. And Hitler. She had him. She would have chosen him as her lover above any other man. The dictator, the conqueror before whom everyone she knew trembled. Could there be a stronger bastion against the void inside her?

I lean over the abyss. I want to understand why she chose to go that way.

I see that the abyss is deep. I can make nothing out there. Confused yearnings. Intertwined dependencies. Emptiness. Confusions, mistakes.

I don't understand it.

But I remember. I remember the Christmas Eve I spent with Eva. I know that her desperation and rebellion were present in the room like an aura. I felt the outrage gathering in her. I guessed that a night can be endless when the phone does not ring, harder to endure than death itself. I understood that this is the logic of depressives. I felt an emptiness from which I myself shrank in horror, a vacuum that I, too, must resist as it tried to suck me in as well. I felt the presence of the Fury of suicide in the room. She spread her wings and brushed us with them as she passed. I, too, was mortally afraid.

I suspect that this contains the answer to my question: How can Eva have loved this man?

But I don't really know the answer. It is hidden in the folds of my memory. The waiting, night, death. The aura of outrage. The Fury rising in the air.

And I knew that Hitler's liaison with Eva had begun with an attempted suicide. She had been waiting in vain for days for a telephone call from him—he was then in the final phase of the Reichstag election campaign—when Ilse came home one evening to find her on the bed in their parents' room, bleeding and unconscious, with a bullet lodged in the side of her neck, its outlines clearly visible.

This kind of thing mustn't happen again, Hitler is supposed to have said to Heinrich Hoffmann. I must look after her from now on.

From the first, death was a partner in their relationship, saying incomprehensible things, expressing itself in riddles as it always does. Let those understand it who will. At any rate, it had the last word.

Go away now, said Eva. Leave me alone.

In no circumstances did I want to leave her alone.

I told her that at this moment her lover was losing the war in the west, and possibly that was why he didn't get around to calling her.

She wasn't interested.

The ground troops can operate only at night, I say. By day the Allied bombers attack them. And the German supply lines as far as the Rhine and the Luftwaffe airfields are under attack at the same time.

I'm not interested, she said firmly.

The Ardennes offensive has failed, that's what Hugh Carleton Greene says, I told her. The German tanks have stopped at the Meuse. They won't make it, he says.

Will you shut up! cries Eva. I don't want to hear any more of this.

I tried another tack. I suggested going out. The bar at the Hotel Platterhof would still be open.

Suppose he calls?

Then you're not at home, I said.

That had the desired effect. Cognac for her woes, and for Hitler the unsettling news that she wasn't at home. If he happened to call. After all, she still cherished the hope that he would. It would help her to get through the night.

Not a bad idea, she said.

The Fury vanished, like a vampire with a wooden stake thrust through its heart.

As she walked out into the glittering night, and our two guards closed the door after us, Eva suddenly stopped.

Did you hear something? she asked me. Was that the telephone?

Oh, come on! I said.

There was a band playing in the Hotel Platterhof, with dancing in all the function rooms. I didn't know where so many women had suddenly come from. Elegant young women in long off-the-shoulder evening dresses, with fur stoles that seemed to be in constant motion against their shimmering skin. They let the stoles slide off their shoulders, made them brush along the floor for a few steps like a pet following its mistress. Then, with an inimitable gesture, they swept them up to their necks again. I was immediately fascinated.

Perhaps the officers have their wives visiting for Christmas, I suggested.

Or perhaps not, said Eva.

We sat down at the bar. No one seemed to be taking any notice of us. The atmosphere was obviously extremely heated. Champagne had been flowing. You could see the silver buckets at all the tables. We decided on champagne ourselves.

I hadn't known you could dance Christmas Eve away at a party. As a bourgeois young Catholic girl I was surprised, and said so.

Well, now you know, said Eva.

We ought to have changed, I said.

No, said Eva. We ought not. And you won't let anyone ask you to dance, is that clear?

Yes, that's clear, I said.

Soon afterward the first hopeful dancing partner began making his way over to us.

We're not dancing, said Eva, before he could open his mouth. Kindly but firmly. Once again I was impressed by the sure way in which she dealt with matters of etiquette.

I saw the barman lean over the counter and whisper something in the man's ear. It wasn't difficult to guess what. Careful, he was saying, that's the Führer's mistress.

I saw the man give a start, and with a slight bow in our direction he disappeared as fast as he could.

This was a crazy idea of yours, coming here, said Eva. Still, we're here now.

I liked it. To hell with good upbringing and the rules of etiquette, I thought. All those boring Christmas Eves with my parents. The silence in our living room. The exclusivity of the nuclear family that celebrated Christmas by strictly isolating itself. The thin singing under the Christmas tree accompanied on the piano by my mother, who had been practicing for this occasion for weeks. I didn't miss any of it.

Oh, I don't need any millions,
Money doesn't make my day,
All I need is music, music, music all the way!

announced the singer in the hall. She was wearing a knee-length vel-vet dress and had her hair pinned up on top of her head in tiny curls that fell forward over her brow. A man in a glittering sky-blue suit had appeared next to her and began to tap dance with her.

Keep your feet still! Eva hissed.

I wanted to dance. Oh, how I wanted to dance. Instead I rapidly tipped another glass of champagne down my throat. Beside me, a be-hind covered with tight-fitting silk brocade settled on a bar stool. A blue fox fur fell head first from the woman's neck and slid with a slightly sinuous movement to the floor, tracing the curve of her hips. A man bent down, picked it up, and looked at me as he placed the blue fox fur back around its owner's neck, with a tenderness that seemed to be more for the blue fox than the woman.

Good evening, he said. I didn't know you were here.

We aren't really, I said. We're just having a glass of champagne and then we're going back.

What a pity, said the Obersturmbannführer. I would have liked to dance with you.

We're not dancing, I said bravely.

Even more of a pity, he said.

The world won't come to an end,

continued the singer in the hall.

Though the skies may now look gray,
Never mind what Fate may send
They'll be blue again some day . . .

The Obersturmbannführer and the wearer of the blue fox fur made their way to the dance floor. They were all making their way to it, joining to form a mass slowly coming to the boil, separate whirlpools uniting around a swirling center. The waltzing couples pressed close together, bumping into each other. They let the crowd catch and support them, dissolved into it, merged with one another, and the voices of the dancers, taking up the refrain, mingled with the singer's voice to make a single sound, the loud roar with which the living strike up a song to defy the chorus of the dead, the fearful to defy the fear in them, the guilty to defy the voice of conscience, shipwrecked mariners to defy the roaring of the storm that will soon destroy them.

I tried to remove my mind from it. I tried to catch something of the silence surrounding us, even here broken more and more often now by air-raid warnings. Allied bomber formations were flying over us in the direction of Munich with increasing frequency. We concealed ourselves under the artificial mist at ever shorter intervals. We still thought it sufficient protection. We still believed in the magic of the mountain, we thought our enemies could not find us there, we believed that the fortress in which we were secluded was impregnable. We still expected retribution to strike others, not ourselves.

We may go round the bend

sang the dancers in the Platterhof,

And our heads be all awhirl
But the world won't come to an end
Not for me, not for me and my girl.

Let's go, said Eva.
The Obersturmbannführer caught up with us at the door.
Wait, he said. I'll see you home.

When we reached the Berghof I offered to spend the night with Eva, but she refused.

Don't worry about me, little one, she said. It takes a lot to get me down, you know.

The two guards we had left behind opened the door of the house for her.

There, you see, said Eva, no harm can come to me.

Did she have no idea what this was all about? Couldn't she help me just this once by letting me spend the night at the Berghof?

I saw the Obersturmbannführer talking to the two men. *I* knew what it was all about. I saw their glances. They were in it with him. Their secret knowledge. Their satisfaction in seeing the suspicions they had long entertained of me confirmed.

I'll take you to the Mooslahner Kopf, he said.

He mustn't. I had to think of some way of stopping him. If I got back late at night Mikhail would be there. I'd have no chance of warning him. He would hear the sound of boots outside the house. He wouldn't understand how one of them could be with me. He would see me letting the man kiss and embrace me. Because I would. By now we had gone so far that it was a certainty. And Mikhail would think I was one of them now and was ready to betray him. I'd never be able to win his trust again.

I'd like to go back to the Platterhof, I told my companion when we had reached the foot of Hitler's stairway.

It was not a solution. Delaying tactics, no more. Just as everything from now on was not a solution, only delaying tactics. From now on my situation was the same as the military situation: desperate, but at no price must I give in. A hopeless tactical gambit; the war of procrastination now beginning could be ended only by the final victory of the Allies. I would have to defend an indefensible position until then. It would take that long.

Are you sure? said my companion. Haven't you had enough of the Platterhof?

I haven't danced yet, I said.

Then let's go, he said, starting out along the path to the Hintereck again. After a few steps he put his arm around my shoulders, drew me close and kissed me. There was nothing for us to lean against. We swayed slightly in the snow, holding each other tight like sparring partners unsure how to emerge from each other's clutches without falling over. Partners in love. Sparring partners. There's a moment when it can go either way. A moment when everything trembles in the balance.

You're a strange girl, he said.

We reached the Platterhof too late. The ball had turned into a boozing session. Hairstyles had slipped, glasses fallen over, ashtrays filled up faster than they could be emptied. Uniform jackets were slung untidily over the backs of chairs. The bar where Eva and I had sat almost alone was now besieged by a dense cluster of humanity. Men pressed close to women, women to men, gently pushing a knee between their legs. Hands that had been clicking cigarette lighters earlier were now laid on the curves of the women's buttocks, stroking them. Makeup was smudged. Cigarettes passed from mouth to mouth. No one minded who was drinking from whose glass now. The threefold ban on smoking, drinking, and using makeup did not apply to the German women gathered here.

The band had stopped playing and was just packing up its instruments.

Wait a minute, said my companion, going up to the musicians and giving the pianist a note—of how high a denomination I could not see. This young lady hasn't had a dance yet tonight. One more song, please. Just one.

And they unpacked their instruments again and switched on the microphone.

For a young lady who hasn't had a dance yet tonight, said the man at the piano with his erotically husky entertainer's voice. Shall we give her a last tune? What do you say?

Yes, yes, yes, called the men and women from the bar. Yes, give her a tune!

A lullaby for a good little girl, want to hear it?

Yes, go on, they cried, let's hear it!

Give me your hands once again in farewell,

sings the man at the piano, accompanied by a fiddle and a double bass, and the men and women standing at the bar join in the refrain with their slurred, intoxicated voices:

Good-night, good-night, good-night,

they sing. And my companion and I dance a slow waltz, our bodies entirely in harmony. It is the continuation of our long embrace, except that we now have the music and our dance steps to keep us balanced in equilibrium, an equilibrium somewhere between a duel and an embrace. I realize that this is what dancing was invented for. I give myself up entirely to his guidance . . .

You'll think of me again one day,

sings the man at the piano,

Lower your eyes and softly say . . .
Good-night, good-night, good-night,

the men and women at the bar join in. I feel their glances lingering on me. I know that in my pleated skirt and my pullover from Eva's winter collection I look like an ugly duckling among swans. I look like a girl with whom a man more than fifteen years older is about to fall madly in love. I know I look like that. I'm acquainted with the rules for falling in love in the Cinderella scheme of things. I bring to it the same elementary advance knowledge as the women watching, who, in their expensive evening dresses, their makeup now smudged, are suddenly confronted with this divergent pattern, which they know to be invincible. There is nothing they can do but be moved, nothing they can do but sing along:

Good-night, good-night, good-night,

like a benediction for me and my dancing partner. They are wishing we will spend a good night together, and the wish unfolds its whole insinuating nature as we dance. They watch us, and they see what in their eyes we are: a couple for tonight. They see the desire in my dancing partner's eyes. The women at the bar feel it themselves. They think of nights long past when a man looked at them like that, fixedly, through half-closed eyes. They move a little closer to their companions. They cannot take their eyes off us. They applaud wildly when the dance is over.

As we are standing at the bar amid all the crush, I hear someone ask: Who is she?

A cousin of the Führer's, comes the reply.

I am too tired to contradict. Too tired and already too much in the wrong to set anything right. I give in to what will happen. I am twenty years old and about to discover love on the Obersalzberg. It will be a Nazi love. A Nazi affair, inflamed by Nazi desire, and it will come to a Nazi end. Not a clean break but a total collapse. If we survive we shall not recognize each other again.

I see myself standing in the crush at the bar of the Platterhof. I see myself from decades away like a daughter I have lost, a child gone astray. I cannot warn her or hold her back. I know what is going to happen, and she doesn't. I see her looking up at the man who has put his arm around her. How small she is. She has that look of being in need of protection, which many men like in women, many men can't get enough of it. I would like to take the glass away from her. She is drinking too much this evening. I see the man do so now. Carefully, he takes it from her hands and empties it himself. She throws her head back, laughing. He is much taller than she is. Taller. More experienced. Older, and in possession of a degree of masculinity to match his military rank. It is only natural for him to be good-looking, it's the result of his masculinity. Nothing in her can withstand him. Everyone can see that.

But there is another game going on between the two of them as well. In this game he is dying of desire for her. He is head over heels in love with her. She can dictate conditions. Let her give the orders. He'll do anything for her, anything.

These are the old rules of the game of seduction, and they apply here, too. It could have been anywhere in the world that she first discovered love, but it's here. It had to be here. On Hitler's mountain. A Nazi love. It can never be undone now, it's a part of me.

I remained *virgo intacta* that night, which I spent in a room at the Hotel Platterhof. He was being considerate with me, as consideration was understood at the time. Men did not expect a virgin to go all the way on the first night, and since on general principle they were more experienced in love they took their time with us.

The hymen I defended with almost ludicrous tenacity was, strictly speaking, my only possession, and I still had it after several nights at the Platterhof.

In fact, diverting our lovers again and again from destroying it schooled our sexual fantasies, increased our sexual ingenuity. It put other ideas into their heads, guided them in other directions. And it was good for their own stocks of ingenuity, too, their ability to empathize. It was all in the cause of tenderness in bed that we begrudged the granting of our favors so long. The men swore the most extravagant oaths. They promised us whatever we wanted. They begged. They showered us with gifts. They could be delightful, tender, in a word irresistible as long as we did not, as one says, give ourselves to them. At some point they, too, realized that what we were withholding from them was of no importance, that this ultimate possession, so highly prized, was really something tiny, something that had long ago been superseded by another ultimate factor, and then—then—the time to give it up had come.

I remember the morning when I lost it in detail. It happened at a moment of inattention, a moment when I really did have other anxieties, when there were other things on my mind.

IT MUST HAVE BEEN IN JANUARY. We had celebrated New Year's Eve at the Platterhof, Eva and I. I had succeeded in dragging her away from the telephone at the Berghof, although in fact Hitler had helped by calling earlier than expected, during the day. She was cheerful and relaxed as we set off down the road to the Platterhof, this time in full evening dress ourselves. I was wearing a pale blue dress from Eva's wardrobe, and Eva herself was a vision in dark red.

I'm so happy, she said, now that the tide's turning.

Turning which way? I asked.

How should I know? said Eva. But the Führer sounded so confident on the phone.

Really? I asked.

You know, she said, those Englishmen of yours don't always know everything.

I'm glad, I said, specially now I hear it from you. Well, are the Americans retreating? Have we crossed the Meuse?

You don't think the Führer tells me such details, do you? she asked. I can tell from his voice if we're winning or not.

Perhaps your Führer had been drinking a little champagne, I said.

No, he never does, said Eva. You can be absolutely sure of that.

He doesn't drink a drop, even on New Year's Eve. No alcohol, no cigarettes, no meat ever.

Must be awful, I said.

That depends, said Eva. There are worse things.

Of course, I said. Far worse.

The New Year's Eve ball at the Platterhof would not have been to Hitler's taste. This was not a party for ascetics. The buffet was for hungry folk: goose liver pâté, larded saddle of venison, eels in aspic, Parma ham, appreciated at the time by only a very select body of connoisseurs . . . it was a party for gourmets. The hungry were elsewhere. Everywhere, in fact: in the camps, in the cities, at the front. Almost everyone went hungry. But here the tables were laid for the rest of us, the lucky few. Here we satisfied a hunger of another kind. A hunger for forgetfulness, amusement, oblivion.

We danced till morning. Eva danced that night, too. She, too, forgot and amused herself. We danced with the officers, the architects and construction managers of the bunker complexes, with the National Socialist Party district heads from southern Bavaria. I danced with Hitler's physician Dr. Brandt, with Bredow the head of the air-raid HQ, with Schenk, Bormann's deputy on the Obersalzberg. I saw sad Frau Bormann, more beautiful and melancholy than ever in the festive crowd, her heavy dark hair parted in the middle, her eyes black and grave, without the slightest expression except for her sadness, which remained always the same, like a woman already drowned who haunts the place like her own ghost, the loveliest depressive I ever saw.

Unlike Eva, who hid behind her cheerfulness, Frau Bormann let herself be seen in the garment of melancholy that clothed her. It clothed her completely, as it does in the portrait Pitthan painted of her in 1940 and exhibited in Munich: a Nazi *Mona Lisa* in a brocade dirndl.

At midnight we welcomed in the year of our downfall rejoicing. The year of countless deaths and unparalleled exhaustion. The year of the mass murder we committed, the year of executions and the end of them. The year of innumerable flights and rapes, the year of captivity, of hunger, of despair. The year of our defeat in more than merely the military sense. The year in which we would be swept away. The year when our disgrace would be made obvious. The year of the beginning of our shame. The year when we did not yet grasp, as in the years that followed, that it would be forever: the shame of our new German sense of nationality, slowly growing in us, making its way very hesitantly, very cautiously toward something new, something never seen in the world before, just as a nation arises from a historical experience: a nation ashamed.

The year we have only to remember in order to know there was reason enough for that shame: Year Zero, as we were already calling 1945 at the time.

Heil, heil, heil, we shouted. *Heil* the Führer! *Sieg Heil.*

I can still see Eva standing there, raising her champagne glass to the many who wanted to drink a health with her. Smiling, she takes on the role of our commander in chief's deputy, receiving New Year wishes on his behalf.

To the final victory! To the final victory!

As usual, there was something like an apology for being at the center of attention in her smile, the smile of a woman who was really rather shy. As usual, I see that she would like to steal away.

To victory! she says with warmth.

It is her last New Year's Eve. The year of her death is beginning. The year of her wedding. In a few weeks' time she will pack her bags for her last journey. She looks charming, in the way shy women look charming when they are slightly tipsy. That is how I would like to remember her. At that moment. Holding her glass aloft in the snapshot taken by my memory.

To what victory? says the Obersturmbannführer, who has his arm around me.

The final victory, I say, rather foolishly.

To *our* final victory, he says softly, leading me out on the dance floor. I shall spend that night in the Hotel Platterhof again. The man who loves me will tell me next morning that he must go back to Schloss Fischhorn, and he is not sure when he will be able to return to Berchtesgaden. I feel his pain at the parting. It confuses me. I myself feel rather relieved at that moment.

A period of grace, I think. Maneuvering for position. Delaying tactics. He must never visit me in the Tea House. Final victory?

Meanwhile, the Allied fronts are advancing.

The Red Army is moving toward the Oder. On January 17 it takes Warsaw; on January 19, Lodz, Krakow, Tilsit; at the end of the month it is somewhere between Frankfurt and Küstrin. Berlin is threatened. In the west, the U.S. Air Force is now attacking the Rhine bridges at Koblenz, Neuwied, and Remagen. The American pincer attack against the German frontal advance in the Ardennes at Houffalize closes in. Suddenly everything happening there seems quite close to us. A pincer attack on our fears.

One morning in the middle of January there is a knock at the front door of the Tea House. The cleaning women don't come until the afternoon. Eva has never been there at this time of day. I'm not expecting anyone.

I don't know where Mikhail is. I hope he hears the knock as clearly as I do.

I rise from my desk. I call on the spirits of cold calm and clever dissimulation. I go through the outer room. I see that the cellar door is closed. I fervently hope Mikhail will stay hidden there. I tell myself he must. He surely heard the sound of boots, I tell myself. Two pairs, I suspect. When they come they always come two by two. I open the door, I open it very slowly, because I am still trying to form a clear view of the situation. Would it have been better to act like a rabbit in its burrow, to pretend not to be here? But they have keys, it occurs to me as I am slowly opening the door, they'd get in anyway. Better if I can shake them off at the doorway.

There is only one man standing at the door. The man who loves me. The most dangerous of all. None of them can be as dangerous as the man who loves me.

He says he knows I'd asked him not to come here, and he respects my wishes. But he has only a few hours before he must go back to Schloss Fischhorn again.

It moves me to realize that he is feeling shy. It moves me in a way not entirely free of the satisfaction of having power over him. Over the dangerous, the powerful man who really has me entirely at his mercy if he wants. I recognize his fear of being rejected by me. If I were to close the door again I would be doing only what he feared on the drive here from Fischhorn. I could do it.

Will you let me in? he asks.

And for a moment I feel so strong that I am weak enough to let him in. He kisses me. I am under the spell of his self-consciousness. It is the self-consciousness that affects lovers when they meet again. A self-consciousness that can be overcome only by the consummation of love. Lovers take refuge in its consummation. They recognize it as the only way to escape their self-consciousness.

He half urges me, I half draw him into the tea salon.

So this is where you live, he says.

This is where I work, I say.

He glances at my notes lying on the table, and at Heisenberg's *Principles*.

You won't understand that, I say, taking the book from his hand.

He shakes his head.

Clever girl, he says.

I can think of only one way to distract him.

Have you ever been here before? I ask.

Good heavens, what an idea, he says.

He says it with awe, positively devoutly. I realize that he is well aware where he is. This little shrine, known to be the favorite place of the deity he reveres, and I, the priestess dwelling in it. I feel how

the aura surrounding me holds him spellbound. I show him the famous view from the Mooslahner Kopf down to the valley of the
Ache from the windows of Hitler's tea salon. The towering peaks,
the blue sky, the sparkling snow. I have that view at my command. I
am generously letting him partake of it, as of a divine supply of salvation over which I preside, allotting it to whom I will.

My God, he says, it's beautiful here.

I hear a noise in the background. As I turn I see Mikhail crouching behind the hearth. Motionless, pressed far into the shadows
between the hearth and the wall, he looks like a wood sprite, a small
and cunning goblin who will leap up any moment and dance around
the room like a flibbertigibbet.

My SS lover misunderstands the movement with which I have
turned to look at the room. We are now facing each other. The dramatic conventions of the moment demand that we kiss now, more
passionately this time. He presses me back against the window frame.
I have to move to one side, since otherwise I shall lose my balance
and stumble over the low window seat. I sink into the flowered linen
curtain. I am afraid of tearing it down. I guide my lover to one of
the deep armchairs. They are wide armchairs with heavy upholstery
and low seats. They seem to be made for giants, huge flowered laps
into which you can let yourself drop, too large for one person, not
large enough for two, so that we are lying partly beside and partly on
top of one another. We sink into the chair and try to find a position
that, if not comfortable, will at least be tolerable. My lover tries to
get us out of it. He sits up. He wants to go somewhere else. He wants
to go in search of my bed.

But he mustn't do that. I adopt and pursue the course of showing
that I am overcome by transports of silent ecstasy. I close my eyes, I
sigh, I bend back as far as my position in the armchair will allow, I let
him see I am beside myself, I can't do anything about what is going
to happen. And I really can't do anything about it! I am indeed beside

myself. I dare not let him be any less carried away than I am, not for a moment. He must not come to his senses. Not for a second. I know the way from the hearth to the door leads past our armchair. There is no other way. But as the one lying underneath—if there can be said to be any above or underneath in our tangle of limbs—it is from my position that I can check the escape route, and as I watch Mikhail's movement toward the door through half-closed eyes, looking into his wide eyes for the fraction of a second, I suddenly feel the pain of something in me tearing, and I realize that I have lost my virginity.

The most sobering moment of a woman's life when seen in the bright light of day. Nothing could be farther from the transports of love than this moment. A rending, a pain, a thought, clear as glass: so that was it. A fine rent, a razor-sharp dividing line. A moment like a knife. Impersonal, never mind who did it. No man will believe us if we say what it's like. A pain illuminating the setting like a lightning flash: Hitler's tea salon. An SS man. A boy in fear for his life. I myself. And no myth will be based on the incident, only the memory will remain.

I hear myself saying: I don't want a baby!

I'll be careful, whispers my lover.

Later I shall be worried about the chair, and scrub at it with soap-suds. Luckily the cover has a flower pattern with a good deal of red in it. I work away with the zeal of Lady Macbeth, returning to the task again and again. I want to undo what has been done. After a while I can't help seeing that I am making matters worse. The colors are bleaching out of the patch of fabric concerned. Hitler will notice at once when he comes home.

Sometimes I try to imagine him suddenly standing in the doorway, having come to drink tea in his Tea House. The mere idea casts me into a frenzied desire to be of service. Where would I find a table-cloth for the table? Has the silver been cleaned? The sugar bowl filled? Do I have enough biscuits to offer him? Where's the tray I ought to use? And what would be the right moment to pass on Hugh Carleton Greene's message? Even in my daydreams I am ashamed of the assiduity with which I am ready to be of service.

These are daydreams of the Hitler period. In the time after Hitler the same dream looks different. I imagine myself handing Hitler a cup of tea on the Mooslahner Kopf. Why not? I ask myself. After all, it was his house. It could have happened. In this daydream I am far from assiduous, I am perfectly cold, resolved to desperate measures. I have laced his tea with poison. I see him raising the cup to his mouth, drinking. . . . It could have happened, I tell myself.

The unwritten history of daydreams. The world of lies in which we walk, which we inhabit. The history of our lies may contain much history that is real. One might perhaps be able to deduce that history from them. From the way our lives change, and make changed characters of us. It is not we who create the lies, the lies create us. Fleeting subjects of a history we do not know. Fading illusions blotting each other out. Is that really me bending over an armchair with a flowered cover, trying to scrub away a bloodstain?

A little over three months later the Tea House will stand in an ashen lunar landscape scattered with ruins and riven by deep craters, one of the few buildings on the Obersalzberg still intact, together with the Kehlstein house, Speer's studio, and the houses on the Hintereck—too removed from the vicinity of the Berghof on which the bombers concentrated their attack.

On that morning I shall not be sitting at my desk as usual, but standing at the window and staring out, turning my back on two men from the security service whose orders are not to let me out of their sight for a moment. I shall be under suspicion of having committed a political crime. I shall be waiting for the arrival of our enemies, and nothing else. Where are they? I shall keep thinking as I look down into the valley of the Ache.

And then they come without warning. Suddenly there they are. They come over the Hoher Göll, and with them comes the urgent air-raid warning signal that ought really to be preceded by an ordinary air-raid warning. Suddenly I shall be aware of the distance to the bunker entrance of the Berghof, and think that they may be locking the doors there.

At this moment the difference between me, the prisoner, and my guards is no longer of any importance. The three of us simply run for it. And no sooner are we out of the house then my guards will leave me behind without more ado, overtaking me as they run, in fact they will even push me slightly to one side on the narrow path in order to get past me on the way to their own safety. They are two young men. What else are they to do? This isn't a matter of courage in the face of the enemy. I am not their adversary, only a woman, and a treacherous woman at that.

And suddenly, when I am already a few hundred meters from the Tea House, it will occur to me that I must have my Heisenberg. Without thinking, I shall run back, and as I come out of the house with the book the first bomb will fall somewhere nearby.

The blast will throw me back into the house, where I shall stand listening in the roaring noise of the four-engined planes overhead. I shall stand as if spellbound behind the door of the house, not knowing what to do next. I can't go out there, I shall think, and I can't stay here either. I shall feel like the only target of this attack. It will seem to me somehow pointless to hide. They'll get me anyway.

Then the noise of the aircraft will die away. I shall wait for the all-clear, but it will not sound. I shall stand listening for a long time, but at the heart of that silence there will be something growing louder, coming closer, a deeply malevolent note like the sound of a murderous swarm of insects in flight toward me, and I shall suddenly realize that the first wave was only the beginning, the next wave is coming, and then I shall run, knowing that I am running for my life, while they come down on us over the mountain peaks to the south, making straight for us. Then the first shock wave will throw me to the ground, and suddenly Mikhail will be there. He will grab me and haul me up the slope. From there, we shall see that the right wing of the Berghof is in flames. Before our eyes, huge fountains of earth will shoot up, rising to the sky and darkening it. The day of devastation is dark night.

We shall crawl far into the passageway, into the womb of the roaring mountain as it rears up, and as I press myself to the quivering rock beneath me I shall feel the book on my breast like armor, for I have put it under my jacket, and I shall think: If we are buried in the rubble it will be buried, too. No one will recognize us. No one will know who we were.

1.20

M. won't speak to me. He isn't touching his food either. I think that's going too far.

1.23

I've tried to tell him how it came about. But he's too young to understand. On the other hand, unfortunately, he's no longer too young to feel like a man. I think he despises me. He said a single word. I guessed what it meant, and looked it up in the dictionary. At least he's eating again, but only if I leave him alone in the kitchen. I'm sorry. I'd got used to our nocturnal conversations. The word means whore.

1.29

Eva says she's worried about H.'s health. She thinks his physician Dr. Morell is prescribing him too many drugs. I wonder if Hugh Carleton Greene knows that? I'm anxious about her.

2.1

Yesterday evening, on the radio, heard H.'s speech on the twelfth anniversary of his taking power. He says he will shrink from nothing to spare us the most terrible fate of all time. What is the most terrible fate of all time? And how can a sick man who swallows over 20 tablets every day spare us that fate?

2.3

Hans was here again. He's getting suspicious. He can't understand why I won't let him into the Tea House again. He says he suspected from the first that there was another man with me there. He has ways of finding out, he says. What am I going to do? I'm afraid of him.

2.4

Now that H. is back in Berlin I can sense Eva's restlessness. She may well go to join him even if H. doesn't want her to. Although we are probably losing the war she always seems certain of victory, is always radiant. Does she know more than the rest of us? There's something the matter with her. She wants to spend her birthday in Munich. We leave tomorrow.

2.7

I think Eva's overdoing it. Celebrating her birthday as if it were the final victory. Singing and dancing late into night. Down to the cellar a couple of times in between. The usual crowd: Schorsch, Mitzi, Kathi, and the others. And Aunt Fanny and Uncle Fritz. At some point I went upstairs. Why are you so quiet? Aunt Fanny asked me. Her, too. I can't understand it. Nobody talks to me. There's nobody I can talk to.

My God, how young I was. How desperate to get it off my chest. I needed to so much. I wanted my cousin's help, her ear, her advice, her support. Her willingness to listen to me, that's all I wanted. Her readiness to know what I knew, understand what I understood. At twenty you are desperate to confide in someone. I almost did.

It must have been in Munich, the day before Eva's birthday, when she is going to be thirty-three. It will be a farewell party. These days every party is a farewell party.

The city is a ghost town now. You count the buildings still standing, not the ruined ones. There is no glass left in the windows anywhere. The window openings have rough boards nailed over them, where they aren't gaping open like dead eyes. There seems to be nothing behind them. Blackness. The city is blind, dark. It looks uninhabitable, although there are still people there. But apparently half a million of the inhabitants have left.

Men and women no longer look different from each other. A race of gray people in woolen caps, old wool coats, long trousers. The children are very well behaved. They have learned that shouting does no good. They are terribly quiet, and very small. The older children were evacuated to children's homes in the country long ago, where it's supposed to be safer, and where they cry themselves to sleep night after night with homesickness.

In 1945 this Munich is the only city we know. We see the destruction and believe it is final. This is Munich, we say. This is what it has become. This is how it will be. We shall live in this city, we say. And we know other cities are the same.

We do not know the word *reconstruction*. We could think up such an expression but we don't, because we can't imagine the possibility of such a thing. We would be unable to think who could have the strength for it. The money. The materials. And above all the work, who would do the work? When this is over we shall be simply too tired for such an effort. We shall be rats living in cellars, emerging now and then to go raiding. We are the race left over when the human world has died out. We are those who will have to live in the former cities, in the rubble, in the dark ruins, like thieving vermin. Nobody else survives in such cities. We do not see them as cities not yet reconstructed. We see them as they are.

We see ourselves in them.

On the evening of the fifth of February we have to go down to the air-raid shelter in the cellar. There are air-raid warnings every night now, although often they portend only nuisance attacks. No one can get any rest in Munich these days.

This time the two of us are alone. We sit side by side on the folding seats against the wall. If it were not so dreadful it could be quite cozy. It gives me the illusion that only the two of us exist, just Eva and me in our fortified shelter from which a corridor leads out into the garden and the open air. Twin children in the womb of the world.

Eva shows me a gold bracelet set with pearls and diamonds. I don't need to ask who gave it to her. She takes it out of a box hidden under the folding seat opposite. It contains many more things of the same kind.

She says that if she dies this is to be mine. She shows me a matching ring and brooch. She tells me she made her will in October, and left this to me in it.

But make sure you get it, she says. They'll try to trick you out of it if I'm not here.

I don't ask who she means. I say: Goodness, what's all this about? You're not going to die. You don't need to make a will.

She says nothing.

Eva, I say, what are you planning?

You know what, she says.

You could go to my parents in Jena, I say.

What would I do there? says Eva.

Nobody there would know who you are, I say.

You haven't the faintest idea, have you? says Eva. Everyone knows who I am.

I realize I have made a mistake. Eva's sensitive spot; her pride in being Hitler's mistress.

But Eva, I say, you're not married to the Führer.

I know, she says curtly.

I only meant, I say, that you can break it off with him anytime you like. You're not his wife. And then you can start a new life.

I know just how hollow my words are. I know I have to tell her she is dying for the wrong man. But whom does a woman see as the wrong man? A criminal? Is that any kind of argument? A criminal on the grand scale? The perpetrator of murder and atrocities in unimaginable numbers? A man who devastates a continent? Causes immeasurable suffering? Is he the wrong man—and is that any kind of argument?

If I had asked Eva the question she would not have held it against me. I'm not even sure if she would have contradicted me. It would not, so to speak, have touched her sense of feminine honor. It would have achieved nothing.

But if I'd told her: I don't like him. I really think he's unattractive. Even stronger: I think he's repulsive. He's old. He's ridiculous. He's worn out. He looks like a loser. I can't bear to think of him touching you—then she might well have hated me, and shouted at me angrily and thrown me out of the house, but perhaps she might have lost the desire for her own grand finale. A little pinprick and all the hot air of heroic sacrifice would have leaked out, leaving only an obscure affair in the life story of my cousin Eva Braun, an affair better not discussed any further. She would have broken with Hitler before it was too late. She would have been able to slip away unnoticed. The rest of the whole sad tale would have been silence.

But I didn't do it. I could not bring myself to say that to her. Anything else, not that.

Since then I have experienced, over and over again, the affirmative power inherent in one's choice of partner. Once that choice is made, and made public, it is inevitably confirmed by outsiders. No sooner is a couple's engagement announced than congratulations hail down. The lover is touched to discover what a wonderful person his or her chosen partner is.

There's no one who will say: Take a good look at this person you've fallen in love with. What strikes you? Yes, quite right: he or she is unappealing.

Does love need the nourishment of other people's hypocrisy in order to grow and thrive? A kind of unspoken, collective conspiracy, interested not in happiness and success but simply in the sealing of a pair-bond? I was part of it myself. I, too, could not bring myself to use the only argument that can dislodge love.

And so, a few weeks later, Eva will receive congratulations on her wedding. She will raise her glass, will smile, look dreamily at the man beside her. He will not raise a glass. Even if he drank alcohol he couldn't because his hand would shake too much. Thank you, Eva will say. Thank you. Many, many thanks. And with that slight touch of awkwardness and timidity that makes her so charming, she will offer her hand to the guests congratulating them. Good luck. Good luck. Good luck, they will say, wishes echoing through the room that lies sixteen meters underground in the midst of death and destruction.

And none of those present in the great conference room of the bunker under the Reich Chancellery, not Hitler's secretaries Traudl Junge and Gerda Christian, not Generals Burgdorf and Krebs, not Axmann, not Goebbels and his wife, and certainly not Bormann, will tell my cousin that she has married the wrong man. Not just any wrong man, but the worst choice of man a woman ever married. They will not say he was wrong for all those who threw in their lot with him, wrong from first to last, wrong, wrong, wrong. And although they have known it for a long time now, although hardly any of them will come away unscathed, they congratulated her sincerely. They congratulated her on her choice. Thirty-eight hours later she will be dead.

I, too, bow to the affirmative power of her choice of partner. I myself will not say to her face what I think about him. (I *find* him old. I *find* him repulsive. I *find* it intolerable to think of him even touching her, and I can guess the rest.)

Get yourself somewhere safe—that is all I beg Eva. Of course she has no intention of doing any such thing.

But *you* ought to go, she tells me. Don't stay here at the Berghof. If they find you, you'll be one of us.

One of what? I ask, stupidly.

Us, she says.

And that phrase echoes on in my mind. For the first time I have some presentiment of a world that will exist after us. A world where we shall no longer be the same. Carefully, I try out categories. We. I. They.

I'm not one of you, I say.

And hearing myself say that, I am suddenly carried away on a wave of confidence, courage, a deceptive sense of my own abilities. Something brushes against me, and I shall recognize it again later: a state of mind that no longer distinguishes between boldness and carelessness. You just want to say everything once, express it that one time. You want to be as free as you feel.

I can't leave, I say.

Are you in love? she asks.

I don't know, I say.

What is it, little one? she asks. If I can help you I will.

I suddenly hear myself talking about responsibility, a responsibility too heavy for me to go on bearing alone.

Are you pregnant? Eva asks.

No, I say. No.

Just then we hear the all-clear, and I realize I was about to give Mikhail away. At the same time I suddenly know how Eva can help me, me and the boy who has taken refuge with me and is endangered by my lover.

I tell her I'm confused about my feelings for Hans. I need time to think. He's pressing me, and it would all be easier for me if we could be apart for a while.

This is the kind of language she understands.

Fischhorn is too near, says Eva thoughtfully. Now, if he were in Berlin . . .

Then you could meet at the Adlon, she adds, suddenly back in familiar waters.

Eva, I say, there's not going to be much left of the Adlon.

I don't want to see her retreating into such stupid ideas.

But Berlin would be just the thing, I say.

It depends on Hermann Fegelein, says Eva. He's his superior officer. They were in the same brigade in the Russian campaign.

Oh yes, I tell Eva. If you do go to Berlin, maybe you could ask Fegelein to fix it as a favor to you. I mean, he's your brother-in-law.

I don't know, she says. I don't like doing that kind of thing.

Do it for me, I say.

I'll try, says Eva.

Later, long after the Nazi period, I shall discover that the SS cavalry brigade commanded by Hermann Fegelein shot six thousand civilians in Pinsk in August 1941.

I'm not one of you, I hear myself saying.

But I was.

CHAPTER 7

THERE WAS A SPELL OF PREMATURE SPRING
weather in February that year. When I look at the notes I made in
my Heisenberg, it suddenly comes back to me. The smell of melting
snow. The warm southwest wind, sometimes rising to storm force.
The colors on the horizon: turquoise blue, yellow. The mountains,
ultramarine and white.

ENTRY IN HEISENBERG, p. 103 (quantum theory of wave fields):
The first blackbird. Eva has gone.
   I didn't enter any date.

FOR TWENTY-FOUR HOURS I act like a husband whose wife has
walked out on him. I am indignant. I'm baffled. I don't believe it.
I say: It's not so much the fact that she's gone. It's the fact that she
didn't say good-bye to me. Imagine just leaving like that!
   I wait for her to call me. But she doesn't call. As there is no tele-

phone in the Tea House I go to the Berghof several times in the evening to ask if she has rung.

No, she hasn't, says the housekeeper. But madam will be sure to come back. Everyone will come here in the end, she says.

I think so, too. What else? When Berlin can hold out no longer, at the very end, there will be only this Alpine fortress left. This is our refuge. We shall defend ourselves against the rest of the world here.

Then you'll be one of us, Eva said.

We. I. They. Against the rest of the world.

But I know from Hugh Carleton Greene that the Allies have reached the Rhine. They are in Kalkar on February 27. The "West Wall" falls. They will get here some time. It won't be long now.

I don't know which I ought to fear most: the arrival here of the Allies or of our own people. Since I don't know I just hope it will be quick. Whatever happens, let it happen fast.

This is the attitude of the trapped, those besieged by the enemy. Our fortress cannot be held indefinitely. We don't know what will happen to us, we only know that things can't stay as they are. No one will get away. We are ducking our heads, closing our eyes. We are acting perfectly calmly, listening for sounds from the world outside. Are they here yet? We fall victim to the apathy of the already defeated. Perhaps it would be a good idea to play dead? Anything that gets us out of this intolerable state will be welcome.

We can no longer tolerate ourselves. Our falsity, our cowardice, our depravity. We want to be released from the web of false loyalties, never mind by whom. We are ready, at last, for defeat. Let it come. Let it come soon.

How much longer can I keep Mikhail hidden? How much longer can I keep the man who loves me and the man who needs me away from each other? How much longer can I protect myself from both of them? How much longer? When will I ever get away from this mountain? It is as if some curse kept me here. I myself am a fortress

that has long been indefensible. Ready to be stormed. Ready to surrender. Tired of defending myself. I avidly listen to the news of the
approach of the Western forces. The Americans! Oh, I wish they
would come. Where are they?

We. I. They. If you stay on the Berg you'll be one of us, Eva said.

I am one of them. I am one of us.

The housekeeper raises an eyebrow slightly. Are you staying on?
she asks me.

Suddenly I am revealed in my true colors: an extra mouth to feed,
a guest who has outstayed her welcome. From today my presence at
the Berghof requires justification.

Didn't my cousin say? I ask.

She didn't say anything, says the housekeeper. She didn't say good-
bye to me either.

That reestablishes a link between us. She's hurt us both by leaving.

I'm waiting here until she comes back, I say. That's what we
agreed.

And will you still be sleeping at the Mooslahner Kopf? asks the
housekeeper.

Yes, of course, I tell her.

Fancy you not being scared, all alone there, she says. If you like I
can have them get your guestroom at the Berghof ready again. Only
if no other arrangements have been made, of course.

Thank you, I say, but please don't worry about me. I'll stay at the
Mooslahner Kopf. I like it there.

I sense that this doesn't strike her as much of an argument, but I
can't think of a better one.

You can still eat at the Berghof, that goes without saying, says the
housekeeper.

I am suddenly aware that it no longer goes without saying. At the
same time it occurs to me, for the first time in ages, that I have no
money. While Eva was still here that didn't seem to matter. Mistresses

don't need money. They don't pay bills. They get all kinds of services free. Nobody asks to see their ticket, their pass, their entrance to the best seats, the boxes where the VIPs sit. Suddenly I had no ticket. Suddenly I realized that if only for lack of funds I had to stay where I was.

Even if one could still have traveled through Germany by train at this time, in March 1945—which one couldn't, for you were in more danger on the railways than anywhere else when your enemies were attacking not just with bombs but with low-flying aircraft carrying air cannon—even if I had felt like risking my life in that way to get home I couldn't have bought a ticket at the station. I don't think Eva did that on purpose when she left me behind on the Berg on my own and went to join Hitler. It was not like her to picture the consequences of her actions in much detail. Not when they were nothing to do with her and the man who was her sole concern. Not when they had nothing to do with the grand finale toward which she was now making her way.

She simply left me behind at the Berghof. Alone, just as I had come. She abandoned me. Was she an egoist? If she had had an ego she might have been. But she had nothing of that sort. No authority working for her own advantage. The opposite, if anything. The egoism of people like her is an urge for self-destruction that reliably prevents them from thinking about other people. My problem was that I had trusted Eva, and kept expecting something from her.

But we can't go serving separate meals just for you, says the housekeeper. Meals for the staff are eaten in the staff kitchen.

Yes, I see, I say.

Then winter returns. Quantities of wet snow bury us in the Tea House. It falls softly, insidiously. Suddenly there is a wall outside our windows on the side of the house facing the mountains. We can see the sky only through their top halves. We haven't known anything like this all winter. And it keeps on snowing.

I wait for a detachment of guards to come and shovel the place free. But no one comes. The morning passes. I don't know how I am to reach the Berghof. I feed the fire in the hearth with the briquettes I still have. They are dwindling. I don't know how long the stock will last. A day? Two days? The snow is over a meter high on the path outside the Tea House. It is heavy snow, a constant mass weighing down where it falls. It's the kind of snow that crushes roofs, sets off avalanches, a malevolent snow.

I don't even have a spade. I try forcing a path through the snow. I give up.

Mikhail tries, too, but I stop him.

That's no good, I say. I'm the one who has to get through, not you.

But even he couldn't get any farther.

He asks me where my friends are.

I guess exactly what he means by that question.

They're not my friends, I say.

When dark falls it begins to snow again.

At home, Mikhail tells me, they used to tie staves from wooden casks under their shoes in winter, and then they could walk over the snow.

I don't tell him I have a pair of skis at the Berghof. Eva, who neglected no form of sport, sometimes insisted on my skiing with her. I hated it. There seemed to me something wrong about it, and when I watch the old sequences of film today, I know why: that playful tumbling about, that romping to the accompaniment of squeals and shouts of glee almost always ended in a fall, and could hardly do otherwise because our bodies had not mastered a crucial skill, and at the time we didn't know what it was. Prewar skiing was simply transported from the hills of Scandinavia to the Alps, and something wasn't right about it.

Not until the 1950s did they reinvent skiing as a sport on the

Arlberg. Strange that our bodies didn't know it of their own accord: a slight shift in the body's center of gravity, a twist of the shoulders, and there you had it: the heavenly, matchless elegance of skiing, taking control of Alpine topography and the human body at the same time. It took me a long time to forget my experiences of skiing with Eva: her dogged determination to get some fun out of the tumbles we took.

I often declined to accompany her, pleading pain in my knee. But now, a prisoner snowed in up at the Tea House, I'd be very glad for a pair of skis.

That evening we share a packet of biscuits. We eat all of them but two. When Mikhail is about to reach for the last biscuits I take them away from him, saying: For the morning.

Just for a moment I am afraid of him, of the savagery with which he snatches them from my hand. Then I see that reason is triumphing over his wolfish instincts.

You not eat, he says, a question in his voice.

I promise I won't.

Now all we have is the stocks of canned milk that the staff kept replenished, as if they might expect a visit from the master of the house at any time. Six cans of condensed milk and some sugar. That's more than many people buried under the snow have as iron rations.

It snows for four days on end, almost without stopping. Around noon we sometimes think the snow is turning to rain. On the valley side, masses of snow slide off the roof and fall like avalanches to the valley. We hear a dripping somewhere. It's the thaw, we say.

But in the afternoon we see thick, solid snowflakes falling densely. A soundless burial. I don't even know if the house can still be seen from its side of the mountain. Perhaps the round tower of the tea salon is still sticking up. We at least can't see anything in that direction. The snow comes up to the roof and may perhaps cover it. If the slope didn't fall so steeply to the valley we wouldn't be here anymore.

It's been a long time since we could open the front door. We're lost without a trace. Even if anyone wanted to rescue us it would be difficult.

But who would want to rescue us? No one at the Berghof knows I'm still here except the housekeeper. As time goes on she assumes demonic characteristics in my mind. Why does she want to murder me? Why is she doing it? What does she know about me? Or is this the way they get rid of guests here when the guests don't go of their own accord? Suppose Eva phones and asks after me? Will she lie then?

On the second day we take a kitchen chair apart and try to make snowshoes out of it. I tie them to my shoes with a sheet torn into strips and climb out of one of the windows on the valley side. But it is so steep that I immediately dive headfirst into the masses of snow, and as I try to struggle out again one of the boards comes off my foot. I am stuck in the snow with a twisted ankle, while more snow keeps falling on me. I can see Mikhail trying to climb out after me. That way neither of us will get back into the house again!

I call to him to stay where he is. I need something to hold on to. I feel the snow giving slightly beneath me. It is nearly noon. Avalanche time. With the temperature rising, if only slightly, I could start an avalanche sliding down to the valley with me at its center. Luckily I realize that only later. At the moment I just feel as if I am stuck here forever, in this icy cold envelope of snow, which is being melted by what body warmth I still have to form a solid carapace molded exactly to my body, enclosing it as tightly as if I were cast in concrete.

I have to wait until Mikhail has wrenched out a floorboard. He has little more than his bare hands and some kitchen cutlery to do it with. It turns out that the floorboard isn't long enough. It won't reach down to me. Mikhail has to tear up another sheet.

Finally, when I reach for the knot, my hands are far too numb to catch hold of it. Mikhail manages to fasten the sheet to the window,

I don't know how. By now I am noticing nothing but the slight give of the snow beneath me. I don't feel the cold anymore, only the pull of the snowy current underfoot, constant, eerie, tugging me away with it. Then Mikhail is with me. He seizes my hand, pulls me up. The sheet holds. I manage to get the remaining board off my foot, reach one of the knots in the sheet with it, and push myself off. Then I feel myself being pushed onto the floorboard. I have a firm foothold now, and at some point we both fall back through the window and into the house. I'd rather die here than out there in the snow.

On the third day the heating packs up. We have used our whole stock of briquettes. It is still snowing. I never knew how much snow the sky could hold. Strange for it to finish like this, I think. There's something embarrassing about being buried by the snow in the middle of war. It doesn't seem a proper way to die. The airmen I can hear fly over us as if in derision, dropping their bombs somewhere else. That has nothing to do with me now; only the voices from the radio still reach us.

The city of Cologne has been taken. The Red Army has reached Pomerania. The German troops still fighting around Danzig are cut off. U.S. bombers have destroyed part of the city of Tokyo in a major raid.

Cologne and Tokyo are equally distant from where I am now. The war has forgotten me, and I have forgotten the war. When the snow melts, I think, they'll come here. Hitler. The Americans. Never mind who. It's none of my business now.

Mikhail and I pile all the blankets and cushions, anything with any warmth in it, on my bed. Then we lie under the pile together. The cold still hurts. That means we're still alive. They say that at the end you don't feel the cold anymore. We assure each other of that. We know it must be true.

I say I read it somewhere.

Mikhail says everyone knows it.

Good-night, I say.

Good-night, says Mikhail.

But the next morning I am still alive. It's even quite warm under our blankets. I remember that Eskimo igloos are said to be pleasantly warm. Perhaps the covering of snow around the house can warm us? It's a pity we have nothing left to eat, though. Even Eskimos can't live without food.

Then I hear voices. Quite close. I hear one man shouting at another.

Here! he shouts. Here! You knew, for God's sake! I shall report you! Incredible! he shouts.

I hear the front door being opened; the next moment the man who loves me bursts in. I burrow my way out of the bed, heaping blankets over Mikhail as best I can. My lover pulls me into his arms.

You're still alive, he says.

The room is full of SS men.

Go on, light a fire, he shouts. Get the bathroom stove working! And bring some breakfast!

Two breakfasts, I say.

Two breakfasts! he shouts.

Three, I say.

Hear that? Double helpings! he shouts at the men.

I try to get him out of the room. You can see there's a floorboard missing in the hall.

I tried climbing out of one of the back windows, I say.

My God, he says. How on earth did you do it on your own?

Soon afterward he is watching me eat breakfast at the kitchen table.

He arrived from Fischhorn the day before, and at the Platterhof they told him that Eva and I had left. No one knew for certain where we had gone. So he went up to the Berghof to find out where we were. He discovered that I was still here but hadn't been seen for days. She supposed, said the housekeeper, that I'd been going to the Platterhof to eat, because I hadn't been back to them since Fräulein Braun left.

And then, says the man who loves me, a terrible idea suddenly occurred to him. He went down to the road and saw that the path to the Mooslahner Kopf was invisible. There was nothing but snow piled meters high at the roadside. It had taken them all night to make their way through to the Tea House.

So here we were, both of us heroes, both of us exhausted. I a mistress of the art of survival, he my rescuer. It seemed impossible to avoid the logical idea that we must now finally belong to one another, our relationship sealed by the overcoming of obstacles, by the harsh trials we had withstood to come together. After that nothing seemed possible but to fall into one another's arms and live happily ever after.

If only I'd been here sooner, says my rescuer, this wouldn't have happened. But it was impossible to make much progress on the roads with all this snow. And even for us it's getting harder and harder to find petrol, he says. Don't worry now. I'll try to get transferred here. I'm well in with the Gruppenführer—he means Fegelein—so it should be possible. Then I can take care of you. After all you've been through.

He takes my hand. He kisses it. He looks tenderly at me. I realize he thinks I stayed here for his sake. Eva, I think, help me. Don't forget your promise. And hurry up about it.

I rise to my feet. I must act. I must take charge before he thinks of making his way to my bed, the bed in which Mikhail is still lying under the blankets.

This house seems like a prison, I say. I must get out of here. I need to see if there's anyone else around. Oh, let's go!

I can see how you feel, he says. We leave the breakfast tray in the kitchen. Butter, fresh rolls, plenty of breakfast left. I know Mikhail will fall on it as soon as we're out of the house.

The path leading from the Tea House to the road is a ravine between walls of snow. The sky clears for the first time in days. A full thaw has set in. We are suddenly surrounded by springlike air, and the war is back again, too: There's an air-raid warning. The artificial mists rise around us, enveloping us. They darken the sun above us again. The next moment the urgent air-raid warning sounds. As we are close to the Berghof we make for the bunker entrance beside the old part of the building.

They're all there inside one of the caves, the domestic staff, the chauffeurs, the guards, even the housekeeper. I pull myself together. I mustn't cross her, I think. Anyway, a bunker with the air-raid sounding is no place to have a quarrel.

I ask if Eva has rung.

The *gnädiges Fräulein*? Yes, she says.

Did she ask after me?

No, she says, she only asked after the dogs. Oh, my God, I forgot the dogs!

What dogs? one of the chauffeurs asks.

Fräulein Braun's dogs. Those two miniature schnauzers, says the housekeeper. Stasi and Negus. I hope nothing happens to them.

Stupid tykes, says the man.

He speaks with scornful precision, as if he were spitting at a particular spot on the ground and meeting his target accurately. His scorn is meant for my cousin and, as I clearly feel, for me, too. Stasi, Negus, and I are all that's left of Hitler's whore on the Berg.

Didn't she leave any message for me? I ask the housekeeper.

Wait a moment, she says. A message? No. No, I can't remember a message.

Think! I say.

Oh, dear me, she says. Perhaps the *gnädiges Fräulein* sent you regards. But everything's upside down in Berlin. She'll have other things on her mind.

Very likely, I say. She'll be back soon.

Stupid tykes. She'd thought of them.

Soon afterward the all-clear sounds. They'd only been flying overhead again. Up here on the mountain we expect no less. We are Hitler's Alpine fortress. They won't dare to bomb us.

We see one of the labor columns outside. The men have obviously taken cover from the risk of an air raid by the tall ramparts of snow at the roadside. They are knocking the snow off their clothes and reforming under the orders of the overseers. Many of the men have no shoes, only rags wrapped around their feet. They must be wet, and the gray cotton drill jackets with the Eastern workers' badges are wet through, too. The men wear them as if trying to crawl into them and become invisible. They are thin enough. Their jackets hang off them like wet sacks.

Look at that, I say to my companion.

It's the late shift, he says. They're working on the bunker extension.

How long does the late shift go on? I ask.

Why should that interest you? asks my companion. There's no reason for you to be interested in that.

They look so worn out, I say. Do they get anything to eat?

Of course they do, he says. After all, they couldn't work if they didn't. They get everything they need. They even have . . . He stops.

What do they have? I ask.

They even have their own brothel, says my companion. With their own Polish whores, so they won't be any threat to the safety of German women. Everything laid on, you see? They're well looked after, I can assure you. I'm sorry, I shouldn't have mentioned that to a lady. I'm only telling you so that you'll know, so that you won't get any silly ideas about the treatment of foreign workers in Germany. They're well off.

Information about the sinful side of life. I haven't been one of the grown-ups so very long, and this kind of thing still embarrasses me.

I have no idea what the world is like, but I begin to suspect that evil is the rule. I'm just too sheltered, too naive, in short too young to understand that sin and depravity are normal. I am not familiar with wickedness. I'll have to learn. Just as long as I don't show my weakness.

Are they? I say.

They're glad to have work here, says my companion. Why do you think they came to the Reich? They're not human like us, don't forget, he says, suddenly very serious as he turns toward me. They don't have the same feelings, the same desires, the same, he chooses his word, the same visions as us.

Visions? I say.

Yes, he says, dreams. Like you and me. Dreams of a life of dignity. Greatness. Distinction. Pride. Courage. They don't know anything about that. We are creating a world of high ideals and values. These people are good for nothing but the coarsest kind of work. They can't do anything else and they don't even want to. Of course you have to treat them strictly to make them work. Those Easterners are lazy at heart. Well, look at them, he says. See what they look like.

I look at him instead. He looks good. I go to the Hotel Platterhof with him. We shall spend all afternoon in bed.

I learn a hateful, a damnable lesson. I learn it too early. I'm too young for it. I learn to separate myself from my body and throw it into the fray on its own. I learn to watch it in the process. I learn to let it do as it likes. I use it. I let it be used. I discover that it enjoys being separate from me. I learn the lesson my body teaches me. It has no conscience, I discover. My body loves what I hate. It lets itself love and punishes me with self-contempt for my wish to despise it. My body, exhausted and sweating on damp sheets, my body, after all, is myself.

It is a whore's lesson I learn. I learn it in revulsion, desperate, horrified. It's not a lesson I wanted to learn.

I shall never be all right again, I think, I shall never be happy, in love . . . I shall never be anything but lonely.

What's the matter with you? asks my lover.

If he touches me again I shall kill him.

I have to go home, I say.

And at that moment Hitler's Tea House does seem like a home, a refuge.

But you can stay here, says my lover. We can dine in the restaurant this evening.

Oh, I can't, I say.

My lover laughs. It is an affectionate, relaxed, amused laugh.

You're not a married woman with a husband expecting you home, he says. One might think you had someone else.

Are you going to have me watched? I say.

Yes, he says. Yes, I am. You'd better not keep any secrets from me. Don't do it.

He is lying with his arms behind his head in the tumbled bed, watching me as I dress. Very much my satisfied lover. Very much my owner.

For instance, why would you want to go to the Tea House this evening? he asks. I'm free until tomorrow morning.

I hate this mountain. I hate him. I want to get away from here. I hate them all. I hate Hitler. I hate the German Reich. I want the Americans to come and liberate me.

All right, I say. I just want to go over and change, and then I'll be back.

Good, he says.

On the way I'm able to look in at the Berghof and fetch my supper from the staff kitchen, for Mikhail.

I thought you'd be eating at the Platterhof, says the housekeeper. But of course we're here for you any time.

Thank you very much, I say.

My life on the Obersalzberg is a fortress that can no longer be defended. Ripe for storming. Ready to surrender. I am waiting for the army that will relieve it. I'm waiting for Eva to help me. She did promise, I tell myself. I am waiting for help from a woman who is arming herself for her marriage to death. I wait in vain.

DURING THE MONTH OF APRIL things changed on the Obersalzberg. They changed imperceptibly, changed while, in an oppressive way, they still remained the same. The anticipation of disaster did not prevent us from going about our usual daily business. A day before the end of the world we were still eating breakfast, setting store by punctuality, noting our expenses.

As before I was spending the mornings with my physics books, drawing diagrams, solving the model exercises in the supplements that led to preparation for the preliminary diploma. I would have passed the exam. I was well prepared. I was sure of my facts. I acted as if the coming trial I must face was a physics exam. I was preparing blindly for the unknown toward which I was making. One had to do something to arm oneself. I studied with a kind of furious sense of duty. I gave myself up to the coasting sensation of autistic keenness. Nothing could exceed the correctness of my results. I would not let the slightest carelessness get past me. I didn't have to compel myself. I was under compulsion already.

Meanwhile, more and more guests kept arriving on the Berg. Suddenly it was crowded. The Platterhof and the Berchtesgadener Hof down in the village were fully booked. The guestrooms in the Bechstein house and the Berghof itself filled up. Every day the limousines of the car pool brought new arrivals: SS men, escort parties, orderlies. . . . It looked as if this was an advance guard, the vanguard of a vanguard, quartermasters preparing for those who would follow, the real VIPs. The camp followers arrived. Wives who didn't understand, disoriented, still hit hard by parting from their children, left behind somewhere with grandparents. Why? What were they doing here? What did it all mean?

My cousin Gretl, heavily pregnant with the child she was to have in May, Aunt Fanny, and Uncle Fritz also arrived at the Berghof. Gretl was absentminded, distracted, almost out of her mind with fear. She was haunted by the notion that her baby would be born dead. Aunt Fanny couldn't leave her alone for a moment. As soon as she stood up Gretl reached for her hand.

Aunt Fanny herself no longer seemed able to find anything amusing in the situation. She talked of nothing but Eva. She was waiting for her. I never again saw a human being wait so intently for anyone as Aunt Fanny waited for Eva then. She was like a mother whose little girl has been abducted and who is now waiting for a message from the kidnappers. I felt sorry for her.

Eva's friend Hertha suddenly turned up, too. Now the entourage was complete. Only Eva was still missing. Everything seemed to suggest that she would soon be back. The court was assembling again. That must mean something.

For the last time, the Berghof ideal was revived: the Berghof as the invulnerable core of what we were defending, our innermost war aim. The Berghof ideal was truth, beauty, permanence in the world now collapsing before our eyes. It was meant to be immune to the evil now imminent, an indisputably solid value, a sense of patriotism that could be experienced even by those whose emotional traditions were not of the Alps. They were now withdrawing here. To this place, where they meant to live on into a future that they hoped must after all be theirs, as one always expects the future to be. There is no other.

They believed they could survive at the Berghof. They were glad to find it so well fortified. They praised Bormann for making sure that so many of them could take shelter in its bunkers. He's done an amazing job, they said. That was all part of their mental survival kit, too: the miracle of German capability and efficiency. If they were to be defeated, then at least let it be here.

They didn't just want to survive. They wanted to save something of themselves for the new life that would come after them, and which they knew there was no stopping now. Something must remain. The Berghof core of their world. They gathered around it like the inhabitants of a besieged castle around the last hearth where a fire still burns.

At the same time, it was the center of the Nazis' emotional life. They warmed themselves here, and gathered strength. They felt at home here. They had withdrawn so deep into the place that they thought, against all reason and in defiance of all appearances, that they would be safe from their enemies and could not be found here. The phantom of a fortress of Alpine stone that now no longer meant only the Obersalzberg but the whole mighty mountain range at the heart of Europe, as if, defying any militarily precise defense strategy, they could finally withdraw into the mountains, that phantom was a delusion so closely corresponding to the desire in their hearts for warmth, security, and some kind of reliability in all they saw breaking up around them that they gave themselves up to it without resisting, congratulating themselves on being safe in their refuge, while really nothing but a little theatrical mist concealed them when enemy reconnaissance planes flew overhead, mist that made the precise location of their refuge obvious on clear days: It was just below the spot where the mists were rising.

I say "they." But what had Eva said? You're one of us here.

We drew closer together.

New arrivals came to the mountain daily. They came and they stayed. On April 20 the Berghof was prepared for a possible birthday party. People were claiming to know that today, his birthday, Hitler would be back from Berlin. These rumors were persistent. Flowers were brought in, tables laid, champagne chilled. The kitchen of the Platterhof was ready to prepare a buffet. But the day passed, one of the last few days before the destruction of what we knew as the Berg, and Hitler did not come.

Nor was the hiding place in his Tea House discovered. Nor was I found out. Nor did they take the boy away and kill him.

I told him it wouldn't be long now before people came to liberate him.

Who are they? he asked.

The Americans, I said.

And the Poles? he said. Are the Poles coming?

The Poles? No, I said. The Russians. The Russians are coming, too. They've already taken Vienna, and they'll soon take Berlin.

Vienna, he said. Is that far away?

Not as far as Berlin, I said.

I did not notice at first how horrified he was.

The Russians—then he must get away, he said.

I promised him the Americans would be here before the Russians.

Where are the Americans?

In Nuremberg, I said. That's quite close. They could get here in two days, I said.

I had no idea what would happen then. I would no longer allow myself to think about it. Like everyone else, the generals, the fighting troops, the army staff officers, the domestic staff, the concentration camp overseers, the antiaircraft auxiliaries, the Gestapo officials, the gauleiters, block wardens, air-raid wardens, Red Cross nurses, field hospital doctors, secretaries, steely Nazi administrators, representatives of the Reich women's organization, holders of the Mothers' Cross, Hitler Youth—like everyone else I simply carried on as before. Hitler carried on as before. So did Bormann, Himmler, Goebbels, Keitel. They all carried on as before. Hitler gave orders that no one obeyed now. Bormann prompted him, offering bad advice whenever necessary. Himmler led his Death's Head units. Goebbels talked grandly, his own emotion moving him to tears. For some time Keitel had been only the empty shell of a field marshal, poring over maps he could no longer read. They were already as they would be when they entered Hell, already entirely prey to a diabolical repetition compulsion, always repeating the same actions, carrying them out with the same pointless fervor—crime and punishment together. They were resistant to redemption.

Who is that man? a Dante of the future will ask a future Virgil. The man clenching his fists in front of his face, the man who has shouted himself hoarse and can't stop shouting now? And who are those others?

Don't you know them? Virgil will ask. Everyone knows who they are.

And the two will pass swiftly on.

Then, in the last days of the Nazi period, we were all under the spell of that repetition compulsion. We had Nazi habits, Nazi anxieties. Nazi ambition was still as lively and strongly motivated as ever. Wehrmacht soldiers were still bursting with pride as they received the Iron Cross. Promotions came thick and fast: from sergeant-major to lieutenant, from colonel to major-general. The social standing of intricately related families still depended on such things, and they still aroused resentment. Intrigues were plotted, alliances forged.

No one said: Another twenty . . . eighteen . . . fifteen days and we won't be here anymore. No Cassandra raised her voice, warning us to consider our own destruction.

There were still another four days to go there on the mountain, in our royal citadel, our Nazi Troy, when Göring arrived the day after Hitler's birthday. He came with a great retinue, Chief Adjutant von Brauchitsch, Reichsleiter Bouhler, Reichsminister Lammers, the whole court of satraps. Emmy and her daughter were with us on the Berg, too.

I happened to be looking toward the Hintereck when the column of cars came driving up toward Göring Hill. I recognized the Reichsmarschall himself in one of the cars. He, too, I thought. He's coming to the Berg, too—what does it mean? What did they all mean to do here? Were we to survive or to die with them?

I would only have needed a close look at the uniform the Reichsmarschall was wearing to tell me the answer, at least so far as Göring was concerned.

Did you see Göring? my lover will ask, for he, too, is here with us at the end. Didn't you notice anything striking about him?

What am I expected to notice that's striking about Göring? Göring is Göring. Everything about him is striking.

Exactly, says my lover. That's why it's particularly striking when he doesn't want to attract attention.

For all of a sudden he has exchanged his silver-gray uniform for a grayish-brown one. The epaulets, usually five centimeters wide and made of gold braid, have been replaced by a plain mark of rank, the marshal's eagle, positioned as inconspicuously as possible. If you didn't know for certain it was Göring you might think you were looking at some American general, says my lover. Or someone who'd like to be an American general, don't you think?

I don't know, I say. I'm not acquainted with any American generals.

Göring is a traitor, says my lover.

He should know, because he has arrested the Reichsmarschall. Göring is under house arrest, under his orders. The whole Berg suddenly seems to be under my lover's orders. He is the man of the moment. (It is April 23, two days before our annihilation.)

It is late evening. When I am about to leave the Berghof, where I have been playing Catch the Hat with Gretl to give Aunt Fanny a rest from her maternal duty of constant hand-holding, a couple of men from the security service stand in my way.

You can't leave here, they say.

I see the muzzles of their submachine guns. I just don't believe it.

This is the first time since last summer anyone has threatened me with a gun.

The easy life, the luxury to which we have treated ourselves, the holiday paradise of our existence on the Berg—yet they have always been there: guns, to be used at any time, even against us, and men who will turn them against us if ordered to do so.

Who's your superior officer? I ask.

It seems as if this is the right reaction to this turn of events for the part I'm playing. I probably picked it up from a film.

We have our orders, says one of the men curtly.

From whom? I ask. I am the Führer's guest, I add. That's my ticket for a free ride. My Open Sesame.

A man steps out of the background, also armed, obviously the one giving the orders around here.

I immediately change my tune. I do it instinctively. I am a submissive little woman in need of help. But I now pay dearly for my ignorance of army ranks.

Oh, Gruppenführer, I say. That seems to me about right. It sounds like a rank without too much power, but a rank not without power either.

Scharführer, the man sharply corrects me.

Scharführer, I say. Sorry.

I think I must have underestimated his rank first time. Later I shall discover that by addressing him as Gruppenführer I have put him up there with the lieutenant-generals. He thought you were laughing at him, the man who loves me will explain carefully. He himself can only dream of promotion to Gruppenführer. It's his great aim in life.

Please, I say, Scharführer. I have to go to the Mooslahner Kopf.

No, you have to stay here tonight, he says. All the buildings in the Führer's restricted area are surrounded, including the Tea House.

I must stay calm.

Who's your superior officer? I say, trying again. Who gave orders to place us under arrest?

The Führer, he says, smiling. Obviously he isn't duty bound to take me seriously.

I'm a cousin of the Führer's, I say as firmly as possible. I want to be told.

The answer I get is my lover's name.

I am surprised. I haven't seen him since the end of March, and I was thinking that Eva had kept her promise to me after all.

I want to telephone him, I say.

Not allowed, says the Scharführer.

Oh yes, it is, I say, you wait and see. Please send a message through that I want to talk to him. I'm sure you can do that.

Ten minutes later my lover arrives. I see that the security men are deeply impressed by this. They are impressed by the fact that the Obersturmbannführer has a liaison with a cousin of the Führer's. And they are impressed by me.

Two days later we shall go under. But we are still the object of admiring glances, a plane of projection for the happiness they envy. We, so close to power. We, so privileged. We, so much in love, so young, so attractive. Whispering to each other after my lover has put his arm around my shoulders and drawn me aside.

He didn't have much time, but he quickly told me what had happened. Göring had tried to seize power from Hitler and take his place. He wanted to hand us over to our enemies without a fight, while the Führer in Berlin was boldly defying them in order to defend our capital from the advancing Bolshevists. As a result, Göring had been arrested and forced to give up his offices under threat of the death penalty.

I thought briefly of Hugh Carleton Greene, and fragments of his broadcasts shot through my mind ("a clique of criminals," "no mercy on their own kind"). But he would hardly have regarded Göring as our savior.

Only later, when all of this was past history and belonged to another world in which we had been other people, did I discover what actually happened: Göring had telegraphed Hitler asking whether, in view of his decision to stay in Berlin and, as could be predicted, die there, he, Göring, was to regard himself as Hitler's successor and take over his official duties, as specified in a law of June 29, 1941. It had been a cautiously phrased question, ending with the hope that Hitler might yet escape from Berlin. What could a man like Göring have betrayed that had not already been betrayed long before?

At the time, and at close quarters, I understood none of this. I couldn't understand why the old dramas were still being acted out on our tottering stage. Dramas of betrayal and faithfulness, revenge and regicide. The protagonists were still declaiming their way through old conflicts, forming new bands of followers. Hotheads were still fanning the flames of insubordination. Intriguers were weaving nets to bring others down. The faithful reported at once and readily offered the loyalty they owed. Those who trimmed their sails hesitated for nights on end deciding which side it would be best to come down on. Toadies bowed low. The stiff-necked remained stiff-necked. Those who had been passed over continued to suffer resentment at being passed over. And although they were in free fall together already, there were some who would still try to topple others if the opportunity arose.

I was on this tottering stage myself, involved as I was in a liaison with one of the less high ranking officers, a young guards officer, a minor character in the drama, of attractive appearance, to be sure, the two of us reflecting and providing a commentary on the main plot on our less important level.

So now what? I ask, rather stupidly.

Now I'm responsible for all security measures, he says. Arresting conspirators, imposing curfews, searching premises.

Searching premises? On the Mooslahner Kopf, too?

There, too.

You must stay at the Berghof tonight, says my lover.

I can't, I say. I don't have a nightdress or a toothbrush. . . . And I don't think they have a spare bed for me at the Berghof.

The question of the bed where I am to spend the night is occupying his mind. I can see it. At the same time I see how drawn he is to his great tasks of imposing order, maintaining the state. The man's double message comes through to me. It says: I have much more important things to think about than you. It also says: Although I have much more important things to think about, you are more important than anything.

It is the message of both his strength and his weakness. It captivates me. I have never tasted such a heady mixture before. I lean back against a doorway. But my lover remains unapproachable. He does not follow my choreographic guidelines. He stands in front of me without moving.

At that moment I would do anything to keep him from wanting anything but me. I want the utmost sacrifice from him, the sacrifice of power. Just now, if he would give me that, he could drive me out of my mind. At the same time it is the aura of his power that unleashes sexual desire in me, that and nothing else. I see the holster of his pistol at his belt. The leather is gleaming. What would he do, I suddenly think, if I were to put my hand on it, just touch it? After all we've already done.

I put out my hand. He takes a step back.

I'm sorry, he says, but it can't be helped. You'll have to stay here tonight.

I spend the night with Gretl, who whimpers quietly to herself in her dreams. I can't sleep. I keep thinking of Mikhail all night. When they have found him, they will come for me, too.

In the morning we are told that no one can leave the house yet. We breakfast in the bay window of the dining hall with its pine paneling up to the ceiling: Aunt Fanny, Uncle Fritz, Gretl, Hertha Schneider, her two little girls, and me. Eva's dogs lie at our feet. We present the perfect picture of a large, talkative family beginning the spring day with a hearty meal.

It is a pleasant place in which to breakfast, there in Hitler's dining hall. In sunny weather like this it is bathed in a flood of warm, agreeable, honey-colored light that makes the fine grain of the wood on the walls seem to glow. Everything in this room suggests solidity. Everything speaks of a sense of well-being conveyed not only by its furnishings, the fine wood, the floral decorations still arranged for the birthday of the absent master of the house, the attractive shades of red in the huge oriental carpet under the dining table that will take twenty-four guests, the curtains patterned in the red of the leather-covered chairs and the honey-colored tone of the wood, but above all by the height from which we look down over the valley as if from a pulpit, enjoying the famous view of the Watzmann massif, the view that appeals so much to the master of the house, particularly on days like this, when an immaculate blue sky extends overhead and the snow has withdrawn to the higher parts of the mountains. It could be a picture from an Alpine calendar.

The situation of the Berghof, halfway up the mountains, tempts one to feel on familiar terms with the great giants on the other side of the wide valley, as if we were as far above the plains below as they are.

Someone opens a window, and the mild air drifts into the dining room of Hitler's Berghof. Spring will come to the mountains now without many preliminaries, forceful and triumphant. Spring will be victorious. There are already royal blue gentians to be seen on the way to the Tea House, and the cowslips, violets, and anemones are in flower. The leaves of the beech trees are unfolding. Trees will soon be in blossom down in the valley. There is something of all that is in the air making its way in to us. It carries a message, the same every year, a message to the poor hearts overwintering within us. Be of good cheer, says the message.

Teacups clink. A curtain moves gently. Everything must change now, everything, our hearts tell us. Even now. I can't believe I am lost, and none of the others around me believe they are lost either.

There are two prealerts at the Berghof during the morning, and the blue spring air is clouded by dark gray mist. The birds fall silent. Bombers thunder overhead and away. It is like a sinister mingling of the seasons. As if we could dispute the spring's dominion with impunity. As if we could soil and humiliate it.

That afternoon I am told I'm to go to the Platterhof. The way things are now, that is an order. I am accompanied this time not by two men following me at a distance, but by one on each side of me as if I were a dangerous delinquent. I don't know if I am being taken to an interrogation or a lovers' tryst.

There are a great many SS men milling around the foyer of the Platterhof. My guards ask what to do with me and take me to one of the doors on the first floor, where I am made to wait.

When the door finally opens I enter a suite of rooms obviously converted into an ad hoc office, the HQ for carrying out security measures after the coup d'état of which Reichsmarschall Göring is accused.

Not a lovers' tryst, then.

But the two SS men flanking me are sent out again, and the door to the next room where a typewriter is clattering away is closed. I am alone with the man who loves me.

What's all this about? I ask.

He looks at me for a long time. I cannot interpret the expression on his face.

We've searched the Tea House, he says.

The spring air of Berchtesgaden comes in through the open window. A superfluous spring that has nothing more to do with me, which excludes and derides me.

So? I say.

I try to sound as indifferent as possible.

We found something, says my lover.

He looks as if he hasn't had any sleep. Like someone carrying a burden too heavy for him. Our conversation is one of long pauses and duels fought by our eyes, which I win more often than he does. But it is clear that it is not a good thing for me to be delivered up to an obviously overtaxed man, and one who, in addition, still loves me.

In the cellar, he says. Someone must have been in the cellar. Someone was sleeping there. Don't tell me you don't know anything about it.

Well, I don't, I've no idea, I say. It must have been before my time in the Tea House. I mean, I'd have noticed. I've never been down in the cellar. What would I want there?

Suddenly the whole thing seems to me farcical. As if we were in an amateur production of a mediocre detective play, acting to an empty auditorium.

Did you notice anything? he asks. Anything suspicious.

No, I say. No, I didn't. That's to say . . .

What? he asks.

I tell him about the suspicious things we'd noticed before I moved into the Tea House. The open fridge door. The used towel in the bathroom.

That must have been him, I say. The man who was sleeping in the cellar. But there's been no one in the place since I moved in.

Are you sure? asks my lover.

I suddenly feel that he is really concerned about something different. He looks at me long and hard. Is he bluffing? Has sentence already been passed on me? Have they found Mikhail? Or did he manage to get away from them? I cling to that possibility.

There's something else, says the man who loves me.

I know that the surprise about to be sprung on me will be no real surprise. I shall know a moment in advance what is coming next. I need to know, so that I am not so vulnerable. But however feverishly

I try to think what it can be, something awkward, some small detail that has escaped me, something hidden, something that will give me away, I can think of nothing, except that his name, his first name by which I have never called him, comes into my mind. That is a dark, obscure spot, the sore point of our relationship: the fact that I never call him by his first name.

Hans, I say, as if I could ward off discovery in that way. As if this were the reason why he had to subject me to an interrogation: my reluctance until now to speak his name. Hans.

I feel I am blushing. I am moving from one level of conversation to another, which is impermissible: a cheap attempt to use our private relationship to win an advantage. Almost an attempt at bribery.

I can see that this catches him off balance, too. The magic of our role-playing game is gone, giving way to a sense of overwhelming awkwardness that exposes us to each other.

Here, he says, placing a sheet of paper torn from one of my notepads on the table.

Not my Heisenberg, thank goodness, I think. All I noted down on those pads was calculations and diagrams.

Look at this, he says.

It is written in indelible pencil in Cyrillic script.

I can't read that, I say.

Nor can I, he says. But I've had it translated. It says, literally:

We last met outside the big barracks gate by the floodlights, dear Marlene—and so on and so forth—But when the smoke mortars generating mist are switched on this evening I shall be by the floodlights as usual, dear Marlene.

Who translated it? I ask.

Trust me, we have translators in the security service for all enemy languages. That's no problem for us. This is in Ukrainian.

It's "Lili Marleen," I say. Someone's translated "Lili Marleen" into Ukrainian.

My lover looks at the piece of paper in front of him.

But the smoke mortars . . . he says.

I recite the last verse to him.

Resting in our billets, just behind the lines
Even though we're parted your lips are close to mine.
When the night mists swirl and churn,
To that lantern I'll return,
My Lili of the lamplight, my own Lili Marleen.

Quietly, incredulously, he joins in with me until we are speaking in unison. It is as if Lale Andersen herself were stepping through the wall. We are chanting, almost singing, with her voice. No song in the world is better suited to speech-song than "Lili Marleen." As in the film, it sounds quiet at first, then grows stronger, and the love theme returns, although we both know that this is good-bye, the finale of our Nazi love story, which will perish with the Nazis themselves, ruined and extinguished. Even the memory of it will be dust and ashes.

Where does it come from? he asks again, in an unrelenting voice. Where did you get this piece of paper? Who wrote it?

No idea, I say.

I know that only lying will help now, but even that, I also know, won't really help. Now that his jealous suspicion of my fidelity has been laid to rest, the other, worse suspicion remains. Jealousy made him weak, laid him open to my little diversionary maneuver. But now it's serious.

There was someone with you in the Tea House who shouldn't have been there, he says.

There wasn't anyone there, I say.

Then where does this come from?

I don't know, I say.

The radio in your room was tuned to an enemy transmitter. Marlene, he says, his voice suddenly very soft, I can't afford this kind of thing. Everyone here knows I have a personal interest in you.

Have you? I say.

He does not reply. I realize I am genuinely making him suffer. I realize how serious he is about the battle he is losing.

Everyone listens to enemy transmitters, I say. How else are we supposed to find out what's really going on? Or haven't you heard that the Americans have reached the Elbe?

We have other sources, he says.

I hope you'll find out in good time when they get here, I say.

You can be sure we will. And we'll give them the reception they deserve, says my lover. But just at the moment we have other things on our minds.

Other things? You mean you think I'm a spy.

You don't understand me, he says. It's not a question of what I think. It's a question of laying all suspicions to rest. Doubt makes us weak. Having a traitor in the camp like Göring does us more damage than any enemies can do from outside. If we are true and keep faith and are blameless, then we're invincible. Then we are German. A true German keeps faith. Don't you understand that, Marlene? No ifs and buts. That's how we are. We don't play a double game. We are absolutely true. Absolutely faithful. Absolutely German. That's our secret weapon. That's what makes us superior to others. And we shall win with it. I say what I tell you now for your ears alone, but we have no other weapon left.

He seems to be expecting me to contradict him. I don't.

That's why it is so important, he continues, for you to tell me the truth now. It's more important than ever, now that everything most sacred to us is in danger, now that our great ideal is endangered. It all depends on us. Who will act correctly, properly, reliably if we don't? There must be something left to cling to. So I beg you . . . I beg you, Marlene . . .

His voice has dropped to a hoarse whisper. He is almost stammering, pleading.

What are you begging me for? I ask.

The truth! he shouts at me.

He is shouting for the benefit of the men in the room next door. And for himself. He has remembered that he's subjecting me to an interrogation.

The truth is that we're beaten, I say. None of this will be important anymore once the Americans are here.

I see, he says. So my sweetheart's already preparing to welcome the conquerors.

An ugly grimace twists his face. He is trying to be sarcastic.

Like all men, he is most dangerous when he is weak, but I am not old enough yet to understand that. I don't realize that he would rather kill me than see me fall into enemy hands. I don't know the pattern, as ancient and simple as it is cruel: The last defiant action of the defeated warrior as he surrenders is to kill his own wife so that she cannot bear children to the victors. It is the scorched-earth strategy of retreat, the spirit in which Hitler's last orders are issued: Leave nothing that the victors can still use. Destroy the bridges, roads, industrial plants, transport routes. Leave the enemy a civilization now turned to desert.

Listen, says my SS lover, his voice dropping to a whisper that certainly cannot be heard outside the room where he and I are alone, I could have you shot, you know I could. But I won't. Oh no, darling. No one is going to touch a hair of your head unless I say so. And I won't say so. Why would I? I love you, you know I do.

I hate the tone of voice in which he is speaking to me. I hate it not because it frightens me, but because I feel that his sarcasm is artificial. I know my lover better than he would like. Nonetheless, what he has just said has not failed in its effect on me. I have understood who is in power—for the time being.

But if even the slightest suspicion of political unreliability is con-firmed I won't be able to do anything for you, he continues. In that case please don't count on me. Personal feelings will never influence my decisions. You know that. You're going to be taken to the Moo-slahner Kopf now and you will stay there until further notice under strict house arrest. And closely guarded. Don't doubt that. No one will come near you without being spotted. You won't be able to take a single step unobserved day or night. Think about it!

When I am outside the door, flanked by the guards who are to es-cort me to the Tea House, I am tempted to turn and say something else. Some kind of clarification to ease the tension, something crucial that has not been said between us. I don't know what. Something to cancel out this all-or-nothing game, this love-against-duty situation. It is an impulse that I shall recognize later in my life, in other love quarrels.

Stop, I have always wanted to say. Let's start again. That wasn't us. A kind of nervous compulsion to laugh sets in, and I have to fight it harder than the fear that lies in recognizing how close misunder-standing, anger, a final break has been to love all the time. Such a small step unleashes it. The Fury of lost love is suddenly so immedi-ately present.

It can be called back. It can be overcome. It is a chained wild beast lurking in every love affair. But now, meeting it for the first time, I know for certain that this is serious. It is the end. I shall not turn around. I shall not laugh. I shall not say: You can't mean that seri-ously! Have you forgotten how we feel about each other? In this first love quarrel of my life it really is all or nothing. A matter of life or death. I can't pretend to myself it isn't. And the wish to laugh that I try to control as I walk down the path to the Mooslahner Kopf between two security men is only the expression of my helplessness and fear: I don't know where Mikhail is. I don't even know if he is still alive.

★ ★ ★

THAT NIGHT MIKHAIL WAKES UP in his hiding place, the narrow passage into the mountain from which he fled on the day when the snow came. Now the snow is melting again, and he is back here. He has made no further progress at all on his way to Korcziw.

But now the time has come. He got the message the evening before. It came in with the air drifting through a window opened just a crack. Winter is over, said the message. Time to go.

And suddenly everything was clear to him. He had only to take the first step. He would go back to Korcziw, whoever were the masters there now—Russians, Americans, Germans, it made no difference. His mother could hide him just as well as the girl here.

In any case, he couldn't believe that from now on there would be any other life for him but a life in hiding. As it was now, he thought, it always would be. He had learned to hide. If there was one thing he had learned it was the art of invisibility. Making no sound. Leaving no tracks. He already felt startled by the sight of his own shadow or reflection. He wouldn't be surprised if there were nothing there at all. Nothing of him. If anyone could manage to get to Korcziw then he could. They wouldn't even be looking for him anymore. All the same, no one must find him. He knew that.

By now he was so much at one with his state of concealment, so closely related to it, that he couldn't believe anything would change even if the Americans came and liberated him. The Americans were masters, too, weren't they? They, too, would want to know who he really was.

So who was he really? The only place where that could be decided was Korcziw. And perhaps the dog was still there. Perhaps he had waited. Mikhail felt sure he had waited.

He filled his lungs with the air coming in from outside. Buds. Earth. Grass. When? he wondered. And as he asked himself that question he already knew the answer: Now. At once.

Shouldn't he wait for the girl? Wait for the food she would bring him? He would need his strength, and from now on he would be living only on what he could steal. (He did not know that there wasn't much left to steal in Germany.) But then he decided to go at once. Darkness would favor his plan. There was still some bread in the kitchen, and he took it with him. Then he put on a lady's woolen pullover, blue with a cable pattern, without guessing that it had belonged to Hitler's mistress, slipped into his gray drill jacket with the wreath of sunflowers on the breast, and left the house.

He had been a prisoner long enough to know that only extreme caution would help him now. He made straight for the bushes, looking for cover, hiding as best he could. But then he saw them. He hadn't expected them to be waiting for him, ready to pick him up as soon as he left the house. Not just two men either, enough to rout him out and catch him, six or seven of them coming along the footpath toward the house on the hillside. Mikhail pressed close to the earth. Where he lay he could feel the ground shake under their feet, a trembling not to be distinguished from his own. He wished he could disappear into the ground entirely, be one with it, nothing but a place on which their boots would tread without feeling a heart beating there, breath going in and out.

Then he suddenly knew the only place where he could take refuge, and when they had passed he crawled to the entrance of the tunnel from which he had emerged six months before, the place known only to him, concealed behind ferns and tendrils, and he hid there.

He had spent all the next day waiting there and keeping watch, well aware that he could leave his hiding place only in the dark. He had seen the restless coming and going of the guards that day. He felt their high state of alert, and thought it must have to do with him. His flight had been discovered. He thought it possible that the girl had given him away. Since finding out that she was the German overseer's whore he had always been slightly wary of her. He was a man, and convinced that when women belong to a man they are subject to him, and will tell him any secret if required to do so.

He is freezing. Sometimes he sleeps briefly. He ate his bread early in the morning. Now, in his second night here, it is hunger that will not let him rest. He thinks of the cold roast meat she often brings. The eggs she sometimes fries for him at night. He tells himself he must have one more proper meal if he is going to make it to Korcziw. Moreover, it is terribly cold. He leaves his cave just before midnight.

All seems calm. He knows the guards have usually already made their round by this time of night. As he comes closer he sees the light in the house, taps on a window, hears a noise behind him and sees that he is surrounded. They've caught him. Next moment she arrives. Let go of him, she shouts. Then he hears her say: I don't know him. I've no idea who he is.

That's how he always imagined her betrayal. Women. They'll tell any secret to the man they belong to.

He is taken to a detention cell in the barracks. At least it's warm here, and they give him breakfast in the morning. He's been worse off in his time. So long as they don't shoot him he doesn't mind. But he suspects that is exactly what they will do.

Most of the time he sees fields of barley behind his closed eyelids, bordered by elder and hazel bushes. He imagines dogs hunting among the ears of barley. He follows the waves rippling through the corn as they chase their quarry, a lively movement dying down and rising again and again. He hears the loud barking of the dogs hunting among the ears of corn.

But then he is suddenly roused by the barking of real dogs. Everything around him seems to be very loud, very agitated. The door of his cell is flung open, orders are shouted. He gets up and follows the guards. But he knows very well that this is about the guards themselves, not him. "Urgent air-raid warning." He knows what that means, too.

They run across the barrack yard to one of the bunker entrances. SS men stream up from all sides, each trying to outstrip his comrades. And Mikhail realizes that they are afraid.

This is the sudden new discovery, a revelation coming into his mind as he runs—the fact that SS men can be afraid—that suddenly gives him the courage to be cunning, the courage of the hare in the barley field deceiving the pack by doubling back, and as the first aircraft appear overhead Mikhail sees his chance. Just before reaching the gateway to the bunker, he turns off into an alleyway between two garages.

He presses close to the wall and sees, looking back, that no one is following him, hears the mighty sound of the engines above him, the whistling and howling, the salvos of antiaircraft fire. Only now, much too late, does the sharp, acrid artificial mist rise from the smoke mortars by the roadside, and he runs into it to hide. But there is no one left aboveground to whom he matters. They have long since closed the heavy steel gates of the bunkers. Anyone still out here is lost. And Mikhail runs on, coughing and breathless. He knows where he is going, and when the first shock wave flings him to the ground he makes himself get up again at once and run on.

This attack is not for him. It won't get him. He will run home at last. No one can stop him. He's on his way.

And when he sees that the aircraft in the sky have moved away again, when he can hear nothing but the crackling of fires from the Berghof, he knows that he will make it. It's now or never. He will be well outside the restricted area by the time the men emerge from the bunkers. Let them look for him. They won't catch him this time. He'd sooner be dead than their prisoner again, forced to go down once more into their deep tunnels, their world without daylight, the terrible, cramped, dark universe of their mountain, but then he sees the girl running down the path from the Tea House, and hears the second attack wave coming.

Stopping for a moment, he sees what is flying over the mountain peaks. It is as if the mountain giants themselves had risen and were hailing projectiles down. They show on the horizon, more and more missiles falling from the aircraft. They descend on Hitler's mountain like a shower of arrows. They will hit it, destroy it, they will leave nothing behind, Mikhail knows that. No one will survive outside the shelter of the bunker complex. And he runs toward the girl. When he has almost reached her the first shock wave catches them both. They fall flat in front of each other, as if a great god had suddenly descended between them, a god before whom they bow down in the dust, shaking.

Mikhail is the first to get to his feet again. They are both bleeding from their noses, eyes, and ears. They don't feel it. He takes hold of her and pulls her up the slope with him. He knows every small rocky projection here, every root offering a firm handhold. He calls out brief orders to her in his own language, and she understands. There are no languages anymore, only the insane bellowing of the mountain as it shakes. As it rears up. And the darkness in which it envelops itself. The darkness of a clear, sunny April morning. A darkness made of ashes, smoke, fountains of soil dispersing as they fall, and artificial mists, illuminated by fires shooting up here and there, after some minutes unfolding into the spectacular glory of a blazing, triumphant conflagration that will leave nothing of what it attacks behind.

Long, long after the bombers have turned away particles are still falling from the air. They drift in the spring wind, play around the charred tree trunks, dance over the heat of the smoldering fires here and there, and finally settle over the mountain in a grayish-white, powdery shroud. Only then does the full extent of what has happened emerge.

A FEW YEARS AGO I spent my holiday in Bayrischzell. I had rented a mountain cabin on the grounds of a sanatorium, a small cabin just for me, but near the main building where I would have company, good cooking, and medical treatment. An ideal place for me to be alone yet not alone, independent and yet well cared for.

I left home in bright sunlight, in a good mood, and with a case full of summer clothes. It was May.

When I reached Bayrischzell a wall of mist arrived at the same time and stayed on, as if it had made an appointment to meet me there. It was noticeably chilly, the electric heater in the cabin either uncomfortably hot or not warm enough. They always did make you feel the cold lying in wait as soon as you ventured into their sphere of influence.

I had not expected the silence surrounding me. Is it true that mist swallows up sounds, or do we imagine it? All that I heard when I strained my ears was its soft trickling sound as it constantly dripped gray from the trees. And you do strain your ears when you can't see anything. Life must still be there somewhere, surely. Mist. There's a horror film in which evil approaches in a wall of mist rolling over the sea. You watch it coming closer, making directly for you. There's no escape. As soon as it reaches you all hell will be let loose.

I had asthma attacks every day. The doctor could do nothing to help me. I told him about my fears. Indeed, I spoke of the most shameful of all the sufferings to afflict me. I told him I was on my own and could not bear to think that if I screamed no one would hear me.

Why would you need to scream? he asked. Do you feel pain somewhere?

No, I said.

The fact was that I was afraid of dying alone. This is surely what all patients confide to their doctors at some time or other. And certainly every doctor has his own little patent remedy for this ultimate complaint with which they approach him. But the prescription he gave me was no use.

Perhaps it might have helped if I had moved into one of the

rooms in the main sanatorium. The cabin, with its back to a wood of tall spruce trees and the famous view of the valley, now veiled in mist, in front, displayed all its terrors to me only gradually. I dared not put on the light because I couldn't be sure if I might not be seen from outside. Sometimes I thought I heard footsteps stalking around the place. I felt as if someone was there watching me. Someone with his mind bent on me ever more frequently, ever more exclusively. When I opened the front door I thought I heard the steps move swiftly away toward the outskirts of the wood. When I came back I had to pluck up all my courage to enter the cabin, where I encountered a darkness that withdrew before me into the corners of the room, but still lingered there.

I left early, but while I drove into sunny early summer weather soon after leaving Bayrischzell, the sense of oppression still weighed on me, and even when I stepped into the familiar entrance hall of my own house something of the darkness from which I had fled was there in the corners, and a waiting silence received me, the sounds of my presence echoing in it like something strange and unwanted, as if a victorious vacuum had spread through my house while I was away, and was not immediately prepared to withdraw now. It had been living there. It regarded the house as its property, and spared not a thought for me.

Only several months later did I have the photographs I had taken at Bayrischzell developed. I had taken them on one of the few days when the mist not only parted a little but to some slight extent lifted. A curious, swimming light had made me take some photographs, with milky swathes of mist playing around the outlines of objects, both giving them a statuesque appearance and veiling them.

I had a shock when I saw the pictures. For a moment I felt as if someone had been playing a practical joke, a bad one, and palmed pictures from my own life off on me. What I saw was the world after its destruction: a gray-white, ghostly world. Fragments of trees rearing up into a ghostly void. Lonely, abandoned witnesses to an extinction that will not even leave its memory behind. The outlines, at which one could guess, of a house standing in a dead wood like its own memorial. A house I shall never in my life enter again.

I recognized the ancient images of a fear that has always accompanied me. It has been kept under control, suppressed, banished to the dark corners of my dwellings. But it has been ever present. Always there.

THE BIRDS RETURN TO LIFE FIRST. They always do. After deluges. After solar eclipses, volcanic eruptions, earthquakes. This is spring, this is spring, this is spring, they say. Test cases bearing witness to the heartless continuance of life, its oblivious triumph.

So there must be something left outside. I feel as if we hadn't moved for several hours. When I crawl out of the cave the sun is near its zenith in the sky, but veiled with a red glow as if it lay on the evening horizon. The world is enveloped in thick, yellowish smoke, which becomes more impenetrable the closer it is to the ground. Here and there shattered spruce trees rise out of it, as if out of mists. From afar the hiss and crackle of the fires can be heard, but a black-bird has perched on a hazel bush close to us and is singing and singing. The world at the foot of the cave in which we lie is still intact, but ashes fall on it like yellowish snowflakes, sallow as they settle on the green. Tweet tweet, sings the blackbird. It can't help singing now that the sun is coming through the haze again.

I lower myself to the path. Mikhail follows me. I am convinced that we are the only survivors. It is just before two in the afternoon. Sometimes I have to stop when the urge to cough gets too strong. When I glance at Mikhail I see what I must look like; we are encrusted with blood, black as miners coming up from underground. No, like the dead and buried who have risen again. I don't yet know that I shall soon see the earth open and give up hordes of resurrected, pale, swaying figures who look like me. *The Night of the Living Dead.*

I can still make out the path along which I have walked so often. Then we lose ourselves in the new desert just created.

It is terribly quiet, and in the midst of that silence something suddenly breaks apart. Something creaks. Something explodes. Something falls rattling to the ground. A fire flares up again with an infernal hiss. Broken fragments clink. We are hearing the sounds of the underworld. Our human ears are tormented by them and cannot bear it. They can bear it as little as our eyes can bear what they see.

We move through the destruction as if through a dream of it, not really surprised; there is a certain strange familiarity in the horror, a familiarity that, amid the ruins, the fragments of concrete tossed about, twisted girders, broken brick and glass, armored doors wrenched from their hinges, shredded power cables, singed scraps of fabric, car parts, charred rafters and doorposts; amid all this immeasurable destruction is the knowledge that we ourselves are uninjured. Here we are, set down in a place of terror as dreamers are, traveling through Hell, as if we had only to wake up to find ourselves back in the intact world of the Obersalzberg, the real familiar world of which indestructibility is the salient feature.

In one of the bomb craters, which are so numerous on the road to the Hintereck that they often touch and overlap each other, I see a car compressed into a lump of metal. I can still make out its Mercedes star. As I skirt the edge of the crater it is so far below me that it looks like a gigantic conjuring trick. As if a giant had bet that he could make it disappear in his clenched fist, just like that, and was now showing us all what was left of it.

The craters oblige us to perform dangerous maneuvers. We cling to iron posts, clamber over swaying concrete slabs perched at an angle, their center of gravity difficult to determine now. We still think we are the last human beings alive. We are as utterly fearless as the last of humanity would be: in principle invulnerable, like people in a nightmare.

Coming to the Zum Türken inn, we have to cross a thick carpet of splintered glass. The Zum Türken inn isn't there anymore. Nor is the HQ of the Reich security service, which was billeted here after they turned the landlord out of the inn. There is no security service anymore. No HQ. No offices. No safes, no telephone network, no typewriters and decoding machines. No card indexes of data concerning suspicious characters. It has all been shredded, burned, laid waste. The lighter particles of debris are still snowing down on us. The heavier particles block our way, mingle with the splintered glass from the hothouse above us on the opposite side of the street, now nothing but a tangle of iron struts, a devastated collection of metal that we will explore in the next few days, making our way into it without caring that we hurt ourselves on broken glass, sharp edges, and pass dangling metal girders that, if dislodged, could bring the whole unstable and confused structure down like a house of cards, just to get at the last few leeks and cauliflowers. For destruction is followed by hunger, greed, and savagery. The last vegetables in Hitler's hothouses, covered by dust and rubble, will not keep long. Still, we shall be frantic to get at them, not just because we are hungry but because the spirit of plunder will enter into us.

Farther up the road, where the barracks once stood, black smoke rises to the sky. The Kindergartenhaus, seat of the administration, no longer exists. We try to climb the road to the Berghof. It is pitted with bomb craters.

The Berghof itself is still standing. Its right wing is destroyed, but the main building and the northeast part are still there. The windows are black holes without any glass. The shutters hang crooked from their hinges. The roof of the main building is like a hat tilted at an angle, the roof of the northeast wing hangs untidily down. The great panoramic window, the pride of the master of the house, his way of revealing himself to the outside world and letting it be known that he regarded it as his own special property, is dark and empty as a mouth opened in a toothless scream. The face of the house is the face of a drunken fool, a fool struck dead in the middle of a blustering stage act before he gets the chance to deliver the punch line of the bad joke he is trying to tell.

At the bottom of the steps I see the first survivor. He stands there, arms dangling, looking down into the valley. I recognize Schenk, chief administrator on the Obersalzberg, responsible for carrying out all the measures ordained by Bormann, constructing the buildings, the bunkers. . . . His raincoat is torn, the expression on his face fixed. I abandon my intention of greeting him as one shipwrecked sailor greets another. Look, a human being. Another human being among us.

I shall never see him again. And perhaps he was only a hallucination.

But what I am seeing now must be real, although it bears every re-semblance to a vision. The graves open and give up their dead, who emerge swaying, blinded, both hands outstretched in the gesture of the sightless, their faces raised and turned to where the sun is still hidden behind a pale red veil, a timeless sunset, apocalyptic as a solar eclipse, a phenomenon casting doubt on the usual course of cosmic events. It is around two-thirty.

They do not seem to see me as they pass me by as if in proces-sion. But I know them. I see the housekeeper and her husband, the kitchen maids, the chauffeurs, Hitler's secretaries Christa Schroeder and Johanna Wolf, who arrived here from Berlin a few days ago. I see Hertha Schneider carrying the younger of her little girls. She is hold-ing the other little girl's hand. The children are silent as angels as they emerge into the light of day.

I see that they all resemble the models for their own funerary monuments. I see the mother with her two children. They should, I realize, be carved in stone like that. This is the Platonic ideal of their existence made sculptural.

At the moment when they emerge from the earth they are all

turned to pillars of salt. The devastation appears like a divine vision before them, announces itself in all its power and terror. The sight of it strikes them down. It shows them, once and for all, who they are. The defeated.

In this living nightmare where I am both present and able to see myself from the outside, I know that I am one of them.

No one has any chance of escaping. They emerge, and see it. Silent and pale, moving jerkily like marionettes, in slow motion, they walk past me. There are no greetings, no cries of recognition as we meet again. We have become indifferent strangers to one another. We are all set down alone on this new desert planet. There are no words for what we see, there is no understanding of it. The only human sound is the dry coughing that attacks them all as they come out of the gates, breathing deeply, after they have climbed the eighty steps up to the light, and then inhale this mixture of soot and dust and smoke that still makes up the air surrounding us.

Slowly, the human beings become part of the picture of devastation, spread over it without animating it. And slowly I begin to hear voices, a swelling chorus of distress and perplexity dominated by the angry cries of the children, demanding, complaining, protesting forcefully against what they see. Then commands come, uttered in male voices. Signals from the fire engines that cannot reach the fires because of the wrecked roads. Somewhere on the mountain there must still be a working siren, which suddenly howls and howls and howls. There is something of the mindless enthusiasm of the birds in it, something of their resistance to devastation.

I still haven't seen any of the members of my family.

I ask about them. The passing figures hardly look at me, just shrug their shoulders. Each of them is looking for something as they come up to the light again. A great, confused search has begun. A backward and forward movement, resembling the drifting of the particles of soot in the light spring wind that stirs the fires. Their eyes are still blank. Most of us are still unapproachable.

I, too, am a part of this pointless bustle in which we express our helplessness. If there were any injured victims we might know what to do. But there are only the defeated among us, only those who have not the faintest idea what will happen next.

With several others, I enter Hitler's house through one of the terrace doors. What we are doing is dangerous, but none of us thinks of the risk of the place falling in. I want to go upstairs and see if Gretl is in her room. Where else could I look for her? I know only the old, well-trodden paths in this new and uncertain world. I make my way over piles of rubble and fallen furniture.

One of the uniformed guards stands at the bottom of the stairs. They are back, too.

You can't go up there, he says.

At this moment it occurs to me that I have parted from Mikhail. I lost him in the snowstorm of confusion. At the same time I know I am no longer responsible for him. Never again. From now on we are all outlaws, each of us is his own survival system. There are no protected zones, there is no refuge on this mountain now. Our enemies have come. I wished them here without knowing what it would be like when they found us.

Like this. It was to be like this. They have found us. And for the first time I feel relief. I am not liberated yet, oh no, and perhaps I never will be entirely liberated. But I suddenly know that nothing is as it was before, and never will be again, and the thought makes me quite dizzy, I feel light, as if this were no longer my body, as if it had gone through the fire, as if it were nothing but what the fire has left, a white shell, light as paper, drifting over the ground, frail, delicate, scarcely perceptible, perhaps entirely invisible, like the dead with whom we do not collide when they stand in our way.

And as I see that we are looking through one another, that we all move as if we were alone, only slightly irritated to find others around and then unerringly pursuing our own way, continuing that aimless search sustained by no reasonable hope, I am suddenly no longer sure whether we are still alive or whether that emergence from the earth was nothing but the arrival of the dead in the realm of death, the colorless, ruined, distorted counterworld in which we find ourselves. And something of this lightness of nonbeing will remain with me, this sense of not being physically present where I actually am but invisible as the dead, weightless and endowed with the gift of passing through walls. A wonderful and entirely new kind of protection.

Perhaps Mikhail is invisible in the same way and similarly protected. At any rate, I spend no more time thinking about him. From now on he has disappeared, and will not reappear. He is good at disappearing, I know. I shall see him just once more. In another place.

You can't go up there, says the uniformed guard.

His uniform, his hair, and his face are gray.

I'm looking for my family, I say.

Go away, he says. No entry anywhere here.

In the great hall I see people carrying out pictures, lamps, candelabra, vases . . . I am surprised that some kind of authority is active so soon and getting things in order. So far I have no experience of the other forces generated by chaos, and how quickly they set to work. Consequently I cannot understand the indignation of Hitler's two secretaries as they watch.

Do you know where my family is? I ask them. I discover that my relations stayed behind in the bunker because they feared Gretl might go into premature labor.

For the time being it is enough to know they are still alive. Now I want to find out whether the Tea House is still standing.

A LATE AFTERNOON IN APRIL 1999. Dirty remnants of snow. The road to the Kehlstein house is not clear yet. The meadows are still brown. The beech trees have not broken into leaf, and not even the anemones and liverwort are in flower. It is too early. Nature is still holding back, but a few warm days and the fields will be full of flowers. Until then April will be the grayest of all months up here. A month full of the past, full of mourning, full of rage. Full of memory.

I look for a path where there is none now. I try to find my way through the trunks of young beech, larch, and fir trees. I keep looking around at the Zum Türken hotel to take my bearings, imagining the now nonexistent Berghof to the right of it.

The ground is uneven and sometimes muddy. Under the wasteland of grass the melt water is trickling down to the valley, collecting in small hollows that I must avoid. It is not an easy walk for an old woman.

Nor is it meant to be. I recognize the place where Bormann's house stood. A level surface, no more. Not a stone, not a suggestion of any foundations. Nothing except that the mountain itself seems to be hushing something up, a trace of the impact of humanity thousands of years old and now reverted entirely to nature, less obvious to the eye than a Celtic oppidum or ring wall that has long ago become a part of the natural topography. And yet there was something to sense after all. Something that this terracelike surface must have pushed back into the hill. But perhaps I am wrong.

If this is really the place where Bormann's house stood, then I must bear farther left. But the ground is too steep for me there. I am afraid of falling. I know that the fear of falling afflicts old women, and I am aware that until a few years ago I was entirely free of it. But if my body is so clearly telling me what it fears, why not listen to what it has to say?

I make my way back to the paved road and try again, farther down this time. Soon I find myself below a slope, among tall gorse bushes and last year's ferns, and I know I am on the right track, although it has not been a track for a long time. I see the top of the Mooslahner Kopf in front of me and make for it. The Tea House should be over to the right. I no longer fear falling. I am twenty years old and I know this path, even if a matted thicket that is new to me and in which I scratch my face and hands looms in my way. Birds fly up uttering warning cries which announce that I am intruding where no one ought to intrude.

Suddenly I find myself in undergrowth. Sloes, hawthorn, firs several years old. I am caught in it. I can go neither forward nor back, and I cannot see where backward and forward are either. Birds perch somewhere over my head, twittering angrily. I stop and try to peer through the bushes and make out where I am. The branches surrounding me are covered with fat, swollen buds, still closed, so that I can see past them.

Looking out across the valley, I see the outline of the Untersberg on the other side. Far below, the ribbon of the Ache winds its way through the valley. I can make out the roofs of isolated farms looking as if they had been scattered about the scene, the world as viewed from Hitler's tea salon, his idyllic toy-town world. I realize that I am where his Tea House stood. Now I can see the rocky outcrop on which it was built. I see that I am only a few centimeters from its precipitous edge, and that nothing is left of the Tea House. They have blown it up, like the Berghof and the remains of Göring's and Bormann's houses. Birds nest there now.

Tweet, tweet, sings a blackbird. Twilight is falling. It will soon be dark.

I KNOW THAT THERE ARE CANDLES somewhere in the place. There has been no electricity on the Berg since our annihilation. For the first time I feel uncomfortable in the Tea House. I do not want darkness to take me by surprise, but I can't find the candles in either the anteroom or the kitchen. All I can find on the mantelpiece is a box of matches.

Of course I am relieved that I still have a roof over my head. The Tea House was slightly outside the periphery of the target area. I have been lucky.

Most of the windowpanes are broken, of course, but otherwise the place is just as I left it that morning. My notebooks on the desk, the remains of my breakfast on the kitchen table, the full ashtrays in the hall where my guards were positioned.

Yet something has changed. The house is different, forbidding, gloomy. Dirty. As if someone abandoned it years ago and never came back. It is probably to do with the dark gray precipitation that has been settling since morning on everything here, as elsewhere. With the acrid, burning smell of it, which conveys a message of pitiless destruction, pain, and violence. The message suddenly reaches me so clearly that I feel the little hairs on the back of my neck stand up.

Only then do I hear footsteps and voices. I am not alone in the house.

What's she after here? I hear them say.

They are women. But my sense of relief is premature and misplaced. They must have clambered into the house through one of the broken kitchen windows while I was in the tea salon. One of them seems familiar to me. But in the gathering darkness I can't make out if she is really one of the cleaning women.

Go away, I say, please go away!

Shut up, says one of the women.

You clear out of here, and look sharp about it, says the other. She is already wearing one of my jackets.

I discover another world that day. A new and surprising world. I never guessed at it. I am learning, learning, learning. I understand that this is the reverse of the coin, but I'm not ready to reconcile myself to it just like that.

What are you doing here? I ask. You have no right to be here.

Asking for trouble, are you? says a third woman, coming out of the kitchen. You can have it if you don't clear off.

Three are enough to surround me suddenly. I feel the blow in my stomach before I see the fist delivering it. My surprise is greater than my pain. No one has ever hit me in all my life before. I discover how inexorably the learning process sets in, like a reflex. A new way of seeing. A new reality. At the same time I am aware that I am weeping. I can't help it.

I see that there is no mercy on the reverse of the coin, in this brand-new world where I find myself. Here, what will happen happens, just like that. Terrible crimes. Miraculous rescues. What is done is done for no reason, without justification, without hesitation, without even amounting to a memory. The women are in earnest. I realize that. No jokes, no mockery, no irony exist in this other world. But it is a lightweight earnestness that can be diverted: fickle, inconstant. At that moment I hear Hugh Carleton Greene's voice from my bedroom. The power is back on again.

Hitler's Alpine fortress has been destroyed, he says, the last hiding place of the Nazis . . .

A radio! the women exclaim, and I seize my chance and run for it. Mr. Greene has saved me. In the end he was the only person I could rely on. The one and only person.

I shall never set foot in Hitler's Tea House again.

Like everyone else still on the mountain, I seek refuge in the bunkers. We live there, discovering the luxury to which we are accustomed. We lack for nothing. Our provisions are stored there, and we luxuriate in tiled bathrooms. We sleep between silk sheets. I reclothe myself from Eva's bunker wardrobe. We ourselves are rather like the looters of a vanished world, our own. All we lack is daylight. And any idea of where we are to go now. An answer to the question of who we are. Who we were. And whom we shall become. We are nobody now. There is nowhere left for us in the world from which we hide down here.

When I come up now and then I see the fires. It is not only the ruins that still burn; these are the pyres of our inheritance.

Hitler's adjutant Schaub has arrived from Berlin. He does not talk to anyone, although he is besieged by questions about Hitler. Is he coming? When will he arrive? Schaub does not reply. He keeps burning things on the Berghof terrace, the stuff he and his batman carry out of the house, files, cartons full of books and letters, the entire contents of the safes.

As soon as anyone tries to approach the fire Schaub pours petrol on the flames from a canister that seems magically inexhaustible. That keeps everyone away, including the SS men, of whom there are fewer and fewer to be seen on the Berg now.

They, too, have begun destroying anything that could incriminate them, anything left on the day of our destruction. For days and days I see them incinerating the end products of vast administrative diligence. They are destroying all those papers as overzealously as they once wrote them. No one thinks it funny. No one thinks it worth despair. Nowhere do I hear the curses, fiendish laughter, and sarcastic remarks that ought to accompany all this.

We drink. We all drink far too much. I don't have a strong head and never did, and I was much too young to tolerate alcohol at the time. But my memory of the days I spent in the Berghof bunkers, or rather of the constant, unbroken night that reigned down there, is as fragmentary and befuddled as only the memories of a drunk can be. It consists of scenes of bright Goya-like radiance surrounded by gloom, framed in oblivion, unrelated, without any context. Scenes from a nightmare that even to this day has not yet been dreamed to the end.

THERE SEEMS TO BE nobody down below anymore. The air is musty and damp, the floor wet. The much-vaunted technology of the Obersalzberg air-raid shelters has failed. Water has got in, and part of the ventilation system is out of order. The used air we breathe still holds the aroma of the mortal fear we were sweating here not long ago. A nauseating, strong smell that serves to drive away superior adversaries. A desperate emergency weapon of Nature.

Hitler's artificial cavern, his elegant living room under the mountain, looks as if a party has been held there. Empty bottles, broken glasses, cigarette holes burned in the red-velour covers of the armchairs, which are copies of the chairs in the great hall. Stains and burned patches on the oriental rugs. I don't yet know that this is only the beginning of the place's return to the wild.

Eva's cavern opposite looks the same. The door to her bedroom is open. A wailing sound emerges.

My cousin Gretl is lying on the double bed. Her belly is a mountain beneath which she lies as if buried. It is a terrible sight. The baby disfiguring its mother and making her suffer like this must be a monster.

Her parents sit to right and left of her. They look at me as if I, of all people, could save them. A family scene: father, mother, and their child who is having a baby herself, amid this underground nightmare of white matte-lacquered Chippendale-style furniture and silk eiderdowns, all bathed in a ghostly dark green light, the faces strange as if on a photographic negative.

Is everything all right? Aunt Fanny asks me. I mean, is it all right up there?

No, I say. There's nothing left up there.

Hush, says Uncle Fritz.

He raises both hands in a gesture with which he is trying to protect himself against me, himself and the two women. He wants to protect them from me as messenger of doom. And as if on an X ray I suddenly realize what holds them together: the wish to conceal the truth from each other. All their bluster, all their efforts to be on the scene of the action and have a good time, Uncle Fritz's membership of the Party, his assumption of veteran status, his patriarchal pride, which, late in the day but wholeheartedly, he has reevaluated in terms of Fascism, Aunt Fanny's cheerfulness, her wit verging on frivolity, the indestructible sex appeal with which she asserts herself against the hesitant beauty of her daughters, Gretl's touching readiness to do what they all expected of her, marrying a man without a conscience whom she did not love—all this was done to shield one another from the truth, which was that through Eva's liaison they were in-laws to evil. They do not warn each other, they do not try to save each other, they just close their eyes to it.

I realize that families are systems intended to hinder true perception, duty bound, for better or worse, to spare each other the truth. Each is aware of it separately, but together they are blind. I see that in the dark green otherworldly light of Eva's bedroom under Hitler's mountain, in a family picture that looks like an X ray.

There's nothing left up there, I say.

I see the truth go home to each of them, and I see them hate me for telling them.

What do you mean? asks Uncle Fritz reproachfully.

I don't believe it, says Aunt Fanny.

Isn't there a doctor here? says Gretl.

Hush, hush, says Aunt Fanny soothingly. The baby won't be coming yet.

They are obstructing the view of reality from each other again.

But Aunt Fanny is right. Gretl's daughter Eva will not be born for another two weeks. By then the baby's father will be dead, like her mother's sister, whose name she bears. The world in which this little girl was conceived in Schloss Fischhorn will be drowned and gone; scarcely anything from it will reach the bank of the future. If it does it will be driven away and sent back to where it belongs, to the Hades of the past, which must have no chance of finding a way to the future—except for these babies conceived under the Nazis and born after the end of the war. An extraordinarily strong generation. There they suddenly were, the children of an infamous population policy. And the children of their parents' lust for life. Both. And there they still are. They are now becoming grandparents, but my niece Eva Fegelein is no longer among them.

Eva is not a fortunate name for a child of the Braun family, the only grandchild that the three daughters ever gave their parents.

She will be born two weeks later in Garmisch. Hertha Schneider will take my heavily pregnant cousin with her when she leaves us on a truck fueled by wood-gas, paying the driver with spirits from the stocks in the bunker. These have become desirable goods: liquor and a lift in an open truck.

There's supposed to be a good hospital in Garmisch, with a maternity department where Hertha had her own children.

Gretl's parents will try to reach Munich. An empty flat does not stand empty for long these days, if indeed it is still standing at all. They have promised Gretl to join her in Garmisch as soon as possible.

They will not be able to keep their promise. In Munich they will discover that they have been bombed out and will be sent to temporary accommodations, a small room somewhere in the country. A communal kitchen, an earth-closet in the yard. The luxury of Hitler's bunker on the Obersalzberg will be the last luxury of their lives.

When her time comes my cousin Gretl will be left standing in the street outside the hospital.

There's no room in this hospital for the likes of you, she will be told. Understand? We're full. What? There must be somewhere, must there? Do you still think all doors will be opened for you just because of who you are?

And my cousin Gretl, in labor and alone, will lie down by the roadside, obeying the law of all women bringing a baby into the world: when their time comes, it will come.

Soon afterward a military vehicle will stop beside her, a U.S. army officer will get out, see what the matter is, pick her up and drive her to the gates of the same hospital.

You'll take this woman in! he will say. Is there no humanity in this country anymore?

It will make no difference whether the nurse on duty at reception understands English or not. The language of the victors is always understood. It gives the orders: that's enough.

So my niece Eva Fegelein will be born in a sterile delivery room after all, not in a ditch beside the road, and her mother will call her after the only person who ever meant anything to her.

The baby will not want for anything. Nor will her mother lack anything she needs to sustain life: peanut butter, cigarettes, chocolate bars, chewing gum, whisky, male protection. The officer will become a kind of godfather to little Eva. He will be captivated by the charm of his role, the role of victor who is also the protector of the defeated, generous, superior, and humane in the manner of victors. Gretl and her baby will be, so to speak, his little substitute transatlantic family, a tender temptation that he cannot resist, the source of his happiness as a member of the occupying forces.

And Gretl? I shall see her again at some point in Garmisch, when I attend a sporting occasion with her, one obviously meant only for American guests. I shall find that, for her, nothing has changed. She is still living in a system of dependency and protection, and living well in it again.

Gretl is a clinging vine, Ilse once said.

Yes, Gretl is a clinging vine.

She has a clinging vine of a child. An enchantingly pretty child with dark curly hair who, at the age of twenty-seven, will kill herself over a man. Clinging vines can never support themselves out of their own strength. They need a host plant. Eva is not a fortunate name for a child of the Braun family.

A child who will find out, one day, the identity of the aunt after whom she was named. Who it was that her aunt loved, and how she died.

In the green light of the bunker world I see the contours of this future life stand out, rising from the earth and growing. Like a freshly dug grave.

Schaub has brought Gretl a letter from Eva. It is a farewell letter, dated April 23.

"The end could come for us any time now," she writes. She asks Gretl to destroy all her correspondence, particularly "the business matters."

What business matters?

"Frau Heise's bills must not on any account be found."

Frau Heise is her dressmaker. It is the last will and testament of a clothes-buying addict. *That* is the trace of herself she wants wiped out. That is what bothers her. She wouldn't like posterity to know about the one sin she is aware of having committed.

And then I know she has finished with life.

I am sure you will be seeing Hermann again, Gretl reads out to me in a faint voice.

She puts the letter down on top of her huge belly.

I shall not be seeing Hermann again, she says firmly.

How do you know? I say.

From this, she says, pointing at two exclamation marks after the sentence.

When we were children, she says, we agreed on the meaning of signs like this. Only the two of us knew about them. Two exclamation marks at the end of a sentence meant that the opposite was true.

She looks content, peaceful as a child who has just been listening to a bedtime story.

She doesn't want to see him again, I think.

Later I shall learn that when Hitler had Fegelein shot in a fit of suspicious fury two days before his own death, Eva didn't lift a finger to save her brother-in-law. Two exclamation marks at the end of a sentence. No one knew those two sisters as well as they knew each other.

Music comes out of Hitler's cavern again. The record collection was stored in a side room. Although there are hundreds of records, someone keeps putting the same one on.

How all our hearts now
Surge like a river!
How all our senses
So joyfully quiver!

And the cognac is passed around.

Someone shouts: Turn that Wagner off! Can't a man even get drunk in peace here?

Never in my life shall I be able to hear Wagner without anticipating a golden, lukewarm sense of nausea, without anticipating an insidious, gentle movement like that of a viscous, oily fluid swirled about in a bulbous glass held between forefinger and middle finger.

Yearning devotion
Swelling and flowing,
Soulfully loving,
Sacred and glowing . . .

It makes me feel quite ill.

ON THE FIRST OF MAY the looters are suddenly in our midst. They even come down to the bunkers, intruding into our private caverns. No one tries to stop them now. They come with bags, burlap sacks, suitcases. They pack everything into these containers—food, crockery, cutlery, tablecloths—they strip the beds in which we have been sleeping; they unscrew the bathroom fittings, the lavatory seats; they chisel the tiles out of the walls, roll up the rugs, cut the telephones away from their wires, carry off the gramophone, the records, the books; they begin clearing out Eva's wardrobes at top speed, and then I join them, too. Suddenly I myself am a looter among looters. I take what I need before others do, and that is probably the nub of it, the market laws prevail now. It's just a different way, an anarchistic way of packing your bag.

We have heard that Hitler is dead.

A great migration has begun, a great removal that appears unplanned and aimless only at first sight. Very soon I recognize new and entirely unexpected hierarchies of command.

One of the housemaids is standing at the top of the great flight of steps up to the Berghof, directing the removal of pieces of furniture from the house. I know her as a shy girl, anxious not to attract attention by doing anything clumsy. Uncertain eyes. A bowed head.

All that is past history. She is directing proceedings with great determination. Even the housekeeper obeys her orders. Neither of them acknowledge me now.

I share this fate with a creature who, in another life, was called Stasi or Negus. I don't know which of the two is the shaggy animal constantly going around and around in circles on the stones in front of the house, like a cat chasing its own tail. Obviously only one of Eva's two dogs survived our downfall.

In this way, still circling around and around itself, the dog approaches the door, only to be kicked every time someone comes out, heavily laden as they all are, and is thrown a little way through the air, whereupon it resumes its strange movement, whimpering quietly.

I approach it cautiously, putting out my hand.

Stasi? I say. Negus?

The dog stops circling. From close quarters I see how dirty and matted its coat is. How thin it has grown.

Negus! I say. Stasi!

It bares its teeth and growls at me. I see from its eyes that it has gone mad, and with all the force of that madness is trying to get back to the place where it was at home, back to the paradise of its blissful lapdog days, the world of a spoiled little animal loved by all, fed by everyone, much fussed over.

Stupid tyke, I say.

And it begins circling around itself again, as if looking for some way out of the scenario where it has ended up.

Can't you give the dog something to eat? I say, turning to the housemaid. It's one of Eva Braun's dogs.

Go away, *Fräulein,* she says. You're in our way.

She is right. I must get away from here. I want to go home. I want to go back to my parents. To my father, who knew what was going on from the start, who can explain all this to me. Whose prohibition I ignored when I came here last summer. I want to go back where I came from, back to Jena, back to my childhood. But there are no trains to take me there anymore. There is nothing now. When I try making plans I go around and around in circles like the dog. I can't find my way out of this scenario either.

I hear the loud crash of breaking china from the terrace. It is a cheerful, relaxed sound, high-spirited like the spring twittering of the birds above us sitting in the bare, charred trees that remain. Eva's china is being smashed, her hand-painted china with her monogram shaped like a four-leaf clover.

I run that way. I recognize the china. What are you doing? I shout.

Two security men are there. Two of those who are still wearing uniform, still expecting someone to tell them what to do.

They explain that anything to do with my cousin's existence is to be destroyed.

But she's still alive, I say.

All we have heard is the news of Hitler's death. On the radio, Dönitz said that he had fallen for Germany, fighting against Bolshevism to his last breath. We don't know anything about Eva.

It's orders, say the men.

And I watch them smashing the green good-luck symbols. I see them shattered into fragments, I see how the men are enjoying it, how destruction puts them in a good mood while they share in the symbolism of the act—an untimely, posthumous wedding-eve party for a couple already dead, complete with the traditional smashing of china—and I find myself wanting to join in, and when there is nothing left secretly regretting that it is over.

Then I see them bring out Eva's coats, Eva's hats, Eva's shoes, everything that is left of her wardrobe, her silk dressing gowns, her towels, her photograph albums, her fashion magazines, I see them open her books and tear out the flypapers on which she has written her name, and I see them make a fire out of all this, a fire that burns high and can be seen from afar. Eva's auto-da-fé.

I stay to the end. I stay until it is all ashes. Until evening, when the last bird falls silent. Until I can no longer warm myself by the glowing embers of the fire of Eva's life.

May 1999
Dear Father

I have been looking for you for fifty-four years. A few weeks ago I found you through the Red Cross. The Russians released thirty thousand names, and yours was among them. Died in the camp in Frankfurt an der Oder, February 23, 1946. They arrested you for taking part in the attempt to get some of the research equipment from the Zeiss works out of the Russian zone of occupation and into the West. You always did know what you ought to do.

You were in counterintelligence. That, too, I have only just discovered. It accounts for all your traveling. Your absence, which was more than just a lack of your physical presence. The absence of explanation for anything concerning you. The way I felt you couldn't be reached even when you were at home.

Perhaps all young daughters feel like that about their fathers. Perhaps it has to be that way. Or was there something you didn't tell me? Something I wasn't to know because it would have been too dangerous for me? Something that perhaps even Mother didn't know? Was it your intimacy with men like Canaris, Oster, and Hans von Dohnanyi that made you so reserved and cold, so unapproachable to me?

Why did you never speak openly to me? What did you want to spare me? Anxiety? The necessity of making up my mind? Or did you think I couldn't keep my mouth shut?

Oh, I can keep my mouth shut. If there's one thing I've learned, Father, that's it. I have kept my mouth shut all my life. Not a word about it, my husband said. And I kept my promise as long as he lived.

He was sixteen years my senior. A clever man. A man who knew all the answers and gave me guidance. The man with whom I ended up, after looking in vain for you so long. Mother and I had no idea what had happened to you, or whether you were still alive. Now, at my age, what was hidden is revealed to me, and I can see the pattern.

Now I realize that to this day I never stopped looking for you.

The most bitter insight of all is to know that one has omitted to do something. The most bitter insight to me, Father, is that I would have seen you again if I had come home sooner that summer after the war, in time to see you before they came for you and took you to the Frankfurt camp. The most bitter insight of all is to know that I could have done it. How can I explain why you waited in vain for me?

I didn't leave the Berghof until we heard that the first American tanks had already reached the Chiemsee. That must have been on May 4. The last opportunity to get out was on a truck supposed to be taking away Hitler's valuable picture collection, which had been hidden in a secret tunnel of the bunker, and driving it I didn't know where. In the end I simply clambered aboard and sat among pictures by Tintoretto, van Dyck, Bordone, and Titian, tied up and packed in covers and sacking, exposed to a bumpy drive over damaged mountain roads.

Only when we reached our journey's end did I see where I had been brought: Schloss Fischhorn, near Zell am See. The last refuge of the Nazis. Ministers, generals, anyone who had made it south out of Berlin came here. On my arrival I saw Frau Göring at one of the castle windows high above, wearing a big sun hat and a white dress.

It was a shock to me. The end of a long odyssey, when you suddenly see that you have been going around in circles, and have come back to the very place you wanted to avoid at any cost.

For I had been there before. I am sure Mother told you, although all through that time in the past you told her you didn't want to hear any more about me. What you didn't know was that I met a man there whom I wanted to see again as little as I wished to return to the place itself.

I did see him again. He was there, too. He was one of those capable of still believing, to the very end, that something can be saved. The kind of men who supervise their own ruin with the same circumspection, the same diligence, they once used in the service of a terrible power.

The victors need such men. They let them continue operating a little longer, watch them directing the work of dissolution with practiced hands, and then arrest them.

At such a place as this the triumph of the victors looks like an act of refined courtesy. It is conducted in the form of conversations on the terrace, where champagne and biscuits are served. Think of Göring after his departure from Schloss Fischhorn, on the balcony of a Kitzbühel hotel, laughing, champagne glass in hand, surrounded by American generals. . . .

I knew a mountain hut, and spent a few days there entirely alone. Then it suddenly filled up with men and women who had exchanged their wristwatches, fur coats, and rings for lederhosen, dirndls, and Alpine jackets: mountain farmers and farmers' wives rather conspicuously speaking standard High German. Mountain huts were highly desirable temporary residences then.

I spent some time on a farm in Thumersbach on the eastern side of the Zeller See. I worked in the stables. This was when I bartered a nightdress of Eva's for a packet of cigarettes. I crumbled up the tobacco and steeped it in water. When I had laid a boiling hot hot-water bottle on my stomach, along with an old heater that I had left switched on for a while first, I drank the brown liquid to the dregs. I knew that if this didn't work I would have to die. But it worked.

I would never have told you about that, Father, not while you were alive, and I tell you now only to explain why I didn't come home sooner, in time to see you again. I still don't know if I was really pregnant or whether the horrors of our downfall had upset my menstrual cycle, in the same way as some dreadful event can make the heartbeat falter.

This was the time when I saw my lover again. I call him that, Father, although I know the word would not please you. But I could never bring myself to call him by his name.

Once, in a bookshop, I picked up a volume entitled Biographical Encyclopedia of the Third Reich. I opened it very quickly, as you *might open a forbidden book, and looked to see if his name was there. I was greatly relieved to find that it wasn't. Not that it made any difference. I remember the cover of the book. It was black. And I thought of those stupid old sayings about black books, and about a golden, invisible, celestial book of accounts in which the balance of good and evil is drawn up. It's a naive idea, but hard to refute. So there was this black book, available on sale in any bookshop . . .*

When I saw him again he was sitting by the roadside. They had let the prisoners keep their uniforms, but removed the signs of rank. A lieutenant strode up and down in front of them, smoking. There were about fifteen of them, former SS men, probably the last to be taken away from Schloss Fischhorn.

My lover looked strangely bored as he was being taken away. Very likely it was the expression he had practiced for this situation. It did not allow him to look up and take notice of his surroundings, or he would have seen me.

Perhaps he did see me. Perhaps I, too, had that deliberately bored expression on my face. You don't have to tell the whole truth to the very end.

A GI with the safety catch off his pistol stood behind the prisoners, along with two armed young men wearing the leather jackets of German fighter pilots and American peaked caps. I knew one of them. A young Ukrainian who had worked on the Obersalzberg. A boy, almost a child still. Crazy with fear, with hunger, with homesickness. With hatred for us.

I was surprised to see him. I had thought he would be well on his way back to his native land. But obviously someone had told him that the Russians were there now, and had also told him what they did to men returning from Germany. And perhaps the lure of a gun had been too tempting for him. The gun and the power it gave him over his former tormentors.

Why am I telling you all this, Father? Because that was the end of

the war for me: an army truck stopping on the other side of the road.
The lieutenant spitting out his cigarette and treading it into the dust.
The men seated there rising at his command, getting into line and cross-
ing the road, where they climb up into the truck one by one. My lover
getting in last. The Ukrainian's pistol pushing against his back. The
black fabric of his uniform wrinkling where the muzzle of the gun
prods him rather more firmly than is permitted. His failing to turn to
look at me as he gets into the truck. The way he lowers himself down
inside the wall of the truck with the same rigid, bored expression. The
way it all takes longer than necessary, and they wait, for no good rea-
son, before driving the prisoners away. The two boys placing themselves
at the very back of the truck. The GI putting the tarpaulin up. The
Ukrainian suddenly turning and looking me in the face. Briefly show-
ing me his pistol, showing me his pride, showing a contempt that in-
cludes me, too. Intentionally letting me know that he is a man now.
And I myself understand that from now on I would be afraid of him.
The truck driving off, enveloping me in a cloud of golden dust. And my
own relief at knowing that I need never see either of them again, real-
izing that it is all over.

For each of us there was this moment of knowing that it was over. It
was different for everyone, unique, a moment that could not be relived.
Millions of untold stories of the end of the war. Each of us was alone
in experiencing it, just as we are alone when we wake up in the morn-
ing. Defenseless, vulnerable, and blinking, the world still upside down.
Then comes a rapid, desperate attempt to find your way into a new
world, a new day. The shameful, irritating, incredulous memory of
your dream, something monstrous and profoundly wrong from which
you have just emerged. Something incredible. Something that demands
suppression. Something that it is entirely impossible to speak, because
every dream is different when you have finished dreaming it, entirely
different; is experienced in quite a different way once you can describe

it. Indeed, the most precise language in which a dream is narrated suddenly means something quite different when it is told. It is something that cannot really be told, something that may never be spoken. And the familiar and commonplace, which came so naturally when we were dreaming it—was so near, so close, as close as we can be only to ourselves—this familiar world to which a part of us would like to return, the tired, sleeping part of us that is unwilling to be surprised by day, suddenly shows itself in all its obscene horror.

I wonder whether there was such an awakening for Eva. A moment when she understood who it was beside whom she was sitting on the sofa when she died, and whose hand she tried to grasp as she bit unhesitatingly into the capsule, hurrying on ahead rather overassiduously, in her usual way.

She was carefully groomed and made up. And if she still felt any regret it will have been to know that there would be no funeral procession for her, no lying in state, no farewell except for the immediate burning of their bodies in the Reich Chancellery garden.

Did she guess at any of the huge relief felt in the bunker as soon as they had retired to Hitler's rooms after what was unmistakably a farewell ceremony? Did she know anything about the party already in progress in the other part of the bunker? Did she know that they were dancing there?

Death by cyanide is instant. An extreme sensation of burning lasting a second. Did she have time to understand anything else? Was it time enough? Or did she reach eternity like that, in her blue wedding dress and understanding nothing? Was the fact that she understood nothing to the very last her share in eternal damnation?

We all have our dead, with whom we are fated to talk. To whom we still owe explanations, and of whom we would like to know one last thing. You are one of them for me, Father, and Eva is another.

Once, years ago in Munich, I saw an old bag lady. It was summer, but she was wearing a fur coat and pulling a handcart full of old rags *behind her. The first thing I noticed about her was her yellowed old sealskin coat. These days you can pick something of that sort up off a tip. In our time it was still a genuine fashion item. It probably represented something like home to her, her only asylum.*

When she raised her head I suddenly saw in her a kind of similarity to myself. She looked like a bad, blurred copy of me. The incarnation of all the misery I have carefully steered clear of and avoided in my life. Like one of the many variants of my own existence that I have not lived—like the worst of them.

As I took my next step I suddenly realized that Eva as an old woman would have looked like that. My likeness to her had misled me, the likeness between us that people so often pointed out. It was the most wretched, failed variant of Eva imaginable who was walking toward me then.

I must have stopped and stared at her. I saw how unwilling she was to meet my glance, I saw the lifting of the brows, the touchy, incalculable anger of an old alcoholic, the sudden bullfighter look flaring up in her eyes.

Go away, will you, go away, she said. You don't know me.

She used the familiar du pronoun.

And I felt my betrayal as I turned away and walked on. I felt her contempt, the contempt of an outcast for those on the inside, of one who has become conspicuous for those who look normal. No one sees through us as well as the wretched. No one knows us better than they do. You could be me, says their glance, if we have not yet looked away. You could be me, and you know it, it says. They know all about us. They know everything we have done to keep from being like them.

I didn't think for a moment that she was really Eva. And yet I was as shocked as if she had been. The dead don't die again. The past does not come to pass once more, and our letters to you who are dead come to no ending.

At some point I stopped wondering why she had said: You don't know me.

Oughtn't she to have said: I don't know you?

Or, We don't know each other?

And why did she say du *to me? Is that just the language of the streets? And ought I to have followed her?*

I have stopped thinking about it. I must stop thinking about it.

ABOUT THE AUTHOR

SIBYLLE KNAUSS, born in 1944, is the author of eight novels, and is professor of dramaturgy and scriptwriting at the Baden-Württemberg Academy of Film. This is her first book to be translated into English. She lives near Stuttgart in Germany.

DATE DUE

FOLLETT